EVASTANY

THE DRAYKON SERIES: 5

CHARLOTTE E. ENGLISH

ISBN: 9789492824219

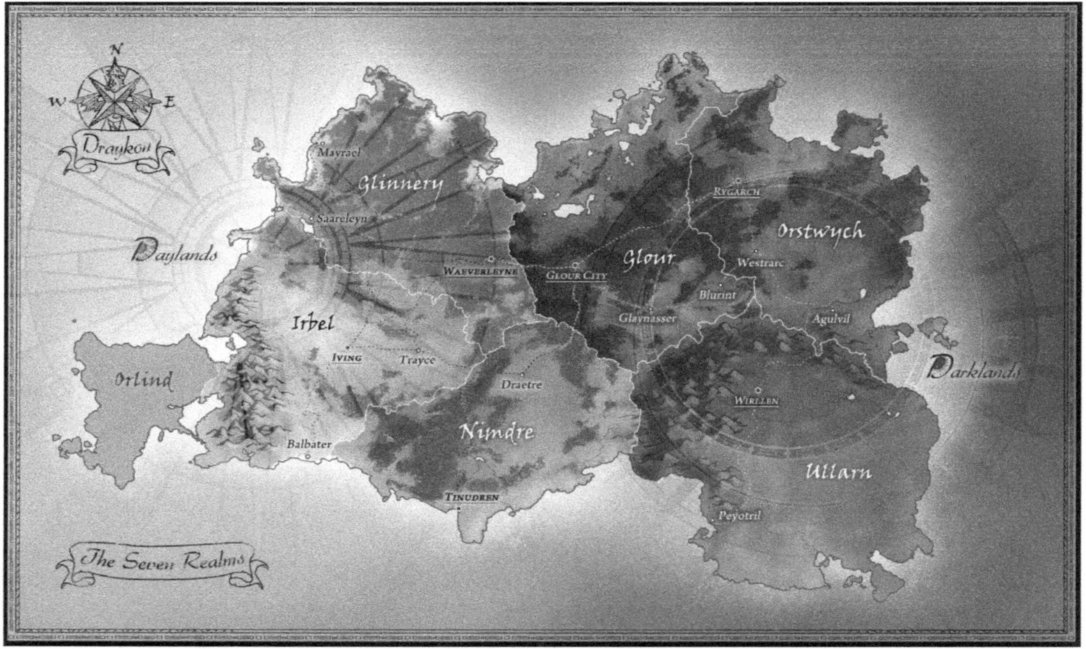

N
W
E
Draykon
The Seven Realms
Daylands
Darklands
Orlind
Glinnery
Mayrael
Saareleyn
Irbel
Iving
Trayce
Balbater
Waeverleyne
Nimdre
Draetre
Tinudren
Glour
Glour City
Glaynasser
Blurint
Rygarch
Orstwych
Westrarc
Agulvil
Ullarn
Wirllen
Peyotril

INTRODUCTION TO THE JOURNALS OF LADY EVASTANY GLOSTRUM

The problem with good intentions is that they are *so* difficult to stick to.

Good advice is even worse. How easy it is to dispense one's wisdom to all one's friends! How difficult it is to follow it oneself!

Yesterday I received the benefit of a visit from a dear friend of mine, Miss Llandry Sanfaer. The girl who made headlines in *all* the best papers not too long ago. Perhaps you read about it? She was a Summoner of Glinnery, though untrained. One of the winged folk. A talented jeweller — I've bought one or two of her pieces, and wear them often. Largely unremarkable for all these things, until the day she Shapeshifted into a draykon and sparked a large-scale revival of that long-extinct race.

It was *spectacular.*

The poor girl has since been burdened with the cumbersome title of "Lady Draykon" (and I would love to know whose fertile imagination spawned *that* absurdity, so I may make a note never to invite them to dinner). At twenty years old, she is co-ambassador between the Daylands realms and these new draykoni settlements that are popping up out in the Off-Worlds, and my goodness, what a mess of problems she has had to manage already. I do not envy her the task.

Naturally, then, I hastened to give her yet another job to do.

I said to her, *Llan, it would be wise to write down an account of your doings for the next few moons!* The draykoni have not exactly made themselves popular thus far, what with trying to destroy the finest city in Glinnery and all that. There will be those who will blame poor Llandry for a great many things not of her doing, and it would be wise for her to have her own account to hand.

Thus far, I was wise enough. I did not err until I assured her that I would be keeping a similar account of my own doings for the foreseeable future, and for similarly sound reasons. I also promised to let her read it! What was I thinking!

Well, yesterday she put into my hands a fat journal written through with a faithful record of all manner of exciting things. It is admirably detailed. I quite feel as though I had been there myself! What a fine job she has done. I am most proud.

The naïve soul was sweet enough to assume that I have been faithfully keeping records all this time myself. That I have, not to put too fine a point on it, been following my own brilliant advice. I had not the heart to tell her that I had not written so much as a word.

What can I say in my own defence? I have been busy, certainly, but that can be no excuse. Llandry has been up to her beautiful grey eyeballs in turmoil beyond imagining, and still contrived to write down her activities.

I feel quite ashamed of myself! No, I really do. I am thoroughly contrite.

So, I begin today. And *today* is… let's see. The sixth of the ninth moon, 1913. Dates are important, one must be meticulous. After all, it is distantly possible that someone may actually read this someday.

I have faithfully read Llandry's account. Every word. I stayed up half the night to do so, somewhat to the dissatisfaction of my fiancé, Mister Pitren Warvel. Not because he disapproved of my late hours, but because I swiped the book first and then would not permit him to read it along with me.

'Eva!' he complained. 'Why do you get to read it first?'

'Because Llandry likes me better.' I snuggled more comfortably into the pillows of our beautiful big bed and turned a page.

'Share,' he pleaded, at his most pitiful.

'You may have it when I am finished.'

He sighed and abandoned the attempt, wandering for the door. I blew him a kiss as he left.

Now, that may seem harsh of me but *really*. Have you ever tried to share a book with somebody else? No two people read at the same speed, and being expected to wait for the other party to finish the page before you can move on is perfectly insufferable. Insupportable! I made him wait.

He will have his revenge by taking the whole of today to read the book, quite ignoring our other plans in the process. I will quietly encourage this, without seeming to do so.

The events outlined in that journal are rather important, all told, and I am glad that Llan wrote them down for us. We are duly informed of a variety of events of which we were previously unaware, many of them pertinent. New draykon colonies all over Iskyr and Ayrien, the Upper and Lower Realms! *Murders,* of a species previously thought unable to permanently die! And, worst of all, more *Lokant interfering*. I had hoped that the latter had finished mucking about with our lovely worlds some time ago, since the worst of them (a chap called Krays) was deservedly eaten by Llan's spouse, Pensould. No such luck! I should have known better than to expect it.

Moreover, we now know why the mountains in between Irbel and beleaguered Orlind tried to shake themselves to pieces a little while ago. There was an avalanche. It was exciting — all the bulletin boards said so! No actual damage was done, but what can I say. It was a slow news day.

It did worry Tren and I just a little, however. The Seventh Realm, Orlind, was held to be as lost as the draykoni for many a long age. I imagine many people still think that, for it will take some time for news to the contrary to travel as far as it needs to.

But Orlind is *not* lost. Just mostly so, and still somewhat contested, because it happens to be the site of the single most powerful and magnificent Lokant Library there ever was.

Or it was until a week or two ago, when the Library blew up.

That was the news Llan brought us, and I can still scarcely believe it. The Library was broken beyond repair and a madhouse, true, but it was special. Many wonderful and precious things were created there, the draykoni not least among them. And now it is gone.

It is good news, all told. Llandry and Pensould are confident that they will now be able to mend the island, get it to grow again. That would be wonderful, of course. They even talk of reclaiming some of its lost land from the sea. But the Library is still a great loss, and the way it came about grieves me indeed.

Well; it is not the purpose of this journal to repeat what Llandry has already written. She has left me with a new task, and to that I must now turn my attention. I could not help but accept it, busy as I am, because she leaves me with worrying news. I assure you, I did *try* to convince myself that it is not my duty to take up this problem; I hoped I might be able to delegate it to some other fool… I mean, praiseworthy volunteer. But I cannot. It falls to me, and I will have to be that fool.

At least she left a pair of scintillating and delicious assistants to help us along.

Perhaps I ought to introduce myself? I now realise that I have failed to do so. Llandry was far more on the ball there than I, and got the dull business out of the way right at the beginning. I, however, have rambled on for pages without offering so much as my name. There can be no excuse. To presume upon your attention without a formal introduction! All ideas of etiquette are grossly violated.

I am Evastany, Lady Glostrum. I am a member of the peerage of Glour, the loveliest of the three Darklands realms (I admit to no bias there whatsoever). I am the second of my name, my detestable father having briefly held the title before me. I was High Summoner for Glour for more than a decade, but I recently resigned that role in favour of…

… well, peril and adventure, for a time, though that was not precisely of my choosing. After the Waeverleyne war, though, and our subsequent exploratory expedition to Orlind, everything calmed down again. I had time to consider what to do with myself next.

I should also mention that I am a partial Lokant, by blood heritage. It is the reason for my white hair, which is *not* a sign of premature ageing, as some of the seedier papers have been so unflattering as to suggest. Lokants are a different race, human in appearance but not by any other characteristic. They have strange powers, stranger ideas and unfathomable goals. They are based on no particular world, as far as I know; instead they organise themselves into structures they call Libraries, which are like miniature worlds floating out in nowhere-in-particular. They are fond of books. They have populated our cluster of worlds with a great many species of plants and animals, as well as the glorious draykoni. They are spectacularly intelligent, far cleverer than any of the rest of us can claim to be. They are also compulsively secretive and completely ruthless. It took me some time to accept my portion of that heritage, or to understand that blood inheritance does not compel me to resemble them in any other way.

I am not the only person hereabouts with Lokant ancestors somewhere in the family tree. There are others, and they are usually easy to spot because the white hair breeds true. If you ever see somebody youngish with snow-white hair, that is a partial Lokant — if not a full one. In either case, please send them to me.

See, some of those distant Lokants have had the bright idea of using partials like me for their various schemes, and to be fair we can be quite useful. It does not tend to work out well for us, however, or for our worlds, so I would rather get in the way of any such bright ideas in the future, and harness the partials' unusual abilities for the benefit of the Seven instead.

Tren and I have been trying to find them all. It is not as easy as I just made it sound, because the fact that they have white hair is all that we have to go on. So in the past few weeks, we have accomplished the following:

- Secured the approval of Glour's Council for the creation of a new bureau, to be dedicated to the identification and training of partial Lokants.

- Secured provisional approval for some funding to be allocated to the project.

- Talked the realms of Orstwych and Nimdre into joining the party, and adding to the funding pot (that last is a particular coup. If you have ever had anything to do with governments, you will know how difficult it is to get them to pay for anything, ever).

- Tried to gain access to Ullarn for the same purpose, but failed (I may have slightly used and then double-crossed my contact there not long ago, which proved to be unwise in the longer term. Though in my defence, he is a reprehensible soul and absolutely deserved it).

- Talked very seriously about travelling into the Daylands to discuss this with Glinnery and Irbel.

- Procrastinated on this last part with great diligence.

All of this done, we have arranged for advertisements to be distributed via the bulletin boards of Glour, Orstwych and Nimdre, asking all those with naturally occurring white hair to communicate with us. We have an office, in a nice house in Glour City. It is one of my own properties, a pretty enough place I had no use for. I went there yesterday, hoping to find a delicious stack of post from swarms of prospective trainees, and found only two letters.

Well, it is a start.

Did I mention that I am also planning my wedding? That is no small task either, for it must be a grand event. It is expected of me, as an aristocrat, to do things in the proper style. Since I deprived society of the spectacle of my marriage to another member of the peerage, Lord Vale, I feel it incumbent upon me to make up for it by at *least* giving the papers a wedding to talk about for weeks to come.

I am not sure that Tren entirely agrees with me. I have hired somebody else to do all the more tiresome drudgery of the thing, however, so he has no right to be too displeased.

Into the middle of this came Llandry, with her news and warnings *slightly* more on the dire side than I was hoping for. I thought her journal would be about trade agreements and minor conflicts with other draykon tribes. Diplomatic relations between Iskyr and the Daylands. Maybe an occasional border skirmish between draykoni tribes. That kind of thing.

I relinquish those fond hopes reluctantly, and with a pang of regret.

That brings me to the two intriguing young men she brought me. One of them is young Mr. Orillin Vanse, a Summoner of Glinnery, one of the first hereditary draykoni of modern times, and incidentally Lord Draykon. He is a lively chap, and appealingly carefree. I like him very much. He is quite at home with us, the grandeur of my family mansion notwithstanding, and ate himself merrily replete last evening.

His companion is unknown to me, and *he* interests me greatly. Gio Maeval, grandson of Krays — the very same Lokant dear Pensould made a meal of a few moons ago. *What* a fine young man he is! And how difficult it is to trust him! But I must.

Llandry assures me that his loyalty has been proven beyond doubt, which I hope is true, because poor Ori has quite lost his head over the boy.

Not that I can blame him. Gio is intelligent, self-possessed, exquisitely polite and *very* handsome indeed. Fortunately he appears to reciprocate Ori's affection, and they do make a charming couple.

It is only unfortunate that Gio is also a full Lokant with a problematic family history. His grandmother, Dwinal, has been getting up to all kinds of mischief and it is my unhappy task to find out what, exactly, that is. With Gio's help.

The woman *wanted* the Library of Orlind destroyed. Wanted it gone! She claimed it is to do with averting future Lokant wars over the place, and that could well be true. They destroyed it once before, after all, and if anybody were to succeed in mending the poor broken mess of it all, perhaps there would be war again.

But when the Library blew up, Dwinal was radiant with glee. So says Llandry. I have to agree with her that the reaction seems inappropriate, considering that the destruction of Orlind also killed its self-appointed guardian, Galywis — a genius looked up to by all Lokantkind, even if he was stark raving mad.

Also, Gio brings unpromising accounts of his grandfather's doings prior to his (un)timely demise, and word that some of his former colleagues have not been content to let Krays's projects die just because he had the good taste to bite the dust early.

What does any of it have to do with our worlds? Maybe nothing.

Then again, maybe everything.

It is all so very tiresome. A plague upon all Lokants! Except for Gio, who looks far too good in an evening jacket to be consigned to oblivion.

I promised Llandry I would do something about this, but here I sit towards the end of truenight, sleepless and at a loss as to how to proceed. Lokants are secretive to a fault and inconveniently inaccessible. Even with Gio's help, how am I to gain access to Dwinal's Library, Sulayn Phay? Supposing that done, how to investigate? They do not exactly welcome outsiders.

I have erred in permitting myself to become so absorbed, for the NightCloak will be coming in soon and the day (such as it is) will begin. I have not slept. I do not think Tren has, either. Today we have a meeting with the ambassador for Orstwych, and I will have to focus on the finer points of our agreement regarding the handover of partial Orstwychian Lokants for training by our new bureau. There is also the slight problem of *how* to train these people once we find them, for there is only me to do the teaching, and I am largely untrained myself. After all this, I have an appointment with my wedding planner in the evening.

At least I will not be bored.

Laying those two problems side by side does give me an idea, however. Ideally we need the assistance of a few full Lokants to provide initial training, at the very least. I have not previously been able to imagine a way to accomplish this, but here is Gio! Fully trained and so obliging. I wonder if he would mind being recruited as a teacher?

I wonder if he would mind being used as a contact with other Lokant Libraries, too? I have lost all of my own, having never expected (or wanted) to need them again.

I suppose it is time to find out just how obliging Gio is inclined to be, and how long he expects to remain in our cluster of worlds. Since that latter question is most likely to depend upon the progress of his relationship with Ori, I shall consider it a priority to encourage their romance by all means at my disposal.

Well, they *are* a happy couple. I do like to see people happy, do not you?

7 IV

I have to say, Gio is rapidly becoming my new favourite person! (Always excepting Tren, of course. I had better spell that out, for he will read this journal someday and I would not like him to be unhappy with me when he does).

'Gio,' I said over dinner on the second night of his stay. 'How would you like turn teacher, and be shamelessly used for my own, nefarious purposes forthwith?' I have always been given to subtlety in my communication, and do not believe in alarming unsuspecting souls with strange requests out of the blue.

Gio, to his credit, took it in stride. I begin to think him unflappable. He blinked at me, a forkful of roast meat halfway to his lips, and said: 'I shall be happy to help you in any way I can, my lady, of course.'

I *told* you he was polite!

I did not tell him how unwise it was to hand me an invitation without limits. I would not put him to any truly nefarious purpose, of course; I was jesting about that. But as I said, there is a great deal I need him to do.

Tren tried, bless his foolish heart. He caught Gio's eye and widened his own, shaking his head slightly in a clear warning.

One which sweet Gio entirely failed to understand. I do think he is a little naïve in some particulars. He certainly has not much encountered humour before, which I think is rather sad.

He stared at Tren in obvious confusion, glanced uncertainly at me, and returned to studying Tren's face as though an explanation might materialise upon closer attention.

Ori took pity on him. 'I wouldn't call her ladyship demanding,' he said, 'at least, not in her hearing. But she is… er, particularly motivated, shall we say? She tends to have about a thousand projects on hand at any given time, and if you are too quick to volunteer your services, you may find yourself urgently busy for about the next fifteen years.' He turned a cherubic smile upon me as he completed this speech, hoping, perhaps, to deflect my justifiable wrath by pure force of adorability.

Unfortunately for me, it worked like a charm.

Gio's face registered consternation — whether because he feared Ori was speaking the literal truth or because he feared he had somehow given offence, I do not know. I swallowed my urge to laugh, and tried my best to appear kindly instead. 'I shall not unduly burden you, I promise,' I assured Gio, with a conciliating smile.

It occurred to me halfway through that my idea of conciliating *might* come across as vaguely motherly. And *then* I realised that, in Ori's case at least, I am literally just about old enough to *be* his mother.

I stopped smiling.

Tren knows me far too well, and instantly guessed the reason for my abrupt alteration in manner. He was so unkind as to convulse with laughter, almost choking upon his meal in the process.

I was tempted to extract some of the exquisite braised carrots from my plate and flick them at him, but I recollected in time that I am a woman of dignity and refrained.

Gio spoke up. 'Uh, my lady? What is it you would like me to teach, exactly?'

First things first. 'Ori has rather misled you, in using my full and proper title.' I directed a quelling look at Ori as I said this, but he only twinkled at me and grinned, so I abandoned my attempts to encourage good behaviour.

To Gio I said, 'Please call me Eva.'

His eyes widened, and he shook his head. 'Oh, I could not.'

Oh, dear. What did I do to the poor chap? I fear I may have inadvertently got up on my pedestal a little, and overawed poor Gio. The house and the furniture and the servants and the jewels probably do not help, either.

Oh, well. If being nice does not work… 'You must,' I replied, 'For I insist.'

He blinked. 'Oh… th-then of course.'

I beamed. 'Good. Well then, what I require is a trained Lokant, preferably a full-blooded specimen with the complete range of powers. We are gathering up partials with a variety of untrained abilities, you see, and they are in sore need of teaching. Most of them do not know what they are, and have no notion whatsoever of what they may do.'

Gio swallowed. 'Ah… I am not much of a teacher, ma'am.'

Ma'am. Not *Eva*, but it was an advance upon *my lady*, so I let it pass. 'You do not need to be greatly experienced at the art of teaching,' I assured him. 'I am sure you will do very well.'

'The fact is,' Tren put in, 'you are the only candidate we have for the post. Easiest job interview ever.'

Gio looked at Ori. It is quickly becoming clear to me that Ori is the driving force in that relationship, odd though that may seem. I do not know what Gio's age might be; he looks more or less of an age with Ori, but being a Lokant, it is impossible to know. He is probably older, perhaps a great deal older, and he is undoubtedly powerful in his own right. But Ori's charisma and exuberance tend to carry all before them, and Gio is curiously unsure of himself for a man in his position.

Well, he has had a deplorable range of influences thus far in his life.

'I will do my best, then, ma'am,' said Gio.

'Excellent.' I paused to consider my options. I could give him time to get used to his first job before I broach the topic of the second, which might be both kind of me and politic. He does give the impression that he might be easily overwhelmed.

On the other hand, perhaps it would be best to get it all out of the way at once. Brutal, but efficient.

'I also need to regain access to a Library or two,' I said, hoping that my casual tone would soften the impact of the request.

Gio choked. Mightily.

Ori handed him a glass of water, which Gio dispatched in three swallows. When he had finished spluttering, he stared at me in consternation. 'You want *access* to a Library?' he repeated. Then he bethought himself of a detail he had missed, and added,

'More than one!'

'Ideally. You see, Lokants are tricky folk, as I imagine you are aware. If one requires information, one cannot blithely go to a single Lokant, or just one Library, and expect to be given the full and accurate truth about anything whatsoever. One would do far better to consult multiple parties, compare their accounts, and do one's best to extract whatever miserable morsels of truth from it that one can.'

'Eva used to have access to Limbane's Library,' Tren said, probably to reassure poor Gio that I wasn't talking complete nonsense.

Gio's brows went up. 'As in, the coming-and-going variety?'

'Everything.'

Gio turned the raised eyebrow treatment upon me. 'Used to?' he echoed.

I suppose it was fairly my turn to be put on the spot. 'I relinquished it,' I admitted, and permitted myself the faint hope that he would not enquire further.

Hopes, dashed. The eyebrow, if possible, arched even higher. 'Oh?'

I drummed my fingers upon the table top, trying to think of a way of explaining my decision that wouldn't make it sound as bad as it was.

Oh, forget it.

'I lost my temper.'

At the other end of the table, Tren grinned, and tried to hide it behind a hastily-taken mouthful of food.

'Limbane,' I continued, 'is a secretive, manipulative, cold-hearted sneak and I wanted nothing more to do with him.'

'Those qualities aren't all bad,' Tren said. 'Under the right circumstances they can be beneficial.'

'They are perfectly acceptable when I engage in them,' said I with a glower for my unhelpful fiancé. 'I do not recall giving Limbane permission, however.'

Tren beamed sunnily upon me and blew me a kiss, following which I was unable to maintain my gravity and began to laugh.

Poor Gio looked hopelessly confused. 'Limbane is no connection of mine,' he warned me. 'I cannot even get hold of him, necessarily, let alone persuade him into restoring your access to Estinor.'

'Estinor?' That word drew a blank.

'He gave you access to the place but didn't tell you its name?' Gio looked incredulous.

I threw down my napkin. 'See, that is what I mean about secretive. Why would he tell me the name of his Library, if he had no particular means to gain by doing so? The most maddening man! And all the rest of them, the same! If they would only stop meddling in our poor worlds, I could go on peacefully ignoring Limbane forever. As it is, your blessed grandmother is up to no good and *somebody* needs to tell me what is going on.'

Tren has developed a bad habit of acting as my voice of reason. It is no real consolation that I perform the same service for him. 'Limbane is hardly likely to be the person to elucidate on that subject,' he opined. 'Even if he has any idea what Dwinal's game is, which may or may not be likely.'

'He is a place to start. The fact is, Tren my love, I am used to leaning upon Limbane's soft parts until he does more or less what I want him to do. I would have to start from the beginning, with anybody else.'

With which statement, I had the satisfaction of observing that I had made all three of the gentlemen uncomfortable, and applied myself to the remains of my dinner in peace.

I left Gio to think that over for a day or two while I occupied myself with other concerns. I'd given him a spacious bedchamber on the third storey, directly next door to Ori's. I wasn't sure if their relationship had progressed to the point of sharing a bedroom yet, and decided to let them sort it out for themselves.

Meanwhile, I had my two letters to reply to.

One was from a woman in Orstwych, who introduced herself in terse terms as Heliandor Rasset. Thirty-three, unmarried, bank clerk by profession. White-haired since birth. Free to start training right away.

I wrote to offer her a bursary on the spot.

The second was from a Faronni Nallay, supposedly from Glour, though her name sounds Ullarni to me. Four-and-twenty, white hair, a painter. It was an artistic letter, all told, though light on actual information.

No matter. I offered her a bursary, too, for we are not

exactly overwhelmed with applicants.

I also remembered someone else: a girl, about ten years old, currently enrolled at Glour City's Sorcerer academy. Susa. She had been tested for Summoner ability some moons back, at my instigation, and failed — sort of.

Let me explain something. For ages now, we have been habitually dividing human magical abilities into two categories. There's Sorcery, which typically involves things like manipulation of light and shadow, illusions, glamours, gates through to the Off-Worlds, that kind of thing. And there is Summoning, my own former field of specialisation, which has more to do with animals — talking with them, working with them, controlling them and so on.

It has taken until recently for us to learn that these things are all derived from the same ultimate source: draykoni heritage. I have a draykon ancestor back somewhere in my family tree, and so I am able to access some small, diluted aspect of their peculiar abilities. We have probably been in error to imagine that Summoning and Sorcery cannot co-exist in the same individual; after all, the draykoni can manage all of the above at once, and plenty more besides. But for whatever reason, those of us with minimal heritage tend to gravitate towards one group of abilities in particular, hence the labelling system.

So, back to little Susa. As a sorceress, nobody expected her to have any ability as a summoner, and so it proved; except that she demonstrated herself capable of controlling beasts anyway, in ways that made no sense at the time. I have since learned what it means to have Lokant heritage, which is much rarer, and brings its own gifts (or burdens, depending upon one's perspective and, frankly, upon one's mood). Susa, with her white hair and her gift for domination of weaker beings, is of Lokant blood, so I am going to need to have her trained.

It is interesting to note that the Lokant trait does not always breed out consistently. Neither one of my parents had white hair. I will check, but it is not especially likely that Susa's parents are white-haired either. And what that seems to mean is that merely having Lokant blood somewhere in the ancestry is insufficient: if one carries the potential to wield their powers as well, it comes with the physical indicator of the prematurely pale plumage. (I realise that plumage is not precisely an accurate word to use here, but I was unable to resist the delicious alliteration of that sentence. My apologies).

Anyway, I fear I have wandered from the point. The *point* is that Susa shall be our third student, and a class of only three will make a gentle beginning for poor Gio. So I rationalise away my disappointment at receiving so few applicants. I know that the white hair is rare, but it is not so rare as this, I think? I wonder what is deterring people from coming to us.

8 IV

I am not precisely sure why Llandry sent Ori to me.

It is not that I object to his presence! Not at all! He is a dear boy and delightful to have around. But since the problem she set me is entirely Lokant-specific, I am not sure what to do with our Lord Draykon.

I can well believe he was reluctant to be separated from Gio, and vice versa, which was probably reason enough. Llandry wishes to see both of them happy, I am sure of it, and would not lightly divide them.

Nor would I. But while Gio is preparing himself to turn teacher, and indeed holding classes, what is poor Ori to do? He looks to me, blithely expecting that I shall produce a task for him at any moment — something worthy of his scintillating brain, something challenging.

I, however, have not the faintest notion of what that might be.

I am reluctant to admit it, for am I not supposed to be infallible? So I stalled by taking Ori with me when I went to see Angstrun.

That's Darae, Lord Angstrun, High Sorcerer of Glour and an old friend of mine. He was more than a friend, once, and that is the other reason why I wanted Ori with me. I will not admit to using the poor man as a human barrier between me and a former flame who is not so delighted with the *former* part, but if you want to draw that conclusion on your own, far be it from me to stop you.

Taking Tren with me would serve the same purpose, of course, but the outcome might be fractionally different. I am too wise to risk it.

I found Angstrun at the Sorcerer School, which fell in line nicely with my hopes. The circumstances were ideal: professional surroundings, the student I wanted to thieve conveniently close by, little chance of being shut up long with Angstrun. I wanted to give him as little as possible to object to about my request, and no time to find things to complain about. A precision operation, conducted with the utmost efficiency.

It is not that Angstrun is especially hard work — or at least, not significantly more so than most men. But it is better not to leave things too much to chance, do you not agree?

Of course, despite one's best efforts it is still possible to be taken by surprise from time to time.

'Lady Glostrum,' said Angstrun politely when I entered his office, Ori in tow.

'Darae,' I responded. Formality be hanged. 'This is Orillin Vance.'

Ori made a casual bow. Angstrun sat in his favourite chair with his feet on the table, and did not trouble himself to move, merely inclining his head to my guest. I thought he would guess why we had come, but if he did, he gave no sign of it. He sat with an expectant expression, looking from me to Ori and back with a creditable appearance of mystification.

'Is there a reason you have brought the Lord Draykon of the Daylands to see me?' he enquired, when I did not immediately speak.

'No, because I haven't. We are here about Susa.'

'Oh?' said Angstrun. He folded his arms and grinned at me, looking pleased about something. Maliciously so.

It isn't that Angstrun objected all that much to my breaking off our largely casual arrangement. The problem is, I did so in order to marry one Lord Vale, a man rather older than myself, and thoroughly eligible. All the right everything, you know. But instead of following through with that unobjectionable plan, I fell in love with Tren.

Tren is a former aide of Angstrun's. If you were not already aware, he is also somewhat younger than both of us, untitled, and the owner of no property. If one were to view the matter in purely pragmatic terms, he has no equitable claim to marrying me, not by way of either fortune or status. In Angstrun's opinion, I threw aside Angstrun and Vale in order to wed someone younger and more handsome than both of those two gentlemen put together.

Well, if dear Darae can believe me to be so shallow as all that, I am not disposed to waste my life worrying over his good opinion.

I crossed my own arms and gave him my best cold stare. If he *would* make me spell it out… 'You must be aware of my endeavours by now. The new bureau proceeds apace, and we are ready to enrol students. I need you to release Susa to me, at least for part of each week.'

Lord Angstrun blinked at me and his eyebrows went up. He looked, much to my displeasure, as though I had lost my mind. 'What are you talking about?'

A question which left me at a loss, for I could not have spoken more plainly. 'Pray do not make difficulties, Angstrun. Tell me at once what the problem is, and I dare say it can be solved.'

'The problem,' said Angstrun slowly, 'is that you have lost your wits. Or perhaps you are here to complicate my day, for some mischievous reason of your own. You must know that I referred Susa to you two days ago. Is she proving unsatisfactory? If you cannot manage her, I invite you to hand her back at your earliest convenience.'

'I what?' Now it was my turn to stare in disbelief, and to doubt whether I had heard correctly. 'Why would you do such a thing?'

'Because you requested it of me.' Angstrun took his feet off the table and sat up, his sardonic expression fading in favour of more genuine puzzlement.

'I?' I echoed, a feeling of foreboding uncurling in my stomach. 'I did no such thing, for I have come here *today* for precisely that purpose.'

'Where did you send her?' interjected Ori.

'Nowhere, especially. She left with you.' Angstrun was looking directly at me as he said that, and I cannot doubt that he spoke the truth. Aggravating as he can sometimes be, I acquit him of any likelihood to torment me by fabricating such an alarming story.

'Darae,' I said in a voice of forced calm, 'The last time I was here was weeks ago. We have had no contact in all of that time, until today. Tell me at once what happened, please, and in detail.'

Angstrun nodded. 'What happened? You came in here just as you are doing right now, demanded that Susa attend upon you instantly for enrolment in your new school, and shortly afterwards left again, taking Susa with you.'

Hmm. 'How did I appear?' I asked. 'How did I behave?'

'You were wearing a new gown,' said Angstrun. He looked me over and added in a bland tone, 'At least, one that I have never seen you wear before. I remember thinking that it became you very well, though it was a trifle more daring than you would normally wear outside of evening engagements.' He made a vague gesture at his own torso, leaving me in no doubt as to his meaning. 'You were imperious, too — more so than usual. I concluded you were displeased with me.'

'I knew your name, I suppose? I understood who you are?'

'You addressed me by name.'

'As Darae?' I pressed.

Angstrun shook his head. 'No, you called me "Lord Angstrun". That is partly why I thought you were angered with me.'

I could not tell if the prospect of my dissatisfaction with him had troubled him at all, or whether he merely dismissed the possibility with a shrug.

Sideline. Focus. 'That was not me,' I reiterated. 'Did this other me give you any clues as to where she might have been taking Susa?'

'To your school,' replied he. 'That is what she said. Or you said.' His eyes narrowed. 'If that was not you, she was incredibly good at pretending to be so.'

I read the direction of his thoughts easily enough, and could not help rolling my eyes in frustration. 'We appear to have a child missing, Darae. Now is not the time for suspicion. I assure you, *I* am the real Evastany Glostrum.'

His brows went up.

I gave a long sigh. 'Close your ears, Ori,' I ordered. The dratted boy looked at me like he had ceased to understand words in the last five seconds, so I did it for him.

While I had Ori so disabled, I proceeded to relate a few particulars of a most intimate character. Now, I am under no illusions about Angstrun. I have no reason to think that I was his *only* liaison all these years. But I do not imagine there are a great many women about who are as intimately acquainted with him as I, or as well informed about certain… details of his private life.

I was only halfway through my monologue when Angstrun began waving his hands in a *cease and desist* gesture, his cheeks turning faintly pink. 'Very well,' he said hastily, raising his voice to interrupt my flow of words. 'Consider me convinced.' He glanced at Ori in alarm, no doubt hoping that I had a good, firm grip upon the boy's tender ears.

I delivered myself of one or two more choice facts before I stopped speaking — driven, no doubt, by some mischievous impulse for which I cannot apologise. What can I say. It was a pleasure to see Angstrun discomfited.

Then I released Ori, who gave me a smile of such angelic innocence that I was immediately convinced that he had heard every word.

So was Angstrun, which did not improve his temper. 'So I sent Susa away with someone who was not you. How is that possible? Believe me, I would never have entrusted Susa to this woman's care had I had the slightest suspicion that she was a stranger.'

'Lokant,' I said, and all mischief left me, for here was trouble indeed. 'It is one of their talents. Or *our* talents, for I can manage it myself. If I wanted to persuade you that you saw something else at this moment, I could.' I demonstrated this by implanting a vision in his mind of my own good self, splendidly naked. It is a sight he was once accustomed to, but has not lately seen, and I had the satisfaction of witnessing a distinct increase in discomfort in our mighty Lord Angstrun.

Understand, it differs from the sorcerous arts in that I made no alteration whatsoever to my appearance. Ori continued to see me exactly as I was that day. It was in Angstrun's perception only that I changed, for I ordered him to imagine that he saw something other than what was. It is an art well suited to a dictatorial personality like mine, and there can be no surprise that I excel at it.

‘I imagine you encountered some other Lokant,’ I continued calmly, allowing my compulsion upon poor Angstrun to fade. ‘Whether a partial or a full-blood I do not know, but clearly it was no trouble for her to persuade you that you were seeing me.’

‘Or him,’ put in Ori. ‘A man may just as easily manipulate Angstrun into believing himself in female company, no?’

‘Fair point,’ I conceded.

‘Someone who knows you, surely?’ said Angstrun. ‘For the impression was most convincing.’ He would be obliged to emphasise that point to save face, I realise, for he would not like any of us to believe that he is easily duped.

On the other hand, whatever Angstrun’s flaws he is not careless. I do believe he would not have dispatched Susa with this person had he had any suspicion it was not truly me.

‘Perhaps,’ I conceded. ‘I am acquainted with few Lokants.’ There is Limbane of course, and Andraly, a female Lokant from the same Library. Plus a handful of others.

‘Or not,’ said Ori. ‘You are a well-known figure, after all, and it does not sound as though this other you behaved to Angstrun as you normally would.’

‘True,’ said Angstrun with a sigh. ‘Your physical appearance would not be too hard to replicate, considering how many images of you are to be seen all over the bulletin boards every week.’ He looked chagrined as he said that, and I wondered whether my inescapability bothered him.

‘Someone was behaving as they imagined you would behave,’ said Ori. ‘Based on your public image. The imperious Lady Glostrum, not at all given to asking when she can command.’

That was not too far from the truth of course, and Angstrun knew it too. Neither of us enlightened Ori. ‘So it could be someone unknown to any of us,’ I concluded. ‘Wonderful.’ I frowned at Angstrun. ‘Did her parents have no objection to your sending her away with me?’

‘She has no parents. Orphan. She has been in the care of the school for the past year or so.’

I spent a little while in thought, considering the facts at hand.

- Someone had a reason to want Susa, urgently enough to engage in subterfuge and kidnapping in order to secure her.

- This enterprising person knew that I would be likely to feel an interest in the child, and that I had both a reason and a right to request her transferral to my school.

- This person may also have been aware that she had no parents to raise the alarm over her disappearance. Perhaps they thought it might be a long time before I swapped notes with Angstrun and realised her absence, or had they concluded that it might never come to pass at all?

Questions aside, we had a child missing and every reason to think that she was far, far away by now. Lokants do not live on our world at all. They settle in their "Libraries" — structures which exist independently of any particular world and are largely invulnerable to the passage of time. Structures which, worst of all for our purposes, can be absolutely anywhere.

There was a chance that the person who had taken Susa was only a partial Lokant, like me, and might not have taken her off-world at all. But not a great one, and even if that was the case: how to follow?

'This matter of altering your perceptions,' I said out loud. 'It is extremely difficult to so manipulate more than one person at once.'

'Somebody might have seen them leave,' Ori agreed. 'A white-haired person with a child? That might be memorable enough.'

'I will enquire,' said Angstrun.

Which he did, and sent the report after us a few days later. Susa had been seen in the company of a woman with white hair. One person described the latter as elderly, but the other said no, she was at most middle-aged. I think the second account is the more likely. When people see white hair, they tend to assume advanced age to go with it — unless they are paying close enough attention to notice the more subtle signs to the contrary.

Nobody saw where the woman and Susa went.

This lack of information was disheartening, but at least it confirmed one thing. We may not have received a clear enough description of the abductor to guess at her identity, but we can be fairly sure that she is female. I am afraid, though, that her traceless disappearance hints at her being a full-blooded Lokant. If she is, she has probably taken poor Susa far off-world to some Library or other, and the chances of our recovering the girl under those circumstances are slim.

11 IV

We asked Gio, of course, but he had no information for us.

'I am sorry,' he said, when we had finished telling him everything we knew. 'I know of nobody who might want a child like Susa, and without a clearer description I can have no way of guessing who the woman is.'

'Can you find out anything?' asked Ori. 'The girl is only ten! We have to help her somehow.'

Gio shifted in his seat, looking most uncomfortable. 'I fear you have an inaccurate idea of Lokant society. You have only come into contact with one or two of our Libraries, I gather, so it may seem as though there are only a few. From there, it is easy to assume that we all know each other's business. I'm afraid that is far from the case. There are many Libraries I know nothing of.'

I thought I could guess the source of his concern. 'Our expectations of you are not of crushing proportions,' I told Gio. 'If you can discover nothing of use, we shall not hold it to be your fault.'

'No, no!' Ori hastened to agree with me. 'Only do what you can, dearest.'

Gio sighed, and rubbed at his eyes. 'I want to recover the missing child as much as you do, I assure you. I will be glad to make enquiries at Sulayn Phay, only… I have rather parted ways with them, and I have treated one or two of them pretty badly at that. It will be difficult to convince them to trust me enough to confide, if indeed they have any involvement in this business.'

Personally I doubt that the woman who took Susa was Dwinal. Firstly because Dwinal is of advanced age and I think it more likely that our second witness was correct: the abductor was a younger woman. Secondly because it would be far too easy if our kidnapper was the same person I am already charged to investigate, and when is life ever that?

That does not rule out the possibility that someone else of Sulayn Phay took Susa, however. We know from Llandry's account, as well as Gio's information, that Phay is divided into factions these days, and who knows what nefarious business they are all getting up to?

I could sympathise with Gio's problem, though. Was he to go wandering around his former home Library, casually asking all he met whether they had happened to kidnap a part-Lokant child recently? And when he spoke of having treated some of them badly, I could guess what he meant. By Llandry's account, he had carved an implant out of the living flesh of one of his former colleagues, in order to gain access to his grandmother's personal chambers.

This is the kind of thing that tends to irritate people.

I would not be in a hurry to send him back there, and judging from the look on Ori's face, I would have him to contend with if I tried.

There is always the possibility that we are dealing with a mere partial Lokant, of course, and Susa is not far away. With this in mind, I submitted the details of the case to Glour City's Investigative Office.

I was outraged to find that they doubted me. Me! The notion that it is possible for our abductress to so convincingly mimic someone else's appearance is too far-fetched for credulity, I am to understand, and I could spend all day explaining Lokant abilities for all the good it would do. I was displeased. The more so when told that, with so few details of the mystery woman's appearance to go on (and conflicting accounts at that), there would be little they could do to find her.

I did not receive the impression that the fate of Susa was of any great concern to them. Is it because she is an orphan child, with no family to miss her? How detestable, if so! It only made me the more determined to find her myself. Though I cannot help admitting that they are right about one thing: with no real information to work with, we begin at a grave disadvantage.

I am not without my resources, however, even if the Investigative Office is disinclined to lend me theirs. I and my Summoner days have parted ways lately, but I have not lost my abilities there; nor have I lost the various animal friends I made during my years as High Summoner of Glour.

Chief among them is Rikbeek, my gwaystrel. Tiny creature. Black fur, webby wings, a tendency to bite. He is difficult to love, I will admit, but we have been friends for so long that I tend to forgive him his faults. He is a marvellous spy, too, being both difficult to spot and almost impossible to deceive. I make use of him a lot, when I want to find things out.

He only grows grumpier with the passage of time, alas. *Rikbeek,* I said to him this morning. *We seek a missing child. If you spot her, inform me at once.* With this command I conveyed to him a mental picture of Susa, as far as I remembered her. It has been a few moons since I last saw the girl.

I received by way of reply the sound of tiny teeth snapping, and the faint scent of blood drifted across my senses.

I am glad we are in agreement, I told him, unmoved by this display of insubordination.

Perhaps it is unwise to let him live in the folds of my skirt. Usually he drapes himself among the outer layers of fabric, but in colder weather (or when he is upset about something) he burrows under and suspends himself, upside-down, directly next to my legs. I can well believe that it is warmer, and therefore more comforting, underneath, but since it also gives him unimpeded access to my poor skin, I sometimes regret my leniency. I was given cause to do so this morning.

I made a mental note to see about having sturdier stockings made.

Besides Rikbeek I have also befriended a shortig hound, to whom Tren has given the fine name of Bartel. Shortigs have a fine sense of smell, and can track anything. I have had cause to test Bartel before, and found him to be unbeatable in this respect. Tren and I went to the Academy this morning and took Bartel with us. I walked into Angstrun's office with tiny Bartel tucked under one arm, and presented him to the High Sorcerer with a smug smile.

Darae gazed upon my little shortig hound in confusion. 'No thank you,' he said.

I frowned. Setting aside for the moment the absurdity of Angstrun imagining I might offer him a gift, why should he object to poor Bart? The very cutest of creatures! Small enough to be easily carted about with one hand, all silky black fur and paws and ears, and the friendliest nature!

'He is not for you,' I informed Angstrun with strong displeasure. 'Particularly if you are going to be so abominable as to reject him anyway! He is here to help us.'

Angstrun cast a glowering look at Tren, and did not reply.

'We need access to Susa's things,' I persevered, ignoring this display of manly rivalry. 'Bartel will take her scent and attempt to track her. Where was she sleeping?'

Angstrun sighed, and to my relief he set aside his sour mood and bent himself to the task of being much more helpful. 'She has a room in the attic, somewhere in the servants' quarters. I will have somebody take you up.'

"Somebody" proved to be another girl of around Susa's age, dark-haired and wearing an expensive dress. They were clearly friends, in spite of the apparent difference in social status, for our little guide questioned us at length about Susa's whereabouts as she led us up flights of stairs into the attic. 'She said nothing about going away,' said the little girl with a mighty frown. 'And it is my birthday soon, too! She must come back, and attend the party.'

'We are doing our best to bring her back in time,' Tren promised, with a reassuring smile for the girl.

I decline to waste my time trying to please children, on the whole. Not that my fondness for fine gowns does not find its fair share of concordant enthusiasm, especially from little girls. But my manner, I must sorrowfully own, is forbidding, and they tend to shrink from me, however attracted they might be to the glitter of my attire. I blessed Tren for being so much less awful a figure, and left him to talk to the child.

She had nothing of use to tell us, of course. 'Twas but a small hope that she might. Susa had never mentioned any new acquaintance, and nothing seemed to have changed in her life prior to her disappearance. Her friend was as confused as the rest of us.

She did lead us straight to Susa's tiny, featureless room, however, and assisted us in searching the girl's meagre possessions. Susa's belongings appeared to consist of one spare dress, threadbare and shabby, and a discarded hat.

'Surely she had more than this?' Tren said.

Susa's friend nodded. 'Three dresses! One blue, one red, and that one.' She nodded towards the closet in which the abandoned dress hung. 'And a coat and gloves and a scarf.'

'Is there any chance that somebody might have stolen them?' I put in.

The girl glowered at me. 'No one would do that.'

Well, I'm sorry, little girl, but people thieve all the time. I admired her naïve reliance upon the goodness of humanity, even as I speculated wearily as to how long it would last. Perhaps she had a few years of such fond imaginings left.

'The door was locked,' Tren pointed out.

True. Our guide secured the key from a housekeeper or something before we came up, and certainly used it to unlock the door. And since there were no signs that anyone had forced their way in, a robbery did not seem likely. Who would go out of their way to steal a key to this little attic chamber, in order to steal a shabby child's dress?

Susa had been given the opportunity to pack her belongings, then. I was unsure how to feel about this. It was an unusually civilised kidnapper that gave her victims chance to prepare themselves for a trip. Could I therefore conclude that Susa was being well-treated in general? I hoped so, though the circumstances puzzled me.

I took down the discarded dress and let it slip off its hanger onto the floor. Bartel I placed beside it, and silently gave him to understand that he was to immerse himself in its aromas forthwith. Our tiny guide, overcome with instant love for my shortig, would have fallen upon the beast at once and smothered him in affection, if she had been permitted. Judging from the gleam of ferocious delight in her pale blue eyes, I would consider Bartel fortunate if he had survived the experience.

Happily for us both, Tren intervened. 'Bart is going to help us find Susa,' he told the disappointed girl. 'He needs to find out what she smells like, so he can follow her trail. He is getting it from the dress, look.'

To her credit, the girl did not object, but held her peace and watched while Bartel stuffed his face into the folds of the shabby dress and noisily inhaled. I gave him the sorry little hat Susa had left behind as well, and he repeated the process.

Smells like child, he informed me when he had finished.

It is difficult to put anything past you, I responded. Bartel gave me a tongue-lolling houndish grin and stood, tail wagging, ready to proceed.

'And now we follow,' said Tren, doing a fine job once again of remembering that children are people and that speaking to them is an option.

I opened the door, and Bartel shot out into the corridor beyond. Once he gets a scent there is no stopping him, and the two of us — er, *three,* childchildchild — had to hasten to keep up with him.

He charged straight for the nearest staircase and rattled down it, a pattern he repeated down the next few flights of stairs until he reached the ground floor. No diversions of any kind, no sidelines; he went for the front door, and the moment I opened it he bounded on through and into the street.

I hoped he would disappear up the street in merry pursuit of a satisfyingly long trail, tail wagging and ears flying all the way. To my dismay — though not, I admit, to my surprise — he merely dashed around a corner, galloped several feet up a narrow alleyway in between the Academy building and its next neighbour, and stopped.

End, he said.

And I sighed, because so abrupt an ending to the trail could only mean one thing.

Susa's abductor might be a partial or full-blooded Lokant, but either way she had access to a Lokant Library. She had taken the girl downstairs — presumably prepared to convince anybody she encountered that it was *me* they saw, in order to preserve the illusion that Susa had merely transferred into my school.

But the moment she was outside, she had translocated off-world into some Lokant Library somewhere, taking poor Susa with her. The girl was far, far away by now, and how could we possibly guess where?

12 IV

Gio found me earlier today in my favourite parlour, where I was sitting with Tren. We were going over the details of a funding agreement with an independent contributor (who prefers to remain nameless, so I may not document her generosity here). His purpose was to lament my lack of relevant study materials, and I could not blame him for doing so. How was he to teach any improving course of study without suitable books?

In my defence, what was I to do? 'It is true that I have helped myself to a range of texts from Limbane's Library,' I told him.

'Thirty-seven of them,' put in Tren.

'Thirty-seven of them,' I confirmed. 'They are mostly relating to the draykoni, though, and those with any relevance to Lokantkind are unlikely to be of use to you. I have one or two general histories, a few language primers, that kind of thing.'

Gio sighed. 'It is difficult to teach any subject when the only resource at hand is the contents of one's own head,' he complained. 'The random recollections of any private individual tend to emerge in no organised state, and I am bound to forget all kinds of things.'

'I apologise,' I informed him. 'No, I do. I fully understand the problem. If I had happened to see any texts lying about with titles like *A Conveniently Simple Account of our Own Arts,* or maybe *Lokant Skills and How to Use Them,* I assure you I would have snagged them with alacrity, for they would have been of great help to me.'

'Snagged?' said Tren, one eyebrow raised.

'Snagged,' I repeated, with infinite dignity. 'It is a perfectly respectable word.'

'I wonder if Harwell's Dictionary would agree,' murmured he, returning his attention to the documents before him. I was not deceived. I could *feel* his mischievous smile, even if he had concealed it behind a casually raised hand.

'I am not in the habit of being dictated to by a book.'

'Not even an especially authoritative one?'

'No. Harwell is a sad, hidebound creature, stuck forever in his paltry *traditions* and *accepted conventions* and deplorably reluctant to keep pace with the developments of modern language. I, however, am a woman of linguistic vision.'

Tren removed his hand, having by then mastered his expression, for he gave me a sober look and murmured, 'Very true.'

I stuck my tongue out at him.

Gio was staring at us both with palpable perplexity. I recollected that he is unused to banter, and feared he might believe us both mad — or at best, impossibly frivolous. I regretted the sticking-out-of-the-tongue incident accordingly, but it was done for sound reasons. Best to move on.

I composed my face into a grave expression to match Tren's and returned to the topic at hand. I smiled encouragingly at Gio. 'If I give you a great deal of paper and ink and a few *very* good pens, do you suppose you might be able to make do?'

Gio's response was to dissolve into consternation. I appear to evoke that feeling in the poor boy rather often. 'I… yes, probably,' he said with a sigh. 'Only I do not think it will be ready before your first students arrive.'

'*Your* first students, Gio,' I reminded him with a smile, in response to which he merely turned paler.

My attempts at encouragement having summarily failed, it fell to Tren to salvage the situation. 'You are not trying to turn out top scholars,' he said. 'There will be no tests for your students to pass, no examinations, no dissertations required. They merely need to develop a sound, practical knowledge of their abilities, and a degree of confidence in using them.'

'So that we may milk their fledgling aptitude later,' I put in, beaming.

'And,' Tren added with a quelling look at me, 'It is unlikely that your students will develop a grasp for all of the possible Lokant arts. Typically, a partial will display ability for some one or two things only. So you see, you will not be teaching all things to all students.'

Gio looked a little mollified, or at any rate less likely to descend into total panic. I wondered briefly what manner of schooling he had received at Sulayn Phay, and how far he expected to follow his own pattern of education in teaching our fledgling partials.

'Ask Ori to help,' I suggested. 'He has brain enough for at least six people, and motivation to match. He will have half your programme written before you can blink.'

I was pleased with myself for this idea, as it brightened Gio up immediately, *and* gave Ori something useful to do. I had no doubt of the truth of my words, either. Those two young men would make a formidable team at most things, I am sure, and anything remotely academic in particular. Away Gio went, taking with him the promised sheaf of paper and supply of ink and pens and what-not.

'Cunning,' Tren complimented me.

'I know,' I agreed.

'Almost fiendishly so.' He looked me over in an appraising way, and there was a certain gleam to his eye that made me regret the busy programme of work I had given us for the day.

'It is why you love me.' I returned the look, gleaming more than a little myself, and seriously considered ripping up my list of tasks-for-the-day and burning the pieces.

These budding plans — undeniably fiendish — were interrupted by the arrival of a missive. It was delivered, rather originally, by bird. I guessed this because Hayes, my butler, appeared in the parlour after a discreet knock upon the door, a slip of paper held in one hand and an expression of distaste upon his elegant features. The paper in question was curled as though it had spent some little time rolled up, and when I accepted it from him I noticed at once the traces of… *aroma* about the message.

I handled it with care.

Your first student arrived at headquarters, eleven hours and thirty-seven minutes past the Cloaking hour.

'Lovely,' I said, delighted, and passed the message to Tren. He accepted it dubiously, and discarded it upon the table-top the moment he had read it. 'I wonder which of them it is?'

The message, I conclude, was sent by Adonia Marle, who I have installed to act as a general assistant at our new bureau building. Secretary, welcomer-of-new-arrivals, handler-of-paperwork, that kind of thing. I admit, her choice of message delivery vehicle was unexpected.

'Let us go and meet her,' I said, rising from the table at once.

Tren's brows went up. 'Are we finished here?'

'Yes.' I mentally swept the competing demands of paperwork aside, delighted, I confess, to have a justifiable reason for doing so.

Tren was no less so, for he rose with alacrity and followed me from the room.

It was not, perhaps, strictly necessary to take a detour to my dressing-room prior to departure, for my choice of gown was adequate to the occasion. Nor was it necessary to take Tren with me, or for either of us to take so very long about it all.

We were happier for the delay, however, so I make no apology.

Adonia Marle is not your typical administrator (supposing there can be said to be such a thing). Her choice of courier may seem odd at first, but seeing as she is a graduate of Summoner school, it is not all that surprising. Her ability at the art is not sufficiently profound to permit her to pursue a career as a summoner, but it is not without its uses to have such a person in charge of our offices.

In other respects, though, she is somewhat… erratic. Eccentric, shall we say? She is a trifle more disorganised than one would typically prefer, though I have hopes this will improve as she grows more accustomed to her new role. Her style of dress I make no objection to, for what can it possibly matter what she wears? If she feels at her happiest, most comfortable and most confident wearing a gown of jonquil and ebony cotton, trimmed with lace and teamed with striped black-and-white boots, far be it from me to object. Happy people make for the best employees.

Today she had selected a pale green shirt of a style more

usually chosen by men, paired with dark trousers (my fault there; I have become somewhat famous for my adoption of the trouser for ordinary daywear). Her abundant brown hair was swept up into a cloudily bouffant arrangement decked in violently green ribbons, and she wore a lip tint of matching hue. Her choices are startling, I admit; I have never seen her wear the same ensemble twice, either, in spite of what must be a modest budget for clothing. I cannot help admiring her boldness, or her imagination, however much my eyes might sometimes protest the combinations.

Tren and I found her in the little office we had assigned to her role. She was not sitting *at* her desk so much as *on* it, cross-legged at one end of the neatly cleared surface with a cup of tea in her hand. Seated at the opposite end was a stranger, presumably our new student. The two were sipping tea and talking animatedly with one another, and it was nice to see them getting along so well, even if their choice of seating arrangements did puzzle me.

I exchanged a bemused look with Tren, and finding him no more enlightened than myself as to what was occurring in there, I decided to ignore it.

Adonia saluted us with her tea cup as we walked in. 'Bosses,' she said, characteristically laconic. At least, she is usually so with us. How our new arrival managed to get her to talk so freely, I still do not know.

The lady in question put down her tea cup and spun around to face us — without uncrossing her legs or getting down from the desktop. 'Ah!' she cried. 'Lady Glostrum and Mr. Warvel! How many times have I seen you both in the news! You are far more splendid in person than I dared imagine.'

This last reflection appeared to be directed more at me than Tren, as her eyes swept over my cerulean silk-velvet gown and bejewelled hair in a perfunctory once-over. I was not able to gather anything about her opinion of my splendour, for her expression gave nothing away.

She appeared to be a little older than Adonia and Tren, somewhere in her late twenties. Her hair, of course, was white, and tied back in an elaborate braid. She was soberly dressed, so much so as to look drab beside Adonia's bedazzling ensemble. She had a pleasant face, though, and an air of cheerful friendliness which I found promising.

‘Miss Nallay?’ I hazarded.

‘Miss Heliandor Rasset,’ she corrected me. ‘Or preferably, Heli. Formality was never popular with me, and Heliandor is such a mouthful, is it not? Far too many syllables. Cannot think what my parents were about in bestowing such a name. My brother’s is still worse, would you believe? And no, before you ask, his hair is sky-black all the way through. Not so much as a single whitish strand on his whole head. My parents are the same. I am the only white-haired oddity we have, which is strange indeed, do you not think?’

She delivered herself of this speech so rapidly and with so little apparent thought, one might be tempted to dismiss her as a brainless talker. But her eyes were busy as she spoke: watching me, watching Tren, taking note of every detail of our appearances, and without losing track of Adonia in the process. I detected a shrewd appraisal going on, and concluded that, far from being vacant-headed, she had a sharp intellect.

I also mentally adjusted my estimate of her age, upwards by a few years.

‘I apologise,’ I said. ‘We are expecting two arrivals in the next day or two, but I rather thought Miss Nallay would appear first, having the least distance to travel. You have come all the way from Orstwych, have you not? I hope you had a tolerable journey.’

Pleasantries were exchanged all round, and since they were predominantly of the very smallest kind of talk, I will not bore you with them. Tren, of course, invited her to use his short name right away. I did not. It can be unwise to establish too casual a relationship early on, if one expects to be properly attended to later.

Heli did not descend from her perch atop the desk and neither did Adonia. Eventually I was able to lure the former down by proposing to show her to her quarters. The house is large enough to provide accommodation to our students on its upper floors, at least for the time being.

With Heli settled and Adonia restored to the performance of her duties (at least in theory), I had leisure to consider the problem of Miss Faronni Nallay. I was genuinely surprised to find Miss Rasset arrived first, for Miss Nallay had given her address as Amori Tovia, a town only a few hours’ carriage-ride from Glour City. What could be keeping her?

'Perhaps she is delayed,' Tren suggested. 'She did not give any projected date for her arrival, did she?'

'Not that I recall. But her letter arrived days ago — six, I think, or seven?'

'She has a life to leave behind. It can take time to effect such a transformation of circumstances.'

He was right, of course, so I quieted my fledgling alarms and focused on the matter of introducing Gio to Heli and assisting them with the awkward business of beginning their teacher-student relationship. Gio has yet to fully accept himself in that role and began much too diffidently. Fortunately, Heli was absolutely awed by him.

Not at all to my surprise, I might add, for Gio can be an awe-inspiring figure. He appears young, but he has the gravity of a much more mature man, especially when he is uncomfortable and, consequently, reserved. He is also spectacularly good-looking, which might be considered an obstacle more than an advantage for a teacher, but it seemed to operate upon Heli in more or less useful ways. Once she had been given a demonstration of his abilities — abilities which, with time and study, could be hers — she lost her tendency to rattle on and soon became a sober and attentive student. Gio gradually remembered that he was not absolutely obliged to maintain a stiffly imposing manner at all times, and lessons proceeded apace.

I was proud. And a little excited, as juvenile as it may seem. Our bureau was operational! Our school was functional! We had premises, funding, recruits, employees, students, everything!

'Next step, the world,' said Tren, observing my enthusiasm with an indulgent grin.

'At *least*,' I agreed.

19 IV

It has been a week or so since the commencement of Heli's lessons, and Ori and Gio have contrived to have their supporting materials completed, which pleases everybody. Except perhaps Heliandor herself, for they have produced seemingly endless pages between them, all of which she is expected to read in due course.

I, however, am delighted. Such excellent work, and in so short a time! I have been most effusive in my praise.

But Faronni Nallay still has not arrived. I confess myself troubled, for we have received no word from her either — no notification of delay, no estimate as to her probable time of arrival. It is as though she never existed. I have even retrieved her letter once or twice and perused it afresh, just to reassure myself that I did not imagine her altogether.

Under ordinary circumstances, one would assume the most mundane of all possible explanations to be the true one. She is delayed by some mind-numbingly ordinary occurrence. She forgot to write to inform us, or her letter went astray somewhere in between Amori Tovia and Glour City. She will turn up tomorrow, or perhaps next week, and there will be an end of it.

On we would all go with our lives.

Consider, though, the fate of Susa, and then tell me that my concern is misplaced. We do not appear to be enjoying the blissful dullness of ordinary circumstances.

I may not have any idea, as yet, why somebody might consider it worth abducting a penniless ten-year-old girl from Sorcerer School. But in impersonating me at the time, whoever was responsible for it created a link between Susa's disappearance and my new school. That person is worryingly well informed about our doings, has clearly been paying close attention to our activities, and I cannot imagine that such surveillance has been undertaken lightly, or without clear motive.

We must consider, then, the possibility that Faronni Nallay's failure to arrive is not the fault of some commonplace happenstance. If, as I fear, she has been abstracted from Amori Tovia in the same way as Susa was removed from school, then she is in need of assistance and it falls to us to provide it.

I considered this full reason enough to abandon all other duties earlier today and depart the capital at once. Tren accompanies me. We go to Miss Nallay's home in search of her.

I write this en route, though the swaying of the carriage does render it a tricky task, and my penmanship is not up to my usual standards. No matter; it is legible. I have some hopes of arriving at Miss Nallay's house to find her still in residence, urgently occupied with the task of removing to Glour City. Tren's disposition is more sanguine than mine, more optimistic, less cynical. He considers it likely, even, that we will find her hale and well and, above all, present.

Let us hope this shall be a victory for optimism over cynicism, for in my experience the opposite much more frequently proves true.

Spoken, of course, like a true cynic.

20 IV

I write from the best inn Amori Tovia can offer, which is not bad at all in spite of the town's modest size. We are installed here for but one night, for our search tomorrow will soon take us beyond the borders of the town, I have no doubt.

You will guess from such a statement that Tren's sanguine hopes were proved sadly unfounded. Let me describe the events of yesterday, as best I can.

Miss Faronni Nallay lives in a poorer part of the town. Her tiny, shabby little house is one of a row of tiny, shabby little houses, most of them ill-kept and unloved. I imagine they usually prove to be rather temporary residences.

Miss Nallay's house is a little better maintained than some, and the pots of various growing-things around the door speak well of her. We saw nothing amiss when we arrived, but having knocked upon the door some three or four times, waiting a minute or two in between, we were soon obliged to conclude that she was not at home.

Tren immediately conducted a speedy survey of her neighbours, most of whom were found to be in residence. The news was bad: no one had seen her in at least a week.

'Time to break in,' Tren decided, and found this task immediately achievable, for a door at the back was unlocked. In we went.

I do not know what I expected to see: a mess, perhaps? The

kind that suggests somebody was forcibly removed from the house, protesting all the way? We saw nothing of the kind. Miss Nallay's house was scrupulously neat inside, and all that was obviously missing was a selection of clothes, for her wardrobe was almost empty.

'So she left willingly,' Tren observed. 'But was she on her way to us, and intercepted somewhere en route? Or did whoever took her give her time to pack, like Susa?'

No way to tell. I abandoned her drab little bedchamber quite quickly, for it had nothing else to tell us.

Downstairs, I conducted a more thorough search of her possessions. I found my own letter to her, inviting her to take up a position with our new bureau. I glanced over it so perfunctorily, it took me a moment to realise that it was *not* my letter, or not quite. The wording was the same, as far as I remembered, and that was my signature at the bottom. But I had invited her to present herself at our office in Glour City, and given the address.

This letter made no mention of it. It merely stated — *in my own handwriting!* — that someone would arrive to collect her, and that she should make herself ready to travel.

I handed this gem off to Tren with a disgusted flourish. A filthy trick. 'Someone has made off with two out of three of our students,' I said to him. 'And as if that were not offensive enough, they have been making free with my handwriting, my signature and even my visage in order to accomplish it!'

'The insult is insupportable,' Tren agreed, perusing the letter briefly. 'I have to say, though, as kidnappings go these are fairly low-key. No forcible abductions, no ransom notes, no apparent violence.'

'All good things,' I had to agree. 'But the fact remains that Susa has been taken away somewhere unspecified, by someone who had no right to do so, and Faronni Nallay has been deceived.'

I paused to think, largely fruitlessly. I feel sure, even as I write, that some degree of explanation ought to be obvious. Here we have a pattern emerging: two untrained partial Lokants taken away, most likely to a Library off-world. Both were prospective students at my new school, and shortly due to receive training. Both appear to have gone along more or less willingly, though whether they had any true understanding of where they were going remains in doubt.

It would not be the first time that Lokants have made use of partials from our world. Krays (a tasteless, troublesome individual whose untimely demise is regretted by nobody) has done so before, though the experience did not turn out very well for the people in question.

It is this that troubles me. It ought to be a good thing, if Lokants are disposed to take an interest in us. They are by far the best qualified to teach us; I am aware how much hubris there is in *my* presuming to set up a school, considering that I am by no means an expert in these arts myself. My grasp of domination is excellent, though I do not think I qualify as fully trained in the business. I can translocate. But Gio is far better equipped to teach such arts than I, and I am entirely lacking in some other Lokant powers — I cannot heal or mend at all.

If I could believe that they simply propose to do a better job of teaching my students than I can, I would have no objection to their interference. But the chances of that are slim. I am persuaded that no Lokant ever did anything for the benefit of others. If they are teaching my students then they are also disposed to use them for something, and it is unlikely to prove to be much to the benefit of Susa or Faronni.

I took the precaution of bringing Bartel along with us, as well as Rikbeek, who goes everywhere with me. This second tracking expedition ended in the same way as the first. We gave Bart some of Miss Nallay's clothing, and he duly followed her scent out into the street. Her trail persisted just around the corner and… then it vanished.

We spent the remaining hours consulting once again with her neighbours, in hopes that she might have mentioned something — anything — that could help us. I did not hold out much hope, for it does not appear that my impersonator communicated with her at all except by the false letter.

We uncovered nothing new, nothing of note, nothing helpful. Miss Faronni Nallay has vanished into the wind, like Susa, and we cannot follow.

I put down my pen with a view to turning in for the night, for we propose to leave early tomorrow. But Tren asked something pertinent and I feel compelled to note it down.

We had identified three prospective students, but only two of them have been taken. My first thought upon considering this fact was mild panic; what if we return to find that Heliandor has likewise disappeared?

'Unlikely,' Tren argued. 'Clearly, whoever is responsible is well-informed as to our doings. They cannot be unaware of Heliandor's existence, and I can think of no sensible reason why they would have taken Susa and Faronni already and simply been late to claim Heliandor. I think that the link between Susa and Faronni must be more complex than we imagine.'

'It is not merely that they are partials,' I agreed. 'Considering the fact that I, too, have failed to disappear into thin air, we can conclude that more is required.'

Tren looked worried by this reflection, and I regretted bringing it up. 'Let's hope that whatever it is about Susa and Faronni that qualifies them for special treatment is something you lack.'

'Apparently it is something Heliandor lacks. But what? The frustrating thing is, we know nothing at all about Faronni. Only basic, largely useless facts.' Nobody we had spoken to seemed to know much about her, either. She was a withdrawn type of person, not much given to socialising, and had no apparent friends in her neighbourhood. And since we have no idea where she works, if anywhere in particular, it will be difficult to find out more about her.

It is a place to start, however. We agreed to learn more about Faronni, by whatever means possible.

'Considering that there are now two missing students,' I added, 'It stands to reason that there might be more abductees, or potential ones.'

'Sending letters,' agreed Tren. 'To us.'

'Ah. Yes.' As minimal an exchange as this last part was, I caught Tren's drift at once.

Who has been intercepting our post, and how?

22 IV

I have learned that Ori and Gio are formidably devious.

I have also learned that Ori has a flair for espionage, and has had a fancy to try his hand at it for some time. I discovered these things because when Tren and I returned to Glour City and revealed our findings, the two of them threw themselves into the problem with an enthusiasm I can only describe as Gusto (believe me, the capital letter is more than justified).

'Right, so,' said Ori, stretching out in his chair in my favourite parlour and putting his feet on my favourite footstool, 'There are a few places it would be possible to intercept post. We can assume, firstly, that this is happening from *our* end, not the sender's, as the interference appears to be designed to discover the identities of the latter. So, it is probably happening somewhere in between Glour City's main sorting office and the letterbox at Headquarters.'

'Big office?' asked Gio.

'I have never thought about it,' I replied.

'Of course it is,' said Tren. 'Big city, big sorting office.'

'It would be difficult to find and intercept two particular letters in a sorting office like that,' Gio suggested. 'If they have no idea where the letters are coming from.'

Ori agreed. 'So they are probably getting hold of them after they leave the sorting office. It might be a question of swiping them off the post carrier en route, or maybe it's been as simple as taking them out of our letterbox before we can get to them. As for the other problem: how are you sending letters?'

He was looking at me, which left me in some little difficulty. 'Um,' I said, and looked at Tren for help.

I had to suffer the indignity of being laughed at in response. 'Eva never thinks of simple practicalities,' Tren said, with a wink at me to show that he was not being malicious. 'It is for others to deal with dull matters like how to get a letter out.'

'I have other things to think about,' I said, and hoped I did not sound as defensive as I feared.

'What do you do with your letters, Eva?' said Ori, in a patient tone I found deplorable.

'I sign and seal them and leave them on my desk.'

Tren put in, 'Adonia probably takes them and posts them.'

'In theory then, anybody could take them off your desk, alter them and put them back before Adonia finds them?'

I nodded at Ori. 'In theory.'

'Supposing, of course, that it is not Adonia herself,' he added.

I was horrified. 'No, I am sure not. I have known her since she was a child. She's a former student of mine. I invited her mother to my wedding!'

'Which wedding?' put in Tren in a whisper.

'The previous one.'

'The… cancelled, previous one?' Tren looked faintly nervous, as though he seriously imagined I might have been married and widowed before and somehow contrived to conceal the fact from him.

'The cancelled one,' I said, heroically resisting the impulse to roll my eyes.

Tren looked relieved.

Ori eyed me with suspicion, apparently unconvinced by my staunch faith in Adonia. 'Do not *doubt* me, Ori,' I told him sternly. 'It is appallingly rude.'

'Fine, fine,' he said ungraciously. 'For the present, we will assume Adonia's innocence and look elsewhere for our culprit.'

'Do we have any security at headquarters at all?' said Gio.

'I have no idea,' said I frostily.

He smiled faintly in response. 'I will attend to that, if you will permit.'

'Feel free.'

'Not yet,' said Ori. 'We can use this to draw out our kidnapper.'

And Ori paused. His only possible motive in doing so was to heighten the suspense, so I had no qualms in bending my most ferocious glower upon him until he started talking again.

'This is a complicated scheme,' said he. 'I see two possible motives for it. One: to ensure that people like Miss Nallay go along quietly. A person who does not realise they are being kidnapped is much easier to make off with, no? And two: to conceal the Lokant's identity, and if possible their activities, from people like us who might object. If they can throw suspicion on you in the process, all the better.

'So, I imagine a few things likely. One, we may not receive any more letters from prospective students. They will mysteriously go astray, because how can we interfere in the removal of more of our students if we are not even informed of their existence? In fact, Eva, I would not be surprised if that has already occurred. You did wonder why you received so few letters. Miss Nallay's was probably swiped a bit late, forcing our kidnapper to arrange an alternative way to intercept her.'

A good point indeed.

'Two: if we assume that all letters addressed to headquarters are being taken before we get anywhere near them, this is potentially of great benefit to us. We begin by pretending that we have no idea it is happening at all. Your ladyship can help this process along by making a deal of noise in public about your lack of applicants and your great disappointment in the failure of your scheme.

'Meanwhile, we will set up a fake applicant. Have a letter ostensibly from that person sent to headquarters in the regular post. See what happens.'

'You mean,' said I, 'that we will try to have one of ourselves kidnapped.'

'Exactly.' Ori beamed upon all three of us.

Tren gave a slight cough. 'Not that I wish to pour scorn upon an excellent plan, Ori, but do you not think that might be a trifle dangerous?'

'Not at all. I suggest we employ Gio. He can camouflage his appearance from whoever shows up, in case it turns out to be someone he knows — make them see a different person in his place. And he can translocate out of wherever it is he's taken to, if he finds himself in danger. They are expecting untrained partials, remember, not a fully-trained Lokant.'

I looked at Gio to discover how he felt about Ori's cavalier attitude to his safety. I was surprised by it myself, but I was prepared to put it down to enthusiasm for the thrilling adventure.

Gio looked slightly nonplussed, but his confidence in his own abilities appeared to equal his lover's, for he shrugged and agreed. 'It is a sound enough plan.'

That won him Ori's full approval, which appeared to gratify him more than enough to justify his being used as bait in a mission of, possibly, some danger.

'If you should happen to be successfully kidnapped,' I told Gio, 'and you should happen to find yourself left in company with Susa and Faronni, please do bring them back with you.'

'Of course,' said Gio.

'But no,' objected Ori. 'That will give the game away! They will realise at once that we have found them out, and our advantage is lost.'

I said, 'They will realise that anyway, as soon as they find Gio missing. Or whoever he is pretending to be.'

'Gio won't come back right away,' Ori argued. 'Or rather, he will come back long enough to collect me, then return and go on pretending to be a student.'

Gio's brows went up at that, though whether it was the former or the latter part of Ori's plan that disconcerted him I could not tell. 'Leaving you to do what?' he demanded.

'Snoop.'

'And how will you get out, if trouble happens?'

Ori shrugged. 'I am not helpless. I'm a draykon. I can take care of myself.'

There appeared to be a severe disagreement pending, so I judged it best to intervene. 'How about this. We go along with Ori's plan, save for one modification: we are going to get all four of us kidnapped. We will do a better job of investigating the problems together, and nobody ends up left to the practice of high espionage alone.'

'Absolutely not,' said Tren. The fierce frown he directed at me expressed his objection clearly enough: he disliked the notion of my putting myself in any danger.

Endearing as was his concern, I dismissed it.

Other objections tended towards the practical, all of which I was able to argue away. 'Gio and I will manipulate the perceptions of our kidnapper, in order to escape notice. Ori, you may shapeshift into any shape you please, no? I dare say you can turn your hair white for a time. And Tren has masqueraded as a Lokant before, with brilliant success. It will be perfectly possible to arrange for all four of us to be absconded with.'

'The one problem,' said Ori, 'is that Heliandor has been ignored. You are right that there's more to their choice of target than Lokant heritage alone. We'll have to figure out what else they want, first, in order to be sure of getting ourselves onto their shopping list.'

'In which case,' I said with a brilliant smile for Ori, 'I charge you to do what you do best: go gather information.'

'Yes, my lady!' Ori collected up Gio, and departed forthwith to conduct research.

'I love academics,' I said to Tren. 'They never tire of digging for facts.'

'Good memories, too,' he agreed.

'And so biddable.' I made a mental note to do something nice for Ori and Gio sometime soon.

22 IV

Allow me to introduce you to the new me!

My new persona is a few years younger (because who would not be, given the option?). She is female. I mean, I could masquerade as a man if I wanted to; I need change nothing about my own appearance, merely my audience's perception of it. I could be green if I wanted to, with three horns, six eyes and a tail. I could be invisible.

But why would I choose to pass myself off as a man? Men are so dull. No gowns, no bosom, little jewellery and sadly minimal eyelashes. What would I be expected to *do* with myself? I'd rather be green and betailed.

I have chosen a name! I considered such delights as *Petrovanka Lorianassan* and *Miss Arabellina De Varsenay,* but I suppose they are a little too flamboyant. Do they sound convincingly like real people, to you?

No. They don't to me either.

I regret this excessively, for I feel that Miss De Varsenay would be more than passingly fond of her parasol, and I have always been attracted to those. However, one must be sensible. I have settled upon *Edwora Selana Crompet.* She shall be a Summoner like me, as I see no reason why I should resign all claim to some of my best abilities just because I am pretending to be somebody else.

I place my character in Orstwych — some town just over the

border will do. I do not wish to have to travel too far. I will ask Adonia to fix upon a suitable address.

… Or perhaps I shall not. A terrible thought has just occurred to me. What if she *is* the person who has tampered with our post! What if my confidence is misplaced and I am being made a sad dupe? I know I was severe upon Ori for doubting me, but it happens that I come to doubt myself.

It is an activity I have rarely indulged in before, and I can tell you, I do not find it an enjoyable experience. In fact it is so particularly unpleasant, I cannot understand why anybody ever bothers with it at all.

I do not see any occasion to mention to Ori that this has come to pass, for he would no doubt imagine himself free to be deplorably smug about it. But if I happen to refrain from confiding in Adonia about this new plan, just in case, I do not see that anybody shall be inconvenienced by it.

Miss Crompet is a woman of some prosperity, sadly orphaned (I do not wish to throw any obstacles in the way of potential kidnappage, and it is perhaps noteworthy that neither Susa nor Faronni appear to be overly blessed with relatives). Her father and mother were traders in… some species of industry. Details are boring. I will reserve the designing of her wardrobe to myself, naturally, but perhaps I can prevail upon Tren to dream up the dull parts.

Ah, I am bored with the idea now. I will put my journal away, and return to the tasks I am supposed to be venturing upon at this hour of the day.

Ooh, what about *Drusilla T. Rosewater?* The "T" stands for Tabitheia.

… Perhaps I had better put the journal somewhere out of reach.

22 IV TRUENIGHT

It occurred to me belatedly that we had forgotten Heliandor's interests in our enthusiasm for espionage. If we all wandered off-world in search of dark deeds, nefarious plans and dastardly villains, what would become of her education? We had assigned her teacher an alternative duty without sparing a thought for her progress.

I was reassured by the recollection that time passes oddly in the Libraries, if it passes at all. You can be in there for what would be weeks of our time, and return to find that a matter of mere hours has passed at home. So, Gio's absence would not, in all likelihood, signify much for Heliandor. We will give her a little holiday of a day or two, by the end of which time, everything should be nicely cleared up.

Ori left Glour City for a day in favour of Amori Tovia. He said he plans to annoy Faronni's neighbours without cease until somebody tells him something useful. I tried to tell him that Tren and I had been more than annoying enough already, but he was unmoved.

Of course, what he will actually do is befriend every one of them and charm them into talking with him at great length. People grow expansive under such treatment, and in the course of ordinary conversation may remember details that do not come to mind under direct questioning from a stranger. It is an art I have never been much good at, because I tend to intimidate people. Ordinary people, that is. Give me a Lord or an Ambassador or a High Sorcerer or something and I will have no difficulty in bending them to my will.

Ori has not yet returned, but in his absence something odd has happened.

I have received a letter.

It is an application for a bursary, from another partial Lokant. Had it arrived yesterday, I would have been delighted, and would have wasted no time in writing to invite this gentleman to join us.

The matter looks different today. I think Ori is probably right: our letters are being intercepted, allowing our unknown opponent to extract whichever partials she requires without interference from us. Why, then, did this letter arrive?

Is it like Miss Nallay's letter? Has it simply been missed, evaded capture somehow? That seems unlikely. I can believe that one letter might slip through the net accidentally, especially when it was sent very early in our campaign — before, perhaps, our opponent had mustered her strategy. I find it hard to imagine that the same explanation applies to this one.

Two possibilities, then, that I can think of. Either this new applicant is like Heliandor Rasset, and somehow fails to qualify according to whatever criteria our Lokant friend is using. Or, the letter is decidedly Fishy and Something Sinister is Afoot.

I suspect the latter. Shall I imagine that, having confiscated all of our post for at least the past week, our friendly local kidnapper would be obliging enough to forward on to us the applications from those students who do not fit her requirements? She might be an unusually polite, unaggressive kidnapper, but such neighbourly conduct is too much to expect.

Shall I imagine instead that we are not the only ones who can conceive of the benefits of fabricating false applicants? I think so indeed.

I showed the letter to Tren.

'Intriguing,' he said when he had read it. 'Are we pursuing it?'

I was firmly of the opinion that it ought to be investigated, and said so. 'If it is a trap, how convenient! Obviously they expect us to be too wary to reply by return of post, and to go in person instead. And clearly, our ultimate fate is to be made off with forthwith, or perhaps just attacked in some refreshingly direct fashion. Nothing could coincide more beautifully with our plans.'

'I prefer the plans. At least we would be more or less in control of the situation.'

I gave a great, disappointed sigh. 'Where is your sense of adventure, Tren.'

He narrowed his pretty eyes at me. 'It dissipated around the time I asked you to marry me, and you agreed.'

'Protectiveness is so limiting.'

Tren grinned. 'Let's say I have a vested interest in your continued existence. Is that better?'

'I have a vested interest in yours, but you don't catch me wrapping you in fluffy things and forbidding you to venture outdoors. And what of Ori! He proposes to propel dear Gio into the very jaws of the whurthag, so to speak, and with alacrity!'

'I do not consider it much to his credit that he does. Ori can be reckless at times, which is his own business, but being reckless on behalf of somebody one loves is difficult to justify.'

'Dearest heart of mine,' said I in my most serious tone. 'If you propose to become poor-spirited, lily-livered and fretful on account of our marriage, I may be forced to reconsider my acceptance.'

Tren's eyes widened. 'Please tell me that is a joke.'

I tried my hardest to maintain a severe demeanour, but failed. I leaned on him instead and said: 'Just try not to ruin *all* my fun, if you can manage it.'

'How about if I go with you?' he offered, apparently by way of compromise.

I looked at him like the idiot he was. 'I have no idea why you imagined you were likely to be excused from that duty in the first place.'

Tren blinked. 'Right. Sorry.'

Nothing went according to either our plans or theirs, of course, but isn't that life?

24 IV

The first thing that didn't happen was kidnapping.

I confess to feeling a trifle disappointed. Half the rest of the partial Lokant population of the Darklands has managed to get themselves kidnapped lately; why not me? Do I present so poor a prospect? Am I so unappealing? It is difficult not to take it personally.

Our new applicant was supposedly called Fostiger DeMarte-Tregoriann, and "he" informed me that he was a resident of Glour City, making his abode in one of our good city's less populous suburbs.

Fostiger DeMarte-Tregoriann. Honestly. I have had a little bit of experience at coming up with likely-sounding pseudonyms, and I ask you. Can anybody with such a name be taken seriously? Could there be a moment's doubt in anybody's mind that there can be no such person? I think not.

Out to the farthest reaches of Glour City went Tren and I, at our most official — because we were still representative of our fledgling bureau, even if we were knowingly in pursuit of a den of filthy kidnappers. It would never do to make a poor impression.

Mr. DeMarte-Tregoriann was an engineer by trade, and lived in exactly the kind of neat, featureless, scrupulously well-kept house one might expect an engineer to live in.

'How thoroughly predictable,' I said to Tren as we approached the building. It was a detached property, not too sizeable, and painted an unimaginative white.

'Deplorably,' Tren agreed.

'As if we would be so dull-witted as to fall for such an obvious ploy.'

'It's unthinkable.'

It appeared to me (impossible as it might seem) that Tren was laughing at me. Something to do with the curve of his lip and the faint twinkle in his eyes as he obligingly supplied just the answers I wanted.

'You're laughing at me,' I observed.

'Never.'

'At least tell me why.'

'Maybe later.'

We had arrived at Mr. DeMarte-Tregoriann's front door by then, so I had to allow him to enjoy the advantage of having the last word. I can assure you, I was suitably ungracious about it.

Tren rang the bell.

Now, considering that I just told you we were expecting to be attacked, it might seem extraordinarily reckless of us to walk nonchalantly up to the door and ring the bell as if naught but a tedious social call with tea and small talk were expected. But it would not do to make our prospective attackers wary, and accidentally scupper their convenient plans. Sometimes one simply has to be dauntless, and take a few risks for the sake of the greater good.

The door opened. We received our first view of our prospective kidnapper: a youngish, white-haired man dressed… well, dressed exactly like an engineer ought to be. He looked at me, and then at Tren, and gave us a nice, slightly shy smile.

'Lady Glostrum,' he said. 'This is quite the honour. I did not expect you to come in person. I have been watching the post for a reply by letter.'

A likely speech, though I wondered why he (or she) bothered. I looked at him closely, trying to catch a glimpse of some detail out of place, anything that might reveal the real person behind the facade. But there was nothing. The vision was thorough, and entirely convincing. We were obviously dealing with a very powerful Lokant.

I did not trouble myself to concoct a reply, for what would

be the point? I stood alert, waiting for something to happen.

Tren, though, stepped smoothly into my silence, stuck out his hand to shake DeMarte-Tregoriann's and said: 'How do you do? We're here to talk to you about your application to the Bureau.'

'Great,' said the engineer, and with a puzzled look at me (still silent and imposingly statuesque), he opened the door further and invited us inside.

Into the trap we went.

The house looked surprisingly lived-in, not too scrupulously well-arranged or too improbably dusted. A nice touch, I thought. Good attention to detail. But how long were we all going to maintain the charade?

Far enough to have the tea and the small talk, it rapidly appeared, for DeMarte-Tregoriann seated us in his comfortable parlour and disappeared off to the kitchen. He soon returned with rather good rosuis tea, a refined blend with a little gloren fruit mixed in unless I miss my guess (and with tea, I never do). He also had biscuits. Good ones, nice and short, with plenty of butter.

I was suspicious.

Tren seemed content to continue the charade while he enjoyed his tea and biscuits, and I was happy enough to let him while I pretended to relish my own.

(All right, I wasn't entirely pretending. It *was* good tea.)

They discussed Fostiger's background and education (moderately privileged, highly academic); current place of work (some Darklands company, I wasn't really listening); experience of Lokant abilities (minimal) and other such matters until I, finally bored, interrupted with:

'This is a fine waste of time, Mr. DeMarte-Tregoriann. I do not know what kind of a value you place upon your time but *mine* is precious, so permit me to ask you plainly: Who are you really, and what do you want with us?'

I was fairly proud of this speech, it being clear, forthright and well phrased. It did not have the effect I was hoping for, however, for Fostiger blinked at me in a befuddled way and said: 'What?'

'I believe you heard me.' I set my tea cup back into its saucer and fixed him with my most severe, no-nonsense stare.

Fostiger began to look nervous. 'I am Fostiger DeMarte-

Tregoriann,' he protested. 'Did you not… um, you did receive my letter?'

Insupportable. I opened my mouth to inform him of my total lack of tolerance for any further dissembling, when I noticed that Tren was trying to catch my eye. I permitted him to do so, and he immediately shook his head at me.

What? I asked him with my eyes.

He widened his. I wanted to interpret that as a sign of something exciting and above all, *useful* about to happen; something that would finally help us to understand who we were dealing with and what they wanted. An attack. An intrusion. *Something.*

But I know Tren well by now, and I could not read anything in his face or his body language to suggest that he was trying to communicate anything so promising. It was a warning all right, but not of that kind.

And I sighed inside, for I had to admit that we had spent almost half an hour with Fostiger DeMarte-Tregoriann without anything untoward happening at all.

I looked at the predictable engineer before me and rapidly revised my opinion of his improbability. 'Your name is Fostiger DeMarte-Tregoriann.'

He nodded. 'Yes.'

'Really?'

'Yes.'

'*Truly?*'

He smiled faintly. 'I'm afraid so.'

I closed my eyes briefly. 'So you are a real person.'

He blinked at that, and looked at his own hands, as though he were momentarily afraid of turning incorporeal on the spot. 'I… thought I was?'

I hope you appreciate my honesty in recounting this incident. It is no pleasant thing to acknowledge oneself so utterly, unquestionably, shatteringly wrong, and my immediate inclination was to leave it out of my account altogether, thereby preserving my reputation for cleverness and infallibility.

But I did promise to write a true account of my doings. If I do not deal honestly with you in this, how shall I expect you to give credence to the rest of my assertions?

So: enjoy this spectacle that I made of myself, but be kind enough to forgive me if you can.

At least it explained why Tren was laughing at me before.

I did my best to sweep aside the odd questions I had just put to the *unbelievably named* Fostiger and hastened on, hoping that my cheeks were not too red. 'Have you received any unexpected letters recently?' I enquired.

'Or even any expected ones, purporting to be from us or the Bureau.' Tren could have capitalised on his triumph of discernment by laughing heartily at me, but he chose instead to help me gloss over my mistake, and to distract Fostiger's attention from my odd behaviour.

When your man still has your back no matter how stupid you've just been, ladies, this is when you know that he's truly a keeper.

Fostiger, happily, proved willing to be diverted. 'Nothing of that kind, though I did not expect to hear anything for a day or two yet anyway.'

I wondered if he still would, but I had to doubt it by then. For whatever reason, our interfering opponents hadn't bothered with Fostiger. They had permitted his letter to reach us and had not made any attempt to make off with him. That made him another Heliandor, and by the by, what kind of considerate, neighbourly opponents are these? People that cheerfully abscond with orphaned children, while simultaneously ensuring that we continue to receive unimpeded access to those of our recruits that they don't seem to want?

I was, by this time, most puzzled.

I debated imparting some of this to Fostiger, by way of warning him. If anybody else showed up at his door purporting to be me, he ought to be left with some way of discovering the lie. I could leave him with some kind of pass phrase, perhaps, some cunning question he could ask of some-other-Eva that she would not know how to correctly answer.

I decided against it. Our shadowy adversaries could have interfered with this one if they had wanted to. They hadn't. It seemed unlikely they would change their mind, and why worry Fostiger in that case?

So we invited him to join us in Glour City within a few days, gave him directions to our little headquarters, and left him to prepare for his journey. He was happy to accept the place, to my secret relief, for he would be leaving a fine career in order to do so and I had to wonder how attractive a proposition our school might appear to somebody in his position.

This is an approximation of the conversation Tren and I had on the way home:

Me: Do we have to tell people about this?

Tren: Any particular people? (*with that damned twinkle in his eyes*)

Me: Any of them. All of them.

Tren eyed my bosom, which interested me a fair bit until I realised his attention was fixed upon the place where I keep my journal tucked away. 'Aren't you going to record it in there?'

(An Aside. Yes, I keep this journal in my bodice. It is a small book, perfectly sized for such a hideaway, and I find it more convenient than putting it into some kind of bag which I then have to remember to carry around. No, I do not have pockets. They ruin the lines of my gowns. Somewhere inside a corseted bodice is exactly the place for such an object, and that is all I am going to say upon the matter.)

Me: Yes, I suppose I am, but all that means is that my nearest and dearest will learn of my folly *eventually*. There can be no reason to be in a hurry about it.

Tren: (gravely) I suppose I don't have to tell all the people.

Me: You are a hero amongst men.

Tren: I think you've said that before.

Me: It's still true.

After which exchange, Tren was kind enough to soothe my ruffled feelings by way of a considerable dose of love and affection and all those kinds of things, and I felt better.

Don't disapprove. We were in a private carriage. It isn't nearly so scandalous as it sounds.

As it turned out, when we got back to Glour City nobody was remotely interested in where we had been or what we had been doing anyway.

This was because headquarters had been broken into, everything had been ransacked and Heliandor was missing.

'I don't know,' said Adonia upon appeal, brushing a strand of grass off her green-trimmed cerise velvet coat. 'I went out for lunch. When I came back, this had happened.'

When I said "everything" had been ransacked, I mostly meant the records room. "This", in Adonia's interpretation, was the litter of papers which covered the floor, in the midst of which we both stood at that moment.

I do not honestly know why people are so messy with such endeavours. If they had been neater about it, we might never have known they'd been there at all. Were they rushed? Perhaps, if they had to find whatever it was they wanted and flee before Adonia came back. But Adonia isn't all that… I mean, it wouldn't have been difficult to distract her, delay her return, and thereby accomplish the business more tidily.

Anyway, who conducts a search for anything by tearing things apart and throwing things around? Whoever did this went through my office, Adonia's office and Gio's schoolroom in similar fashion, in addition of course to their kind attentions to the records room.

Maybe they got tired of waiting for us to share our information by way of the post, but even so, it seemed to me as though a great show of disruption had been made in order to ensure we knew they'd been here. But that's absurd. Why would anybody do that?

As for Heliandor, who knows? Why overlook her to begin with, and then come back and snabble her later? I no longer pretend to have the faintest idea what's going on. None of it makes any sense.

It did occur to me that Fostiger might not be as safe as I had been happy to assume, not long before. I immediately pinched one of Angstrun's more competent sorcerers and dispatched her to pick the poor man up. He might need a bodyguard after all.

But then why did his letter get through to us? We *know* that someone has been meddling with the post, and general interception is the only reasonable explanation for the lack of applications we've been getting. I could just about bring myself to believe that no one's interested in our school if I tried, but it is genuinely unlikely. We're offering generous bursaries with guaranteed employment thereafter. Partial Lokants are rare, but not *that* rare.

I don't know anymore. I admit this freely.

I did hope for a little while that Heliandor had simply gone out somewhere, and would soon return. No such luck, for a day has passed without any sign of her. I know I mentioned giving her time off from her studies while Gio and the rest of us were busy conducting espionage, but I hadn't yet given her leave to go, so there is no explanation for her absence save that she, too, has been absconded with.

All right, so. When is it going to be my turn?

25 IV

Ori reappeared, but without bringing much of use to relay.

'Nallay,' he pronounced, consulting a sadly small sheaf of notes. 'I found some records for her, plus a little bit of gossip. Uninspiring academic career leading to not much in the way of employment. Makes a little money here and there as a painter. Her neighbours assume she's not much good, but nobody could say they've ever seen any of her work. No known family to speak of. One person thought she'd flunked out of Sorcerer School—'

'Stop,' said I.

Ori looked at me enquiringly.

'Sorcerer school. Did you check that out?'

He slowly raised one eyebrow, and stared me down. 'Of course I did.'

'Because Susa was swiped right out of Sorcerer Academy.'

'I know,' said Ori slowly. 'I remember, because I was there.'

Oops. 'Right,' I said crisply. 'Of course you were. And?'

'Angstrun let me at the records. Faronni Nallay attended for one term, seven years ago. She had a little aptitude but no application, and never came back for her second term.'

'Hmm. So, she's a sorcerer, albeit an untrained one and perhaps not especially powerful. And so is Susa. A link!'

'Yes, and I was quite excited about that, too, until I came back and found Heliandor missing. I checked while I was there. No record of anybody by that name attending the academy, ever.'

'Which doesn't absolutely mean that she isn't a sorc, but it's persuasive of it. She's never claimed any sorcerer or summoner abilities, nor shown signs of possessing any.'

'Right. So it's shaky to conclude that Lokant partials with Sorcerer skills are the goal, but it's interesting information. I'll look into your Fostiger DeMorte-Tregariat—'

'DeMarte-Tregoriann.'

'—That one. He didn't mention having any other magical abilities, I suppose?'

'No. Unless you count mathematics.'

'Haha. No.' Ori folded up his notes, packed them away, and only then thought to look around my otherwise empty parlour. 'Where's Gio?'

Good question. Shall you despise me too much if I admit that I forgot about him? Naturally I didn't say that to Ori. 'Working on his lesson plan, I suppose?'

Ori bounced straight up out of his chair and made for the door. 'Righto, up I go.'

And off he went, but he was back again only two minutes later. He stuck his head around the door, observed the comfortable posture I had taken up in my favourite armchair without, I think, really seeing me at all, and said: 'Are you sure he's here?'

'No,' I admitted. 'But if he has gone somewhere else, he did not mention it to me.'

Ori withdrew with a frown, and returned again after another five minutes. He threw the door open this time, strode into the middle of the parlour, and announced: 'He is not here.'

'He didn't leave word for you?'

'No. But perhaps he didn't expect me to return before he did.'

I beamed. I couldn't help myself. 'This is fantastic. Perhaps he has been kidnapped!'

Ori gave me a flat, unfriendly stare. 'I fail to see cause for celebration in that.'

'But it was our plan!'

'For all four of us! Not Gio by himself! Anyway, how could he possibly? He had not yet set up with a false identity, was not pretending to be anything other than himself.'

'True.' My fledgling hopes faded. 'Then, what?'

'Probably he has just stepped out to buy something, or…

taken a walk.' But Ori frowned as he spoke, clearly concerned. I couldn't blame him, considering everything that had lately happe…. oh.

An unpleasant thought occurred to me.

'Come to think of it,' I said — with, I confess, some reluctance to admit of my neglect — 'I haven't seen Gio since headquarters was broken into.'

Ori glared at me. 'You mean since Heliandor was discovered missing.'

'That's what I mean.' I felt uncomfortable under that stare, for he was right to be angry with me. How had it not occurred to me to look for Gio? Just because I expected to find odd things going on with our partials and therefore focused upon them, it didn't excuse my negligence.

'So he might have been taken along with her.'

'It's possible.' I had to own that it was, though I did not think it likely. Why would a person take Gio? 'Do you suppose he might have been mistaken for a partial? The differences are not immediately obvious.'

'Maybe, but I do not think we are dealing with anyone so… poorly informed. Are we? We know that we've been watched, our post intercepted—'

'Do we though?'

Ori blinked. 'I thought we agreed on that.'

'It made sense at one point, and we do know that somebody sent Miss Nallay a falsified copy of my letter. But that only means that one or two of our letters were interfered with. Since then, Fostiger's arrived without incident, and nobody appears to have tampered with him at all.'

Ori sighed. 'That leaves us with nothing much to go on.'

'I think Gio will be back,' I said firmly. 'He is far from helpless, after all. And perhaps he will return with useful information.'

Ori flopped into a chair and cast me a piteous look. 'I hope you're right, because I'm faint with worry.'

'I will order luncheon,' I said, recognising my cue.

That won me a tremulous smile.

Hurrah, that I should be proved a Prophet! And upon such a point, too! I hope that it has somewhat restored my credit with Ori.

Gio returned just as Ori, Tren and I were reaching the end of a leisurely luncheon. I was moved to believe that Ori was deeply worried, because he ate only half of his usual heroic portion, and sat sipping listlessly at a cup of tea. When the door to the dining room creaked open and Gio's face appeared around it, he bounced up at once, upsetting the tea, and fell upon Gio with touching gusto.

Tren and I politely averted our eyes while this reunion took place. Once the two had recovered their composure, it was time to hear Gio's tale.

'I went home,' he explained, accepting Ori's offer of a seat at the table and a plate of food.

'Home?' repeated Ori and I in chorus.

'To Sulayn Phay.'

'I thought you couldn't,' said Ori. 'Or wouldn't.'

'I wasn't planning the trip,' Gio agreed. 'Or I would have mentioned it.' I suppose we all thought he would progress immediately to explaining what had become of him, but instead he asked, apparently at random: 'How would you describe Heli Rasset?'

An odd question, but all right. I went with it. 'Thirtyish? Moderate height, not short. Thin. Hair usually braided. Blue eyes.'

'More specifically?'

'Umm….' I floundered a bit, unsure what Gio was getting at.

Ori saved me by extracting a piece of paper from his notes and making a quick sketch of Heliandor upon it. I was impressed by its accuracy, having never had any idea that Ori could draw.

Gio looked at me and Tren. 'Would you both agree that's a fair portrait of her?'

We did, in response to which Gio took a piece of paper out of his coat pocket and spread it out before us. Upon it was a sketch of someone who looked not wholly unlike Heliandor Rasset, but her features were markedly different in a few important ways.

'That's who I saw. The person you describe is someone I've met before, but not around here. Her name is Ylona Duna, and she's my grandmother's main rival for leadership of Sulayn Phay.'

Well, that was a facer. 'All right,' I said, concealing my utter surprise behind my favourite — and so often used — Coolly

Composed expression. I mentally reviewed everything I had ever seen or heard of Heliandor, and tried to remember what I had talked to her about, without much success in any instance. I had hardly tried to get to know her, merely dumped her with Gio and Ori and gone about my business.

More fool me.

'So we've had a spy right in our midst all along,' said Ori grouchily, slumping in his chair. 'Wonderful.'

I think all of us felt a bit foolish. For all our caution and cleverness, it had never occurred to us to suspect those already inside headquarters. Except to cast aspersions on the probable honesty of poor Adonia, to whom I felt like apologising.

I began to understand how Llandry felt a moon or so ago. When you realise your shady and unscrupulous adversaries are easily running rings around you, it's… not a pleasant feeling.

'What happened at home?' I enquired of Gio.

'Well, first… you should know that Ylona didn't ransack headquarters.'

I had to focus to remember that Ylona is Heliandor. We hadn't known her long, but I had already got used to thinking of her as Heli. 'She didn't?'

'No. We discovered that together, and she was not happy about it. I would swear that she was sincere. She was surprised, and angry. She asked me some questions about the security I'd set up — which, I am sorry to say, I had not got very far with at that point, though I have since rectified this oversight — and seemed dissatisfied with my answers. After a while I began to realise that her questions were far too discerning for the person she was supposed to be, but before I could follow that train of thought to any useful conclusions, she grabbed me and translocated. We ended up in Sulayn Phay, whereupon she hauled me off to her private rooms and promptly tried to convert me to her cause. It seems word of my row with Grandmother has spread, and I appear to be a highly tempting recruit. I've got inside information on Dwinal, *and* the doings of your Bureau, both of which appear to be of great interest to Ylona.'

'Why?' said I at once.

'No idea. She wouldn't tell me.'

'A poor attempt at recruitment.'

'I know? All I wanted was for her to tell me every facet of

her plans on the spot, without the smallest guarantee of my loyalty thereafter. I didn't think it was so much to ask.'

'So disobliging,' I agreed. 'What did she tell you?'

Gio smiled faintly. 'She abused my grandmother's character and morals — cautiously at first, in case I might be suffering from any lingering family loyalties. I gave her to understand this was not the case, after which she was more forthright in her disapproval. Ylona is determined to win the leadership from Dwinal, and there is an election coming up soon.'

'How does she plan to win it?'

'That she did not tell me. I probed a little, but to no avail. She wants to feel confident of my support, I believe, before she will open up about it.' To my surprise, he grinned rather mischievously. 'So I joined her team on the spot, and I am happy to inform you all that I am now a double agent. Triple, in fact, as I am charged with winning my way back into my grandmother's good graces so I can spy on her, too.'

Ori beamed at Gio, his smile shining with approval and pride and love. 'You are a marvel.'

Gio gave a half-bow, but his smile faded. 'I hope so. I do have to pull it off without getting myself… um, diced.'

Ori sobered at that idea. 'Right, well. You're going to need help.'

'I was hoping you would say that.'

Tren raised a hand. 'Anything I can do? I like the sound of this party.'

'Me too,' I put in. And I did! I might have been suffering some mild impulses to dice and slice duplicitous Ylona myself, but at least we knew who we were up against.

Mostly. 'So, questions,' I continued. 'Who searched our headquarters, if it wasn't her? Who forged the letter to Miss Nallay, since I sent it before Ylona reached us? And for that matter, is Faronni at Sulayn Phay, and Susa?'

'I get the impression Ylona might have one or two over-enthusiastic supporters,' Gio said. 'Though I'm unsure. I will try to find out. As for Faronni and Susa, I don't know yet but I assume so. There seems little doubt that Ylona is behind their extraction.'

'I'd like to talk to this Ylona,' I said, hopefully without sounding too murderous about it.

'I'm working on that,' said Gio. 'I did subtly suggest to her that if she was looking for partial Lokants, she could hardly do better than you. She pointed out that a person would have to be an idiot to walk off with so public and powerful a figure as Lady Glostrum and expect to gain by it, which is fair. Your willing co-operation might not be declined, however.'

'Noted.'

This journal-keeping is an interesting business. It forces one to pay unusually close attention to the details of one's daily doings. For instance, I have never before had occasion to notice how much of our important business is conducted over dinner, or possibly luncheon. What a merry band of hedonistic epicureans we are.

I say "we", but since this is my house and I am the generally acknowledged leader of our various endeavours, does that mean it's all my fault?

Possibly. Very possibly.

Anyway. Interesting news. I took careful note of Gio's words, particularly the part about my *willing co-operation.* If Gio can pretend to be an enthusiastic convert to Ylona's cause, I dare say I can, too.

Everything's getting a trifle complicated, I have to observe. I had *one* ordinary, promising student who had not been made off with and she turns out to be no less than the mastermind of those very same abductions. Somebody *else*, meanwhile, has trashed my precious headquarters in search of who-knows-what and we still have little idea what Ylona proposes to do with the two people she has thieved from us. Somebody is intercepting our post… or perhaps not? It grows difficult to keep track.

All very much par for the course with Lokant business.

Gio we cheerfully dispatched back into the jaws of danger, with strict instructions to find out as much as he could about Ylona's shenanigans. We also encouraged his triple-agent activities as far as his grandmother is concerned, though the poor boy was visibly less sanguine about that prospect. I suffered a pang or two of guilt on his account, but what can be done? We need information, and Gio is best placed to retrieve it.

'If you will, Gio,' I said before he left, 'Do please invite Ylona — most cordially, of course! — to cease absconding with my students. It is highly inconvenient and insufferably rude.'

'I can try,' said he doubtfully.

'It is fair to note that there is no established programme of etiquette regarding the claiming and counter-claiming of students. I ought to write one, perhaps, though I do not have time today.'

Gio gave me his precious bemused look, the one that says he cannot tell whether or not I am joking.

'I am joking,' I told him.

'Oh.'

'Mostly.'

He blinked twice, opened his mouth, and said nothing.

26 IV

I noted that everything is becoming disappointingly complicated. Naturally, then, Limbane chose *this* moment to show up.

Lim…*bane of my life.* We were friends, once, or something vaguely along those lines. That was back when I fondly imagined he might deal fairly with us, or tell us things that would be useful for us to know, and maybe refrain from double-dealing, manipulation and other such unfriendly activities.

No such luck. He *is* a Lokantor after all — a Master of one of their Libraries. I sometimes think that compulsive secretiveness and an uncontrollable need to manipulate others are prerequisites for the job, so Ylona should be a perfect candidate for it.

I digress. I was hoping never to have to deal with Limbane again, so I wasn't best pleased to walk into the breakfast parlour this morning and find Limbane sitting at his ease in my favourite chair. He had availed himself of the dishes set out upon the sideboard and sat with a cup of tea before him, *and* a cup of cayluch. When I walked in, he merely raised his eyebrows at me and took another sip.

Limbane is the very image of an unthreatening old man. He's like your favourite grandfather, all untidy white hair, smiley wrinkles and drab clothing. It is probably his most dangerous weapon, because in truth he is nothing like you'd imagine from looking at him.

(An aside. *Again,* we cannot seem to do anything useful

without eating through it! But this time, I disclaim all responsibility! I can only assume Limbane was hungry, and timed his visit accordingly).

'Good morning, Limbane,' said I with perfect dignity. I let none of my surprise or distaste show, because if he wanted to play at *pretend this is a completely normal occurrence* then by all means, I can do that too. I went to fill a plate with my own breakfast — I concentrated mostly upon such favourite delicacies as dried and stewed fruits, fried bread and syrup, whether or not they are unhealthy — and sat directly across from Limbane. I mean, I might have been privately hoping never to encounter his irritating face again, but if he insists upon invading my home in his urgency to see me, I want to be able to see *him* clearly. Who knows what nefarious mischief he's planning.

I sat and sipped and supped and waited for the manipulation attempts to begin. He would suggest he has something that I need, perhaps, and try to persuade me that I cannot manage without him. He would dangle mysterious hints before me, suggesting that he knows all manner of things I am desperate to learn of and would share them… for a price. I mustered my resources, strengthened my will, dampened my desire to explode with temper in his aggravating face, and waited.

'I need your help,' he said.

I choked upon my tea.

'Do you really?' I said, trying to look elegant while I applied a napkin to the small river of tea flowing down my chin.

'Yes.'

Typically, he did not elaborate.

'All right,' I said ungraciously. 'Why do you need my help?'

'Because Dwinal is set to become the kind of problem I need to not have, and I want someone to get in her way.'

'You have a great many people at your disposal who are more powerful than I,' I had to point out, much as I hate to admit to my own inferiority.

'Dwinal knows all my people, and I need not explain to you the grave impracticality of anybody's trying to masquerade themselves in that kind of company.'

'So you want *me* to try?'

'Of course not.' Limbane looked suitably scornful of this idea, which I took as an uncomplimentary reflection upon my abilities. As such, my mood did not exactly improve. 'I understand you have Dwinal's grandson here.'

'How do you know that?' I asked without much hope of receiving an answer. He would say something fabulously and irritatingly vague like, 'I have my ways,' and I would punch him.

'Word travels,' he said, and I punched him.

Well, no, I didn't. But I was tempted to.

'Gio isn't my puppet. If you want his help, go see him.'

'He is in your employ. Besides, it is not just Gio's assistance I am hoping for. Dwinal appears to have developed an overpowering interest in the partial Lokants of your world, and as such I imagine she would be more than happy to … talk with you.'

'Dwinal?' I repeated dumbly. 'Isn't it Ylona who's kidnapping my partials?'

Limbane raised an eyebrow at me. 'Is it?'

I took a deep breath, expertly mastering my desire to break something against his face, and took a calming sip of tea. 'Why don't you tell me what you know,' I suggested in a deceptively mild tone, 'and then tell me what you want. Then I can tell you my price, and we can proceed to a negotiation.'

'Find out what Dwinal is doing,' he replied, smoothly ignoring my first request. 'I mean, find out what she is *really* doing, for while I have my suspicions, I find her to be annoyingly adept at hiding the truth.'

'How frustrating for you,' I murmured.

He did a little glaring, an expression I returned with a placid smile.

Tren came in. Do you notice the delay? Have I mentioned before that he sometimes takes longer to dress than I do? It's true.

'Limbane,' he said, with a suspicious narrowing of his lovely eyes that I found heart-warming. 'What a surprise.'

'I have come here to grovel,' said Limbane, which surprised me, because I hadn't noticed a great deal of grovelling happening up to that point.

'And Eva hasn't thrown you out yet? She must be in a good mood.' He bent to kiss me in passing, and retreated to the sideboard and its proffered dishes.

'Or perhaps she wants something from me, too,' suggested Limbane.

'Of course not,' I said. Immediate denial is always the best policy, even if — damn him — he was right.

'Isn't there something we want?' Tren enquired. 'There usually is.'

Well, fair. 'I expect to be able to come up with something,' I conceded.

'You did mention a *price,*' said Limbane.

If Tren tried to hide his grin, he didn't try very hard. 'Naturally.'

All right, I'm bored with Limbane. The rest of the conversation proceeded roughly as follows:

Me: I want unimpeded access to literally every piece of knowledge ever uncovered by the whole of Lokantkind, forever.

Limbane: No.

Me: Some of it, forever.

Limbane: No.

Me: Some of it, for a while?

Limbane: All right.

Me: I also want proper training in my Lokant abilities, and the use of a range of teachers for my school.

Limbane: … fine.

Me: Really?!

Limbane: Well… yes.

Me: You really are desperate.

Limbane: You have no idea.

27 IV

So, we have a new assignment. It is essentially the same as our old assignment, only it makes our old assignment that much more confusing by way of a bonus, which is always nice.

Limbane had nothing much of use to tell us, or nothing that he would share. He wouldn't explain what he means by his "suspicions" about Dwinal, because he might be wrong and he wouldn't want to prejudice our thinking. Annoyingly, I couldn't even argue against that because it *is* logical.

Gio was not happy. He returned looking whiter than usual and evaded our questions regarding his grandmother. From which I concluded that he hadn't approached her and really didn't want to.

Well, considering what I know of his background from Llandry's account, I can hardly blame him.

So, alternative plan. Guess who gets to play double agent instead?

That's right: me. If we already have Gio positioned with Ylona, we need somebody else to butter up Dwinal. I can easily pass myself off as a ruthless, ambitious socialite who will stop at nothing in pursuit of power. It's what half the world seems to think of me anyway. I don't know how they think my forthcoming marriage to Tren fits into this programme, but then one doesn't expect people to be either consistent or rational.

The question is: how to get Dwinal's attention? Trying to get ourselves kidnapped no longer seems a viable idea, because…

…Well, no, perhaps it *would* still work. Limbane hinted strongly that Ylona isn't necessarily our kidnapper. Meanwhile, Ori's information is useful after all. Susa and Faronni are both sorcerers! We rejected the significance of that link because Heliandor isn't one, but now that Heliandor proves to be no partial Lokant after all, I'm minded to reconsider.

We have three partials associated with the Bureau. The two who also possess sorcerer abilities have been taken. The one who doesn't, has not.

So. I wonder if summoners would count, too? And I wonder, once again, whether somebody might find *me* a tempting target, if I arranged a suitable opportunity? Ylona might have rejected the idea, but if Dwinal is our abductress, that hardly matters. And Dwinal, by Llandry's account, is sometimes more ruthless than sensible.

Tren, of course, is a sorcerer. If we create a fake partial-Lokant persona for him and put the both of us somewhere conveniently out-of-the-way and easy-to-access, I wonder if we might manage to get ourselves made off with after all?

'Darling,' said I to the love of my life soon after this period of reflection. 'What do you think of the name Archivere?'

'Most elegant,' he said promptly. 'Are we choosing baby names already? Do you have something to tell me?'

'No!' I uttered the syllable instantly and forcefully, which provoked a laugh from Tren. More like a cackle. Alas, he is so lamentably adept at winding me up.

'It is your new name,' I informed him. 'Archivere Dalsy, of Orstwych. A man of mixed sorcerer heritage and some Lokant blood. Together, you and I shall present an irresistible picture to Dwinal. Or Ylona. Or whoever it is that's making our lives difficult lately.'

Tren thought that over. 'We can't just make up a partial-Lokant persona. They have those timelines, remember? Family trees going back centuries? If they've tracked draykoni families that closely, I can hardly imagine they've neglected to keep track of their own.'

'I think they have done exactly that. Why else do they need our Bureau, and our information? If they knew who all of their distant Seven-Realms descendants are, they could have claimed them long ago. I think that tracking Lokant families is harder, because the heritage doesn't manifest in everyone who happens to have a Lokant ancestor somewhere back in the mists of time. With some families, generations can pass without a white-hair emerging. I think their descendants are randomly scattered all over the Seven, and they have almost as much of an idea of where to look for them as we do.'

'They can't be that ignorant. Limbane seems to know exactly who your ancestress is.'

That brought me up short for a moment, because I had forgotten that. I was briefly intrigued. Who was the Lokant woman who had spawned my branch of the family? What was her story? Would she be someone I would like?

And how *did* Limbane know about that, anyway?

Never mind — distraction.

'Probably they are not *all* that ignorant,' I conceded. 'But I doubt there is any centralised records system in this respect, or, probably, in any other. Lokant Libraries do not seem to play nicely together.'

'Fair point,' Tren conceded.

'So I think we may fabricate an Archivere Dalsy, and everyone will simply assume he is somebody else's family. Probably they do not much care. If we are right, they want sorcerer-Lokants and possibly summoner-Lokants; in other words, people with mixed Lokant and draykoni heritage. Where exactly those people came from is, I would wager, less important.'

'I can see you are committed to the idea, so I will argue no further,' said Tren graciously, and was so polite — and so *mocking* — as to bow to me.

'It is the name I like,' I admitted. 'It has such possibilities. I am reluctant to abandon it.'

'I can only agree with you. Nobody called *Archivere* could be anything less than a man of vast character.'

I beamed at him. 'I knew you would understand.'

Truthfully, I was a little discomfited by Tren's obvious doubts. I have not exactly covered myself in glory thus far, having produced one or two conclusions already that were flat wrong, and made more than one mistake. Perhaps Tren was right, and no one would be fooled by our ruse. They would know right away that no such person as *Archivere Dalsy* had ever existed, and would realise that they had encountered a con.

No matter. I did ask him, later, if he had any better ideas, and he had to admit that he did not.

So, we turned Tren into Archivere Dalsy — giving him a whole new wardrobe in the process, an activity from which I freely admit to deriving immense enjoyment — and installed him in a little house in Orstwych. We inserted all the right records for him at all the right places. We sent him a letter from me, with enough fanfare to ensure that (if anybody was, indeed, watching our post) somebody would take notice. The letter arranged a time when I, Lady Glostrum, would arrive to visit Archivere Dalsy, and discuss the possibilities of a bursary with him.

We dispatched Gio plus Ori back to Sulayn Phay — well, they hate to be separated, which is hardly surprising, and anyway I prefer for Gio to have somebody reliable by his side — and away went Tren to Orstwych. I remained behind alone, with no one but Adonia for company.

'Wonderful hat,' I informed her by way of conversation, soon after Tren's departure. Well, it was lonely, and I had to talk to somebody.

She adjusted the splendid thing, clearly pleased by the compliment. It was a wide-brimmed affair, the kind that curves and dips and positively explodes with effusive adornment. There were at least eight colours involved, which I am sure you will agree is far more than should ever be boasted by a single hat. I strongly suspected that she had decorated the thing herself.

'I made it myself,' she declared, with a bright smile.

I tried to look suitably impressed.

Since she was wearing it with a blouse of cerise silk, a voluminous violet skirt and spiky shoes, I could not look at her for too long.

'Adonia,' I said. I briefly considered bestowing a lecture on such elusive concepts as *complementary colours* and *less is more* but the dewy, delighted expression upon her face following my insincere compliment defeated my resolve.

Instead I said: 'You may find that the Bureau is a little empty for a day or two, as we have business elsewhere.' (I had not, of course, informed her as to the nature of the business. Nor had anybody else. Our plan was concocted exclusively among the four of us — Tren and I, Gio and Ori — and nobody else was taken into our confidence).

'I need you to keep track of any further applications we receive, send them a letter of acknowledgement, and hand me the correspondence the moment I return. Any urgent problems may be taken to Lord Angstrun. Any questions?'

She blinked at me, wide-eyed. 'Do you think this hat would be improved by another feather? A larger one, the curling kind, right on the brim.'

'No,' I said, this time choosing the brutal truth.

'Oh.' Her face fell.

I could not suppress a sigh. 'Oh, why not? Just one more feather, though. Too many more and you will not be able to hold up your head.'

The delighted smile returned, and I left before I could be betrayed into encouraging any more such excesses.

I did not tell Adonia, of course, that I had privately tasked Angstrun with keeping an eye on her. I didn't want to suspect her of duplicity, and since Heliandor's unmasking it seemed particularly unlikely that Adonia had anything to do with anything. But one has to at least consider these possibilities, much as I dislike the idea. He assured me that he would have Some of his People discreetly watch her doings and make sure that correspondence arrived at, and departed from, Adonia's office as it should.

As such, I was able to depart upon my espionage mission with something approaching peace of mind. Irritating as Darae can be, he can also be useful, and surprisingly supportive on occasion.

If Tren had not been blessed (or cursed, however one wishes to look at it) with such powerful abilities as a sorcerer, he could have been an actor. I have had occasion to observe this talent in him before.

When I arrived at his borrowed house in Orstwych in all my aristocratic state and rang the doorbell, the person who answered the door was scarcely recognisable to me. If I were not in on the plan, and besides that so intimately familiar with Tren's beloved features, I would never have guessed that it was he. The man who opened the door appeared to be rather younger than Tren, barely into his twenties, and he possessed a demeanour of abundant, youthful enthusiasm which Tren (for all his optimistic temper) has never displayed. His hair (now artificially whitened) was untidy, apparently because Archivere Dalsy had a habit of fidgeting with it when he was excited about something. His clothes stopped just short of dandified (as committed to our mission as Tren is, he would never consent to be badly dressed, not for any reason whatsoever).

He had a pipe in one hand. A *pipe.* An accoutrement which, you must agree, might more naturally be expected of a much older character, for the youth are not known for their fondness for pipes. The things are not considered fashionable. Archivere was unabashed, however, and seemed to regard his with a fondness bordering upon the manic, for he puffed upon it without cease and I never saw him without it in his hand.

'Lady Glostrum!' cried he, and swept me a bow. 'How delightful! How marvellous! I have been so eager for your arrival I have hardly slept, hardly eaten, I cannot tell you how delighted I am at the prospect of joining your magnificent school. Do please come in. I have refreshments — doubtless not up to your usual standard and of course I apologise, but I have done my little best! Do watch the step! I should hate for you to trip on those glorious skirts and injure yourself in some way. There, I shall just close the door behind you. The wind is quite chill, is it not? The parlour is this way.'

On we went, and on *he* went, maintaining such a ceaseless flow of chatter I could hardly get a word in. I could hardly keep a straight face, either, which was inconvenient. He served me good things and chattered while I ate them, and perhaps we both privately wondered how long it would be necessary to maintain the charade before anything useful happened.

If anything useful happened. It was all a bit of a gamble, after all.

I found it within myself to tell Archivere Dalsy all about our Bureau and our school, and the bursary we were inclined to offer. I believe I managed to do it reasonably convincingly, though I cannot but admit that acting is not my strong point. Tren says it is because I am too decidedly, resolutely *myself* to have the capacity to become someone else. He is probably right, though that sounds like a passingly unflattering reflection to my ear. Too self-satisfied by half! Why would I ever want to be someone else when I can be Lady Glostrum?

Anyway. Time passed, tea was drunk, many words were exchanged, and nothing happened. Nobody came to the house, nobody appeared spontaneously in Archivere's parlour, nobody broke in through the window. Nothing.

We began to exchange faintly concerned looks. How wretchedly disappointing, to go through such a charade for nothing! Not that Tren hadn't enjoyed it. It was probably worth it for that alone. Still, it was not quite a productive use of our time, if the only advantage it afforded was giving Tren the chance to play dress-up for a couple of days.

We were about to give up — expertly communicating this by way of meaningful looks alone — when there came, at last, a ring upon the doorbell.

'Aha!' said Archivere, and jumped up at once. 'I cannot think who that can be! I rarely receive visitors, Lady Glostrum — I could not say I am a *sociable* man, exactly. I wonder who this could be! Do, pray, forgive me the interruption! I am sure it is nothing, and will be resolved in an instant. And then I shall promptly return.'

He left, the latter part of this speech wafting back to me as he dashed for the front door.

To my frustration, I could not hear what passed between him and whoever had arrived. I discerned only a low babble of voices, one of which was certainly Tren's (though even his voice was somewhat modified in his persona as Archivere, is that not impressive?) I could tell nothing about the visitor, save that I thought the second voice was male, too.

After a few minutes, Tren — or no, *Archivere* — returned.

'What luck, what fortune!' he was saying as he came in. 'That you should happen to arrive just when her ladyship is with me! Thus we may easily kill two birds with one stone, no? Lady Glostrum, I believe you know this gentleman! He is here with an interesting proposition for us.'

And there, walking into the little parlour behind Archivere, was Limbane.

My instinctive reaction was to feel something like revulsion. Our least favourite sneak was sneaking again, and interfering; sticking his nose in where he was not wanted, following us around, pushing his way into our schemes! Did he not trust us to carry out his request without needing to keep a watch upon us? Terrible man.

Then I recollected who I was dealing with. *Lokants.*

'Why, Limbane,' said I, with every sign of surprise but none of the wariness that I felt. 'How long it has been.'

'Lady Glostrum,' said Limbane, with a degree of courtesy unusual for him. He even bowed to me. 'I trust you are in good health?'

That clinched it. Limbane has never been remotely interested in my continuing good health. 'Oh, perfectly, thank you,' I assured him, and we spent another minute or two exchanging the usual pleasantries.

Then I enquired, naturally enough I do hope, about the reasons for his *happening to show up* at a tiny house in Orstwych, occupied by a fictional partial Lokant, just when I was visiting there myself.

I phrased the question rather more naturally, of course, and contrived to keep my sarcasm to myself.

'I came to meet my great-grand-nephew,' Limbane said, with a pleased smile at Archivere.

Uh huh. 'How lovely!' I exclaimed — and for all Tren's conviction that I cannot act, I must say that I slipped into a charming, easily pleased, pleasantly unsuspicious version of myself which, I hope, was well suited to the occasion. 'I had no idea that Mr. Dalsy was related to an old friend.'

'Neither did I,' murmured Archivere, and the tone was so dry, so wry, and so utterly *Tren* that I almost laughed. I shot him a warning look, and saw his lip twitch in response.

He launched back into Archivere. 'A great-and-some-other-greats-uncle! Goodness! What a pleasure, for I have long been without much family to speak of. It will be the greatest delight to make your acquaintance, sir. That is—' and he paused, his expression turning from delighted to troubled in an instant. 'I hope that you do intend to stay a little while? How sorry I shall be, to meet you only to wave you off again!'

Good man! I puffed up with pride, for whoever was pretending to be Limbane immediately said: 'No, no! I come with every intention of forging the closest of family links, I assure you.'

He looked at me, and I waited. The choice of Limbane as

camouflage could only be directed at me, of course; there could be no reason to imagine that an Archivere either knew or cared who Limbane was. That the scheme was designed to appeal to me, and to persuade me into something, I did not doubt. And how excellent.

'Lady Glostrum and I are old friends,' said apparently-Limbane with a smile. 'And her new endeavour is of great interest to my Library.'

'Oh?' said I politely.

'It pleases me greatly that you are giving training and purpose to such as my great-grand-nephew. It is of benefit to them as well as to your world. And who can say when it might not be of use even to our Libraries, to have such a base in the Seven Realms, a series of contacts who know us and understand us and have worked with us in the past? Who can offer us teams of our own people, with our own abilities, and an understanding of your world which we lack? It would be wise indeed for us to assist you, which is what I come to propose.'

All of that sounded far too plausible to me. I had to work a little to keep my suspicions off my face. 'We would welcome assistance, certainly,' I conceded (and it was true). 'We struggle to teach even so few students as we have thus far secured.' (Which was also true).

Limbane smiled. 'Allow me to invite both of you to Estinor for an extended visit, then. I will get to know my nephew, and your ladyship and I may discuss the requirements of your organisation, and see about what we can do to help.'

How lovely. How neat. Something for everyone, and so civilised an arrangement. I suffered a mild pang of regret that it was all a lie.

I agreed, of course, and graciously. So did Archivere. I spent a little time surreptitiously watching this Limbane, hoping to detect some betraying sign that it was not he. I failed, of course. These people are irritatingly good.

28 IV

And away we went to Estinor. Supposedly.

The problem here is as follows.

Estinor is (apparently) the older of the two Libraries, and Sulayn Phay (Krays's Library) was built afterwards. Krays appears to thrive upon success-by-emulation, so he promoted the functionality, practicality and general excellences of his rival Library by modelling it closely upon Limbane's.

The result is, the two Libraries are eerily similar. I know this because this is not the first time I have been out in these places; because I have heard it mentioned, amid much grouching, by Limbane before; and because of Llandry's account, in which she describes being taken to "Estinor" by Gio, and only later discovering that she had actually been exploring Sulayn Phay.

So, to Estinor we went… or was it? I am certain that this Limbane is not the real Limbane, and that his part is *most likely* being played by a librarian of Sulayn Phay. But that's a guess. A sound one, I would like to think, with much to back it up, but a guess nonetheless. Our mystery Limbane could be one of Limbane's own people, and we might be in Estinor after all.

The only thing I can be certain of is that it's not Limbane. This person does not seem to be aware that Limbane and I have spoken recently, and besides, the man claimed ancestry over a fictional character.

So, "Limbane" took us to a Library which looked exactly like the Library I remember from my sojourn in Estinor before. He took us via translocation, of course. If you've never seen or heard of that, it consists of near-instantaneous travel by means of willing oneself out of one location and into another. It's not as magical as it sounds. In order to do it, one must have a set destination fixed upon what they call the PsiMap (a sort of shared mental vision of the world, or worlds, by which means one may sense those transloc-points that others have set down and put them to use). When it comes to the Libraries, it's also necessary to have official permission to travel into them. I gather they can do this by bloodlines, but if you aren't a blooded relative of any of a given Library's tribes (or even if you are), you're given access by way of an implant.

Yes, it's literally implanted into your flesh. It contains whatever access codes they're using at the moment, and it has to be updated from time to time to keep pace with the Library's changes. I used to have one, which granted me unlimited access to Limbane's Library for a time (you may be very sure that I milked it for every possible advantage). Limbane himself taught me how to translocate. I relinquished the implant in the end, wearied to death as I was with the whole sorry lot of them, and not expecting ever to need to come back to these cursed places.

I've had occasion to regret that decision, here and there. I certainly do right now, for I have no way to tell which Library we're in. I think it would be far too audacious (and risky) for anybody to pose as Limbane in his own Library, however, and I cannot see what would be the point, so for now I am going to assume that we are in Sulayn Phay.

What we are doing here remains in question. It is necessary to assume that everything that has thus far been said is a lie. Sooner or later, someone will reveal to us what's really going on.

In the meantime, Tren and I have a pact to snoop as much as possible.

Limbane showed us to rather handsome adjoining suites, in a part of the Library I have never been to before. They have those wonderful and alarming locks which operate by touch alone (we tested later. Tren cannot open mine and I cannot open his, so obviously they work. Somehow). There he left us, with instructions to rest (why? We haven't done anything). He would return for us as soon as he could, he assured us, and then all the wonderful things would begin.

He withdrew, leaving Tren and I to discover with pleasing inevitability that our locks only respond to our touch from the *outside*, and therefore that, once inside our suites with the doors closed, we are unable to leave again. There aren't even handles on the doors.

It was a neat, efficient abduction, in which the willing victims were removed with the minimum of fuss, ushered into our prisons with a polite bow, and left to enjoy all the comforts of luxurious incarceration until needed.

We were able to communicate, for there is an adjoining door in between our suites (locked of course) through which we could just about make ourselves heard. And so, we spoke.

Tren: Love. While we have successfully carried our point, I cannot help feeling that we have not come out altogether ahead of our adversaries.

Me: Much as I hate to admit it, you are perfectly right. Boxed and gift-wrapped! How lamentable!

Tren: Embarrassing.

Me: No! For we are where we need to be, even if our explorations are somewhat curtailed.

Tren: Options eliminated, possibilities deleted —

Me: Darling, I fear you have forgotten your role in this relationship. It is for *me* to be cynical, pessimistic and bleak. Your job is to be upbeat and hopeful.

Tren: You were not being despairing enough. I had to do something.

As amusing as this conversation was, it was largely nonsense. One does not expect to be kidnapped and then left to wander one's prison at will, of course. The purpose of being abducted was to ensure our passage into the very heart of our enemy's lair; that goal is accomplished! Huzzah!

From here, it is our duty to play along for a while, until we learn enough to act. One does that by being biddable prisoners, not too troublesome and not too bright.

But not *too* obedient. We have a plan, I am happy to inform you, and I expect said plan to come into effect very soon.

I won't say what it is right away, in case it should all go horribly wrong and end in dramatic failure. I would be far too embarrassed to write of it afterwards, for have I not admitted to more than enough mistakes already?

Instead of laying out my optimistic (hah) expectations in this journal, I took a few moments to explore my suite. It consisted of a flatteringly large bedroom with a very good bathroom attached — a *very* good bathroom indeed. They do know how to do plumbing out here! I'll say that for Lokants! I spent a little time searching, perhaps a trifle half-heartedly, for a means of escape. I didn't expect to find one. My little apartment had two doors: the outer door and the one into Tren's suite. Both were locked, neither responded to my touch, and neither had handles or even visible keyholes. There were no windows.

That settled, I availed myself at once of the large bath tub, with its amply flowing hot water and delicious bubbly goodness. After that I went to bed, because why not? I had nothing else to do.

I was woken some time later by the sound of the door opening. I sat up at once, heart pounding, unsure who to expect. Would it be my jailer or my rescuer?

I beheld: the latter!

'Gio!' cried I. 'My dear boy, I have never been more tempted to kiss you.' In my defence, his presence there demonstrated the excellence of my secret plan (hah!), and he represented all the potential-for-investigation-and-future-escape that I could wish for. His arrival also confirmed which Library we were in, which was nice to know.

His eyelids flickered. Two or three seconds of dead silence elapsed, during which I was free to imagine just how distasteful the prospect of my kisses might be to Gio (considerably, I have to conclude, given that he vastly prefers a sweet boy like Ori). 'Hello,' he said, when he recovered his power of speech.

I got out of bed. Whoever had prepared my prison had thoughtfully laid out a selection of spare blankets and pillows for me, in case of need. I had brought a portmanteau along, containing my own clothes, and so I was attired in my own nightgown, buried under six or seven layers of warm things and propped upon several gorgeously squishy pillows. I did not especially like having to get out of bed under these circumstances, but the matter of escape was undeniably important.

I also adjusted the lights. I am a Darklander, which means I am unused to bright lights under any circumstances. Tren and I had made sure to carry the necessary equipment with us, when we travelled out here: namely sets of dark glasses, adept at filtering out as much light as possible. When alone, though, it is still much more comfortable to leave them off, and keep the lights off too. I am used to seeing my way in darkness, I do not need chamber lights. But Gio does, so I donned my glasses once again.

Gio shut the door behind himself. I don't know how he got in, for there is no likelihood that he is supposed to have access to these rooms. But he's a full Lokant, spawn of such devious and ruthless minds as Dwinal and Krays, and he used to live in this Library. None of us doubted that he could get into wherever we ended up, and our faith in him has been fully rewarded.

He held out an unpromising-looking metallic *thing*. Inelegant language I know, but I have no idea what to call it and the word "thing" was coined for precisely this purpose. The *thing* was tiny, perhaps half an inch across, and… I do not even know how to describe it otherwise.

'What is that?' said I, my tone ripe with suspicion.

'Your new implant,' replied Gio.

I shuddered. See, I was not especially aware of the process by which I was given an implant before, or the later procedure which removed it. I didn't really want to know the details. I didn't want to know what it looked like, how it worked, or where in me it went. The whole idea makes me feel rather sick, I don't mind admitting, and I felt a wave of nausea upon beholding the implant in Gio's hands.

Wonderful,' I said weakly.

Gio smiled. It was a sweet smile, rather gentle, the kind that said he knew exactly how I felt and deeply sympathised with my distress. I revised my opinion of him a fraction.

'Grit your teeth,' said he.

'What?'

Gio grabbed my arm. I felt a jab of something sharp piercing my flesh, after which my whole arm went numb. When I saw the flash of a blade in Gio's hand — the really horribly sharp scalpel type of blade — I squeezed my eyes tightly shut, gritted my teeth *very hard indeed,* and tried to sing happy songs in my head until he was finished.

Sweet Gio, adoring of and adored by lovely Ori, friend of

Llandry's and of mine, whose heart could often surprise me with its depths of love. *That* Gio coldly carved a hole in my arm, stuffed the implant into it and sealed me back up again. Happily for me, swift and efficient healing is a Lokant art. They do not so much patch the body up again as persuade the body to patch itself up; it's an ability related to general domination over the will of others. To my regret, it is something I have never managed to master, but Gio was excellent at it.

'You can open your eyes,' he said after a while, and though it may have felt like a century or two I am fairly sure it was only about twenty minutes later.

I cracked one eye open, expecting to see a ruined arm with a horrific scar and pints of blood everywhere.

I saw… my arm. The sleeve of my white nightgown was pushed up to my shoulder, and everything below it was as it should be. Pale, smooth skin, no marks, no scars, no blood.

'How did you do that?!' said I. *And how can you?*

Gio gave me that crooked smile. I thought he looked grim, perhaps sad, but any fleeting glimpses of emotion soon vanished behind his usual composure. 'I do what needs to be done,' he said, which didn't quite address the question I had asked, but did answer the question I'd wanted to ask. 'Why don't you test it? I should not linger.'

I shut my eyes and, for the first time in several moons, I sought to access the PsiMap. It took me some effort to remember how, and for a while it was like trying to see through thick fog.

But then! There it was. I saw the Library laid out in my mind's eye, a system of plans in which each room was distinct. There were translocation points everywhere, including into Tren's suite.

I popped next door.

'Hello, love,' said he. He was lying on his bed, looking pretty comfortable, if a trifle morose. But he lit up at sight of me, and immediately came to embrace me.

'Hello,' I replied, though I did it more with kisses than words.

'Nightgown,' he noted, looking me up and down. 'Were there pillows involved?'

'Many.'

'Blankets?'

'Several.'

He grinned. 'That's my girl.'

He implied, of course, that my attire was not the most practical choice for our forthcoming sleuthing adventures. This was perfectly true, so I flashed back to my own suite with Tren in tow. Gio had already gone, which I observed with some regret; I had not thanked him, though he had gone to a great deal of trouble and probably placed himself in danger in order to provide us with the means to investigate.

'We will catch up with him again soon enough,' Tren said, correctly guessing the reason for my brief dismay.

I could only hope so, for we have no idea where Gio and Ori are. I do have this nice mental map of the Library, now, but its layout assumes a certain familiarity with the place. It is pretty bare. There are no handy labels saying things like, *zone allocated to the nefarious and untrustworthy followers of Krays,* or even more helpfully, *Dwinal's Lair.* The Library is huge, and where in it Ylona might be hiding I cannot guess. I do not know where Susa or Faronni might be, and since Gio said nothing about them, I have to assume he has yet to discover their whereabouts either.

Never mind. It is now time to be intrepid, courageous and just a little bit reckless. There are risks involved with wandering off, of course. Whoever is wearing Limbane's face expects us to be here, and may come back at any time; how can we guess how long he will take?

I'm concerned for Gio. If they find us gone, it will not take them long to realise who helped us. So, Tren and I agreed to proceed with caution. Meanwhile, I am privately hoping that Gio had sense enough to cover his tracks, and to protect himself — if he can.

But we could not simply wait to be retrieved. It is one thing to retire to bed when one is genuinely helpless to achieve anything of use. It is quite another to do nothing when one is empowered to get up to all kinds of (useful, productive and entirely blameless) mischief. And we do, after all, have missing people to find.

And so out we ventured.

Exploration at that time was not *quite* as risky as it may sound. We were both of us suitably white-haired (Tren's hairdo might have been fake, but it was convincing). I had wandered Lokant

Libraries enough in the past to know that they really are huge. Most people know most other people, but not all; it's not uncommon to see unfamiliar Lokant faces rambling the corridors. So, if one dresses the part and acts like one belongs, people are not too quick to challenge. Provided one does not get too close to anywhere they consider to be especially secret or important, anyway.

So, Tren and I donned our best grave, wise, we-are-very-knowing-people-engaged-upon-important-business faces, adopted confident postures matched with twin airs of pomposity, and ventured forth.

The first thing we did, of course, was to search the immediate area for Susa and Faronni. Since Limbane-not-really had dumped Tren and I into adjoining suites, it would make sense that the others would be somewhere nearby, too. But not every room had a translocation point, and we could not access most of them. We were unwilling to make too much noise, but tapped upon doors and called for the missing girls as loudly as we dared. No signs of life did we detect in response. Our suites were situated halfway along a corridor of several doors, most of them presumably leading to other, similar accommodation. The area seemed to be deserted, as far as we could tell; we had been placed at a distance from the main, populated areas of the Library, and if our fellow abductees had been housed anywhere near us, they were not presently at home.

'What next, then?' murmured Tren, kindly deferring to my authority.

Kindly? Not a bit of it. I felt a sudden, suffocating pressure. All right: I was the partial Lokant here. I was the one with the implant and the ability to use it. In our relationship, I have always been the one with the greater power, the greater influence, the habit of command. I was used to leading, and Tren was used to following. It has always worked well for us. We make a splendid team.

But in that moment, under those circumstances, I suddenly felt utterly inadequate to the demands of the occasion. When it came down to it, what did I really know about Lokants or their Libraries? No more than Tren did, certainly. By what right was I better placed to decide how to proceed? How could I be trustfully relied upon not to mess everything up? What if I did exactly the wrong thing, went the wrong way, followed the wrong ideas, and got all of us into deep trouble?

I am not accustomed to self-doubt. It is a horrendously unpleasant feeling, and I felt a stab of sympathy for poor Llandry, to whom the state is sadly familiar. I also felt a new admiration for her courage, for I can tell you: it is far, far harder to lift your chin, put your best foot forward, and stride away into the unknown when you feel acutely aware of everything that can go wrong, and hopelessly inadequate to prevent any of those myriad disasters from coming to pass.

Well, enough of that. Am I Lady Glostrum or am I not?

Why, I *am!* Dauntless Lady Glostrum! She who always knows what to do, even when she has no idea. She who has led others, confidently and successfully, since she was fifteen. She who never lets her doubts show, even on the rare occasions she actually feels them.

I am equal to anything, I told myself.

And I am. I really am.

So up went my chin, back went my shoulders, and on we went.

We found Faronni.

This came about in an odd way. See, it only belatedly occurred to us that we had no idea what she looked like, but there we were bumbling through Sulayn Phay trying to find her anyway. What were we expecting to encounter? A mysteriously locked but conveniently penetrable door, behind which a woman would lie, bound and gagged and obviously kidnapped?

'You must be Faronni Nallay!' we would say, as we breathlessly worked to unbind her poor hands and feet.

She would look meltingly at Tren while he removed her gag, and then say, with the deepest gratitude, 'My rescuers! Thank goodness!'

After which we would all be best friends for life.

That's not what happened.

We wandered away from the cluster of prison-suites and, after venturing down a few more corridors and turning a corner or two, we encountered what appeared to be a collection of classrooms all arranged around a central parlour. We took some care here, braced to encounter company, but the area seemed to be deserted, so we relaxed.

Well, it was deserted until it wasn't, of course. Seated in a chair in a corner of that parlour, so neatly tucked away that we'd failed to see her, was a woman in her twenties. White-haired of course, clad in a simple red cotton dress, she sat with a huge book open upon her lap and a cup of some warm beverage in hand. We had obviously disturbed her studies, for the first sign of her presence we received was the kind of annoyed cough that strives to come across as polite.

'This is a private area,' she informed us, scowling. 'Quiet zone. Learning in progress.'

'Our apologies,' murmured I.

She had barely glanced at us before, her attention focused upon her book. But upon these words of mine, she looked up. Her face brightened.

'Lady Glostrum!' she said in delight. 'How kind of you to visit! I mean, I know you are busy, I hardly imagined you would come to check on my progress. I am busily employed, as you see, and doing great justice to the bursary.' She smiled at me, and tried to get up and curtsey without dropping her enormous book.

I could see that this venture could only end in disaster, but fortunately Tren contrived to collect the book from her before it could tumble to the floor.

All of this took me by surprise, as you might imagine. The last thing I'd expected was to encounter somebody all the way out here that I knew (besides Gio of course). But it did not take me long to understand what had happened.

We knew that Dwinal — or Ylona, or whoever — had been using my visage when they approached my students, the better to lull them into conveniently trusting, docile behaviour. I hadn't quite anticipated that they would carry the charade still further.

Faronni was being trained! I do not know what I had expected our abductors would do with her or Susa, but diligently schooling them in the very arts I had proposed (but struggled) to teach them myself was definitely not it. Furthermore, they had taken the simple expedient of pretending that their classrooms were my school. As far as Faronni knew, nothing had ever gone awry; she had ended up exactly where she had expected to go, and appeared to be quite happy with everything.

Very clever indeed. I was impressed, I admit, with the efficiency and smoothness of the whole operation. But, what was the point?

I tried not to let on that I had never set eyes on Faronni in my life before, because it did not seem quite the right moment to explain to the poor, perfectly happy woman that she had been abducted and deceived. And besides, I may yet be able to make use of this unexpected advantage. So I expressed my delight at seeing her so studiously occupied and, apparently, so happily contented (none of which was feigned, I really was pleased. And relieved. I had never had real cause to imagine she was being poorly treated, but to have this belief in her essentially decent treatment confirmed was good news indeed).

I pumped her for information, without seeming to do so. To be fair, this kind of subtle interrogation is almost second nature to me by now. It is an art that has frequently come in handy in my political life. Faronni innocently relayed all kinds of fascinating things. We learned that she had received a great deal of training in her Lokant abilities (she excelled at the more medical arts and domination, apparently, while showing little aptitude for translocation). She did not know much about her teachers; she knew them merely as "Miss" and "Sir", and apparently had no social contact with them at all. She got on well with the other students (students! Plural! I felt reasonably confident that Susa would be one of them, but who was the other? Or others? Apparently they had discovered some partials of which we were unaware after all, but it was difficult to enquire into the matter when I, Lady Glostrum, was supposedly acquainted with them all. I had to lay it aside for later investigation).

Then Faronni said: 'Lady Glostrum, forgive me if I seem over-eager, but I am more than ready to begin with the other programme. Is there a tutor found?'

Erm. Help! What other programme? What tutor??

'Not yet,' said I — stalling magnificently, as I'm sure you will agree. 'We are hard at work upon the problem, I assure you. Er — what is it about the new programme you're especially looking forward to, if I may ask?'

Not too shabby, right? Faronni became enthusiastic at once. 'Well — it's been so fascinating to learn of my Lokant heritage, and I could not be more interested in developing my abilities. But my other nature! My… failure disappointed my mother so terribly, and I have always wished for an opportunity to try again. I can do better, I know it.'

Reading between the lines there… somebody proposed to teach her sorcery, and Faronni was eager to learn. What had Ori said? At school, she had shown aptitude for sorcery but no application. How reformed a student she now appeared to be.

Interesting. We had stumbled over a fine little programme which proposed to turn out well-rounded Lokant-Sorcerers. Why? Good question. No Lokant ever did anything for unselfish reasons, so I am sure they expect to benefit by it at some point. In the meantime, though, Faronni is receiving decided advantages which I and my fledgling school cannot, alas, give her.

It's growing harder to resent these abductions, though I still deplore the deceitful nature of the operation, and question its usefulness besides. If their goals were much the same as mine (at least as far as training these people up is concerned), why not seek to form an alliance with me? Why not do as Apparently-Limbane claimed to desire, and pool our resources? I don't understand the secrecy, the deception, the manipulation. Even Faronni would clearly have come out here full willingly, if she had been told the truth about where she was going.

I exchanged an uncertain look with Tren, and read in his face a lot of the same kinds of thoughts. We would need to discuss all this, and soon.

'We will secure a tutor very soon,' I assured Faronni, and I felt I could say that with impunity, for no doubt our Lokant hosts would seek to fill that particular post as soon as possible. Which begged a few interesting questions. Where were they expecting to get a fully trained sorcerer from? Who did they plan to approach?

'Where are your fellow students today?' I asked Faronni.

'They are in class.' She blushed faintly. 'I was excused from transloc because I am hopeless at it.'

'That's all right,' I said, moved to a little pity by her obvious embarrassment. 'I am terrible at mending myself, which clearly you excel at.'

She looked briefly delighted by the idea, though her demeanour soon turned to scepticism. 'Really?'

'Really.'

She smiled. I tried not to feel too disturbed by her obvious joy in my failures.

Her attention turned to Tren. Or rather, to Archivere. 'Is this a new student?' The smile she gave him was *very* welcoming, which raised my hackles a fraction. Ah well, who can blame her? He looks excessively handsome with the white hair. And the black hair. He'd look excessively handsome bald, come to that.

'Archivere Dalsy,' Tren introduced himself, and made her a bow.

'Welcome!' she enthused. 'Erm, did you only just arrive? Shall I show you around?'

Tren looked at me, and I gave him a gracious nod. I didn't altogether love the idea of leaving the two of them alone together, not considering how overjoyed Faronni clearly was at the prospect. But I shoved the jealousy aside. What better way to investigate than to receive a tour of the operation from someone who was thoroughly familiar with it? It was a little risky, of course; if the other lessons ended before the tour was concluded, Tren might be caught out. He was not, after all, supposed to be out of his suite. But needs must. I trusted him to figure this out for himself, and to take all due care.

I could help out a bit, though. 'It's a little unorthodox,' I said with a confiding air. 'Mr. Dalsy has yet to be enrolled. He hasn't even met the tutors, yet, and I'd rather he do so via the official channels.'

'I'll keep it quiet,' she promised, and flashed Tren another smile.

Excellent. With that, and feeling only a little bit heroically martyred, I returned a gracious nod to Faronni's curtsey and Tren's bow and watched as she led him away.

So. Turned loose in Sulayn Phay, by myself and equipped with a shiny new translocational device, what did I do?

Well, I went to dinner.

My logic was as follows. I have already noted that lots of interesting and useful things seem to happen over meals. This is because mealtimes gather people together, and when people get together they do fabulously interesting things like talk. A lot. If I wanted to find out what kinds of people lived here, and what sorts of questionable and fascinating things they were getting up to, it wouldn't hurt to present myself at the nearest dining table.

I've already said that it wouldn't be unusual for them to see a stranger wandering around. And it might prove to be handy. I could pose as a newcomer to the Library, and it therefore wouldn't seem odd if I asked questions. Famous as I might be at home, I didn't expect to be recognised in Sulayn Phay. I'm pretty sure the ordinary, day-to-day life of the average Sulayn Librarian doesn't include reading the gossip papers of the Seven Realms.

I was also hungry. Hunger is an unpleasant state in which to exist, and I never see any reason to bear it if I do not have to.

I did not know where to find a dining room, of course, but the map in my head was not without its uses here. It did not have anything helpfully marked as kitchens, or dining parlours, or any such delights. But I could identify spaces which contained larger rooms, sized to accommodate such activities as group cooking and eating, and I made for those.

After a while I was able to follow my nose, for I began to smell something delicious cooking.

You may wonder how I was so sure that such activities as *being fed* would prove to be communal. After all, we may call these places *Libraries* because the nearest translation we have for the word *Lokant* is *Librarian;* even so it's not unfair to suggest that they could more reasonably be compared to a village or perhaps a small town. People live in their own quarters and go about their own lives.

In Limbane's Library, though, there were central kitchens which supplied a few dining areas. People were free to live entirely separately from everyone else if they so wished, but they were strongly encouraged to share mealtimes and some recreational activities as a group. It worked pretty well for Limbane, for it kept everybody in touch with one another and helped to discourage exactly the kinds of factional disputes which were dividing Sulayn Phay.

Seeing as Sulayn was modelled upon Estinor, I fully expected to find its day-to-day workings largely reminiscent thereof, too. Even if (one might reasonably conclude) they had not been quite so successful at maintaining such comfortable things as basic social order and general harmony.

So it proved. I discovered a large, airy, thoroughly delightful dining room, filled with succulent things to eat, and well-supplied with other diners.

Perfect.

As satisfactory as this was, my fond hopes of going unrecognised were almost immediately dashed. No sooner had I walked in, mustering all my confidence in order to appear as though I belonged, than I was spotted and stared hard at by a whole table full of people situated several feet to my left. There were lots of tables with lots of people sitting at them — a veritable sea of colourfully-dressed people with sleek white hair, it was an attractive sight — but to this particular set, my appearance was apparently significant.

So I stared back with a questioning air, but I did not stop. I went straight for the food. (It *was* my primary motive in seeking the dining parlour, after all. Hunger does not conveniently vanish just because one has other things to do!) Then, having chosen an array of tempting things, I drifted back in the direction of the table full of curious people.

As I'd hoped, I was invited to join them.

The flaw in this otherwise splendid plan was soon revealed, for though they chattered, they were not chattering in my own language, nor in any other that I recognised. I don't know why this surprised me. Perhaps because Limbane and others have always talked to me so comfortably in the languages of the Seven, I have fallen into the habit of assuming they are as natural to Lokantkind as they are to us. They *did* make us, after all; it is not unreasonable to imagine that they also gifted us with their languages.

The words that fell from these people's lips were close to my own, so close I could almost understand them. But they were not exactly like, and I recalled with some chagrin that I had heard such speech before.

So there I was, trying to eat and accomplish a little espionage at the same time, and foiled by so rudimentary a problem which I ought to have anticipated. And for which I had no solution. There was only one way they could have recognised me, you see: if they realised I was the real Lady Glostrum, I do not think I would have been permitted to continue walking about with such insouciance, for the fact of my escape must have been obvious. Probably they were not even aware that Lady Glostrum herself was in the Library at all; they took me for whoever it was that had taken to pretending to be me, and treated me accordingly.

This was handy, if they were going to talk to me of Secret Things which I otherwise would never have heard. But of course they expected me to speak their language.

Nothing to do but brazen it out.

'We have a new student,' I said in my own tongue.

This caused a little consternation, and some mild confusion as they tried to work out why I was speaking a Seven Realms language. It came down to what they would consider more likely: that whoever they thought I was had simply chosen to maintain the facade even in such company as this, or that some random woman from the Seven had somehow gained access to their Library and was now wandering around unsupervised. Moreover that such a person had possessed the gumption to stroll nonchalantly into their dining hall and rob it of several particularly fine dishes.

The latter, of course, struck them as impossible.

'All right, all right,' said a youngish man seated across from me, with a roll of his (admittedly rather pretty) eyes. 'We award you full credit for dedication.'

'Who's the new student?' said someone else, a petite woman with short hair and a violently blue dress.

'A sorcerer.' I was feeling my way carefully here, wary of messing up. Best not to say too much.

Some sceptical brows were raised. 'Another one?' said somebody.

'The more, the merrier,' I murmured.

'What about that draykon?'

I looked sharply at the speaker, a man who looked roughly of my own age. He had a grim face, most unwelcoming.

Of course, I wanted to say *what draykon??* and immediately demand a full explanation. Did they have a draykon here somewhere? Was he or she intended to be a student, or a teacher?

If the former, a student of *what*?

I could say none of this, of course, so I settled for a noncommittal shrug. If I hoped the gesture might provoke a more informative response, I was disappointed, for the grim-faced man shrugged too and returned to his food, apparently abandoning the subject.

Hmm.

I was beginning to receive some curious looks, perhaps due to my reticence. I had been laconic to the point of remark, after all, and for all I knew I was impersonating someone with a tendency towards loquacity.

Time to go. The fact that I had finished my meal might also

have influenced my decision, though that point I can neither confirm nor deny.

'Back to it,' I murmured, hoping to convey that I was busy and off to do a range of vitally important things.

Nobody objected to my departure, to my relief, and I left the table feeling like I had got away with it. My heart *might* have been pounding a bit, but that point I can neither confirm nor deny either.

I was halfway to the door when I realised one of them was coming after me.

I was tempted to throw dignity to the winds and beat the hastiest of all possible retreats, but nothing could have been more foolish or more cowardly. So I forced myself to slow my steps, and allow my pursuer to catch up.

It was the woman with the blue dress. She looked sideways at me, and then said in a low voice: 'Gio is back.'

'Oh?' I said, in a neutral tone.

'You didn't know?'

'How long has he been back?'

'I don't know, but Myla saw him earlier. He's running with Ylona's lot.'

Well, whoever she thought I was, it wasn't Ylona. 'Interesting,' I said.

'Mm.' She walked along beside me in silence for a time, and we exited the dining parlour together. 'He hasn't been to see me,' she said after a while.

'Nor me.'

'That's clear enough then, isn't it?' The woman sounded bitter, which intrigued me. I might have thought she was some kind of… *connection* of Gio's, save that I had never seen any sign that he felt that kind of an interest in women. Why was she dismayed by his absence?

She said nothing more, taking her leave of me a moment later. I walked on alone, deep in thought as I made my way back to my suite. It was time to place myself back where I was supposed to be; I had been long enough absent, and to stay away longer would be to unnecessarily increase the risks of trouble.

I went past the classrooms on my way, and retrieved Tren. He and Faronni were getting on swimmingly, and I almost had to drag him away. He later explained this by assuring me that Faronni had given him *masses* of useful information, and who knows what else she might impart if given more time? I perfectly believed him of course, but I may have given him cause to imagine that I did not.

It does not hurt to give one's beloved reason to sweat a little, from time to time. It is unwise to allow them to become too comfortable, lest they begin to take one for granted.

We returned to my suite, and hastily swapped notes. I told him about my adventures with the woman in blue, and he told me about the school. Faronni had given fairly minute descriptions of the two tutors, though I was not able to match them to anybody I had seen in the dining parlour. By her account, her course of study was rigorous and demanding; they were serious about training her up. Susa was the star of the class, quite the pet of both the teachers, and expected to be a great success.

To my disappointment, however, nobody seemed to know what this "success" constituted. It had been strongly implied that they were intended to fulfil some ultimate purpose, but what that might be had been left unspecified. There were merely nebulous promises of "rewards" to be won by those who were sufficiently talented, motivated and generally brilliant.

'We had better make sure you have a chance to milk her some more,' I observed, when Tren had come to the end of his tale.

He blinked, and I had to privately admit that my turn of phrase might have been unfortunate. 'I would be delighted to milk her,' he informed me, his eyes all a-twinkle.

I narrowed mine at him. 'Meanwhile,' I said sternly, 'this question of a draykon. Did you hear any mention of that?'

'None whatsoever. According to Faronni, all of her fellow students are like her: partial Lokants from across the Seven, a mix of Daylanders and Darklanders by the sounds of it. All of them are either sorcerers or summoners as well, though few of them are especially talented at those arts — or perhaps they're merely untrained. I don't know. I thought it an interesting implication, that those with Lokant blood have typically done poorly at sorc or summoner school.'

Interesting indeed. 'I wonder if the two are poorly compatible, somehow.'

'Could be.'

'And I wonder if these people realise that.'

'Perhaps they do. I hear that Susa's sorcerer skills are a bit beyond what was expected for the group. That's partly why she's the star.'

'Mm. So they're looking for the rare ones who are fairly adept with both sides of their heritage.'

'Supposing any such exist. Yes.'

'Of course they do. Am I not proof of it?'

Tren looked sheepish. 'Incontrovertible proof.'

I thought about all of that, but no obvious conclusions jumped to mind. 'I need to see Gio,' I said. 'I wonder if he knows that he's been rumbled.'

'I don't suppose it would surprise him.'

'No, perhaps not. Intrigue, intrigue. Family politics! Dark rumours! Gossip! It is most exciting.'

Tren made a grimacing face. 'Too exciting. I am tired.'

'Then go to sleep. Now that we know the girls are well, it falls to us to be docile and dutiful for a while, and do some waiting. They will come for us eventually. Best to be well-rested when that happens.'

Tren agreed to this. Our leave-taking might have taken rather longer than was strictly necessary, but at length I had him safely deposited in his own room, and me in mine.

Having already napped, I was lively enough to retrieve my journal from its customary spot and make all of the updates you are now enjoying. (You are enjoying them, are you not? Please say yes. I positively *refuse* to write a dry, staid account of my doings, over which people will yawn and fall asleep. If necessary I will start to embellish — include more improbable events, more colourful occurrences, more… *pizzazz*. Just say the word).

I have now done. You are brought all up to date, and I have only to do some waiting. In keeping with my desire to entertain rather than bore you, I will not force you to wait with me. Away goes my journal, and I will write more only once something interesting and preferably exciting has happened.

I, meanwhile, resign myself to all the dullness of some hours, or possibly days (…possibly even *weeks*? Oh goodness please say no…) spent waiting alone. Wish me luck.

29 IV

I now find myself with the same problem as Llandry, in that it becomes extremely difficult to keep track of time out in a Library like this. I have tried to organise my account chronologically, as she did; it is the only system that makes any sense. But how do you write by date, when it is impossible to know what day it is at home? I feel like a day or two has passed since my last update, so that is what I have written down.

If I return to the Seven to find myself, ultimately, weeks off the actual date — which I imagine very likely — then I apologise in advance.

Having smoothly excused myself from all possible reproach on that score, I shall move on.

We had (as I have said) approximately two days of time with nothing to do. Tren and I amused ourselves by playing games — sometimes in person, sometimes by way of tapping upon our adjoining door with various parts of our anatomy.

Don't ask. It is amazing what one can find entertaining, if one is only bored enough.

We speculated wildly as to what they were doing with all this time, though without drawing any useful conclusions. I will spare you the details. We were fed, which briefly alleviated our boredom but not by much. The food was not delivered by a person; instead, a kind of hatch-thing (forgive my imprecision — engineering is not my talent) opened in the floor and a little platform-thing rose into view, bearing plates and dishes and cups all full of good things. Once I had finished eating, it was all taken away again. Lovely. I couldn't decide whether that meant these apartments were always used for captives — indeed, had been especially designed for the purpose — or whether this function had been originally intended for the convenience of more voluntary occupants. That question occupied many a dull hour, I can tell you.

My torment was briefly lifted by the appearance of Gio. Under the circumstances I felt rather like kissing him again, but I wisely kept that fact to myself this time.

I saluted him instead, from my comfortably recumbent posture upon the bed. 'Hurrah, the cavalry!'

Gio surveyed me. I called myself *comfortably recumbent* but it might be fairer to say *hopelessly inert* or *dejectedly unmoving*. 'You look bored,' said he.

'Yes. So I hope you have brought some exciting news.'

'Actually…' he looked apologetic. 'I was hoping you might have some.'

I sighed deeply and flopped back into the blankets. 'Ylona strikes me as an insufferably dull person. Does she do nothing of note or interest?'

Gio shrugged. 'I begin to think that her plan for winning the leadership largely consists of dishing enough dirt on my grandmother. She does not appear to have a great deal of competition, otherwise.'

'It's a time-honoured tradition, I suppose.'

'Yes. So. Any dirt to dish?'

'Not much yet, but Gio…' I sat up and regarded him with earnest concern. 'What have you done with Ori?'

'What have I done with him? He's with me.'

'Do people know what he is?'

'A draykon, you mean? No, we've kept his identity quiet. As far as Ylona knows, he is a summoner from Glinnery and my lover and that's it.'

'Are you sure?' I told him about the blue-garbed woman and her reference to a draykon.

Gio's eyes narrowed. 'Short hair, fond of blue? That sounds like Lania. She's a cousin, of sorts. I didn't realise she was back.'

'Threat or not?'

'I don't know. She has always behaved like grandmother can

do no wrong, but then, so did I, once. One tends to know what's good for one's health.' He frowned, and thought, and shook his head. 'I am pretty sure it's not Ori she's talking about. He's been careful to do nothing that would give him away, and I don't think they have any way to sense a draykon soul the way the draykoni can amongst themselves.'

'All right. Good.'

'I haven't heard of a draykon up here, but I'll ask around. Ylona might be interested to hear about that, anyway.'

He took his leave soon afterwards, looking cheered. It occurred to me that he had probably buttered up Ylona by promising her information about Dwinal — and subsequently allowed her to believe that he was collecting that information himself. It was much more comfortable for him to keep his distance from his grandmother, however, and use me as a source. I wasn't sure how to feel about that.

At length, they came for us. I was stretched out upon my bed at the time, comfortably clad in my nightgown, wearing all the blankets, and staring at the ceiling with (most likely) that expression that says: *just kill me, I would enjoy it more.* When the knock came upon my door, I almost died of fright. I shot out of bed, heart furiously a-pound, and ran for the door.

Only to conclude, of course, that I couldn't open it anyway. What was I doing? Why were they knocking?

'Come in?' I said, rather doubtfully.

The door opened, and it was Limbane again. That surprised me. Considering my two-day incarceration, I had expected the masquerade would have been abandoned. Why bother, when we must realise ourselves to be captive? (At least in theory — I do not anticipate that they know of my implant, yet).

'Lady Glostrum,' he said, with a scrupulously polite inclination of his head.

I merely eyed him, and did not reply.

This show of rudeness did not faze him. He offered me his arm. 'We are ready to begin discussions, with my apologies for the delay. If I may escort you?'

'The *delay*?' I repeated in high disgust. I was not disposed to let him off so easily. 'Was it really necessary to leave me waiting for two days together, and with no means of egress from this room?'

He hesitated, and I watched as his gaze travelled to the door and back to me. How would he explain the captivity?

Apparently he wouldn't try. 'My apologies,' he said again. 'Arrangements took longer than I had anticipated.'

I narrowed my eyes at that. Surely he could not imagine that I would be satisfied with such slippery language, such a total lack of explanation?

'Will Mr. Dalsy be allowed out?' I prompted. 'What explanation do you have for his incarceration either?'

I realised at once that I had erred, for if I had been locked in this room alone for two days, how could I know that Dalsy had been imprisoned likewise? 'That connecting door is rather thin,' I added smoothly. 'We have striven to entertain each other, by such means as we have available.'

'I apologise.'

Really, that was it? He had nothing to offer but repeated apologies? I lost patience with the charade on the spot.

'Permit me to make a guess,' I said to him. 'You are… Hyarn?'

His eyes widened, and I had the satisfaction of observing that I had temporarily robbed him of the power of speech. At length he gave a slight cough, backed away a step, and eyed me with a new wariness which afforded me great satisfaction. 'Hyarn?' he repeated.

'Hyarn. A close associate of Dwinal, who is the current Master Lokantor of this Library. You met some of my friends, not long ago: Llandry and Pense, of Nuwelin, and Orillin Vance of Glinnery.' I could have added, *And you murdered Galywis,* but I decided such a comment would be both dangerous and rather useless at that moment.

His lips curved in a faint, rueful smile. Then the vision of Limbane faded, and before me stood a stranger: a man much younger than Limbane, with close-cropped hair and an air of energy. 'I had not thought that relations between you and Miss Sanfaer were so close.'

'We communicate,' I assured him.

'Clearly.'

'The masquerade was entirely purposeless, I assure you. I knew immediately that you were not Limbane. What can you have meant by it?'

'Ah — we thought you would be more comfortable with a familiar face in charge.'

I snorted. It was spectacularly unladylike, but I couldn't help it. 'You thought I would be more comfortable with *Limbane*? Your information is sorely lacking.'

His eyebrows went up and he waited, perhaps hoping I would elaborate. But I have learned my lesson. With these people, never give away anything that you don't have to, for *they* certainly will not. Why put oneself at a disadvantage?

He was not wrong to imagine that I might have felt more comfortable with someone else in charge, however. He killed Galywis. He had defended his own motives in doing so, not wholly without success; Galy had been mad beyond recall, and had done some terrible things himself. Still, entering into negotiations with a man who has recently proved himself capable of committing murder in cold blood was not a circumstance best calculated to inspire confidence in the proceedings.

Then again, Dwinal was hardly any better.

'It would have been preferable,' I informed him severely, 'if you had approached me in better faith, without the deception you appear to have thought necessary.'

'My apologies,' he said for the third — or fourth? — time, and I gritted my teeth.

'It would also have been nice if you had not abducted me.'

Hyarn tilted his head. 'There was no abduction. You came willingly.'

'Under false pretences.'

'Not at all. I told you where we were going, and I did not lie to you about our reasons for seeking counsel with you.'

'At the same time, you pretended to be somebody else.'

'But you knew I was not Limbane.'

'Yes.'

'It did not deter you.'

'I had reasons.'

He blinked. 'Which were?'

'I came in search of my students, who you absolutely *have* abducted.'

'Not at all,' said he serenely. 'They were invited to train their Lokant abilities, and we provided them with the means.'

'You pretended to be me! You, or one of your people.'

His faint smile returned. 'As I implied. People feel more comfortable with familiar faces.'

And it was easier. I could extract Susa from Angstrun's academy with the greatest of ease; but imagine the paperwork if Dwinal had sought to do so openly, on behalf of her Library!

'Your behaviour throughout has been highly suspect,' I informed him. 'You have been deceitful, manipulative, high-handed and dishonest. Why should I or my organisation have anything to do with you?'

'Because there is much we may do to assist one another. Your organisation will benefit enormously from our help, as you must realise.'

I did, of course. I have already discussed the many problems we have faced, particularly our lack of suitable tutors. 'And how will it benefit you? I am nowhere near naive enough to imagine you would assist us out of the goodness of your hearts.'

He smiled. 'All this shall be discussed, if you will come with me.'

I did not trust him, of course, but what could I do? I needed to hear whatever he had to say, even if I knew he would lie and dissemble all the way through it.

'Archivere Dalsy comes along with us,' I said.

'May I ask why?'

'Because he is not Archivere Dalsy at all. That's my husband and I want him with me.'

That earned me a narrow, somewhat displeased look, which only exasperated me further.

'What? If you treat us with deceitfulness, expect the same in return. I had to get your attention somehow, as you had apparently decided against approaching my organisation openly.'

He sighed, and his lips tightened with annoyance. Oddly, I did not receive the impression that it was directed at me, and I wondered what troubled him.

It was soon gone, and replaced by… calculation. 'Tren Warvel,' he said.

'Yes.'

'A sorcerer?'

That made me wary. 'Yes.'

'One of the best, I understand.'

I did not like the direction his thoughts were tending in, at all. 'Let him out, please.'

Hyarn smiled radiantly, and bowed. 'By all means.'

Oh, dear.

'Hello, darling,' I said when Tren joined us moments later. 'You can take off the wig.'

Tren did so with obvious relief, and I did not blame him. Those things are mighty uncomfortable, so I hear. 'I take it the game is up?'

'Or rather, abandoned,' I replied. 'I have been trying to explain to Hyarn that his typical Lokant attitude of deceit first, dissimulation afterwards and a healthy pack of lies in between is somewhat counter-productive.'

Tren's eyebrows rose. 'Any luck with that?'

'Not a great deal.'

Hyarn had the grace to look faintly embarrassed. 'May I suggest we proceed?'

Tren took my arm, with perhaps a hint of protectiveness. 'Lead on,' he invited, but without his customary smile.

Once outside of our various prisons, Hyarn simply translocated us to another part of the Library. I surreptitiously checked the Map, afterwards, but it availed me little: we were near nothing that I recognised.

He led us into a spacious room, handsomely fitted up with wood and crystal and enlivened with more colour than was customary. It was a pleasant room, and since my approving nose detected the aroma of cayluch the moment we arrived, I was immediately rendered more comfortable.

A long, wooden table occupied the centre of the room, and Hyarn led me to a seat at one end of it. Tren he seated opposite. There were two others present, both Lokants, both women. One was of Limbane's approximate age, rather elderly by appearance, with a wild mane of hair and plain black clothes. The other was somewhat younger, more neatly turned out, with unusually vivid green eyes. Both of them nodded to me.

'Allow me to introduce our Lokantor,' said Hyarn, confirming my suspicions. He indicated the elder of the two women as he spoke: this, then, was the infamous Dwinal. 'And Tynara, her aide.'

Dwinal looked at me, and at Tren, and offered no comment.

I scrutinised her with some interest. Here was the woman Llandry had described: the grandmother of Gio, who had treated her poor grandson with such a casual lack of concern that I could not think well of her. Like so many Lokants, she saw others as tools to be used, manipulated, lied to at will — even her own family. Here was the woman who had sought the death of Galywis, even if she had not delivered it herself, and who had greeted the destruction of so magnificent a construction as the Library of Orlind with glee.

Also the woman who had taken a degree of interest in my students that I could only find unnerving. The good treatment Faronni had obviously received mollified me somewhat, but only a little. I was by no means pacified, and I privately resolved not to leave that room until I had learned what she and Hyarn intended to do with their harvest of partial Lokants.

If I was not satisfied by the end of the discussions, I would be taking Faronni, Susa and all others I could find, and leaving.

Nobody spoke. I sat sipping cayluch, unmoved, waiting.

'Well, Lady Glostrum,' said Dwinal at last. 'I understand you are in need of teachers for your… establishment.'

'Not so much anymore,' I told her with a bland smile. 'Most of my students appear to have been recruited to an entirely different school.'

'They could be relocated, under the right conditions.'

And a number of things fell into place in my mind. We have been much confused by the behaviour of our opponents, have we not? Their tampering with our post, and making a show of searching our building; their absconding with our students; their absconding with *me,* and Tren, only to abandon us in locked rooms for days thereafter. And now, to offer us *back* the very students they have gone to such trouble to procure?

It has been a sustained effort to intimidate; a show of power. We have been shown that the Librarians of Sulayn Phay can interfere with us on every level, and in every conceivable fashion. In short, we and our fledgling bureau are at their mercy, and if we ever expect to establish our school, we must first satisfy Dwinal.

They are more than capable of manipulating us, to my chagrin. My fine, clever scheme has only landed us right where they wanted us: in Dwinal's Library, listening dutifully while she offers to ransom our students, and blackmails us into the bargain.

'What conditions might those be?' I tried to keep my tone neutral, and show little of my irritation. I do not know how well

I succeeded.

'If I was satisfied as to the standard of teaching at your school, I would be more than willing to negotiate.'

'Why not continue to teach them here? Then you may be certain that your standards are being met.'

Dwinal looked me over. Probably she was considering how many lies she could get away with. 'Have you noticed any common features among those who have been invited to Sulayn Phay?'

'They are of mixed blood. Draykon and Lokant.'

'Indeed. They ought to be trained in both sides of their heritage; whatever skills they possess by way of sorcery or summoning ought not to be neglected. We lack the capacity to offer this kind of training, but you certainly do not.'

So this was why she needed us. I wondered about that draykon I had heard mention of. Had they tried to acquire a tutor from among the draykoni, and failed? I would not be surprised. They had a history of harvesting draykon bone and putting it to all manner of questionable uses. What draykon would consent to work with them? I, however, was known to possess close links with the very heart of the new draykon world. If anybody could recruit their aid, it would be me.

'You removed Susa from the Sorcerer's Academy,' I reminded Dwinal. 'There she was receiving precisely the kind of teaching you describe.'

'But her Lokant heritage was neglected. Besides, many of your students have been failed by your "Sorcerer" and "Summoner" schools, have they not? Their aptitude is not considered sufficient, or they do not progress quickly enough. They drop out, or they are invited to leave. They deserve better. There needs to be a new kind of establishment: one that nurtures both sides of these students' heritage.'

'Why should any of this interest you? Your concern for the future of my students is touching, but I fail to see why the standard and breadth of their education should matter one whit to you.'

She gave me that considering look again, and I braced myself. 'We are planning the inauguration of a new … establishment of our own,' she said. 'One which must be peopled and staffed by those such as we have discussed. Men and women with mixed blood, adept at a range of arts previously thought incompatible with one another. Skilled Lokants, trained sorcerers or summoners or whatever you shall come to term these things in future. In exchange for our aid, I wish for you to refer your very best graduates to me. That is all.'

'What kind of establishment?' I said immediately. Such vagueness could only mean bad news.

But she was unmoved by my question. 'It would be difficult to explain it to you.'

I smiled. 'That is insufficient, as you must know. Be frank with me, please. I assure you, I can bear it.'

She inclined her head. 'Then to be frank: I will not answer this question. The matter is no concern of yours.'

I wondered whether that meant it was highly suspect in nature, which seemed probable. I could try to give her the benefit of the doubt, I suppose, and believe her to be telling the truth: it probably wasn't any business of mine, so why should she waste either her time or mine in telling me about it? But these are Lokants, and she's a Lokantor, and I don't believe a word of it.

No matter. If she won't tell me, I will find out for myself.

Tren had let me do all the talking up until then, but something was bothering him; I knew from the perplexed frown that he wore, and his silence. He was thinking.

In due course, he spoke up. 'What is it that you wish for these sorcerers or summoners to learn?'

Dwinal gave him the kind of stare that suggested she was wondering why he was alive. 'Why do you ask?'

Tren's lips quirked in a wry smile; he understood the meaning of that look just as well as I did. 'Let me start by revealing that I am one of the finest sorcerers in the Darklands. I do not say that to boast. It is a fact, and being so, it is likely that I will be having a great deal to do with the training of your fledgling recruits. Therefore, it would not be a bad idea for you to answer my questions.'

Dwinal acknowledged all of this with a faint, grudging nod.

'Excellent. Well then, I ask because I fail to see why the existing academies are so incapable of satisfying your requirements. Misguided their programmes may be, but they are still the very best at teaching the arts we call sorcery and summoning. Furthermore, their assessment of the students is likely to be accurate. If the Academy of Sorcery in Glour City felt that Faronni Nallay was blessed with only minimal talent and quite without the means to expand upon it, they are, in all likelihood, correct. Why do you think that we will be able to do any better, and in what respect are we to try?'

Fair questions indeed. I sat back to listen, glad now that I had insisted upon Tren's being brought along.

Dwinal was nowhere near so pleased by the question. Her face registered annoyance, or something reminiscent thereof. 'As I have just said,' she began coldly, 'Your schools are out of touch. They are… limited. Of course they are. They are vast, grand, ancient organisations, entrenched in tradition, stuck in their ways. They are following programmes laid down generations ago, largely unchanged, I would wager, for the past century at least. What's needed here is a new, broader-minded, more flexible approach. Consider. Students deemed inept in the few and limited arts taught at such academies might excel at other, related powers, might they not? But if it is left to your schools to discover these talents, they will forever go undeveloped.'

All right. So Dwinal is not interested in the usual things that sorcerers and summoners do. In other words, Tren might be one of the finest sorcerers in the Darklands (and he is, no doubt about it), but he is highly skilled at all the regular stuff. The same goes for me. We are both products of precisely the academies she so despises, and have been trained only in the recognised arts.

Full-blooded draykoni, of course, can do a great deal more than we can. They can shapeshift. They can regenerate themselves, raise others from the dead. Is that the kind of thing Dwinal is talking about? Is she hoping that the likes of Faronni Nallay might suddenly manifest an ability to change shape?

I highly doubt that will ever come to pass. According to Llandry, those higher arts (I call them higher for the sake of convenience; let's not argue about the relative value of shapeshifting versus, say, opening portals in the fabric of the world) — those higher arts are accessible only to those with significant draykon heritage. She seems to measure it by a simple rule: if a person can take draykon form, then he or she is close enough to a full draykon to access everything else as well. If a person cannot shapeshift, then…

… well, then what? I suppose we have been behaving as

though these two categories are all there can be; you are either a draykon shapeshifter, or you're stuck being a mere ordinary sorcerer or summoner. There is no middle ground. But perhaps this is misguided, too. Those with partial *Lokant* heritage tend to manifest some of the characteristic powers, but not usually all. What if I had only ever been tested on my ability to heal? I would have been written off as a failure, and sent packing from school.

What if Dwinal is right? What if there *is* a middle ground? What if someone like Faronni, unable to shapeshift, hopeless at the kinds of things at which Tren excels, might actually be quite competent at other draykoni arts?

I was electrified by this idea, and so was Tren. We exchanged a long look, and I saw he was as fired up by the idea as I was. Gracious, what if Tren himself can do more than we've ever supposed? If he is amazing at everything they teach at sorcerer school, maybe he's amazing at the things they don't teach, too. Even if he can't shapeshift.

'We accept,' said Tren.

Dwinal was flatteringly (in my case) or insultingly (in Tren's) unwilling to take his word for it, and looked to me for confirmation. Confirmation I quickly gave. Why would I not? I mean, I have no intention of placidly handing our best students to Dwinal, not when we have no idea what she intends to do with them. But that's a problem for later. In the meantime, there are two inescapable points to bear in mind. One: much as it galls me to even pretend to cave under the kind of pressure she has seen fit to apply, we need to get her out of our hair. And two: she is right, about everything.

'Excellent,' said she, with her first smile of the meeting. It was the unpromising kind, a bit too wide and much too toothy, but I tried not to let that bother me. 'Then I will give you Tynara and two others for your school, on temporary secondment. I also give all of our currently enrolled students into your care, provided your facilities are able to accommodate them.'

'How many are there?'

'Eight, so far. There will be more sent to you, as we discover them, and I imagine you will uncover more yourselves.'

I felt reasonably confident that we could accommodate twenty or so in our current building, which ought to cover our needs for a while, so I made no objection.

And that was it, the meeting was over. Dwinal, having apparently got everything she wanted, departed soon afterwards with Tynara in tow. Hyarn — who had said nothing whatsoever for the entire meeting, slightly to my confusion — rose to escort us back to our apartments.

'You will have a little time to meet those students you are unacquainted with,' he assured us. 'And to see what we have been doing with them thus far.'

Good, because there were some things I wanted to look into before we left.

I also needed a little time to think about where to get a few more draykoni from. Hiring tutors from within the sorcery/summoning establishment obviously wasn't going to be good enough. I'd finally have a use for dear Ori, of course — and what better teacher could I expect to find! He is not only the easiest person in the world to get along with and possessed of endless reserves of patience, he also has just the sort of enquiring mind that would delight in the challenge.

I can't expect him to manage the job alone, however. He will need help.

Which means, we need to go talk to Llandry.

In the interests of not boring you, allow me to skip over the bit where we toured the school and met all the students. They were much as you would expect of a group of eight disparate people, with nothing in common save a certain accident of birth. We all exchanged nods and pleasantries and they eyed me curiously and I eyed them speculatively and that was that.

As for the school, the "Miss" Faronni had spoken of turned out to be Tynara. "Sir" was a man of around Hyarn's apparent age (it's so hard to tell with Lokants) who was introduced as Dan. He had a sloppiness of dress and a laid-back demeanour which interested me, for it set him apart from most of the other people I met up there. Our third teacher was to be… Gio. All very good, except that it would interfere with his espionage activities where Ylona was concerned — something I could hardly expect Dwinal to realise.

Complications, complications.

Anyway, by the time we were kindly escorted home, we were fully up to date with all the official things, everybody was very happy with everybody, and blah blah blah.

I may have sneaked some time to go wandering about the place in hopes of stumbling over this mythical draykon Lania talked of, but I found nothing.

29 IV

Confusingly, we returned to Glour City to find that it was… approximately two hours after we had left. Time runs strangely in those Libraries, mostly in that it doesn't. I think the inhabitants are all about ten thousand years old as a consequence, but most of them don't look over forty.

How I hate them, sometimes.

Anyway. I discovered the date by the simple expedient of confusing Adonia.

'We are returned!' I said to her, sweeping into her office with the air of one long absent (to me it had been some days, after all).

She, however, blinked at me as though I was mad, or perhaps just making fun of her. The latter she does *not* like, not at all. We quickly learned to stop making mild jokes about her clothes. 'From… where?' said she. 'When are you leaving again?'

'I have left, and come back!' I don't know why I said this with the air of a woman making an announcement of great importance. If I expected Adonia to be delighted, I was soon disabused of any such expectation.

'Oh,' she said, and blinked. 'That was fast.'

Then she went to her desk, sat down, and began reading a magazine.

'Yes, well, we thought we would be longer away but the business was completed rather quickly…' I didn't fancy trying to explain Lokant Libraries and relative time to Adonia, but my attempts to find an alternative way to excuse our remarkably brief absence might have been spared. Adonia merely nodded vaguely, her eyes fixed upon her magazine.

'I'll be in my office,' I said, and withdrew.

Adonia said nothing.

Ori came back, overflowing with enthusiasm as I had expected, and entered into our new project with gusto. 'I've thought about the possibility before,' he told me, and I wasn't much surprised. 'I'd love the chance to look into it properly.'

'I would love you to do so,' I informed him. 'Though surreptitiously, please. I want Dwinal to feel that we are addressing the matter, but not *too* expeditiously. Any discoveries we make should be kept quiet, for now.'

'Naturally, naturally.'

'Where's Gio?'

'He went back, for now. He'll follow soon.'

'Hm. Ori, I need you to do something else first.'

He beamed at me with limitless enthusiasm and said grandly, 'Anything.'

I raised a brow. 'That's dangerous, as you well know.'

His grin widened. 'I trust you.'

'Fool.'

He visibly braced himself. 'Very well. Out with it!'

'I need to see Llandry.'

'Oh, but that's easy!'

'It is? You know where she is?'

'She'll be on Orlind.'

'Exactly.'

Ori shrugged. 'It will take a little time to get there, but it's not hard.'

I have been to Orlind before. In fact, I was part of the very expedition which discovered the place was *not* lost, as we'd long assumed. It's only an island now, and a tiny one at that; once it was the Seventh of our Seven Realms, and every bit as significant as the other six. Its decline is a sad tale, but the important point is, Orlind *is* still there.

It is… not easy to get to. It lies beyond Irbel, and there's a vast and inhospitable mountain range in between. Those mountains are very high. And where you have high mountains you also have high winds, snow, and in short, *cold*.

I hate the cold.

I tried to be encouraged by Ori's nonchalance. I know he has been back a few times since, and he assures me that Orlind itself — once so chaotically broken that it was extremely difficult, unpleasant and frightening to visit — is now quite safe.

All right, then. If Llandry can muster her courage and venture places she would infinitely prefer to avoid, so can I.

I won't burden you with the details of our miserable journey. I will spare you the pitiful vision of me, bundled up in thirty-five layers and still uncontrollably shivering. I will certainly spare you the details of my gritted teeth, wretched mood and embarrassingly poor temper. In some ways, I think I bore with our first journey thither much better. At the time, we were swept up in adventure, travelling with a sense of high urgency and vast possibility. It was a voyage of discovery, and too fraught with danger to leave me with much time to think about the cold or discomfort. Returning in a more leisurely fashion, minus the sense of impending doom, wore my resilience to shreds and I am not proud of my behaviour.

So let's move on. I will merely state that Ori conveyed Tren and I over the mountains with inexhaustible patience and good cheer, no matter how I complained, and on the other side… well, we received a view, which was new. No enshrouding fog, this time, no clinging mists to hide the island from our sight; it lay before us, a floating disc in the sea, barren and dead. I was prepared for this, but still, it was a sorry vision. Very little was growing down there, and to be honest with you, it looked like nothing ever would. It was basically a desert.

Ori soared gracefully over the water and landed on the southern edge of the island. Nothing was nearby, not the smallest sign of life, and I could not refrain from asking him (rather waspishly, I am sorry to say) why he had chosen so desolate a spot for our disembarkation when our purpose in coming was to find the *people*.

He waited until Tren and I had slithered our way down to the ground from his broad back, and then he shifted human. 'Because,' said he gravely, 'I thought you might like to get comfortable first.'

It was a lot warmer down on the island than it had been up in the heights. I walked about a bit, bouncing and rubbing my arms and indulging in all the usual antics we could call *I am freezing help me*. After a while I realised that Ori had meant more than merely warming up; he was tactfully suggesting that my appalling mood did not perfectly fit me for company just then, and I might want to (bluntly put — why beat about the bush after all?) *get a grip*.

I did that, with Tren's assistance, who proved adept as ever at both warming me and cheering me. I am terribly hard work sometimes, am I not? I made a mental note to make it up to both of them later. I made another mental note to remember, another time, that cold and discomfort are not the end of the world; they almost certainly won't kill me; and, as a grown woman, *I can deal with this*.

Once we had recovered both our warmth and our equanimity (I say *we* because it did belatedly occur to me that the other two are by no means cold-proof, even if they bore the weather with more grace), Tren and I returned to Ori's draykon back and we did a little bit more flying. There was not far to go after that — it is a small island, as I have mentioned. We flew until we encountered a little settlement set up upon the bleak, dead surface of Orlind, a knot of makeshift houses made from who-knows-what. They looked like they were dreamed up in a hurry, and they probably were. Llandry's people had some building materials, I suppose; the Library of Orlind, once blown to bits, left a fine debris of stone and wood everywhere. But the products of such broken chunks of stone, hastily erected, were not beautiful.

Not that it mattered. The place had a welcoming atmosphere, and an air of industry and cheerful activity which could not but appeal. And since one of the first people we saw was Llandry, I immediately felt quite at home. She was in her draykon shape, all misty-grey scales and graceful curves — beautiful. But when she saw Ori, already landed and shapeshifted, she flashed into her human shape in an instant, becoming the girl I had first known: slim, brown-skinned, her abundant black hair pulled back into a tail.

'*Ori!*' she squeaked, and hurled herself at him. I mean that literally. Shy Llandry Sanfaer, reserved, timid and tightly controlled as she has always been, went for Ori at a gallop and leapt on him.

'What's this?' he asked, laughing. 'You'd think I had been away for a year.'

'It must be at least a moon, which is almost as bad!' she told him, tickling him with shocking ruthlessness. 'I've regretted sending you away!'

'Now, now. You wouldn't dispatch poor Gio into Lokant territory alone, would you?'

'Never,' Llandry agreed, letting Ori go with visible reluctance. 'Where is he?'

'Um. Well, he's in Lokant territory alone, just at the moment.'

'Oh.'

'I'll explain. But you've ignored poor Eva and Tren.'

Llandry's head whipped around, and it immediately became apparent that she had not seen us. She was pleased — I think I can say that she was pleased. It was difficult to tell, for all the overflowing exuberance with which she had greeted Ori vanished without trace, and her greetings for us were much more subdued. But she smiled, and looked happy, and said some appropriate things. She even consented to hug Tren, though she did not hazard an embrace with me. Nor did I offer.

The fact is, I think Llan is a little in awe of me. Possibly even afraid. She is always on her guard around me, more reserved than ever, clearly trying to be on her best behaviour at all times. It is flattering, I suppose, as far as it goes, but it somehow obliges me to be on my best behaviour, too. So, friends though we are, much as we've been through together, we treat each other with a careful, slightly stilted politeness which cannot but put something of a damper on things.

'To what do we owe the pleasure?' said Llandry (do you see what I mean? Ori she almost knocked flat in her delight; to me she says *to what do we owe the pleasure!*)

'We come seeking aid,' I said, hoping that an admission of need might put her at her ease. 'We have one or two problems.'

The gambit succeeded beyond my wildest dreams, for Llandry beamed at me with such delight that I was somewhat nonplussed. 'Really!' she declared. It was not so much a question as an expression of jubilation.

My tendency towards sarcasm got the better of me, I am

afraid. 'Really,' I assured her. 'But they are not of the gravest kind; you need not be so excessively concerned.'

Happily, she took this sally in good part, and grinned at me. 'I'm only thinking of all the times I have come to you with a problem, and landed all kinds of complications in your lap. I shall be happy to return those many favours, if I can.'

'Excellent,' I said briskly. 'Then we had better begin by relaying the news, for there is quite a bit of it.'

Llandry listened to everything I had to tell with spellbound fascination. I wish I had such an audience for my every communication, it is most satisfying! Only perhaps poor for my ego, were I always to be treated with such deferential attention. I believe Llandry thinks I can do no wrong, too, and I am sorry to say that I encouraged that belief by lightly glossing over the various mistakes I have made lately. When she reads this journal she will know all, and I hope she will not judge me too harshly.

When I reached the part about needing draykon assistance, her eyes lit up in a fashion that struck me as… calculating. Can I possibly express how strange that was? Llan is the last woman in the world to manage cold-blooded calculation. She's the sensitive type, very feeling, diffident and unsure of herself (though that last part, I am happy to say, seems to be fading quickly; she is taking to her new life better than I might have expected). Anyway, she is more likely to break herself to pieces trying to help someone else than to operate under ulterior motives, and seize upon an opportunity to advance her own cause. That speculative light in her eye made me uneasy — and also intrigued. This new Llandry was not known to me. What would she do?

'How many teachers do you need?' she said, smiling.

Uh oh. Something about that smile worried me, too. 'Well, we are hoping to retain the use of Ori, for a while. We do expect Gio to come back from Lokant-Land eventually, and besides, we like Ori.'

'Thank you,' said Ori gravely.

Llandry looked a little disappointed, but she did not oppose my request. 'Of course, if that's what Ori wants to do.'

Ori gave her a hug. 'I'll come back,' he promised. 'Just not quite yet.'

Llandry nodded, but her face was thoughtful and her gaze strayed back to me. 'But you want one more, right? At least one more, or you would not be here.'

'Yes. I have at least eight students to manage already, and we expect more. Possibly many more. I'd like Ori to have help.'

May I admit something here? You may be wondering why I had gone to all the trouble of visiting Orlind myself, especially considering how much I hate the passage over the mountains. I could have sent Ori by himself, with instructions to collect a friend. It would have been far easier, and it is not as though I don't have a thousand other things to do.

The fact is, I have missed Llandry, and Pense, and Avane and all the rest. It has been pleasant having Ori with me; more so than I would ever have anticipated.

For a time, Llandry and I were bound up in the same adventure. Our paths often crossed, we worked together, we had the same goals. It was a difficult time, but a lively one, and we accomplished so much.

But things changed. Llandry's duties took her away to Iskyr (the Upper Realm), and then to Orlind. Pense and Ori went with her, of course. They have survived adventures aplenty since then — adventures I have had little to do with, because my own duties took me back to Glour City and (ultimately) Off-World altogether.

I miss our old fellowship. Nothing would please me more than to whisk Llandry back with me, install her in my school, and keep her at my side for as long as I can. Pensould, too. He is her mate, one of the ancient type of draykoni with no human blood at all. He's… intriguing. He came wandering up about halfway through our conversation and stood nearby, listening with the impassive face, and interpolated only a brief comment, the substance of which I cannot remember. But there'll come a moment where he will know exactly the thing to do, precisely the piece of information we need, and he will proceed to get things done with a kind of blunt practicality that has nothing to do with ordinary human behaviour. It's refreshing. And effective.

I cannot take Llandry, or Pense. They are needed here. Reviving Orlind is *a mission of grave importance* (I love being able to say that), and I cannot justify removing those who are leading the project. Even if they would consent to come, which I doubt.

I might, however, be able to get away with taking Avane. She is like Llandry and Ori, a human shapeshifter rather than an ancient pure-blood. What's more, she is a Darklander like me, a native of Glour, and near enough my own age. I like her a lot. I always wanted to get to know her better.

I know she is important to Llandry, too, so I broached the topic with as much subtlety as I could muster.

'I want Avane,' I told her.

Well, sometimes directness is best.

Llandry blinked. 'Oh.'

She looked… crestfallen, which was as I had expected. But I was rapidly forced to revise my conclusion, for it was not that kind of dismay that I saw in Llandry's face.

'But…' said Llan, and hesitated. 'Surely—'

'Avane would like to go, I think,' said Pense, who blinked his black, black eyes at me and attempted something that was probably supposed to be a smile. 'She suffers under the light.'

As well she might, being used to the comfortably dark conditions of Glour. 'Perfect,' I enthused.

Llandry nodded. 'Oh, you may borrow Avane with my blessing, if she would like it! I can have no objection to that.'

'Then, what?' said Pensould gently, for he could see as well as I could that Llandry had something else on her mind.

Llan beamed at me. 'Only two teachers! That is a good start, but should you not like to have one more? What if you get many more students? And besides, three minds to grapple with the problem would be far better than two, no?'

'Doubtless,' said I, watching Llandry's face with decided wariness.

'You will have two human shapeshifters, which is great! They will know exactly how to relate to your human-Lokant students, and I am sure Ori and Avane will do wonderfully. But should you not like to have an ancient along, too? They see things differently, you know. They have an entirely different perspective.'

Very good point, which is one reason why I'd gladly walk off with Pensould if I could. If we need people who are less hidebound by our age-old assumptions, traditions and beliefs, who better to entreat for aid than someone who predates all of it, and has never understood any part of our human interpretations of their arts anyway? I encouraged this line of thought, though I didn't lose my sense of foreboding. Llandry was being far too strenuously helpful.

'Best of all, an Elder!' she said. 'Nothing could be better! They are stronger, older, wiser, more powerful, they know *everything* there is to know about the draykon arts—'

'All true, but do you not need your Elders here?' I interjected. 'I understood you were finding them most useful yourself, and were rather shorter on supply than you would like.'

'Oh, that's changed now,' she said airily. 'We have a few floating around, and I can easily spare one for you.'

Ori cast her a suspicious look. So did Pense.

So did I. 'Who do you have in mind?'

Llandry gave me a winning smile, and beckoned. 'Come with me.'

I followed.

Llandry led us around to the back of the ramshackle houses. Someone had made a pool there, all clear waters and wisps of steam — it was heated! It looked a bit sad somehow, though, for it was adrift in an expanse of dead and barren dirt. The water was not all that clean, and the air smelled odd.

Draped listlessly by the pool, half in and half out of the water, was an unusually large draykon. When I say unusually large, please understand that the draykoni are by no means small, even at their most diminutive. This one was probably not much smaller than my house. Or, well, if that's an exaggeration… you get the idea. He was all sinuous lines and impressive bulk, and his scales were deep, solid black.

He was also the very picture of boredom. He lay totally inert and did not move, not even when the several of us trooped up to stand right by his head.

'Hello, Ny!' said Llandry brightly.

His eyelids moved in a slow blink.

'I've brought people,' she persevered. 'You don't know Eva or Tren, do you?'

This was productive of nothing whatsoever, for Nyden still declined to react. Only his tail moved, in a lethargic *swish* which sent a tiny spray of water up into the air.

'You may not,' I said grimly, 'but we know you.' At Llandry I directed a rather displeased look, for this couldn't possibly do!

Nyden featured prominently in Llandry's journal. He has much to recommend him, undeniably: he is indeed an Elder, which means he's the most ancient of the ancients, one of the very first draykoni ever to exist. He uses their peculiar arts with an insouciance, a confidence, an aptitude which far outstrips most of the rest. He is also supremely unconcerned with notions of *limitations* and breezily oblivious to such obstructions as *entrenched conventions* or *expected manifestations of power*. What Nyden wants to do, Nyden does.

That is probably of use to me. There are one or two problems, though, the main one being that Nyden, for all his fine qualities, is…

…quirky, shall I say? Quirky in ways that lead me to suspect he would prove to be insubordinate, difficult, slow to take instruction, let alone orders, and a liability in several exciting ways it probably wouldn't enter my head to consider.

When he's fully involved in something that interests him, and about which he cares (as far as he's able), I can well believe that his talents, his bright mind and even his attitude can be of great use and benefit. But if he is bored, having him around is probably more like having your own personal plague to hand.

Which is no doubt why Llandry was so eager to get rid of him.

Llandry crouched down by Nyden's head, and smiled at him. 'I know you have been bored. I am sorry. I thought it would interest you, what we're doing here, but I can see I was wrong.'

Nyden's tail lashed again, harder this time. 'I,' he said, slowly and deliberately, 'hate growing things.'

'Well, yes. So we have learned, and I apologise.'

'It is so dull,' he continued. 'What do you even do? You take some tiny grain of a thing you can't even see and shove it in the ground. Then, you expend a ton of effort — *tons* of it, Llandry — and after all that sweating and straining you get—'

'I know,' Llandry said hastily, shooting a look at me. She patted his face in a vain attempt to soothe him.

'—you *get*,' Nyden continued, flatly refusing to be hushed, 'a… a *leaf!*' He wailed the latter word in anguish. 'And it's not even a whole leaf! Just a miserable, sproutish, *potential* leaf that might, if you're very lucky, become a tree. Someday. In about a thousand years.'

Llandry sighed. 'Yes, well, we've been through all that. I have something else for you to do.'

Nyden's tail stilled. 'You do?'

'Eva does.' Llandry indicated me.

Nyden finally found it possible to acknowledge my existence, though not by way of anything so polite as a greeting. He squinted at me, sucking upon one protruding fang in a manner that struck me as thoughtful.

'Awfully human-looking, isn't she?' he decided. 'Draykony bits in there somewhere but not strong, Llandry. Not strong at all.'

'She's actually one of the better summoners in the Seven,' Llandry said quickly, and I was touched by her eagerness to defend my prowess, though I did not feel at all dismayed by Nyden's lack of approval.

'One of the better what?' Nyden lifted his head to peer at me, as though Llandry had said I was unusually well-supplied with heads, or limbs.

'Summoners. It means she uses our magics in some specific ways, and she's good at it. She talks to animals and she works with them and—'

'Eh.' Nyden fell back into his listless heap. 'No idea what you mean.'

'I'll take him,' I said.

Everyone looked at me funny. Tren looked quizzical, Ori dismayed, Pensould bemused. Llandry's face was such a comical mixture of shock and elation that I was tempted to laugh.

'No really, I will. Did you hear that? He has no idea what we're talking about. Any of us. Sorcery? Summoning? It's all nonsense to him, and that's exactly what we need.'

'Um, Eva?' said Ori, eyeing Nyden with undisguised scepticism. 'May I talk to you for a second?'

I graciously consented to this and we moved a little apart from the others. Ori lowered his voice. 'Are you sure about this?'

'Yes!'

'Really? Because he can be, um, difficult…'

'I know. But I hope to keep him interested, and I think as long as we can do that he'll be great.'

Ori cast a doubtful look Nyden's way. 'Do you think that will work?'

Privately, I highly doubted it, but I considered it worth the attempt. 'If it doesn't, we'll send him back.'

Ori grunted, though whether the sound was intended to express agreement with the suggestion, or a lack of conviction either way, I could not tell. 'He will drive Avane nuts, too.'

I had forgotten that. His *interest* in Avane was entirely

unreciprocated, but she was too soft-hearted to successfully repel him. 'If he irritates her too much, we will send him back,' I repeated.

Ori rolled his eyes. 'Llandry!' he called. 'Do you have any other Elders up here right now?'

'None I can spare,' she called back firmly.

'No ancients? It doesn't have to be an Elder, does it?'

'No! I need them all. They're vital. You're already taking Avane!' In other words, they were putting themselves to use in Orlind, unlike Nyden whose idea of productive activity was to lie in the pool. Half in the pool. He couldn't even be bothered to immerse himself properly.

Was I making a huge mistake? Maybe. But my choices were few.

There was a desperate, beseeching quality to Llandry's gaze which worked powerfully upon me, too. Yes, she wanted to help us, but Nyden was clearly driving her crazy.

'We're taking him,' I said, and hauled Ori back to the pool.

Nyden grinned at both of us, his fangs prominently protruding. 'We're going to be the best of friends,' he promised us.

Ori sighed, and ran his fingers through his hair. 'I can't wait.'

When patient, good-natured Ori is so rude as to express his doubts about another person out loud, and to their face, one would do well to pay attention. And I did. Nyden was clearly going to need some management.

The question of who best to appoint to the task occupied me for some time. Avane would have been the obvious choice, if I hadn't felt that I would be condemning her to weeks or moons of cruel and unusual torment in the process. Ori obviously was not disposed to be landed with the job, and neither Tren nor I would have the time to be always at hand.

I needed a perfect candidate: someone who would know exactly how to deal with Nyden, who would have the patience (or something like it) to manage him without going mad, and who had a good chance of keeping him interested.

Lacking such a perfect specimen, I gave him to Adonia instead.

This may seem like an odd choice, but let me explain. Adonia is just the kind of oddity to appeal to a mind like Nyden's, or so I believe. She has quirkiness enough to match his, with some to spare. And she is probably as much in need of a challenge as Nyden, considering that she, too, tends to exist in a fog of palpable boredom enlivened only by an occasional gossip magazine.

When I got home, I said: 'Adonia, I have brought the most charming but also the most annoying man alive back with me and I need you to keep him in line.'

Her eyes lit up at once, and when she saw Nyden, she practically purred. 'Yes, boss,' she said, and I knew I had done well.

But I'm getting ahead of myself. Having agreed upon the matter of Nyden and secured Avane's consent to the business (what a sweet and obliging woman is Avane! I like her so much), we made preparations to leave.

I wanted to linger a great deal longer, of course, but I could not justify it at the time. We stayed only long enough to hear Llandry's news — of which there was not much, yet, though she declared herself cautiously optimistic about the future of Orlind — and then we left. Tren rode with Ori on the way home, and I accepted Avane's invitation to travel with her. I found the return journey more peaceful, though whether that was because of Avane's presence or because I had got my grouches out of my system on the way over, I cannot say.

One other thing happened before our departure. You might have noticed that I referred to Nyden as a *man*, a few paragraphs back. That I introduced him to Adonia as such, and failed to mention that he was anything other than human.

Well, I could hardly take Nyden back with me as he was, could I? Apart from anything, there is no way he would fit into our classrooms.

So we had a talk, he and I, after the others had drifted back to Llandry's house. Nyden might have been offered the reprieve he was desperate for and had new and exciting prospects laid out before him, but he still did not appear to consider this reason enough to move. He lay inert as ever, still partially submerged, though the fog of deep gloom had lifted a little. I even thought I saw a faint, fangy smile hovering about his mouth.

'Nyden,' I said with my nicest, most conciliating attitude.

His smile vanished at once. 'Yes?'

'I am going to need you to change your shape.'

'No.'

'It is not negotiable.'

'I never shift!'

'You do! I have read of it. You Changed yourself into something small, so that Llandry could carry you out of the Library before it blew up.'

Nyden sniffed. 'That was different.'

'It was not.'

'It was an emergency!'

'It still counts.'

'Why do I have to Change? Am I not perfect as I am?'

He was indeed a perfect specimen of draykoni…dom. Draykonhood? Let's go with that one. A perfect specimen of draykonhood. But that was entirely beside the point, so I didn't make the mistake of agreeing with him.

'You are too big,' I informed him. 'Far too big. You will be associating with human-sized and human-shaped people in human dwellings, and I need you to fit in.'

He grinned at me and purred, 'Then make the dwellings bigger.'

'I can't do that.'

'I do not see why not.'

'Because the houses are not flexible, but you are.'

He crooned a tune under his breath, keeping time with his tail. 'That is your problem, Eva, not mine.' The wretched creature sang the words along with his mad little melody, and ended with a few whistled bars.

I folded my arms. 'Insubordination will not be brooked!' I declared, losing patience with him. 'You cannot have this assignment if you will not comply with these terms. It is physically impossible for you to perform the role in your current shape.'

Nyden looked at me out of one eye. He looked calm, thoughtful, not at all like he was about to mount a rebellion, and I relaxed a bit. He was probably more reasonable than we all expected, he just liked to make a show of—

I had to abandon the thought because Nyden streeeetched luxuriously and then… he began to shrink. He contracted in size until, from the tip of his nose to the tip of his tail, he was about as long as I was tall. 'Will that do?'

As I was struggling to control my temper, a voice spoke from behind me, so suddenly and unexpectedly that I jumped. 'What you have to do,' said Pensould, 'is… well, I will show you.' He walked past me, went straight up to Nyden, and kicked him in the ribs.

'Ow,' Nyden observed.

Pensould kicked him again, much harder.

'*Ow*. I said ow already!'

'Saying *ow* does not mean that the thrashing will stop,' said Pensould. 'It stops when you cease doing whatever it is that earned you the thrashing.'

'I wouldn't be human,' Nyden said sulkily.

'Why not?'

Nyden squirmed. 'Because it's so untidy, that's why. Look at you, with your bits flapping around everywhere. Isn't it uncomfortable?'

Pensould blinked, and looked down at himself. He was looking neat and tidy in simple trousers and a shirt, boots, a good coat. Nothing messy about him. 'What bits?'

Nyden opened his mouth, but — most uncharacteristically for him — he withheld whatever it was that he was planning to say. 'Never mind.'

Pensould nudged Nyden with his toe. 'Do it.'

'It's so demeaning.'

Pense's eyes narrowed. 'You're going to get kicked again.'

'Fine.' Nyden sat up and Changed, so fast that I had not even had time to register that he had capitulated.

The miniaturised, black-scaled draykon disappeared. In his place stood a tall, elegant man in a dark suit, his skin darker still. He had night-black hair swept back from a widow's peak, and inky-black eyes. He caught my eye and smiled a smug, smirking smile, smoothing back his hair with one immaculately-manicured hand.

'Better,' said Pense.

Nyden looked at me, clearly waiting for me to be impressed.

I narrowed my eyes. 'Nyden,' I said.

'Yes?'

'You have done that before.'

'Never.'

'You have. You must have. So polished a vision of masculine urbanity does not spring from nowhere.'

Nyden frowned in annoyance, and licked the tip of one fang. I noted his incisors were still rather longer than they should have been. 'I do not know what you are talking about.'

'Mhmm. There's just one thing.'

'What's that?'

'Your skin. It's too black.'

'Don't be ridiculous.'

'I am serious. Many humans there are with gorgeous black skin, but it's… not like that.'

See, Nyden was proving himself a little too attached to his blacker-than-black scales. He had given himself black skin like onyx, solid black, like he was carved from marble. He would have made an exquisite statue, but that wasn't quite the effect we were going for.

Nyden thought about my comments for a moment, and then said: 'Is that better?'

'No,' I replied, having failed to discern the slightest alteration in his appearance.

He sighed deeply. 'Humans,' he growled. 'So limited.' But he adjusted again. His skin didn't lighten exactly, but he altered and blended the depth of the colour until it looked more real.

'Lovely,' I assured him.

Nyden admired the back of one of his own hands, and gave a satisfied smile. 'I know.'

5 V

I did remember to ask Llandry about that mystery draykon out at Sulayn Phay.

'I haven't heard anything about that,' she said, but she looked troubled, and I wondered whether the possibility had sparked off something in her mind. But she would not be drawn further on the subject, merely adjured me to consult her if anything else about it came to light.

By the time I reached Glour City, the matter had largely faded from my mind. We returned to find that our two Lokant tutors, Tynara and Dan, had arrived and were kicking their heels at HQ with Adonia. Neither of them were delighted about this. They had brought our students with them, and Fostiger had arrived as well, so we had nine partial Lokants to house and five tutors to settle in. It made for a busy week, I can tell you.

Within a few days, though, we had everybody comfortable, lessons were underway, and our little school was officially functional. And all right, there were some problems. Tynara and Dan found us unsophisticated, poorly organised and risibly ignorant, and they made no secret of the fact. Some of the students apparently concurred with their opinions, and were not best pleased to be relocated to Glour City when they could have stayed at Sulayn Phay (and how is that for ingratitude! Rescued from the clutches of their vile kidnappers and they saw *us* as the oppressors!) Nyden clearly had no idea how to behave like a responsible human (sort of) being and had to be guided (if not pushed) through every part of his day.

Avane and Adonia between them made fairly short work of Nyden, however; the students mostly settled in; and I found it possible to ignore Tynara and Dan. And lo, we did all exist in peace and harmony for…

… a day or two. After which point it began to occur to Ori and I that there was still no sign of Gio, and that this seemed like a bad sign. Ori began to look meaningfully at my arm — the wrong one, but I could hardly expect him to remember which bit of me his boyfriend had carved a hole in — and murmur about "going to check on him".

At first I felt only that Gio's continued absence was inconvenient, considering that we were deprived of his services, and all the diligent lesson planning he had done with Ori was going to waste. But as the days passed I became concerned, too.

'He's probably just, um… busy?' I tried.

Ori looked sceptical, to say the least. 'Busy doing what?'

'Being indispensable to Ylona?'

'And he hasn't come back even once, to catch us up? To make sure we know he's okay? I find that hard to believe.' We were in my office at HQ and Ori couldn't sit still. He had occupied my visitor's chair for about five seconds and then got up and paced about. He was still pacing.

So Gio was absent and one of our draykon tutors was largely incapacitated by worry. And much as I hate to admit it (I like to at least *pretend* to live up to my reputation for cool, unruffled composure), I was not much less anxious myself. When you are dealing with Lokants, anything that seems wrong… probably is.

I watched as Ori danced another agitated figure-of-eight around my visitor's chair, chewing upon his fingernails and generally presenting a picture of abject misery. It struck me how hard on him it was to wait, lacking the means to follow Gio himself. He had to rely on me.

'Where is Tren?' I said, rising from my own chair where I had been reclining at my ease.

Ori understood my gist at once. He shot me a grateful look, said breathlessly, 'I'll get him!' and charged out of the room.

I took a few moments to inform one or two people of where we were going — Avane, specifically, for I trusted her the most out of those we were leaving behind — and awaited Tren and Ori at the office door.

They soon arrived, Ori looking desperately anxious but also a bit relieved (to be doing something productive about Gio's absence, no doubt).

'So we're going?' said Tren.

'Immediately,' I replied.

'Good. I don't like this silence.' He took hold of my left hand, and Ori my right, and I translocated us away.

Translocation is a fairly easy process, once you get the hang of it — that is, translocating alone. Taking other people along gets a lot harder, because people are heavy and one has to more or less drag them through the fabric of the world. I am not all that physically strong. Taking two fully grown men along with me was not the most pleasant experience.

I'd chosen a transloc point near the schoolroom we had now emptied out. We all but fell into the room, with an embarrassing lack of grace. Ori was raring to go in search of Gio *at once and immediately* but I needed a breather. My arms hurt, my head hurt and I was gasping for breath.

'Hold up a moment, Ori,' said Tren, while doing that nice solicitous thing he does when I have done something either exhaustingly impressive or impossibly stupid (or both).

'Sorry,' said Ori with a sigh, but he could not stand still. He paced the corridor, peered through the door into the schoolrooms, paced a bit more.

'I'm all right,' I said, only slightly untruthfully. 'We should not go haring off willy-nilly, however.' (Willy-nilly is such a wonderful word, is it not? I don't get nearly enough opportunities to use it). 'Let's think. Where is Gio likely to be, and what might reasonably have happened to him?'

I looked at Ori as I said it, because he had spent time up here with Gio before. If anybody knew where Gio had lately taken to lingering, it would be Ori. I only knew that Dwinal was probably the last person to have lately seen her grandson.

'I know where his new quarters are,' Ori volunteered. 'He ditched the ones in Dwinal's wing but Ylona gave him new.'

'Excellent,' I said. 'Lead on.'

Ori hesitated. 'I, um. Don't know how to find them from here.'

'Which part of the Library are they in?' I summoned the Map

in my mind, and tried to mentally muster the strength for another transloc.

'It's, um.' Ori blinked.

I waited.

'I don't know,' he said, shame-faced.

I suppose there had to be something our star scholar was no good at. Apparently, finding his way around wasn't always his strongest point. Will you blame me if I admit to feeling a tiny, *tiny* flicker of relief? It is unnatural for a person to be so entirely without weakness or failing as Ori has thus far appeared to be.

It was an inconvenient time to manifest such a flaw, admittedly. I looked at Tren, vaguely hopeful of some small miracle. Perhaps he, somehow, would know where to look?

He shook his head with a rueful smile, and my hopes were dashed.

And both of them stood there, waiting for me to figure out what to do.

Egads.

I mentally reviewed our options. Asking someone was the most obvious solution, but it raised one or two difficulties. One was simply how to explain our presence in the Library at all, considering that I wasn't supposed to have an implant. And what were we going to ask?

'You know, I think we are in Dwinal's wing,' I offered. 'That dining area I went through is nearby, and it was pretty full of people who seemed to be her associates.'

Ori and Tren nodded thoughtfully. 'So,' said Tren, 'That means…'

'That means we are probably on the wrong side of the Library. Ylona does not like Dwinal at all, why would she base herself and her supporters anywhere nearby?'

'It's the best logic we've got,' said Ori dubiously.

'Thanks.'

He gave me a sheepish grin. 'Sorry.'

I collected up my unhelpful gentlemen, braced myself, and whisked us off to the other side of Sulayn Phay. I'd picked a transloc point at random; over there was uncharted waters as far as I was concerned, and I had no idea where we were going. Time to be intrepid, if we wanted to find Gio.

We came out in a library. Fitting, I suppose; we were in a *Library,* capital L, and hitherto I hadn't seen much in the way of books or records or suchlike. It was a pretty room, long and narrow with a staggeringly high glass ceiling. All of the walls were fitted with shelves as one would expect, but the library otherwise deviated from the classical structures with which I was familiar. One side of the room was crowded with objects I would recognise as *books*; leather-bound, for the most part, and scrupulously dusted. Most of the other shelves housed an array of objects I did not recognise, made from unfamiliar materials… I would hazard a guess that they are for the storage of information, too, but more specifically than that I cannot say.

'I like this place,' said Ori, staring at the book-crowded side with undisguised avarice.

It would have been so beautifully convenient if the library had been empty, but of course it wasn't. Seated in a chair underneath the grand, clear, arching window was Hyarn.

'Perfect,' I muttered. So much for my brilliant logic.

It was too much to hope that he might not have seen us, of course. Absorbed in a book as he appeared to be, he nonetheless looked up when we blew in, and greeted us with a polite, even kindly, smile.

That smile put me on my guard immediately.

'Hello,' I said, trying to be casual.

'You are looking for a book, perhaps.' He took in my two companions with mild interest, and apparently decided to pretend that we had all come in by the door, for he said nothing about our mode of travel.

'Actually,' — and I decided on the spot not to bother dissembling, because it grew tiresome and we lacked the time — 'We are looking for Gio.'

Hyarn closed his book. 'I can assist you there. Gio is with his grandmother.'

'What?' Ori blurted.

'I know, it may surprise you.' Hyarn regarded Ori with that same kindly smile. 'I am happy to tell you that there has been something of a reconciliation between the two. They are on excellent terms, and Gio has returned to his old quarters. You may find him there.'

That rang false to all of us, but I was not unduly worried. Gio had mentioned that Ylona wished for him to return to his grandmother's side, for the purposes of learning about her doings. It did seem oddly abrupt, considering how little I knew he liked the assignment, but doubtless he had his own reasons.

'Thank you,' I said to Hyarn. I hesitated a moment, wondering whether he was minded to say anything else, for he had the air of one about to speak. But he said nothing, and we went away — via the door, like ordinary people. I think it unlikely in the extreme that Hyarn remained unaware that I had been translocating around his Library, but why make that problem worse?

Rikbeek shifted in my skirts, and began muttering darkly in my mind. He was thinking about biting, and I almost sent him after Hyarn just because. The man irritated me, and he had killed Galy. He deserved to be munched upon.

I managed to hang onto my essential decency, however, and left Hyarn unmolested by tiny gwaystrel.

'I don't like it,' grumbled Ori as we left.

'Calm,' I advised. 'We will soon learn what's afoot.' I shared the same sense of foreboding, though I did not want to admit to it.

'If you can get us to the main library building in Dwinal's wing, I can probably find Gio's old quarters,' offered Ori. I remembered that he had spent some weeks up here with Gio before, prior to the demise of Orlind.

'Wonderful.' I realised with a sinking feeling that I would now have to cart everybody back across the Library again. What joy is mine.

I did so without complaint, which perhaps you will agree was gracious of me. I managed not to scream on the other side, too, for which I was proud of myself. My poor body. It did not appreciate such treatment.

I had no real idea which was the main library building, of course, but it wasn't that hard to guess: the Map made it easy to pick out a room that was bigger than all the others, and thither I went. It proved to be much like the room in which we had encountered Hyarn, only much larger.

'Onward,' I instructed Ori, who led the way briskly and with an air of purpose.

Gio's rooms proved to be situated a few minutes' solid walking from the library. It is striking how vast those Libraries really are. We wound our way down many corridors, through a few more libraries of varying sizes, and a number of rooms of ambiguous purpose. At last, Ori stopped at the end of a short corridor lined with doors.

'This one's Gio's,' he said, tapping on the blue door before which he had halted.

I summoned the Map. 'Are you sure?'

Ori looked sharply at me. 'Yes. Why?'

'There is no transloc point around here.'

'There has to be. There was, before.'

'Then it has been removed.'

Ori began to look genuinely afraid. 'I don't know what to do,' he admitted. 'There is no way we can get through that door, if we can't translocate. And I cannot think why his transloc point would be gone.'

Tren tried the door. Optimistic, but of course it was locked.

'It was worth a try,' he shrugged.

I looked at the lock. It bore no keyhole; no point of entry for anything resembling any kind of a key, either. That made me think of the doors upon those lovely suites in which Tren and I had been briefly housed.

I looked at my arm. 'I wonder…' Gio prepared my implant. Had he modelled it on his own?

'Try it,' said Tren.

I laid my hand against the panel I thought might house the lock.

Nothing happened.

'Damnit,' muttered Ori, and began again to pace.

Undeterred, I moved my hand about, trying various parts of the panel. I had no idea how those locks work (I still don't). Obviously they respond to touch somehow, if you are a person with designated access, but how that operates I don't know. Do you have to touch some particular part of the lock, with some particular part of your anatomy?

I tried this, applying my hands, palms, fingers, until at last… a click, and the door drifted ajar.

'Gio planned this,' I said. 'Or he expected… something. He built access to his quarters into my implant.'

'*Yes,*' hissed Ori, and instantly ran inside.

'Ori—' I tried, eager to advise caution, but he was gone.

'We can but follow,' observed Tren, and as he was right, that is what we did.

Gio's quarters consisted of a small complex of rooms, the first being a mere antechamber. Three doors led off it, all of them open. Ori had charged ahead of us into the room on the right, and there he had stopped, blocking the doorway. We had to push him aside to see what had provoked such a reaction, and that gave me a thorough scare, I can tell you. I had visions of Gio's limp corpse strung up from the ceiling, or strewn across the floor in dismembered parts…

How shall I prepare you for what we found inside? I cannot, I think. It was too unexpected, too shocking. For a full minute, not one of the three of us could speak or, I think, breathe.

We found Lania's draykon.

The creature was not dead, I hasten to reassure you. I have made everything sound most dire, and so it was, but it was no slain corpse that we discovered.

The room had probably been used as some kind of parlour at one time, but by then it was cleared of furniture. The atmosphere in there was odd; it prickled at my senses, my *other* senses, as Llandry would call them. The part of my soul that derives its nature from my distant draykon ancestor did not at all like whatever was going on in that room. It made me dizzy, nauseated.

Stationed in each of the room's corners was an energy collector. We have seen those before, on the island of Orlind during the battle with Krays. He built them, he put them there. Their purpose was to siphon off the energies of the place, energies known as *amasku*. Those energies are the source of the powers of the draykoni, and as such, they have long been of interest to people like Krays.

On Orlind, that energy had been corrupted beyond repair. Galywis had diverted Krays's collectors; instead of collecting and siphoning off energy, they were simply directing it around the island in a safe circuit, keeping it from spreading and infecting the rest of the Seven.

The collectors in that room were doing the same thing. Someone had set up a vortex of *amasku* — the unhealthy kind, I was certain of it — and kept it moving in a tight, ceaseless whirl. Each machine was fitted with lengths of that pretty, lovely draykon bone, and they flared silver with power.

The draykon occupied the centre of the room. It was smaller than it should have been, smaller by far, otherwise it could never have fitted into the parlour. I remembered Nyden's shrinking trick of only a few days before and felt sick, because I doubted not that this poor drayk had somehow been forced into performing the same feat. The creature was immobilised, though I could not tell how. Oh, it was tightly bound, but I did not think that the restraints were what was holding it still. Its eyes were blank and there were no signs of life about it at all, save that it was — just barely — breathing. Its hide was marbled in celadon and gold, but those prismatic scales were dulled and faded.

I stared, but I could not work out what was going on. No powerful draykon am I, just a summoner. 'Ori?' I whispered, when I'd found my voice.

Ori swallowed. 'They are, um. Using it.'

'For what?'

'To… generate energy.'

'You mean… amasku?'

He nodded without speaking.

Nobody spoke, for a while. We were all trying to process the horror of it — and the strangeness.

'They *who*?' said Tren after a while. 'And what in the world is the poor thing doing in Gio's room?'

A horrible possibility occurred to me, of course, even if it didn't occur to trusting Tren. I could guess from the sick horror on Ori's face that he was thinking the same thing.

What was it doing in Gio's room? Perhaps Gio had put it there. He was a Lokant, after all. Some small part of my heart — the part that was frustrated beyond sense with the likes of Limbane and Krays, that would infinitely prefer to forget that they had ever existed — was ready to condemn poor Gio on the spot as exactly like the rest of them, everything he had ever said to us a lie.

But my better self struggled. I remembered everything I had seen about Gio that spoke well of his heart, his mind and his good sense. I thought of everything Llandry had written of him in her journal; how difficult it had been for her to come to trust him, and how she had come to do so in spite of herself.

Gio had done nothing to deserve my distrust, and this was mere circumstantial evidence. I banished my unworthy suspicions, and laid a comforting hand on Ori's arm. It was not that he was any more eager than I to condemn Gio, nor any less likely to trust him. It was pure fear that shone in his eyes, terror that he was mistaken after all, that he'd been made a fool of.

'There will be an explanation,' I told him.

Either the words or my calm tone steadied Ori a bit, for the terror faded and he nodded.

'I am going to check the other rooms,' said Tren softly, and departed. Ori cast him an agonised look as he left, and I felt the same: what if there were more to be found, more draykoni like this?

But Tren soon returned, with a shake of his head that said he perfectly understood our thoughts. "Empty."

I looked back at the suspended draykon, feeling an urgent need to help the poor creature. 'We need to do something.' I went forward, stepping carefully, half expecting to feel a backlash of energy or something if I got too close. But nothing happened, and I fell to inspecting the bindings that strapped the draykon's wings against its sides and bound up its legs. They were shockingly tight, and made from something indestructible, or so it seemed. I pulled at them uselessly, unable to affect them in any way.

Tren went to the nearest energy collector and began to wrestle with it. 'I can't find a way to shut it off,' he said rather desperately. 'There's nothing, no switch, lever…'

Gio's voice interrupted, speaking from the doorway. 'Don't do that!' He ran to Tren and shoved him away from the machine. 'You don't understand, just… don't touch that.'

Tren stared at Gio in dismay, and confusion. 'Don't shut it off? But the draykon—'

'I know.' Gio looked at Ori, and I couldn't fail to notice the worry in his eyes, the beseeching look. 'This… I feel like a character in a cheap melodrama in saying this, but this isn't what it looks like.'

'I never imagined it was,' said Ori, probably not with perfect truth.

Gio approached the captive draykon and crouched, staring into the creature's eyes with anxious concern. 'I don't know who did this. I got in touch with Grandmother, made things right, which… wasn't as easy as I just made it sound. But she gave me my old rooms back, and when I came here, this is what I found. I don't know who put her here but I don't think it was my grandmother — why would she send me here, only to find this? I haven't been able to help her. I shut off the collectors right away, but it only… hurt her, somehow. I do not know if she was dying, but she began to scream… I had to power them back up, and only then did she quiet again.'

'Why didn't you come for us?' I couldn't help saying it. What was the absurd boy doing, dealing with this alone when he had assistance to hand?

'I did! When I got back to headquarters nobody seemed to know where you were. I've just spent ages going all over Glour City trying to find you, and finally someone said you had gone in search of *me*. I came back, eventually ran into Hyarn who told me he had sent you here…' He shook his head, frustrated. 'I don't know what to do!'

I thought of Hyarn, and his calm as he dispatched us to Gio's rooms. Interesting.

'Ori,' I said briskly, 'you've the best chance of working out how to solve this. Can you?'

'I don't know.' Ori joined Gio before the spellbound draykon, and the two tightly gripped hands. 'I have never seen anything like this, never heard of anything… she's bound somehow, bound up in the flow. It's sort of symbiotic. It's draining her but also, somehow, keeping her alive… I don't think I can break it alone.'

'So we need help. Gio, we have Avane and Nyden at headquarters. I'm going to get them, I'll bring them straight back. All right?'

Gio blinked vaguely at me. 'Nyden? Wha— never mind. Tell me later.'

Tren wanted to go with me, I could see it, but he knew it would be hard enough for me to bring two draykoni back here without having to try to carry him along as well. So he contented himself with an intense look that said, *You had better be all right.*

I treated this with the contempt it deserved. Of the two of us, he was the one who would be stuck in dangerous territory, however briefly.

Away I went.

As easily as I can use transloc points, I cannot weave them. Happily, Gio can, and he had long since equipped himself with a few in useful places around Glour City — including inside our headquarters. I materialised in the main hallway, startling two students who were loitering there.

'Avane and Nyden,' I barked. 'Where are they?'

One of the two looked too surprised by my appearance and

manner to know how to answer. The other, though, was Fostiger, and he had wits enough about him to make me a reply. 'Classroom three.'

I nodded thanks and left at once, taking the stairs at a run.

Lessons were obviously over for the day, or so I hoped, for I found Nyden reclining upon the floor in front of the desk. He looked thoroughly at his ease, but Avane did not. I wondered distantly what she was doing in there alone with him. 'I need you,' I informed them. 'Both of you. Quickly, please.'

Nyden made to object, but to my surprise Avane instantly shushed him, and ruthlessly. 'Obviously an emergency. Get up.' She nudged him with her toe, so forcefully I could almost have termed it a kick in the ribs.

Even more to my surprise, Nyden instantly rose, dusted off his suit, and nodded to me. 'We follow, wise leader.'

I eyed him, finding his compliance highly suspect, but I didn't have time to think about it just then. I grabbed his arm and Avane's and dragged them bodily through the aether back to Sulayn Phay, ignoring the way my muscles screamed and my head pounded with the effort. I couldn't take them straight back to Gio's rooms, of course, so I chose the closest transloc point I could find and then hauled them to Gio's on foot.

I entered the strange parlour again to find everyone unmoved. The draykon was unchanged; Ori and Gio crouched still before it, inspecting her predicament without much hope of discovering a solution; and Tren stood near one of the energy collectors, eyeing it with a professional interest tinged with disgust and desperation.

I heard twin gasps of horror and revulsion from Avane and Nyden as they entered the room behind me, and spared a moment's regret that I had not had time (nor had it occurred to me) to warn them before I had brought them here.

'Before you ask, nobody knows how this happened,' I said. 'We need to get her out of there.'

The two of them stared at the beleaguered draykon in heavy silence, and Avane looked as stricken and helpless as Ori. They were both out of their depth, too new to their powers, their understanding of their own abilities still incomplete.

Nyden, though, acted at once. I felt a rippling pulse shudder through the room, and the walls shook. 'This is an abomination,' he snarled.

I wanted to admonish him, tell him this was not the time for anger, or railing against the unknown perpetrators of this atrocity. But I did not have to. He spat the words as though they tasted bad, but the moment passed; his eyes closed, and I felt him…

… I don't know, exactly, but I compared notes with Ori later and we agreed that it felt like Nyden had joined himself with the flow of energy, become a part of it — or made it a part of himself. The effect was immediate, and appalling. He grimaced with pain and shuddered, a violent, uncontrollable, painful-looking tremor. And his vitality dimmed… whatever had dulled the draykon's vivid scales took the lustre from his skin, the shine from his hair, the light from his eyes. He withered before our horrified gaze, visibly diminishing.

'Nyden,' Avane whispered.

He shook his head violently, held up a hand. Avane let it go, and we watched, appalled and afraid, as Nyden struggled to conquer whatever it was that held the draykon bound.

For a while, I thought it would conquer him. Elder though he was, stubborn though he was, he was failing that battle. His skin turned grey, and though he gulped in air with great, desperate gasps, it didn't seem enough. My heart sank a mile down and I thought, *I did this. I took Nyden from his home, only to break him…*

But gradually, slowly, something changed. Nyden gritted his teeth and held on, and the rapid deterioration of his health ceased. He took a more natural breath, and another.

Movement. The bound draykon twitched, and shuddered.

'Steady her,' rasped Nyden, and Ori and Avane ran to obey.

In another breath, it was over. The draykon's bindings snapped as one and fell away, and the appalling tension in the air broke. If she had not been supported, she would have fallen to the ground in a boneless heap.

'Careful, careful,' cautioned Avane, as alarmed as I by the creature's obvious weakness. The two of them eased her down and proceeded to do what they could to stabilise her, make her more comfortable; I do not know how they tended to her, but *they* quickly began to look tired, while the prone draykon almost imperceptibly began to revive. Her scales flushed with returning colour, and she took deeper, stronger breaths.

Avane looked at Nyden. 'That was amazing,' she said softly.

But Nyden did not respond to this compliment as I might have expected. It barely seemed to touch him, though it came from the woman he adored. He had spent most of his own energy upon the rescue, and looked drawn and withered himself. More than that, he looked deeply, profoundly troubled, and that frightened me almost more than anything else. Care-free, flippant Nyden, congenitally incapable of taking anything seriously whatsoever, who had to be coaxed into performing even small duties… Nyden was worried, and disgusted, and angry, and that told me clearly enough that we were in for a world of trouble.

The rest of that day was chaos and exhaustion, and I do not like to think of it now. You may imagine, perhaps, with what effort we succeeded in removing the once-captive draykon from Gio's rooms. I do not need to describe the mood, as we settled Nindrinat — as her name proved to be — at HQ, and watched as Nyden fussed and fretted over her like she was his own child. This new, responsible, serious Nyden was frightening us all, and we were glad enough to leave him to it for a time.

'We cannot convey her to Orlind,' Tren said, as we convened in the kitchens. We were all utterly exhausted, but there was no time for sleep; not then. It was cups of cayluch all round, and an emergency meeting right away.

I had to agree. I was not up to trying to cart her there myself, and anyway, there were no transloc points on Orlind yet. 'She needs serious help. So does Ny. And Llandry needs to know about this.'

Llan and I had anticipated a need for reasonably fast communication, and had agreed upon a plan before my departure from the island. There are birds aplenty across Glour and Glinnery, some of which are as comfortable flying at night as they are during the day, or vice versa. I had already taken the precaution of befriending a few of these, and encouraging them to stay close to Headquarters. It would not be difficult for me to task some with taking a message to Orlind. I'd choose the three fastest, and beseech Llandry and Pense to join us in Glour City right away.

Nyden joined us just as this point was settled. He still looked drawn, unhealthy. I was worried about him.

I handed him a cup of cayluch in silence, which he stared at without seeming to see it.

'How is she?' asked Avane.

'Weak. She suffers.'

'Will she be all right?'

'With the right help, yes. Probably.'

I told him of our plan to entreat aid, and he looked relieved. Also, to my surprise, slightly alarmed. 'Do not bring any Elders here.' He said this grimly, without a trace of his customary humour.

'Why… why not?' I faltered. I felt no doubt that Nyden had been able to help Nindrinat precisely because he was an Elder; if we had not had him with us, what could we possibly have done?

'Nindrinat is an Elder,' Nyden said. '*Alyndim.* And that is not a coincidence.'

My mind went in a few directions at once.

Ori had said they — whoever had captured and bound her — were using her to generate *amasku.* Of course she was *alyndim.* Considering everything Llandry had discovered, what other draykoni could be thus employed?

If one Elder had been put to such a purpose, Nyden was right to advise caution. Here we were, up to our eyeballs in Lokants, and some of them would slap Nyden in chains as soon as look at him. I felt a pulse of fear for Ny himself. How had Nindrinat's captors known she was *alyndim*? Would they realise the same about Nyden, if they saw him?

And another thought drifted through my mind: a note from Llan's journal, a question she had never managed to answer. Gio. He had been sent to Nuwelin, Llan's draykon village on Iskyr, by his grandmother — and she had sent him there with instructions to find Elders. He had rebelled, in his quiet way, and reported back that she had no Elders in residence, thus shielding Nyden. But no one had ever learned, or guessed, why Sulayn Phay's Lokantor had an interest in identifying *alyndim* draykoni in the first place. The question became rather buried, I think, by the doings of Galywis, and the greater and more immediate threat that had posed to the Elders of the race at the time.

Was this the reason for Dwinal's interest? Was she behind the capture of Nindrinat? It looked all too likely. Who else had access to Gio's old room?

Then again, why had she cheerfully dispatched Gio there,

knowing what he would find when he arrived? Without warning him, without explanation? And why would she have chosen such an odd spot to keep her captured Elder, anyway?

For that matter, why capture Nindrinat at all? How had she done so? What was she trying to achieve?

I shared these reflections. They are the sort of questions which raise yet more questions, and quickly.

Ori was particularly struck with the question of how a Lokant, or group of such, could possibly capture and bind an Elder so effectively. 'Back on Orlind,' he said, 'we were afraid for a while that somebody of ours was betraying Elders to whoever was killing them. I think we discarded the idea once we found out about Galy, because he did not really need an informant. But perhaps we shouldn't have. Whoever did this — Dwinal, if it was her — needed draykon help, powerful help. Especially if there are more held captive somewhere in Sulayn Phay, and that seems too probable for comfort.'

Nobody could find sound reason to argue against this likelihood, which left us with so many problems we hardly knew where to begin. Had I been wrong to think that Dwinal could not secure draykon help without using me as a go-between? Had she somehow found herself a draykon ally?

Somebody needed to search Sulayn Phay for more such victims, and extricate them at once. And somebody needed to investigate how, and through whose help, Nindrinat and possibly others were being captured, and put a stop to it.

Tall orders, both.

7 V

A few tense days passed. The school proceeded, but in a state of some disorder. I was conscious of Tynara and Dan in our midst, people who were loyal to Dwinal, and who must not learn of Nindrinat's presence if we could possibly help it. This was not easy, with everyone housed in the same (admittedly large) building. We achieved it by assigning attic quarters to Nindrinat, in a disused chamber no one had any other cause to go into. But the necessity of secrecy, of tending to the draykon without alerting any more of our number to her presence, placed an extra strain on Ori, Avane, Tren, Nyden and me, one which we would have gladly done without.

We were all thinking similar things: were we now training our part-Lokant, part-draykon hybrids by order of Nindrinat's tormenter? What exactly was she planning to do with our most talented graduates, anyway?

Another question: if Dwinal conceivably had draykon help with projects like Nindrinat, why did she need us? There were too many holes in everything, too many questions, too many reasons to doubt everything we thought we knew.

Nindrinat revived enough to speak, but she refused to address anybody save Nyden; she was too cowed, I believe, for she would not willingly suffer anybody else's near presence, and shrank back if we approached too near. She and Nyden engaged in long conversations, of use to us only in one particular.

Nindrinat did not know how she had come to be bound and enslaved in the middle of a Lokant Library. She did not remember any attack, because there had, in all probability, never been one. She had come awake to find herself alone in an enclosed space she did not recognise, unable to move, and in a state of some pain. Last time she remembered being awake… well, Nyden had not been able to establish precisely when that was, but that it was an extremely long time ago was not in doubt.

You know, I imagine, that the draykoni can revive each other from death? They do not think of it as death, even: they call it the Long Sleep, because to them, that's more or less what it is. If a draykon dies, and its body decays to nothing but bones, it is not necessarily the end for them. If the skeleton is whole, the spirit still lives and the assistance of sufficient of its fellows is at hand, the dead draykon may be restored to life. It is a startling ability which is shared by no other species of creature in this world. It fascinates the Lokants no end, because though they created the draykoni they did not anticipate that the creatures would be able to do anything so marvellous as that.

What we can conclude about Nindrinat, then, is that she had "died" long ago, slipped peacefully into her Long Sleep, and remained in that state while the ages passed. Until somebody discovered her skeleton, conveyed it to Sulayn Phay, and — we conclude — there revived her to life, bound and at their mercy.

In other words, this was proof positive that other draykoni must have been involved. How could Dwinal discover her skeleton, otherwise? The Off-Worlds are vast. One cannot simply go out there with a shovel and dig, expecting to stumble over draykon bones at any moment. But the draykoni can sense each other's presence, including the near presence of the dead — that is how Llandry came across Pensould.

And how came she to be revived? The draykoni ability to rejuvenate took their creators by surprise; it is not impossible that Dwinal, or someone else, might since have developed a way to restore a dead draykon themselves, but it seems unlikely. In all probability, a draykon (or more than one) found Nindrinat's skeleton, delivered it to Sulayn Phay, and rejuvenated her in captivity.

It is a chilling, horrible thought, is it not? That Nindrinat spent some time in conditions of the worst kind, put to the most painful and degrading use, and was not likely to be released alive, is horrific enough. That she was probably condemned to it by people of her own race — people who were far better able to understand what it would mean for her, how it would feel, than any Lokant — is still worse. I was sickened by it. Ori, Avane and Nyden were so appalled they hardly knew how to react.

The arrival of Llandry and Pense came as a relief. It felt like a breaking of the status quo, a flicker of hope. Even Ori's unfailingly cheerful spirits had suffered, and begun to flag; I could imagine how he felt, too, considering that the death of Galywis and many *alyndim* happened very recently, and he was deeply involved.

Llan and Pensould flew in late this afternoon, and Ori greeted their appearance with the kind of enthusiasm that's usually born of desperation. It was his turn to almost topple Llandry with the force of his affection, and she responded with similar fervour.

They were not happy. The ease, the cheer, the optimism they had displayed only a short time before, was all gone. Now they were as troubled as Nyden, and requested to be taken up to Nindrinat without delay, their faces as grim as their manner was tense.

Nyden was with Nin, as usual, but I dared not follow. I knew that my presence would only disturb Nindrinat more, and she already had two unfamiliar draykoni to cope with.

So I waited with Tren below, anxious and chafing at the delay, but determined not to show it. As was he. We made a fine, unconvincing show of insouciance between the two of us, then gave it up as hopeless, and occupied ourselves with a survey of the classrooms and a show of interest in how our students were progressing.

They were progressing well, not that anybody cared overmuch that particular hour. Three or four passed before Llan and Pense came down from the attic, and when they emerged, Nyden was not with them.

'She is from a part of Ayrien we've never been to before,' Llandry reported. 'It is unclear how they found her, but… most of my people, and Avane's, have been over at Orlind for the past moon or so. There could be vast search parties going on across the Off-Worlds and we might not have even noticed.'

'I doubt they would be so obvious,' I ventured. 'Subterfuge is a Lokant speciality.'

'What took so long?' asked Tren. The question was not a reproach; it was a genuine enquiry, mildly stated, and I'd wanted to ask the same thing myself. They had not spent three or more hours up there with Nindrinat merely to ask her where she was from.

Llandry chewed her lip. She looked worried; Pensould was grim and silent. 'You remember the way Orlind was, until recently?'

'Messy?'

'Yes. Corrupted, broken. Nindrinat's heart's energy is somewhat the same. It is making her very sick. Nyden has been trying to mend her, as she hasn't the strength to mend herself. We've been assisting.'

Judging from the looks on their faces, it had not gone well. 'No luck?'

Llandry shook her head, slightly impatient. 'It isn't that. Ny is making progress, and we think she will be well in time. But… it's confusing. Those maddened Elders we saw, the ones that went insane. They were broken in the same way, their *amasku* all askew, and we tended to conclude that the two things were related — that the one causes the other. But Nindrinat is only ill, she is not mad. She is perfectly lucid.'

'It will kill her,' put in Pensould. 'If she is not healed. And if she dies in such a state, it would be difficult to revive her to health. Perhaps too difficult.'

Llandry nodded. 'That's the other thing. We have encountered this before, but mostly in Galy's memories of Old Orlind. This is the first time we have had chance to study a living example, and… it is not promising.'

'So,' murmured I. 'The question is… was she in such a state before? Did she die of it, centuries ago? Or was she healthy when she revived, and something that has been done to her since has caused this mischief?'

Pensould nodded. 'We have not been able to answer this question. Nyden says that the energy in that chamber was all corrupt, but its flow was so bound up with Nindrinat's, he could not tell where the trouble had started. Was it that Nindrinat's sickness infected the energy around her, or was it vice versa? We do not know.'

'I wonder if whoever left her there had any idea what was

going on.' It is a question Llan raised in her book: Lokants cannot sense *amasku* the way the draykoni can. How much do they really know about it? When it is corrupted, can they tell? We are used to thinking of them as all-knowing but that must be to give them too much credit: nobody knows all, however wise or well-informed.

'That we do not know either,' said Pense.

Mm. So many questions.

Tren had spent a few minutes in silent thought, but he spoke up. 'I wonder what they were trying to power?'

Pense blinked at him. 'Power?'

'They were using her as a kind of energy generator, were they not? Surely they wanted it for something.'

'We need Gio,' I decided. 'And Ori.'

The first thing Gio said, upon hearing all of this news and our subsequent thoughts, was: 'I couldn't tell, about the corruption. And I have some limited draykon ability. If I cannot tell, I doubt that… well, it would take something special for Grandmother to be able to monitor it.'

"Something special" could mean anything. My understanding of Lokant arts and technologies is not, on the whole, profound. Perhaps they have developed some wondrous machine that will monitor such things, as Gio put it. But if so, why leave Nindrinat in that state?

'Gio,' I said. 'We are swimming in questions and we badly need information. You have spent weeks with Ylona and your grandmother, and you know the workings of Lokant society in general and Sulayn Phay in particular better than anybody else we have access to. No pressure, but you are our only hope.'

Gio stared at me. Did he turn paler, or was that my imagination? 'Um, right,' he said. He took a deep breath, glanced once at Ori for encouragement (which he received by way of a huge smile), and began. 'Ylona is deeply angry about a number of things. The "nonsense" that Krays got up to, as she called it, in particular. I am not the only Lokant — partial or full-blooded — who was doctored as part of his experiments, and prior to his death, he was becoming renowned for his ruthless treatment of his own people. Ylona thinks he was an obsessed glory-seeker, fixated upon exalting himself at any cost, and she is probably right.

'She despises my grandmother. She says it is not only because Dwinal was once wedded to Krays. Grandmother consistently swears that she was not involved in Krays's doings, that she did not support them. She resents people's assumptions upon that score, at least publically. But Ylona believes differently. She is convinced that Dwinal was a full partner in all of Krays's projects, and that she continues his work now that he's gone. To Ylona, if my grandmother differs from Krays at all, it is in the details only. She believes that Krays and Dwinal had some bigger plan in view, one which Grandmother is still committed to.'

'Ylona doesn't know what it is?' I asked.

Gio hesitated. 'I… I don't know. Ylona says that my grandmother and Krays were trying to… to cross Lokants and draykoni, somehow; to produce a race which combined the best abilities of both. All the visionary intelligence and unique powers of my race, combined with the best of the draykoni — rejuvenation, impermanent death, shapeshifting, all that.'

'That makes sense!' I said, feeling a rush of excitement. 'Krays was trying to achieve that, by implanting draykon bone in Lokant subjects — like you. But it was only ever of limited success, wasn't it? You cannot change your shape, nor access any of the more powerful draykon abilities. So Dwinal has taken a different approach. That is what she is doing with her school, and ours: taking those who are already of mixed blood, and trying to enhance and encourage their abilities to the required levels. That is why she wants our most talented graduates.'

Gio nodded, but cautiously. 'I do not think Ylona is wrong about any of that. I agree with your conclusions. But I fear that is not all there is to it, and so does Ylona. Why do Krays and Dwinal want to achieve this? Is it purely for glory? It might be — some are powerfully motivated by the prospect of fame, of being remembered down the ages.

'But my grandmother… has something else in hand, I think. I have not yet been able to extract it from her.'

I winced a little at his choice of words. *Extract.* A process which sounded painful, and perhaps it would be. Gio was certainly not afraid of pain, neither of inflicting it nor of suffering it himself. Lokants can be so chilling.

Gio continued. 'The one thing I feel sure of, is that Ylona is misguided upon one crucial point. She is passionately opposed to Dwinal's leadership of Sulayn Phay. She hated Krays, and hoped that, with his death, the Library would elect a worthier leader. She was devastated when Dwinal won, and has dedicated herself to overthrowing her ever since.

'But I do not think my grandmother cares for the leadership. I cannot find out that she ever campaigned for it at all. I think that the residents of Sulayn Phay voted for her out of fear, or perhaps habit, or merely because she was familiar. Or perhaps she has followers who did the campaigning for her — I do not know. But Dwinal does not appear to care for it; I think she would hand it over to Ylona without the smallest regret. Whatever she has in mind has little to do with Sulayn Phay, and upon this point, Ylona appears to be blind.'

Tren said: 'Dwinal may have given us a clue, there.'

Gio looked sharply at him. 'What?'

'When she approached us for help, she said she wanted talented mixed-blood practitioners for a new establishment of hers. Before you ask, no, she did not say what this new establishment is to be.'

Gio mulled that over. 'I have heard nothing of this. But our "reconciliation" is nowhere near as perfect as Hyarn claimed. Grandmother knows I am not to be trusted, and she knows that I will never again trust her. The possibilities are limited. Still… I wonder why she told that to you?'

'It may not be the truth,' Tren conceded.

'It may not be. Then again, it might.'

I made a swift decision. 'I am going to light a fire under Limbane.'

All three of the gentlemen looked at me, nonplussed. 'What?' said Ori.

'He's been sticking his nose in, remember? Because Dwinal has him worried. He would not tell me how or why, but I suspect he knows more about this mysterious plan of hers than he let on. I intend to make him tell me, probably by singeing off his eyebrows until he capitulates.'

'How are you finding him, exactly?' Ori gave me the Sceptical Brow.

'I refused to help him at all, unless he gave me a way to contact him.' I beamed. It was a smug smile, I freely admit it. 'I have a kind of… voice box.'

The voice box is an invention of Llandry's father, who is a talented chap in the way of tinkered, mechanical things. They come in pairs, and if you speak into one, your voice will be heard through the other. Usually. They can be prone to faults, but to be fair to Aysun, it is a recent invention; I have no doubt he will refine it to perfection in time.

The Lokant equivalent is, of course, about five hundred times better. Also a lot smaller, and neater-looking. It is a rounded metal thing, with… with a kind of grid pattern on it, and… oh, never mind trying to describe it, I have no idea how it works and I don't much care. It's a tiny object which is activated by saying Limbane's full name. Anything I say after that is recorded, and conveyed somehow to him.

My sending him a message does not compel him to present himself to me, of course, but I hope I made it clear that I expect him to respond, or he can go whistle for his assistance at Sulayn Phay.

Wise man that he is (hah), he came. He was even on time, more or less, insofar as it did not take him a whole week to appear. He was civilised enough to arrive by way of the front door, and even rang the doorbell. He was shown into the parlour by Hayes, my butler.

'Good of you to come,' I said, and awarded him a smile.

He did not trouble himself to smile back, though he was not so grave in manner as he had been on his last visit. In fact, he seemed eager. 'What have you discovered?' said he without preamble, and did not even take the chair I graciously gestured him towards.

'Nothing, yet.'

His eyebrows flew up. 'Then what am I doing here?'

'I have questions.'

'The arrangement was for me to ask the questions, you to bring information.'

'Well, you asked one enormous, vague question and left us with nowhere in particular to look. Tell me what's bothering you so much about Dwinal.'

He fell into the chair with a long sigh. The movement was unusually graceless, and it occurred to me that he looked exhausted. 'I told you. I have nothing but vague suspicions, and

I would not wish to prejudice your interpretation of anything you should uncover.'

'I know, I know.' I paused to think. He wasn't wrong, but I needed more from him. How could I persuade?

It went sorely against the grain to do it, but this was an emergency. I decided to beg.

'Please,' I said.

This was a feeble effort, and it produced predictably poor results. 'No,' said Limbane.

I sighed, swallowed my pride, and tried again. 'Please? Please!'

'No!'

'This is me begging. I never beg.'

Limbane's glower deepened. 'I have… lost some people,' he said.

This response was so unexpected, my brain heard "no" again, and it took me a moment to process his actual reply. 'Lost?' I repeated dumbly. 'You mean, they were taken?'

Limbane shook his head, though he hesitated. 'I do not think they were taken against their will. I think they left of their own accord. Since they were among my brightest and best, I am inclined to take exception to this.'

'You think they were lured away from your Library.'

'Mm.' Limbane looked mightily affronted by the idea. 'And two of them had lately made Dwinal's acquaintance, that I know of.'

'Two, out of?'

'I have lost four.'

'Were there any common qualities, between the four of them?'

'Not particularly. Two of them were among our oldest, but the others were youth. They excel at different arts, specialise in different subjects. I cannot see that they had much in common.'

Hmm. 'She seems to be collecting people,' I said slowly.

'As I have just told you.'

'No. I mean, not just your people — if indeed she is the reason for their absence. There are my students, too, and… we have reason to think she may have formed agreements with some of the draykoni.'

That interested him. 'Tell me,' he ordered.

I went through it as quickly as I could. 'She also told us she is forming some kind of new establishment,' I concluded. 'Though she would not say of what nature.'

'And you said you had discovered nothing.' Limbane's lips twitched.

'We haven't! She told us that last part herself, so it may be a pack of lies. And the rest is speculation, about as reliable as yours. It could be somebody else playing games with the draykoni.'

'There is an emerging pattern, however, I must agree.' Limbane lapsed into silence for a while, and I recognised his impassive expression as a sign that his mind had wandered far from me. 'A new establishment,' he mused at length. 'I wonder if she is minded to found a new Library?'

'With draykoni…?'

'Mixed blood, mixed arts. Lokants who can shapeshift, draykoni who can translocate. If she could pull it off, it would be quite the coup.'

'Undoubtedly. Is it difficult, to found a Library?'

'Yes.'

I ought to have known better than to expect Limbane to volunteer information. 'Why?' I prompted. 'What do you have to do?'

'For one thing, it is expensive. You will understand how far that is an understatement, I am sure. Such structures as Estinor and Sulayn Phay are the work of generations.'

'I can imagine.' So I could. Impossibly huge and wondrous in their every feature; how did one set about creating a new Library?

'It also requires a great deal of support, as well as approval from our governing council. This latter part I suspect Dwinal intends to skip, considering that no application has been made.'

That interested me, for it was the first I had heard of Lokants having any kind of overarching government body. They had always struck me as anarchistic, in a broad sense, though their individual Libraries had structure enough. 'Are you a member of this governing council?'

Limbane narrowed his eyes at me, but he slightly inclined his head.

'Then you will know if Dwinal files an application.'

'Yes, but I do not at all anticipate that she will. Neither she nor her husband were ever much concerned with rule or law.

Krays was held in contempt of the Council for so many years, it is frankly absurd. It mattered not one whit to him.'

'All right. I would like details as to who your lost people are, if you please. Pictures, if possible. I intend to be haunting Sulayn Phay for the next while, and if they have joined Dwinal, that is probably where they now are.'

'I will arrange it.'

!!

I like this new, co-operative Limbane. I mean… it's highly suspicious, but I like it.

Rikbeek shuffled about in my shirt — I was wearing trousers that day, so no skirts for him to hide in — and politely requested to bite Limbane. I say politely; for Beek that means there was a minimum of snarling involved.

I granted this request.

'*Ow,*' said Limbane, and slapped at his neck. He looked around wildly for the source of the transient pain, but Rikbeek was quicker than lightning and had already dived back into the folds of my shirt.

'Something bite you?' I enquired, at my most casual.

'Must have.' Limbane touched his neck and examined his fingers; I saw a flash of red.

I smiled.

This might seem childish of me, especially when Limbane was being so (relatively) helpful. But I had a few scores to settle with him, and it was only a little bit of blood!

Rikbeek was getting both hungry and grouchy, too, and if I hadn't found someone else for him to munch on, he would have cheerfully made a snack of me instead. Which would you have chosen?

10 V

So, we have a lot to do.

Llan and Pense waited for Nindrinat to recover enough to accompany them back to Orlind. With the help of those two plus Nyden, Ori and Avane, she achieved this within a few more days. Llan left with promises to care for her, and still graver promises to find out what was going on in the Off-Worlds that was ending in the capture of draykoni like Nin. She looked uncharacteristically grim as she said it, and I felt a fleeting moment's pity for whoever was responsible. Considering that face, and Pensould standing behind her looking as grave as death, the consequences were not going to be good.

I requested a set of her father's voice boxes before she departed, too, but no promises could be made. 'They're all broken,' she said. 'Sort of. Pa is either fixing them or improving them or… something. But I will see what I can do.'

My own assignment was no less demanding. We had multiple problems on hand, and the following objectives:

- Find out if there were any more captive draykoni in Sulayn Phay, and liberate them;
- Confirm who was responsible for this charming little project, and ruin them;
- Learn more about the draykoni who were complicit in the plan, if we could, and hand them over to Llandry to ruin;

- Learn the details of Dwinal's Master Plan, and ruin that, too;
- Gently discourage the whole lot of them from meddling in our worlds in the future;
- Somehow keep our school running at the same time, because life goes on;
- … there are probably more that have slipped my mind at the moment.

Our assets:
- Two hereditary draykoni with a wonderful attitude;
- One Elder draykon with a terrible attitude;
- One devastatingly handsome sorcerer;
- One devastatingly handsome full-blood Lokant (I am sorry, Tren my love, but it is true);
- One me;
- One gaggle of incredibly poorly trained students;
- One assistant with too many outfits and not enough organisation;
- One Limbane, as dubious an advantage as he may be;
- Probably some other things I am not remembering right now.

(Do you see a pattern emerging here? I keep lists because otherwise I forget all sorts of things. I've been taking all my lists out of all my notebooks and pockets and studying them *most carefully,* so I hope I have not forgotten anything vital).

There are some practical problems with application, of course. As Ori put it: If we propose to search the entire Library of Sulayn Phay, we are going to need some proper manpower. How are we supposed to sneak that many people in? How to explain our presence, besides? Trying to conduct an exhaustive search of a building that size without being detected could only be a hopeless prospect.

'We need an unassailable, unobjectionable, completely justifiable reason to show up there in force,' I said, with a beatific smile. Tren, standing not far away, instantly gave me a suspicious look.

From Ori, I was awarded a flat stare. 'I am not understanding you. You don't expect them to grant permission, surely?'

'Asking permission is a fantastic way to give someone an

opportunity to say no.'

Ori's eyes narrowed. 'You have that face on again.'

I immediately tried to make myself expressionless. 'What face?'

'The one that says: I have come up with a spectacularly daring idea which everyone will hate, and I am excessively pleased with myself.'

'You won't hate it!'

'Are you sure.'

'Perfectly! It is brilliant!'

Tren stretched and rolled his shoulders, with the air of a man preparing for a bout of combat. Or in other words, a man preparing to take a beating. 'Go on, then. Let us have it.'

'We're moving in.'

There was silence, every moment of which I relished. All right, I was playing it for the drama, but who doesn't get a thrill out of inspiring stupefying awe in their friends once in a while? No one!

I let the silence stretch a little too long, and received notice of it from Tren by way of a faintly irritated look.

'Sorry,' I said, more or less genuinely. 'Headquarters is becoming crowded, don't you think? So many people to fit in, so much classroom space required, and I have all those new employees coming in soon. We are going to need more space.'

'What new employees?' Tren asked.

'Um, the ones we will need in order to run the Bureau when… it's bigger. And then there's the flooding in the cellar which is most inconvenient—'

'What flooding!'

'The flood that happened when the pipes burst, or *will* happen when the pipes burst, which I feel is likely to occur very soon indeed. It may even spread to the ground floor. Wouldn't that be terrible?'

Tren nodded seriously. 'These kinds of problems are fatal to the fortunes of any fledgling school. Our sponsor would be compelled to do something about it.'

Ori folded his arms. 'I take it you are not planning to write to Dwinal, lay these phantom problems before her and entreat her assistance.'

'No, we will just move everybody back to the old schoolroom at the Library. But they aren't phantom problems,

Ori!'

'HQ is not flooded.'

'Not yet.'

His eyes widened. 'You propose to flood out your own building?'

'I can't have Dwinal popping down to check our tale and finding we've left a perfectly useable building behind.'

'There has to be a better way.'

'Can you think of one?'

He struggled with that, but was obliged to give up the endeavour fairly quickly. 'Ruthless!' he gasped.

In response to which accusation, I shrugged. 'It is just a house. It can be repaired.'

'Ruthless *and* reckless.'

'Ruthless, reckless and wealthy. Money has to be of use at some point, wouldn't you say?'

'Ruthless, reckless and rich,' Tren murmured.

I blinked, halted mid-flow. 'What?'

'It's alliterative, that way. Sounds better.' He smiled brightly at me.

I kissed him, because it was better than slapping him. 'If we are finished debating, shall we go?'

Tren made an *onward* motion. 'No time like the present!'

We relayed this plan to Tynara and Dan last of all, of course. I might have subtly given them the impression that we had discussed it with Dwinal first, and received all due permission.

I also flooded headquarters beforehand, so they could hardly argue against there being any need to move. Will it sound too strange to you if I admit that I rather enjoyed it? There is something satisfying about deliberately damaging things, especially of such size and grandeur as an entire building. This is probably why people find destruction cathartic. The pleasure is considerably enhanced if one is destroying something of one's own, knowing that the means are at hand to mend it again at will. I broke the pipes — or actually, I ordered some other, stronger people to break the pipes — and then withdrew for a few hours. I returned just in time to watch the waters swirl up to the foot of the stairs and lap gently at the handsome and expensive carpets. It was beautiful.

It occurs to me that this glimpse into my psyche is unlikely to do me very many favours with my readers, so I will move on.

All in all, the relocation went well. Gio and I ferried everybody up to Sulayn Phay in groups, whereafter we sailed into the old schoolroom with the air of people who had every right to be there (which indeed, we did; that's what made it so beautiful!) By the time word of our arrival spread as far as Dwinal, we were comfortably settled in.

She swept in without warning, perhaps a few hours after we had installed ourselves in her facilities. I'd positioned Ori and Gio's class at the front of the complex, and Dan and Tynara much further back. I wanted Dwinal talking to us first, not her own people.

My two bright young men were instructing Susa, Fostiger and another woman in the differences between Lokant and draykoni methods of healing. It was a good topic to show off to Dwinal, and genuinely interesting besides; I considered it no hardship to officially sit in on it.

As such, I was at hand when Dwinal arrived. The door swung open and she stared at all of us with a mighty frown, fixing at last upon me.

'I thought you were to base your school at your own premises?'

I smiled my most gracious smile, and did the necessary explaining. Gio supported every part of my story, though privately I wondered how much use it would be; did Dwinal really trust her grandson, or did she realise he was up to something?

I do not think she fully believed either of us; it is in the nature of Lokants to be suspicious, I suppose. But she could muster no reasonable grounds upon which to throw us out, and I knew that she would find my story in order if she chose to check it. So I treated her graciously, and she treated us with suspicion, and at length she went away and left us to it.

'We will have to be careful,' I said later to my partners in subterfuge. 'I think she realises there is more to our sudden reappearance than we've said, and of course she would rather we were minding our own business safely back in Glour than running around her Library.'

'The flaw in the otherwise perfect plan,' said Tren, with an apologetic sideways glance at me, 'is that, with our presence here known, Dwinal and company will go to greater lengths to hide anything they do not wish to share with us.'

I let pass this uncharitable reflection upon the brilliance of my plan, because it was true and I could hardly deny it. 'We will prevail,' I said confidently.

Gio had other concerns. 'Eva, are you sure they are safe here?'

'They who?'

'The children.'

'What children? There is only Susa.'

He shrugged. 'The students, then. I was glad, when we took them home. So were you.'

'Desperate measures.'

I shouldn't have spoken flippantly, especially when I did not mean it. Gio looked dismayed, and troubled. 'I think you underestimate my grandmother.'

'We have them under careful watch, and constant protection,' I reminded him more gently. 'Anyway, none of us has been able to discover that anything untoward occurred to any of them at all, when they were here before. Dwinal's methods of "inviting" people to her Library may have been suspect, but once they were here, all she seems to have done is have them taught the very subjects they wanted to study in the first place. There is no reason to feel that they are in any danger.'

'Except that we still don't know what she wants them for. Vague speculation only.'

'True, but whatever they might be destined for, that is not to befall them until they are deemed to be graduates, and suitably talented ones at that. This is unlikely to happen for some time — if any of them meet Dwinal's requirements at all.'

I tried not to let Gio's words infect my confidence. I believed every word that I spoke, but his concerns were not unreasonable, and they stayed with me as I went about the rest of my day. I resolved upon being doubly careful and triply observant.

What I didn't tell Gio, or anybody, was how many doubts I felt myself. I had been relieved to leave the place behind. When I spoke of desperate times, though, I spoke the truth. We cannot fully protect all the students and ourselves, *and* the draykoni I feel sure are held captive somewhere up here. If we are to have any hope of discovering the latter, we need a pretext to be up here for a while. This is the only one we have got; it will have to do.

The problem of Nindrinat and her conspicuous absence from Gio's room is another matter entirely. Gio has opted to follow the path of denial. No one has mentioned Nindrinat to him, and until someone does, he will not mention her to anybody else either.

'If whoever left her there wants to know what became of her, they can come and ask me,' he said grimly. 'But I do not think anyone will. That would necessitate an admission of their own guilt, after all.'

Tren and I installed ourselves back in one of our former suites, though without the captivity this time. As I suspected, the rooms were delightful once we were no longer prisoners in there (theoretically, at least; thanks to Gio, our period of genuine confinement had been short-lived). As for my implant, I stopped hiding it. If we had a solid reason to be at Sulayn Phay, then I also had a solid reason to have free access to and from the place, and Gio could not be blamed for obliging me with the necessary means.

So much for our official activities! The interesting stuff happened in between, of course. We arranged a schedule. Two of us were always free of teaching duty, at any given time. Those two were charged with finding pretexts for wandering the Library, and for finding their way into all manner of secret nooks and promising-looking dark corners. Gio or I went along at every opportunity, seeing as we had the means to hastily extract ourselves and our fellow spies at need. Gio also committed himself to having our implants… adjusted. With Ylona's help, he intends to ensure we are given access to as much of the Library as she can contrive. He claims to know a disenfranchised follower of Dwinal's who will grant us much of the rest, too, so we should be relatively free agents.

Ylona, Ylona. I am conscious that her name keeps coming up, but I still have yet to meet her — properly that is, as herself and not as the charming but fictional Heliandor Rasset. I resolve upon changing that, as soon as I can do so without attracting Dwinal's suspicion.

In the meantime, so settled we into a life of alternate education and espionage. It occurred to me, after some days of this, that I have not thought about my previously all-important wedding plans in weeks. I cannot say that I am sorry for it, either. The unexpected benefits of dark plots, dire threat and immense complications? I do not think we can get away with recommending the approach to frustrated brides-to-be in general. It is unlikely to catch on.

12 V (?)

Today I received a visit from Hyarn.

I say *I* rather than *we* because it was a private visit, paid to my private suite, at a time when Tren was absent. I got the impression that Hyarn knew this, and had deliberately arranged his visit accordingly.

It was also oddly low-key. Considering that he appeared to have made a special point of presenting himself, I assumed that he must have had something particular to say to me — something important. But he knocked politely upon my door, asked after my health when I answered, and accepted my offer of a chair with an air of quiet serenity that hinted at no urgent purpose whatsoever.

'And how are your endeavours progressing?' he enquired, with a smile.

'Moving was an unfortunate necessity,' I said, with outrageous untruthfulness. 'It was sadly disruptive to our programmes of study, and set back our progress a little way. But we are all settling in, I believe, and my tutors inform me that classes proceed more or less as desired.'

Hyarn nodded thoughtfully. He did not say anything for a moment, and I took the time to observe him carefully. If I say that he was the kind of person who seemed to be going out of his way to be bland, will you understand what I mean? He was of indeterminate age, neither young nor old; his clothes, the arrangements of his hair, were unremarkable; he had no particularly memorable features of any kind. I cannot quite believe that a person could be so featureless by accident. Perhaps it is merely my suspicious side talking, but I felt that there was some manipulation occurring, some calculated display designed to encourage me to overlook him.

I think that my response was not what he was looking for, somehow, for he tried again. 'All of your… projects, are going well?'

How casual a question, and how probing. My hackles arose, for here was Dwinal's closest associate, cornering me alone in order to do a spot of digging. 'Which projects, exactly? We have so many in hand.'

I watched him think. At length he decided not to answer the question — an approach he seemed often disposed to fall back upon, to my distaste — and instead said: 'If you need any extra assistance, Lady Glostrum, I hope you will consider me at your disposal.'

That was unexpected. 'What kind of assistance?'

'I am second-in-command at Sulayn Phay, and I have a great many resources at my disposal. While our Lokantor may find herself too busy to pay you or your associates much attention, I hope you will believe that I am differently disposed.' He looked intently at me, and added: 'If any of your projects, official or unofficial, could benefit from my assistance, please approach me at once. You will find me more than ready to support you.'

He took his leave soon afterwards, leaving me to mull this over. I did not return much more than a gracious acknowledgement to his peculiar offer, being too confused to know what to make of it. What did he mean by, "official or unofficial"? Had he truly intended to criticise Dwinal, with his very mild reproof? If so, what did that mean? For he *was* second-in-power, and had always appeared to be thick as thieves with the Lokantor. What did he imagine our "unofficial projects" might be, and how did he propose to help us? *Why* did he propose to help us?

Few people have managed to confuse me more, or with fewer words. I did feel, though, that we have been too quick to focus upon Dwinal, and have consistently overlooked Hyarn.

'Don't forget,' Tren pointed out later. 'It was he who sent us to Gio's rooms, where we found Nindrinat.'

'Yes, but there may be nothing in that. It's natural enough to send us to Gio's rooms, when we said we were looking for him.'

'There may be nothing in it, or there may be everything. He also killed Galywis, so we know he is a man of… resolution, to say the least.'

'Hmm. All right, we will keep more of an eye on Hyarn. Somehow.'

Tren hesitated. 'Shall we… give him a try?'

'What. You mean, ask his help?'

'Why not?'

'With what, exactly?'

Tren grinned. 'With one of our "unofficial" projects.'

'The man is in Dwinal's pocket! She probably sent him to find out what we are really doing up here. I know she suspects that we have an ulterior motive, and Hyarn's the perfect person to send. He's unassuming, unintimidating (his being a confirmed murderer notwithstanding), and does a fine job of appearing very obliging. Our going to him with a problem is exactly what we are supposed to do!'

'So, call the bluff. We can try him out with something unimportant. If the result is that Dwinal comes straight down on us in a blaze of retribution, we know not to trust Hyarn.'

'Beautifully reasoned, but I'm sure they can predict that's what we would do.'

'Yours is a suspicious nature, my love.'

He wasn't wrong, but was that so bad? 'It's necessary to be on one's guard with these people. At all times. They cannot be trusted, you know this.'

Tren sighed. 'I think it's just possible that they aren't all manipulation and lies, all the time. Once in a while, somebody probably wishes us well and genuinely wants to be of use.'

'So Hyarn came here to help us, out of the goodness of his heart? I am sorry, love, but I can't believe it. He killed Galywis. We have no reason to imagine that he possesses anything resembling a heart.'

'No, but supposing he does have an ulterior motive of his own, that need not preclude his ability to be helpful to us, too. If our various goals align, it would be advantageous for us to approach him.'

'Tren. I love you, but—'

'Uh oh.' Tren took a step back.

I ignored this. '— but we have every reason to distrust Hyarn, and none whatsoever to give him the benefit of the doubt.'

'We need help.'

'Yes. But I am still enjoying faint hopes that we can find someone else to ask. Someone less… risky.'

'Like who?'

'I am still working on that part.'

My thought was to make better use of Gio. He was the only one of us who could freely approach both Ylona and Dwinal, and who was acquainted with many of the people of Sulayn Phay already. This conversation did not go as I was hoping.

'They don't trust me,' said he.

'They who?'

'Any of them.'

'I thought you were reconciled with your gra—'

'More of an uneasy truce, and even then I don't think she believes it for a second. My suspicion is that she's planning to use me much the same way that you are: I am her window into your world, and possibly Ylona's.'

Hm. 'Your cousin—'

'Doesn't trust me, won't speak to me.'

'Do you have friends who—'

'They don't trust me and won't speak to me. My split with this Library was widely publicised — the Lokantor's family tends to be prominent, as I am sure you can imagine, and I am Krays's grandson besides. I am broadly seen as a traitor, and treated with hostility. My best chance of acceptance is with Ylona's people, who might be inclined to embrace me for the same reasons the others reject me. Believe me, I am working on her, but it's a slow process because she doesn't trust me either. In her mind, it's vaguely possible that the whole argument with Dwinal and my subsequent departure was staged purely to position me to infiltrate her faction later.'

I felt a stab of remorse. I hadn't given any serious thought to what it might have been like for Gio, trying to come back to a Library from which he had parted on such poor terms. I had serenely sent him off to make nice to Ylona, and Dwinal, and anybody else he could get near, forgetting to consider how difficult, unpleasant and downright soul-destroying it might be for him to try. What was it like, returning to the only home you'd ever known only to be treated with unflagging hostility by all those you had once known and trusted, and to be treated with suspicion by the rest? None of them had accepted him, not even Ylona's people, whom he had approached in good faith. They were all trying to use him, and I had been no better. He had sought refuge with us, and I had merely slung him back into the fray with blithe unconcern.

I felt deeply ashamed of myself.

I tried to apologise, but it was hard to express everything I was then thinking in a mere few words. I don't know if I managed it.

'It's all right,' he said. 'These things are important. I am glad to be of use.' But it occurred to me that he looked strained and tired, and though his words were generous they lacked the ring of conviction.

I should apologise to Llandry, too. Yes, she left Gio with me in the belief that he could be of help, but she also expected that I would care for him, and I haven't. What kind of a leader uses her followers like that, and neglects their well-being? Did I really think I was any better than Dwinal?

What to do, though? It was a bit late to pull him out, and anyway he was right: this *was* important, more so than any individual one of us.

What I should have done from the beginning was take on more of the tasks I had offloaded onto Gio myself, instead of deciding that my other duties took precedence, or that it would be easier, somehow, for Gio. Clearly, it was not.

'I can help, I think,' I told him. 'I need one more thing from you, in order to do it. A small thing.'

Gio tried to look obliging, but I detected a wariness hidden behind it. 'What would that be?'

'Nothing onerous,' I assured him.

Later that day, I was conducted into the presence of Ylona Duna, would-be Lokantor of Sulayn Phay. The woman I had first known as Heliandor Rasset *looked* the same, in the physical sense, but in every other respect she was different. Her cheery manner, her friendly smile, were nowhere in evidence, and her plain, unassuming clothes were gone in favour of a livelier style. She greeted me with a quiet confidence I did not recognise — nothing resembling the breathless chatter she had displayed when I first met her.

The one familiar aspect of her behaviour was that slight eccentricity of manner, that preference for informality, that led her to sit herself atop a desk with Adonia rather than taking a chair. Considering Adonia's predilection for eccentricities of all kinds, I suppose I had assumed that she had taken the lead in the sitting-atop-desks exercise, and Heliandor had chosen to follow suit. I revised that opinion, for when Gio conducted me into Ylona's office she was sitting cross-legged on top of her own desk, straight-backed, surprisingly elegant for such a posture. She did not choose to come down when we approached, but rather held out her hand to me from where she sat, and shook mine with no apparent consciousness of oddity in her behaviour.

'I am delighted to meet you,' she said, with what appeared to be a genuinely welcoming smile. 'I have been anticipating your visit for some time.'

It was obvious that Ylona was an accomplished actress, so I made a note not to take her behaviour at face value. Nonetheless, that smile reassured me, and I welcomed the suggestion that I would not have to fight my way into her favour.

'I should have asked Gio sooner, clearly,' I observed.

Ylona's head tilted. 'Why didn't you?'

Good question. Why hadn't I? I decided to take a page out of Hyarn's book and dodge. 'An oversight.'

Ylona scrutinised me intently, as though she was trying to read my mind by examining my face. 'I cannot tell whether or not you are Dwinal's creature. Gio says not. Is he right?'

'Will you believe anything I tell you?'

'I might.'

I will be honest with you, I didn't like the way this was going. I was supposed to be interviewing Ylona, not the other way around. She had taken the upper hand, instantly and with an ease that left me uncertain how to respond. Me! Unsure, and made to play the supplicant!

I tried not to react to this by instantly hating her to her very core, and swallowed my dissatisfaction. 'I have no sympathy with

Dwinal whatsoever. None of us do. She is behind the death of a friend of ours, a man we admired, and she is the former wife of a man we opposed in everything. There can be no reason to imagine that her goals and ours will ever be aligned.'

Ylona smiled, and some subtle quality about that smile struck me as… odd. I suffered a sudden, horrible doubt.

Was this Ylona? I had briefly forgotten how easy it was for some Lokants to disguise themselves, to make me believe that I saw someone else instead. Had Dwinal decided to test me? Was I fooled? Was Gio fooled? I looked sharply at him, but detected no signs of unease in his characteristically impassive face.

Ylona grinned, guessing my thoughts. 'Confusing creatures, are we not? Don't worry, I am not Dwinal. How is Adonia getting along?'

I could see she meant this as proof that she could not possibly be Dwinal, for otherwise how would she know that "Heliandor" had been so friendly with my assistant? But it only enhanced my confusion, because I had no proof that Ylona had been the person behind Heliandor Rasset either. What if that, too, was Dwinal?

My mind whirled and I felt a little sick. Conspiracies leapt out at me at every mental turn, and I felt all my certainty in the world around me sliding like an avalanche. Could I trust anybody at all? Was even Gio who he claimed to be?

'Eva?' said Gio, who was looking at me with some concern. 'Are you all right?'

I took a deep breath, and pulled myself together. 'I am well,' I told Gio — feeling a little humbled by his concern for me, considering how little I had thus far shown for him.

To Ylona I said: 'Do you know anything about the captive draykon that was, until recently, housed in Gio's old chambers?'

Ylona response to this was surprise. Genuine, as far as I could tell. She looked sharply at Gio. 'You said nothing of this to me.'

Gio gave a slight cough. 'Because I wasn't sure that you had nothing to do with it.'

'The best way to find out is to ask me,' she pointed out. 'As Lady Glostrum has done.'

Gio merely gave her a sceptical stare, which clearly questioned her likelihood of responding with the truth.

'Yes, yes, fair. No, I did not put any draykoni in Gio's

chambers, and I am… intrigued, to hear of this news. You know nothing of how it came to be there, I gather?'

'Nothing whatsoever.'

'Or its purpose?'

'There, we have more of an inkling.' I explained, as best I could, about the *amasku* and Nindrinat's apparent use as a power source.

This news alarmed Ylona. She grew more disturbed as I talked, and when I had finished, she let herself down from her perch atop her desk and began to pace her office in circles.

'A power generator,' she mused. I began to explain further, but she waved my words away. 'I know about *amasku,* though I cannot pretend to understand it any better than the rest of my people. What interests me is: what could anybody want with a supply of so… odd an energy? So specific to your world?'

'Our theory,' I offered, 'such as it is, is that it is part of Dwinal's project to create a new race — a superior species to the draykoni, possibly one combined with Lokant abilities.'

'An aim she shared with her dead husband? Yes, I can see the sense of that idea. Thank you, by the way, for ridding Sulayn Phay of the disease we knew as Krays. I understand you were significantly involved.'

I inclined my head.

'Interesting theory,' she repeated. 'Wrong, I think, but interesting.'

'Wrong?' I echoed. 'Why do you think so?'

'Because I think her attention has shifted away from Krays's experiments. It was he who was determined to outdo Galywis, though he lacked the vision and the talent to truly create something new. All he could do was imitate. I could well believe that he would use a draykon as you have described, and with such an aim in view. But Dwinal? What would she expect to achieve by it? How would it fit in with her goals? I cannot see how it makes sense.'

'So you do not think it was Dwinal who captured Nindrinat?'

'I did not say that.' Ylona leaned against her desk, arms folded. 'She may well have — she herself, or her people. But if she did, I don't think she was harvesting its energy for the reasons you give.' She raised one brow at Gio. 'Besides, it would be odd indeed of her to anchor the creature in your rooms, just when she had restored them to you. She would have known you would find it, and given how much time you have been spending with draykoni lately — that you are romantically entangled with one of them, even — she must have realised that you would immediately extract the creature, and remove it from the Library. Does any of that make sense to you?'

Gio opened his mouth, alarmed. 'How do—'

'Yes, yes, it is known about you and Orillin. And Orillin's nature is understood as well. Don't worry, I do not believe anybody cares.'

'But Ori—'

'Is in no danger, most likely. The bound draykon was an Elder, you said? Orillin is no such thing, and if anybody wanted to put him to such use, I imagine they would have done so by now. They will not. There are easier targets, safer to use, and more powerful.'

'Have you heard of anything like this before?' I put in.

Ylona regarded me gravely, and shook her head. 'No… not exactly. There has been talk of draykoni about the place, but not in the fashion you describe.'

That interested me a great deal. 'What talk? Somebody of the draykoni must be helping Dwinal.'

'I do not know, specifically. Rumours, rumours. Whispers that there are draykoni hidden amongst us, shapeshifted to look like us. Mere gossip and conspiracy, I *had* thought, but perhaps not. I will investigate.'

'I want to search for more captive draykoni,' I said. I was taking a leap of faith in saying any of this, but why not? My spiralling loss of confidence in the reality of anything around me had taught me one, useful thing: if I could be certain of nothing, everything was risk. So why worry? 'I came to solicit your aid.'

Ylona's lips quirked. 'Oh? Why did you think I would help you?'

'Because this is most likely Dwinal's happy little project, and since you oppose everything she does, that makes us natural allies.'

'Mm. I cannot argue with any of that.' Ylona inclined her head to me. 'In truth, I have long felt the same; hence wondering why you had not approached me before. But I could have approached you, could I not? We have both held back, waiting for the other to be the one to entreat assistance. I salute you for having that courage, which I did not.'

I did not know what to say to so unexpected (and peculiar) a compliment, and could only blink stupidly. 'Thank you,' I managed to utter at last.

She grinned. 'I will help you. I have no especial reason to care for the draykoni, but this policy of enslaving other beings is both unwise and rather repugnant. And if it would ruin Dwinal's day to find all her pet draykoni going missing, I shall be delighted to be a part of that.'

I revised my opinion of Ylona on the spot: we were going to get along splendidly. 'Wonderful. I have one further question.'

She waited, listening.

'What do you know of Hyarn?'

And Ylona went still. It seemed to me that she was trying hard to conceal her reaction, whatever it might have been. 'Hyarn?' she repeated. 'What of him?'

'He is behaving oddly, and I am curious.'

She folded her arms again, a defensive posture. 'I know little of him. He is Dwinal's top aide and, apparently, her best friend. Some whisper that they are involved, in a closer sense, though I do not personally think there is anything in that rumour. He supports her in everything, and she relies on him completely.'

'That is about as much as we know of him,' I concurred, though privately I wondered. Her assessment matched with everything we had *heard*, but not fully with everything we had *seen*. I was disappointed. I had hoped that Ylona would know more, and her response troubled me. Why was she so defensive?

'He offered to help us,' I said, watching Ylona closely. 'With *anything* we might need. I received the impression that he made this offer without Dwinal's knowledge.'

Ylona's eyes narrowed. 'How co-operative of him.'

I left it at that, satisfied that I had planted thoughts in her mind that she would, in all probability, follow up on her own. If she learned anything of use about Hyarn, I hoped she would share it with us.

In the meantime, the draykoni. 'The problem we have is one of access,' I said. 'It is all very well deciding to search the Library for captives, but it is an enormous structure, and those places we are most likely to find secrets are, of course, the very places we cannot get into. Gio thought that you might be able to help us there.'

'To some degree, but if we are correct in thinking that

Dwinal is behind this, it is her wing that will be employed as prison space. I cannot get you into most of that.'

'Can't you?'

She looked back at me in silence for a moment, and then capitulated. 'I can get you into some of it,' she conceded.

I smiled. 'That would be of great help.'

'Not all of it,' she cautioned. 'Genuinely. We devote considerable time and energy to finding a way into their chambers, but they of course devote at least as much time and energy to keeping us out.'

'I understand.'

She gave me that odd smile again. 'Were you thinking of asking Hyarn?'

'I was, actually.'

Ylona nodded, slowly and thoughtfully. 'I see the sense, and the dilemma. Will you take the risk?'

I thought for a moment. 'I think I will.'

That earned me a smile, and a tiny salute. 'You are an audacious woman. I respect that.'

I curtseyed. 'Why, thank you. Let us hope I am not about to audaciously get us all slung out of the Library.'

So I discovered a series of personal failings, solemnly vowed to rectify them, listened to my spouse (albeit belatedly), learned to open my mind and be more trusting and actually set forth to act upon all of these things in the same day. Astonishing, is it not?

It is a shame I never got the chance to do much with these bright, shiny impulses after all.

Avane, Nyden and Adonia formed an odd little alliance as soon as we arrived up here. I have barely seen them since, for when not teaching (in the case of Avane and Ny) they have spent their time wandering the Library in search of more captives.

Imagine my surprise, then, to find all three plus Ori and Tren in occupation of my suite when I returned. And they had brought a stranger with them. A social visit, I thought, as everyone was comfortably seated in chairs. But the atmosphere was wrong for that. There was an odd tension, and the room was too quiet.

'Good afternoon,' I said pleasantly as I swept in, Gio at my heels. 'What a charming surprise.' Truthfully I was a little irritated to find them there, as I wanted to discuss Ylona and Hyarn with Tren.

Tren, though, looked gravely at me, and I recognised the expression as his Meaningful Stare. I couldn't have a hope of guessing what he meant by it, of course, which only enhanced my irritation.

I waited, but everybody seemed to be waiting for somebody else to speak.

'Who have you brought me?' I prompted.

The stranger in question was a broad-shouldered man, white-haired like everybody else up here, though he was bulkier and more… shall we say, developed, than most of the Lokants I've seen? He wore a plain robe and looked fabulously uncomfortable in it. His eyes interested me: they were deep-set, on the large side to say the least, and spectacularly green. All in all I might have said he was dreamy, only something was definitely amiss here. Adonia looked serene and unconcerned as ever, but Avane looked worried, Tren was still trying to signal something to me with his eyes, and Nyden — Nyden was simmering with ill-concealed fury.

Hmm.

Tren gave up on telepathy. 'My dear, this is Rastivan. A fascinating man, most unusual. We knew you would want to meet him. We have been awaiting you, or Gio.'

Me *or* Gio? Then presenting this fascinatingly unusual man to me was not the true goal of this meeting. I realised they had put Rastivan in the centre, with two flanking him on either side, which was probably not a coincidence. He was also right at the back of the room; if he wanted to reach the door, he would have to make it past all four of them first.

I heard Gio shut the door behind me.

Me or Gio. What did the two of us have in common? We were the only Lokants of our little group, and… the only ones with a way out of the Library.

'How nice to meet you, Rastivan,' I said, with my blandest smile. 'I am always delighted to meet fascinating people, of course. What do you do in Sulayn Phay?'

Rastivan's eyes flicked to Gio behind me, and then back to my face. He looked cowed, and I wondered if he had only just realised that he'd landed in the centre of a fine trap. 'I am a, um.

Research specialist.'

'Oh?' said I politely. 'How interesting. What is your subject?'

Rastivan did not seem to know what his subject was, for he hesitated. His eyes flicked to Gio again.

The more I looked at Rastivan, the more I felt that something was amiss with him, some small subtlety out of place… was it his eyes, a brighter green than I had ever seen before? Was it his features? He reminded me a little bit of Pense in the early days of his shapeshifting, when he had not yet fully grasped how humans tended to look…

Enlightenment dawned, just as Nyden spoke.

'This is boring,' he announced. 'And stupid.'

I opened my mouth to enquire as to his meaning, but Rastivan's survival instincts chose that moment to fulfil their assigned purpose. Aware all at once that the scenario could not possibly end well for him, he made a swift, hopeless leap for the doorway.

Nyden was ready for this. He surged out of his chair and leapt at Rastivan, brought him down in a brutal tackle, and ruthlessly beat the bigger man's head against the hard floor until he passed out. Then Ny looked at me with an unpleasant smile. 'Give us a lift home?'

I concealed my surprise. 'By all means.' Gio came too, to my relief, because dragging Nyden plus that massive side of meat around would not be easy on me. We bundled them up between us, and made the leap back to HQ.

'Draykon?' I queried, once we had safely come out in the entrance hall of my poor, flooded building.

'Draykon turncoat,' said Ny, and bared his teeth at the unconscious form of Rastivan. We had let the side of meat slip from our grasp as we'd arrived, and he now lay in a damp heap on the sopping-wet floor. 'Sneaking around at Phay with his shoddy disguise, cosying up with Dwinal. We heard him, talking like an idiot. How easy it is to trap a draykon, if you grab them straight from the Long Sleep! How many more he can deliver! He's an ancient. He should know better.'

So here was our informant, the person responsible for handing over the likes of Nindrinat for enslavement. 'I wonder what he was getting out of it,' I mused.

'I don't know.'

'Are there others?'

Ny shrugged. 'No sign of any more, but maybe. Keep an eye out.' Rastivan stirred, his eyelids fluttering. With a broad, delighted smile, Nyden viciously kicked him in the head, and Rastivan subsided into unconsciousness once more. 'We let him think we were at Phay for the same reasons. The competition, if you like. Invited him to a co-operative meeting.'

'Very clever.'

Nyden gazed down at Rastivan with such fury, even I felt uneasy. 'I will deal with him,' he said to me with chilling glee.

I surveyed Ny, thinking. I could see that Rastivan's fate was not going to be pleasant. If I left Nyden to his own devices… how far would he go? How much could be justified?

Draykon business. I decided not to interfere. 'Thank you,' I said.

Perhaps Nyden guessed at my deliberations, for he gave me a more genuine smile and a bow. 'Come get me in a day or two.'

'Yes, sir.'

To my surprise, Gio looked more concerned about Rastivan's possible fate than I was. Gio, who carved holes in his own people without a qualm, if need arose.

'He sold Nindrinat into slavery,' I reminded him.

'I know, but…' Gio watched Nyden, who in turn was watching Rastivan with the intense anticipation of a predator about to enjoy a particularly succulent meal. 'He'll take him apart.'

'Good point.' I tapped Ny on the shoulder. 'Can I ask him a couple of questions, before you take him away?'

'Interrogation!' said Nyden grandly, and stepped aside. 'I was forgetting that.'

I shook my head in mock dismay. 'Some spy you are.'

'I cannot help it if I am better at the violent bits.'

'Everybody has their strengths.' Nyden had clobbered Rastivan nicely; I had to wait a few minutes before he began to come around again. In the meantime, I had Nyden restrain the captive, which he accomplished by sitting on Rastivan's chest. His hands changed: long, wicked claws erupted from his fingertips, and these he sank deeply into Rastivan's shoulders. When the draykon woke, his first sight was of Nyden's face close to his, long teeth bared. His first sensation, pain.

'Welcome awake,' growled Nyden.

I wasn't going to waste time asking Rastivan questions and

hoping he would reply. Too risky, too long-winded, and too much of an encouragement to Nyden, who I was sure would take great delight in torturing him.

I do have these sparkly Lokant powers, however, and I am rarely afforded so beautiful an opportunity to use them.

So Ny threatened, and I smacked Rastivan around with a nice, blunt compulsion. 'To whom do you report?' I asked him.

Rastivan blinked at me, his face blank. 'The one called Dwinal.'

'How many draykoni have you delivered to her?'

I waited in confident expectation of another prompt answer, but none came. To my distaste, my compulsion wasn't holding; it was running off him like water, his eyes were clearing, he was moving. I'd forgotten that draykoni are somewhat more resistant to the art than humans — or perhaps it is merely that my ability is lacking, for Gio stepped in. *His* idea of a nice, blunt compulsion made mine look like a light caress with a feather. He smashed Rastivan's mind with the mental equivalent of a ton of bricks, and snarled: '*How many?*'

'Sixteen,' panted Rastivan, who seemed unable to breathe.

We ignored his sufferings. *Sixteen*? 'You lie,' I said faintly.

'No.'

I exchanged an appalled look with Gio. We had expected there would be more draykoni held at Sulayn Phay, of course, but privately, I had imagined there might be one or two or three… *sixteen* changed everything. Sixteen made for a whole different set of problems. Sixteen meant that finding them was no longer the biggest challenge we faced; getting them out was going to be far more difficult.

A fight broke out at my feet. Rastivan was throwing off Gio's compulsion, too, ignoring all further questions, and generally getting belligerent about everything. Nyden was taking him apart, as Gio put it, and enjoying himself immensely. A brief survey assured me that, as powerful as Rastivan might look, he was no match for Nyden, and he knew it.

'He'll be fine,' I told Gio, referring to Ny. 'Come on.'

I had spent about three minutes reviewing our options, which was sufficient time to conclude that they were limited. We had badly underestimated the extent of the problem; now that we were better informed, the time for creeping, careful action was past.

'We are going to need help,' I told Gio as I went outside. 'Lots of it.'

My manner worried Gio, but he was too wise to try to stop me. 'What do you have in mind?'

'First, we need to get in touch with our allies.' I went to the post box and rummaged within it. I found a number of letters, all of which I discarded, for they were mere paper and could not contain what I was looking for. There were no packages, no parcels.

'Damn,' I muttered.

'What are you looking for?'

I told him about the voice-boxes made by Llandry's father, and her promise to try to secure one for me.

'Did you tell her about the post shenanigans we had happening?'

'I… yes, I imagine I did.'

'Llandry's too clever to send it here by post, then.'

'Wise man that you are.' I did some thinking. If Llan wanted to deliver something important and she was unwilling to trust it to the post, what would she do with it?

'It's a long way to travel, just to drop off a voice-box,' Gio said. 'She might have sent it somewhere else?'

I rolled my eyes, momentarily exhausted by my own stupidity. 'Like my house, for instance. She knows where that is. Hayes has probably got it.'

Thither we went, the quick way, for Gio set up a transloc point outside my front door some time ago.

I rang the bell and Hayes appeared, all neat black coat, perfectly groomed hair and raised eyebrows. 'My lady?'

'Dear Hayes. Has an odd-looking package arrived for me recently? Possibly marked "incredibly, unimaginably important" as well as "shockingly fragile"?'

'Yes, my lady,' he said, and I swear I saw his lips twitch. It is not easy to make Hayes laugh; he is far too self-possessed. 'I will fetch it.'

He did so with marvellous promptitude, and within a few moments I had a voice-box in my hands once more. It was an odd feeling. The last time I had one of those things, there was a war going on.

'I hope it works,' I muttered, and tried it. It was much simpler than the one Limbane gave me, clunky and almost juvenile by comparison. But a promising *fizz* of sound emerged when I activated it, and I spoke at once. 'Llan.'

Nothing happened.

'Llan?'

Nothing.

'LLANDRY!'

'Yes.' The box buzzed. 'Yes! Eva!'

'Dire emergency!' I warned. 'Darling that you are for arranging this thing! We need all draykoni on hand at my house, as soon as you can get here. There are at least sixteen like Nindrinat somewhere in Sulayn Phay, and we need to move.'

'Sixteen?!' I heard the awe in Llandry's voice, and she fell silent for a long time. Too long.

'Llandry!'

'Yes. Sorry. We are coming.'

The box stopped buzzing. 'Excellent,' I murmured, and tucked it away. 'Onward.'

Gio and I returned to Sulayn Phay to find an empty suite of rooms. The silence unnerved me; it was starkly at odds with the urgency I felt, with the turmoil in my mind. The peacefulness seemed wrong.

'Where is everyone?' murmured Gio.

'I am sure they're well,' I said firmly, though I felt a twinge of concern. Never mind that now. 'Gio, we need to get into your grandmother's rooms.'

I had been hoping I'd never have to say that to him, for the effect was immediate: he turned white, and took an involuntary step backwards. He swallowed. 'Eva… you… have no idea what she'll do if she catches us there.'

'I have an inkling, I think, and I am sorry to ask you to place yourself in such danger. But matters are too urgent to admit of any further delay. Thanks to Rastivan, we are now certain that Dwinal was behind the capture of Nindrinat and the others. We need to know why. We need to find out what this "new establishment" of hers is supposed to be. If winning her confidence through winning back her trust isn't working, then we must try a more direct approach.'

He nodded, but I could see that he felt neither reassured nor resolved. He looked like he wanted to be sick. With a long sigh, he rubbed at his eyes. 'Do you think, once this is all over, we will manage to have a quiet life for a while?'

'I hope so,' I said fervently. 'I want to get married and live happily ever after.'

That prompted a tiny smile from Gio, and he said softly: 'Me too.'

'Sadly, the best way to secure such a future is to send Dwinal packing.'

He nodded, more thoughtfully this time. His colour was returning a little. 'I do not have access to those rooms,' he admitted. 'She has never trusted me enough to grant me that again, and I didn't really expect her to. So, I will have to do as I did before: find someone else who can get in, and um… make use of them.'

I remembered well how he had previously achieved that. I wasn't present myself, but Llandry wrote of how he had cut an implant out of someone's arm — someone to whom he was possibly related — and used that to open the door. 'Do you think your grandmother might be ready for that possibility, this time? Would it still work?'

Gio opened his mouth, and nothing came out. He shut it again, and grunted.

'I think I am minded to gamble,' I offered.

Gio's eyes widened. 'Gambling is… risky.'

'Highly. It is not for the faint of heart, certainly. Will you hear my idea?'

He nodded once.

'I think that there's trouble in Dwinal's camp. All is possibly not well between her and Hyarn. I think that when Hyarn came here and offered to help with "anything we might need", he was trying to tell me that he was disposed to support us in opposing *her.*'

'You're going to ask Hyarn to let us into Dwinal's chambers?'

'Exactly.'

Gio gave me the wide-eyed stare of a sane man confined in close quarters with a madwoman. 'You must be joking.'

'No. I did say that matters are becoming somewhat urgent. Time to be bold.'

'Is that bold, or crazy?'

'Sometimes the two are indistinguishable.'

'What about what you said before? What if it's all a trick?'

'The best way to find out how a trap works is to spring it.'

'And be trapped.'

'What choices do we have? Being *careful* and *wise* and *tentative* has only wasted a lot of time. While we were doing that, Rastivan and company were out enslaving sixteen draykoni. We need to stop this, immediately.'

Nothing Gio said could dissuade me, I am afraid. You might have noticed, I can be stubborn once I have set my mind on something. The poor boy came up with a few alternative ideas for getting into his grandmother's personal space; all of them struck me as shaky, unlikely to succeed, and scarcely less risky than approaching Hyarn. Eventually I decided the debate by leaving the room, leaving Gio to trail helplessly in my wake.

I was fairly sure I knew where to find Hyarn, but I wanted to visit the schoolroom first in hopes of finding Tren there. In this I was disappointed, but I did find Avane, enjoying a drink in between classes. She looked, as ever, worried.

'Nyden is well,' I told her, for I had a suspicion that question was on her mind. Her manner toward him had changed somewhat, since he had shown signs of a better nature (or at least a different one). 'We left him making mincemeat of Rastivan.'

She smiled faintly and said, in her soft way, 'He will enjoy that.'

'He was taking great pleasure in it, when we left,' I agreed. 'Where has everyone gone?'

'Ori's teaching with Tynara, much to his disgust, because everyone else has gone in search of captives. There was an agreement to launch a major search. I had instructions to send you and Gio after them when you returned, for you've access to places they do not.'

'We have another errand first, after which we will gladly join the search.' I told Avane what our errand was — somebody needed to know where we had gone, in case all was disaster and ruin. Avane was no happier about the plan than Gio, but she did not argue as he had done. She merely gazed at me, huge-eyed, with the air of one taking a final, fond look at a dear friend whom she would never see again.

'Be careful,' she said.

I liked that she did not try to dissuade me. If one overlooked her obvious certainty that it would only end in catastrophe, it made for a pleasant vote of confidence.

Avane set down her cup, and rose. 'I must take over from Ori in a few moments. I'll tell him where you are.'

I pictured Ori tearing after us in a blaze of fury that I could dare to put his lover (fiancé…?) in danger. 'Perhaps better not, right away.'

But Avane proved unexpectedly immoveable. 'He has a right to know, and you may need the help.'

Fair, and fair. I didn't argue further.

We left. 'Are you and Ori planning to wed?' I asked Gio as we returned to the corridor.

He blinked, taken aback by the sudden question. 'Ah… why do you ask?'

'Your desire for wedded bliss appears to equal my own.'

He said nothing right away. 'I have not asked him,' he admitted.

'Shall you?'

'If I can find the courage.'

That might have been the moment for a pep talk, for I had no doubts about the likelihood of Ori's accepting such a proposal. But it was not my place to interfere (you hear that, Tren? I chose not to meddle!), and we were in a bit of a hurry.

'Away we go,' I warned Gio as I grabbed his wrist. I translocated back to that little library on the other side of Sulayn Phay, where we had found Hyarn before. He had looked so at home there, I'd got the impression that it was possibly a favourite space of his.

To my relief, there he was, reclining in the same chair as before. A stack of books rested on the table beside him, and he held one open on his lap. He looked up as we materialised before him, and smiled.

'Lady Glostrum,' he greeted me. 'Maeval.'

Gio's face twisted in disgust. 'Don't call me that.'

His reaction puzzled me for a moment, until I remembered that Maeval had been Krays's family name. Apparently it was also Gio's, and he was less than happy about it.

Hyarn responded with a respectful nod. 'Gio, then,' he amended.

I felt emboldened by this kindness towards Gio, small as it was. Could I reasonably take it as a sign that Hyarn was more kindly disposed towards the grandson than the grandparents? Was that wishful thinking? Did I give Hyarn too much credit?

I took a moment to wander the library, surreptitiously checking whether anybody might be near enough to overhear our conversation.

'We are alone, if that troubles you,' said Hyarn mildly. 'This is my library. Nobody enters without my permission.'

'Except for us,' I said, feeling faintly abashed. 'Sorry.'

Hyarn merely smiled. 'As I said: nobody enters without my permission.'

Well, now. If I was hoping for a clear sign, I was unlikely to receive any clearer a sign than that. 'You did say…' I began, and hesitated. I felt uncharacteristically uncertain, which I hate. And what a moment to falter! Having brutally overridden all of Gio's doubts: *now* to question myself!

'Are you in need of assistance?' prompted Hyarn.

I looked at Gio, who stood like a man condemned. He looked back at me, unspeaking, his face unreadable.

I took a breath. *Now for it.* 'Dwinal has been capturing draykoni,' I said, and I managed to speak as though I had never known doubt in my life. 'We discovered one.'

Hyarn nodded.

'In Gio's old chambers.'

Hyarn nodded again.

His complete lack of surprise confirmed my suspicion. 'That was no coincidence, was it?'

'It was not.' Hyarn closed his book and set it aside. 'I knew that Gio, and his new friends, could be relied upon to do whatever was necessary for the creature.'

His dispassionate use of the word *creature* seemed at odds with the apparent interest he was showing in Nindrinat's well-being, and I was unsure what to make of it.

Gio was shocked. '*You* placed her there? Why?'

'For the reason I have just stated.'

'But… but you are Dwinal's second-in-command.'

Hyarn's eyes twinkled, a faint smile curving his lips. 'And you are Dwinal's grandson.'

'Did Dwinal know that you had done that?' I asked.

'No. It is my duty to accommodate Dwinal's… guests, and she takes little interest in how I choose to perform that task.'

My heart leapt. 'So you know where the others are?'

'Yes, but so do your friends, by this time. Did you not wonder where they are?'

'You led them to the others?'

'Subtly. I believe they are under the impression that they have discovered the whereabouts of the captives unaided.'

Hyarn was obviously in possession of a devious nature rivalling my own. I was impressed. 'Why are you assisting us?'

'I am not, precisely. I am obstructing Dwinal, which amounts to the same thing.'

'And you are obstructing your Lokantor because…?'

'Because someone needs to.' Hyarn smiled at us, and rose from his chair. 'You came to me with a specific request, I imagine? Would you like me to take you to the draykoni?'

I thought fast, and reached a swift decision. 'No. Our friends will be doing everything they can to stabilise them, and for the moment we lack the manpower to do much more for them. It's on its way. In the meantime, it is information about Dwinal that we need.'

'Such as?'

'We came in hopes that you might let us into Dwinal's chambers, but perhaps you can answer our questions more expediently. Why is she capturing, and draining, draykoni Elders? What is the new establishment she is trying to create? What is any of this *for*?'

Hyarn looked as though he did not know how to respond. He stood, lost in thought, and we waited in silence as he weighed up his options. I could guess at some of his thoughts. How far did he dare help us? Would he risk being seen in our company, anywhere near Dwinal's rooms?

'Come with me,' he said at last.

He translocated us out of his library — and may I say, as an aside, how humbling an experience that was? I have never known anybody accomplish the process so smoothly, so imperceptibly. I felt nothing; no rush of movement; certainly none of the sickening lurch that tended to plague my own, miserable efforts. I did not realise we had moved at all, until I noticed that our surroundings had changed.

We had come out in a large… room. I know that's an unhelpful description, but its purpose was unclear. It looked like part laboratory, part workshop and part library, mixed up with a range of other things. I saw energy collectors stored in one part of the room, one or two of them set a little apart from the others, as though recently used. There was a draykon skeleton, fully intact, probably awaiting rejuvenation by Rastivan (or another). Books, of course, were prominent.

What interested me the most was the vast drawing that occupied one entire wall. Incredibly detailed, it looked like a blueprint for a building, if such an impossibly complicated structure could exist. It was broadly star-shaped, with five distinct wings and five smaller ones offset. I drifted closer, fascinated. I could read none of the notes which covered almost every part of the drawing, but the level of detail was mesmerising.

'This looks like a Library,' I said.

Hyarn came to stand beside me, and we gazed at the marvellous blueprint together. 'It is.'

Gio joined us. 'It is not the plan for any existing Library, though, is it?'

'No,' said Hyarn. 'It is the layout for a new Library. Visionary. Whatever her flaws, Dwinal has a bright, great mind.'

So, Limbane was right. This was the new establishment Dwinal was trying to develop: a new, great Library, one to be populated not only by pure-blood Lokants but by partials as well, those whose blood was mixed with that of the draykoni.

'Are they always so spectacular?' I asked. 'All of your Libraries, I mean.'

'No.' Hyarn looked long at the drawing, his eyes sad. 'There was one other, once. Just one.'

'Orlind,' said Gio, and Hyarn nodded.

'This is to be a new kind, is it not?' I said, electrified. 'One heavily inspired by the lost Library of Orlind. That is why she requires a significant supply of *amasku.* She seeks to bind it into the creation of a new Library, just as it was woven into the fabric of Orlind. And then, perhaps, she will be able to develop a new species, something to rival the draykoni. Or perhaps even to build upon them.'

'Such a project can only go the same way as the Library of Orlind.' Every word Hyarn spoke was laden with regret. 'For a time, it would be a wonder, one we would use to create many marvels. But eventually, inevitably, there would be war.'

'Dwinal herself said something similar,' I remembered. 'To Llandry. She said that the Library of Orlind had to be destroyed, or it would be a source of conflict for your people forever.'

'A mere manipulation, I'm afraid. The prospect of inciting war does not trouble Dwinal, provided she feels secure of coming out on the winning side. That is part of her motive for the school you are presently running, in point of fact. She hopes to identify all the strongest partial Lokants, all those whose brilliance and blended skills offer the brightest prospects. Not only will they assist her in every project she seeks to complete with the use of this spectacular new tool, they will also make a splendid and fearsome army, should it come to that someday.' He paused, and sighed, and added: 'For all the violence of my actions of late, I do not support war. If I have killed, I have done it to *avert* war, not to encourage it.'

His tone had turned from regretful to bitter, and I began to understand. Dwinal had manipulated Hyarn, too. She had convinced him that she was as committed to avoiding further conflicts as he was, had used him as a tool to remove Galywis and by extension the Library of Orlind, had told him whatever she had to in order to retain his loyalty. Then, somehow, he had found her out.

However, I detected a flaw in his logic. 'Such a Library would fulfil all the dreams of those who most regretted the loss of the Library of Orlind,' I said. 'It would relieve Sulayn Phay of Dwinal as Lokantor, which ought to be satisfy Ylona. Only those who essentially agree with Dwinal's approach would join her at the new Library, which would nicely get them out of your hair. And who knows, they might indeed produce something genuinely visionary with such a tool. Are you so certain there would, ultimately, be war?'

'History can only repeat itself. I have lived too long to question this fundamental truth. Over and over again, I see it happen.'

'So you would like to stop Dwinal from founding this Library?'

'She must be prevented from creating this Library. She must be prevented from performing any further abuse of the draykoni in the pursuit of it.' He looked sideways at me. 'Or of your students. Her cheerful willingness to turn even our own descendants to use is similarly questionable. I could wish you had not brought them back here. She must not be allowed to "recruit" any of them.'

'I never had any intention of permitting her to claim them,' I assured him. I could not resist adding, 'I might not have felt driven to resort to such measures, had I known sooner that we had an ally here.'

To his credit, Hyarn acknowledged the justice of that with a nod. 'I could not tell how far you were in agreement with Dwinal.'

Gio had absorbed most of this in impassive silence, but Hyarn appeared to be irritating him. 'Grandmother's abuse of her own descendants is no new thing,' he snapped. 'You work in close proximity with her, Hyarn. You know her methods. You know that no one is safe from her ruthlessness, her brutality — not me, not you.'

'I know it.'

'She must not be allowed to found a new Library, and not only because of the prospect of war! Ylona is right, she is not fit! You know what would become of such a place, of those who are fool enough to support her. It would be a waking nightmare for those inside, and an eternal blot upon our society. And if she succeeds, do you imagine she will stop there? What do you think she will do, with such a tool at her disposal? Nothing we would ever wish to see!'

'We are in full agreement,' said Hyarn gently. 'My question is only: how is such a feat to be accomplished? Long have I thought and thought, sought a way to sabotage Dwinal somehow, to divert her attention, to *remove* her if necessary. But she is inexorable. Unstoppable, I fear. We were freed from Krays, but I do not believe any such stroke of luck is likely to relieve us of his wife.'

'Luck?' I repeated, disbelieving. 'There wasn't a scrap of luck involved. We went to great lengths, huge risks, to remove Krays from the world, and justly celebrated our success.'

'But—'

'No. Luck is a fabrication; there is no such thing. Luck is made, through *action.* You do not lack for resolve. Are you so afraid of Dwinal?'

Hyarn and Gio exchanged a look between them. Clearly they thought me sadly deluded.

'Never mind,' I said. 'We will deal with her.'

'You put me to shame,' murmured Hyarn.

'Then do better,' I said. Brutal, I know, but I cannot bear

feebleness. The best way I know of to fail is to give up before you've even started.

My train of thought was interrupted by a distant buzzing, of which I gradually became aware. Some seconds passed before I realised what it was.

The voice box.

I grabbed it, my heart pounding. This was it. Llandry had arrived, and all her people with her. It was time to act, time to carry through on the rash promise I had just made. For all my bold words, I was not impervious to the fear.

'Llandry?'

'Eva! Thank goodness. I had no idea if it would work at such a range, I'm so glad to get hold of you, I thought— the worst thing has—' She broke off, and I heard her taking a deep breath.

My heart rate about tripled. 'Steady, Llan. What's gone wrong?'

'Eva, I know this will sound insane, but you have to believe me.'

'I will.'

'Promise?'

'Yes! Tell me!' Honestly, I would have shaken her if she had been before me at that moment. The suspense! Intolerable!

'Orlind is gone.'

My heart froze. 'Gone? Orlind? The entire *island*?'

'All of it. Vanished.'

'What… how did that happen? How can it have been destroyed?'

'*Vanished*, Eva! Not destroyed, or I *hope* not. I came back and rounded everyone up, we set off, and the moment we got as far as the mountains into Irbel, the island… that mist came in, you remember how the island used to be? You couldn't even see it under all the fog? That came back, and when it dissipated the island was gone. Just gone. Empty sea.'

'What…' I was so shocked I could barely speak. 'What—how—'

'I was hoping you would be able to answer that.'

With an effort, I pulled myself together. 'Actually, I probably can, but that isn't going to help us get it back.'

'What do we do?'

'I don't… I don't know, Llan. Where are you now?'

'Still on the border of Irbel.'

‘Who is with you?’

‘Pense, and all of Nuwelin and Anshalin. Pretty much everyone.’

‘All right, just… just stay there, for now. I need to find out what’s going on.’

‘Right.’ The box went dead.

Gio and Hyarn were staring at me, probably wearing the exact same expression as my own: blank shock, mixed with horror.

‘Couple of questions,’ I said, as mildly as I could. ‘This Library. It… moves around, does it not? I am sure I heard that somewhere before.’

‘Yes,’ said Hyarn. ‘Most of them do.’

‘Whereabouts is it stationed at the moment?’

Hyarn coughed. ‘Ah… actually, it is anchored in your world.’

‘Not far from Irbel, let me guess?’

‘Not very far from Irbel, indeed.’

That explained how Llandry could reach me with the voice-box. ‘Is it the Library building that moves, or the land it’s built upon?’

‘The… all of it, everything.’

‘Uh huh. Do you happen to know where Dwinal was planning to build her marvellous new Library?’

‘She was looking for a suitable place—’

‘Apparently she found one!’ I lost my temper a little, for which I apologise. The pressure was getting to me. ‘Did you know about this? Either of you!’ I may have shouted. I know that I advanced upon the pair of them, most likely a vision of fury, because they both backed up a step.

‘No!’ said both of them. ‘You have to understand—’ (this was Gio) ‘—Grandmother doesn’t have confidantes! Not for things like this!’

I glared at Hyarn, who echoed Gio’s words. ‘To the last, she told me she was looking — searching for the perfect place — I had no idea she had her sights set on Orlind! I have fought with her, since Galywis, questioned her. She does not trust me as she used to.’

Composure, composure. Screaming at people is productive on occasion, but right then wasn’t one of those times. ‘That vision of old Orlind,’ I said. ‘Llandry told me of it. Gio has seen it. It isn’t just a memory, is it? It is a blueprint, a far more developed one than that.' I waved a hand at the drawing on the wall, which had now assumed a new, much more ominous character. 'Memory it might be, but it's also a vision for the future! Dwinal isn't trying to found a new Library, she's trying to recreate an old one! That's why she was so damned happy when Galywis blew up Old Orlind, broken as it was beyond repair! It got it out of the way, so she could re-use the spit of land it was sitting on.'

I wondered, then, whether our worlds had ever really been composed of Seven Realms at all. I think we had all assumed that the island we call Orlind had once been a far larger piece of land, and joined to the rest of our realms. Originally no island at all, it became so during the literally earth-shaking conflict that destroyed the Library that once stood upon it.

Maybe we were wrong. Perhaps it was always an island, just a larger one. Maybe Galywis and his colleagues anchored it off our shores in the first place. And now Dwinal had merrily unanchored it, and spirited it away!

Bitch.

I took a few moments to think. For all that I have a reputation for unflappable composure (and a carefully cultivated reputation at that), I can be shaken. I can be at a loss. Just then, I felt frozen in panic. What to do? What could we possibly do? Too many problems faced us at once. There were the sixteen draykoni who urgently needed to be extracted from Sulayn Phay, and taken home. Dwinal had to be stopped and the island of Orlind somehow retrieved, but in order to do either of those things Dwinal had first to be *found* and the island, too. The people we needed in order to accomplish either task were spread all over the Library of Sulayn Phay and the Seven Realms — where was Ny, right then? Our only Elder and I had let him wander off with Rastivan, leaving behind himself nothing but an airy promise to come back *in a day or two*!

I wasted some little time cursing myself, as Gio and Hyarn debated in low, urgent tones and nobody arrived at any useful conclusions whatsoever.

Then I remembered who I was supposed to be. I was the person looked to for solutions. I was the unflappable one, by my own connivance. The one with all the answers, the one who always knew what to do and had the gumption to do it, too. I could panic later.

'Gio,' I said. 'I imagine Ori can be found wherever those captive draykoni are. Hyarn will tell you where to find them. Will you join him, and the others, and see what can be done for them?'

'Of course,' he murmured, though he looked uncertain. 'What of—'

'Hyarn,' I continued. 'I will need your assistance in locating the island of Orlind. I imagine there is *something* you can do to help us discover where it has been taken to.'

Hyarn looked uncertain, too, and the look he exchanged with Gio was faintly pleading. But Gio said nothing, and Hyarn found his courage. 'Very well,' he agreed.

'Good. Gio, I will need a report from you, or from Ori or Tren, as soon as possible. Find out the status of those draykoni. We will need Llandry's aid in getting them out, but right now the combined citizenry of Nuwelin and Anshalin are hovering on the Irbellian border awaiting instructions. Since we may also need their assistance with the matter of the island of Orlind, I am reluctant to bring them here until we have better information, in one direction or another. Is that clear?'

'Perfectly.'

'Good. Go then, please.'

Gio left.

Now, then. We come to a convoluted part of this narrative, and as you may very well imagine, I could not be everywhere at once. I cannot relate every step of this story myself, so I beg your leave to turn this journal over to the direction of others, as appropriate.

Beginning with the matter of Nyden. We left him carting Rastivan off for an unpleasant chat, full of bloodthirsty plans and positively quivering with rage. Since the outcome of that little meeting proved more significant than I had imagined at the time, I have invited Nyden to recount it.

NYDEN

On the Little Matter of Rastivan, the Traitor

I don't do hatred.

I really don't. Not ever. What would be the point? Life is long, people are foolish, the world continues regardless. Why waste energy on fury, futile resentment, hate? It is tiring. I dislike being tired.

Besides, who is there to hate? Little Llandry, sweet tentative girl that she is, hiding her fierce draykon heart behind her layers of doubt and fright and too great a desire to please? Pense and Larion and Meriall and all the others, very good fellows all? Or mighty Eva, with her wit and her excellent table, always replete with succulent delights?

Why would I hate Avane, whose scent alone is sufficient to drive me into paroxysms of delight? Why would I despise the delicious little chicks from Ayrien she has taken under her ample wings?

I cannot even be bothered to hate Eterna, leader of my old colony, who cannot help but start wars wherever she goes. Why her followers continue to accept her leadership is beyond me, but what can I say? Blind fury sells. Conflict sells. War is sexy. So turns the world.

When I tell you, then, that I hate, hate, *despise* traitors, I hope you will understand my full meaning. Eterna may err, over and over again, but at least she acts in the fashion she *believes* is best.

But a traitor? Is there not something particularly wicked, especially unforgiveable, about the man who betrays his own friends, his own kind, for naught but personal gain? For that is what it's always about. If I do *this,* hand over *this* person or *that* friend, something good will be awarded to me. Something *I* want. And what could be more important than my receiving everything I could possibly want in life?

So when I found myself left in sole possession of one Rastivan, he who cheerfully sold his own kind into Lokant slavery and felt no remorse, I was *elated.* And enraged. I wanted to kill him. Tear open his lying throat and drink his traitorous blood; watch the undeserved light die out of his filthy, too-pretty eyes; tear him limb-from-limb and scatter his parts to the far corners of the world.

Eva knew this, but she let me take him anyway. She did not send anybody along to intervene. She did not even say, *Now Nyden, nothing too permanent, hm?* She merely patted me on the head (figuratively speaking), wished me good hunting (again figuratively), and departed.

Leaving me with a whole day — *two* entire, delicious days! — to spend encouraging Rastivan to see the error of his ways.

Tricky, tricky, because much as I would like to tear open his chest and devour his heart, I could not help feeling a mild curiosity as to why he behaved as he did. What did he stand to gain from selling out his own kind?

I regretted the delay, but this question had to be answered. What if there were more Rastivans out there? Probably there were. Rastivan would tell me *aaallll* about them.

I took him down into the cellar of Eva's abandoned headquarters. The water had mostly subsided by then, but the place was still dank, partially flooded, dark and freezing cold.

How perfect.

I slung Rastivan in a careless heap in the middle of the floor, making sure that his head landed in one of the deeper puddles of cold water. Then I locked the only exit behind me, and waited for him to wake up.

When he did, he found me crouched over him, a vast, looming shadow in the darkness. My hide is night-black, unblemished by anything so vulgar as *colour*, and I am excellent at creating a certain impression.

I bared my teeth in his pseudo-human face, and he screamed.

That last part might have been because I had my claws buried deep in his shoulders. 'First,' I told him in a low, purring voice (I had plenty of time to practice while he lay unconscious and allow me to assure you: no more menacing words were ever spoken). '*First,*' I said, 'I must make sure you don't run away.'

When you are as big as me and your victim is wearing a flimsy human shape, it is not difficult to tear off a man's leg with your bare claws. He screamed and screamed and I smiled and smiled and some part of me hated myself, but I could not stop. I didn't want to.

'You have three limbs left,' I pointed out, when he had finally stopped screaming. 'Four, if you are so obliging as to return to your proper shape and allow me to get at your tail. Do not doubt that I shall take all the rest, if you do not satisfy me.'

He looked properly, gratifyingly terrified, but he was also beginning to be angry. I saw the fight flicker to life in his eyes, and made the prudent choice to sit on his chest for a while. That knocked the air out of him altogether, and all he could concentrate on was the effort to breathe. I *am* rather large.

'Tell me,' I purred. 'Why did you betray our people to the Lokants?'

He tried to speak, but of course he had not breath enough. Reluctantly, I eased the pressure of my weight a little.

'They,' he panted, 'created us.'

'So it has been said,' I agreed. 'And good for them! But that does not answer my question.'

'They *made us*,' Rastivan repeated. 'Without them, none of us would ever have lived at all. Not me, not you.'

'Nor the people you gave into slavery, so that justifies it, does it?' I stuck my claws into his other thigh, motivated more by anger than expedience. I am not proud of it, but I *did* promise Eva to be honest in this account. So I am telling you the unvarnished truth, as they say. Despise me if you will; what do I care?

Rastivan gasped and writhed, but I held him fast. 'They made us,' he said again, shuddering with pain. 'They could unmake us just as easily.'

'Could they? How?'

Rastivan had gone a bit too pale, and I realised that maybe removing his leg had not been the best idea. He was bleeding so much. Oops.

'I do not know!' Rastivan protested. 'But they could. They said they could and I believe them because I… have you not heard? You are an Elder! You must know how they have died around us, picked off one by one, or in groups! They are unstoppable, *she* is unstoppable…' He trailed off into a daze of pain.

'That was not Dwinal,' I told him. 'She did not kill any of those Elders. It was a man called Galywis who did that. Galywis was the leader of the project that resulted in our existence, and he slew his own creations because he was mad.'

But Rastivan shook his head. 'No,' he panted. 'Or if he did, *she* gave him the idea. She told him how, she put him up to it.'

'Why would she do that?'

'She said we are broken and cannot be mended. That we should have been terminated long ago, that something better might have been made.'

It could be the truth. I could picture Dwinal going after Galywis like that. Galywis was old and confused and deeply mad. I could see her needling him about the faults in our species.

Did *you* know that Elders are flawed somewhere inside, that we sometimes go mad? Just like that, without warning? Mad beyond hope, beyond recall? I didn't, not until recently. I like to pretend that I still don't know it. The prospect of my own mind's suddenly flipping inside out at a moment's notice does not add much sunshine to my day.

Was Galywis the type to regret such a flaw? Probably. So says Llandry. She said he was tortured by the errors he made, the imperfection of his work, and the pain suffered by those like me, when that odd little something went wrong and madness was the result.

But did he come up with all of that guilt himself? All of a sudden, so many centuries after the fact? He might have. But somebody else might well have put the ideas into his head, goaded him, blamed him, belittled his work and sent him into a deeper madness. The kind of madness where you think that throwing all your work away is the only sensible thing to do. He killed many of my kind. I was not impressed with him. If Rastivan was right and Dwinal had something to do with that, well… I was just a shade or two less impressed with her, too.

But that said…

'Why would that matter to her?' I repeated. 'If she wanted to make something "better", she could do that without destroying us first.'

Rastivan did not answer, because he had died.

Oops.

So I bound up his ruined leg and revived him. It is a tiring process. I do not like being tired.

My mood, when he returned to life and consciousness, was a bit worse. 'Why does Dwinal care?' I repeated, my teeth an inch from his face. 'Why do you? Why were you helping her?'

'So she wouldn't kill me, too,' he whispered, grey in the face.

Something was off. I looked at him, still all human-shaped in an inert heap beneath me, all the fight gone out of him. And I wondered. A draykon, threatened by another draykon and in grave danger, does not sit meekly in human shape, taking whatever punishment is meted out and making no effort at self-defence.

'Why did you not Change?' I demanded.

'I cannot.'

'You… you what?'

'I cannot!' he spat. 'She took that. Trapped me like this… someday she will… release me.'

I was too filled with horror to speak. 'How?' I roared at him. 'How?!'

'Don't know,' he whispered.

'So you handed sixteen more into her revolting keep?' I was roaring in earnest now, too angry to think clearly. 'How could you?!'

'What else could I do?'

'You should have come to us for help!'

'What can you do?' he smiled faintly, though it was more a grimace of pain. 'She will kill you, too, before long.'

He was about to die again and I had no problem letting him. But before he expired for the second time he said in a hoarse whisper: 'There is something else you should know.'

'*What?*'

'She sent me to find your friends.'

I froze. 'What? When?'

'Today. It was no accident that they found me. I found *them.*' He grimaced. 'I was to ingratiate myself with them, spy on them… if I had known what— what would happen—'

He did not finish the sentence, for life fled and left him an empty husk. I played with that husk for a while, roaring a bit more and getting the cellar very bloody indeed. But at last I managed to recall myself to sanity, and sat a time in thought.

This did not bode well, not well at all. Dwinal had wanted us to encounter Rastivan. Which means she *wanted* us to know about him. She wanted us to know about the others she had taken. She must have known we would take him to pieces and patently did not care, so she was finished with him. Did that mean she was also finished with the sixteen others?

Why had she wanted us to know about any of this? Why had she gone to such lengths to make *sure* that we did?

Eva needed to know about this, and immediately. I surged out of the cellar, filled with an angry energy, bursting to set forth and make things right *at once*.

It was only once I reached the hallway that I realised I had no way to return to Sulayn Phay, no way to reach Eva or any of the others, and no way to communicate with them either.

ORI

The Sixteen

Let me tell you about the draykoni captives. (Eva did float the notion of my sharing the narrative with Gio but he developed an acute case of stage fright on the spot, and declined with the fervour of a man refusing an invitation to, say, jump off a cliff or be eaten alive by a pack of worvilloes. So it will be just me).

So Eva vanished, carting Nyden and his prey (otherwise known as Rastivan) off to Somewhere Else so he could dine in peace. Gio went with them. I asked him later why he did that, for Eva did not require the assistance. He said he was worried about leaving her alone with a ruthless traitor like Rastivan and a madman like Ny. I mean, Ny is a good man but he did seem rather out of his mind just then, so I couldn't altogether argue with the logic of that. See why I love Gio? He has such a kind heart.

Once they had gone, that left me with Tren, Adonia and Avane at hand but with no obvious course of action to take. We had not been sitting long with Rastivan, when Eva found us. Conversation had been halting and tentative, because we were afraid of scaring him away. Looking back, though, I am not sure why we were. We should have let Nyden go to work on him there and then.

Anyway, Rastivan had not told us where the draykoni captives were being kept. Perhaps he would have, if we'd had more time, but we were not too worried. Either Nyden or Eva would get that information out of him soon enough.

As it happened, we did not have to wait for that occurrence. Five minutes later, when we were in the midst of a friendly argument as to what to do next (wait for Eva and Gio right there, or take ourselves off in favour of some more productive pursuit?), there came a knock at the door.

I opened it to find a young-looking Lokant woman on the other side. She looked nervous.

'May I come in?' she whispered, and glanced about as if unwilling to be seen standing just there.

'Why, of course,' I said with as much gallantry as I could muster, and opened the door wider. Perhaps it was foolish, for I had never seen her before. But she was patently afraid and I could not leave her standing there.

She scuttled inside like a wole whisking out of the rain, and stood staring at my companions with obvious trepidation. 'I am sorry to interrupt,' she whispered, and I marvelled at this miraculous thing, a tentative, polite Lokant with exquisite manners. 'I heard that you were looking for… information.'

Now, this was more than possible. We had spent many days up there, quietly but persistently poking our noses into everything, peeking around all the doors (as far as we could), asking questions, and generally making nuisances of ourselves in the most unassuming way we could manage. It was a fine balance to strike: making enough noise to attract the notice of helpful souls like this lady, but without drawing too much attention from people such as, say, Dwinal, who might like to take our faces off for it.

Success! And finally! For I cannot say we had achieved much by it before. 'What kind of information?' said Tren, with one of those reassuring smiles I am a little envious of. I swear, the man could put anyone at their ease in seconds flat, no question.

'Don't be afraid,' added Avane in her soft way. 'You are doing the right thing, and all will be well.'

Tren's smile and Avane's reassurance worked on the girl, for she smiled back and said: 'About… about the draykoni?'

That electrified everybody at once. I practically had to hold Adonia down; her enthusiasm was such that she looked ready to pummel the information out of the poor girl. 'Where are they?' she all but bellowed.

The girl, whose name turned out to be Unaris by the way, shrank back from Adonia and took cover nearer to Tren. 'I am one of those charged with caring for them,' she admitted, her chin drooping in shame. 'I am… I am a Maeval, you see. Dwinal is my several-times-great aunt. It is hard to deny her anything, but those poor creatures… will you save them? I can show you where they are kept.'

Now, if Eva was present this display of sweet, tender consideration and down-trodden mistreatment would have had her hackles up in an instant. She would have narrowed her eyes, looked Unaris Maeval over like she was three months out of fashion, and *up* would have gone those eyebrows.

Truthfully I experienced a few of those feelings myself, for how pretty and perfect a picture did she make! And how conveniently timed! For all our attempts at finding just such an informant, we had consistently failed — until that day, when both Rastivan and Unaris had suddenly fallen into our nets.

I had my suspicions. But what to do? Dismiss her? She might be telling the pure truth. Even if it was some kind of trick or trap, she might still have real information for us, and that we desperately needed.

'Show us,' I said.

'We'll help them,' added Tren, with another of those smiles, and I swear I saw her fall in love with him on the spot.

'Come with me,' she whispered.

We ended up a long way from Eva's suite. I cannot rightly say where, for after a certain number of identical, winding corridors I tend to lose track. Unaris led us to a door so plain, one would naturally assume it led only into somebody's frightfully dull office or something.

But then she opened it, and of course there was a large hall on the other side, and *dull* it really was not.

'Oh,' breathed Avane, and went inside at once. I tried, belatedly, to grab her, to point out that checking for dangers, threats, traps et cetera might be a wise start, but she was gone. Honestly. I *adore* Avane for that beautiful tender heart of hers, but sometimes she can be such a twit.

Thankfully, nothing sprang out to eat her alive. She crossed the wide hall apparently unscathed as the rest of us poured in behind her, and went at once to the prone figure of a bound, captive draykon resting in a lifeless heap on the far side. Almost lifeless. I could feel the *amasku* whirling around that place, bleeding out of the two prone draykoni in a ceaseless trickle, every wisp of it caught up and drained off. Another lay on the other side of the chamber, slumped against the plain white wall, as helpless and inert as the first.

What was to be done? We had no Nyden, because he was busy tearing strips off Rastivan. We had no transport, because Eva and Gio had gone with Ny. What we had was two hereditary draykoni, one sorcerer and a secretary.

Nowhere near sufficient for the demands of the situation.

'Tricky,' I muttered, eyeing the nearest captive in despair. It's a fiendish little binding they put on those poor souls, horribly hard to unravel without causing intolerable pain and possibly lasting harm to the drayk.

Of course, we also had a crowd of students… poorly trained ones as yet, but not necessarily useless for all that. And…

…and Ylona. Why didn't I think of her before? If she wanted us to help her, let her help us, too.

'I'll be back!' I cried, and did not wait for anybody to object. I was out the door in moments and barrelling down the corridor. In my enthusiasm and urgency I forgot to pay attention to where I was going, or to make note of how to get back to the hallway again. Eva would say I am terribly absent-minded about such things, and she would not be wrong.

Fortunately Unaris came after me. 'Wait!' she called. 'Where are you going?'

I slowed and waited for her to catch up. 'I need to talk to Ylona. We will need help extricating those two draykoni, and there is no one else to ask just now.' It *then* occurred to me that I had no idea where to look for Ylona, either, and I sighed. I really am absent-minded. 'Er, you don't happen to know where to find her, do you?'

Largely, Unaris did, and when she didn't, she papered over the gap by the simple expedient of asking directions. Asking directions! I get so used to sneaking around that I forget about the more direct approach.

We ended up outside of a featureless grey door that looked exactly the same as all the rest. Seriously, they do not go in for creative decorating out there. I knocked.

'Thank you,' I told Unaris. 'You don't need to stay, if you would rather be elsewhere.'

She gave me a single nod and hastened away, for which I did not at all blame her. It wouldn't do for a Maeval to be seen actually going into Ylona's rooms; she had risked enough by openly asking where to find her.

The door opened, and there she was.

'Hello, Heli,' I said.

She grinned. 'Mr. Vance! To what do I owe the pleasure?'

'Dire emergency.'

'Oh. In *that* case, why don't you come in and tell me all about it?'

It took me only half an hour or so — it might have been a little more — to wear down her reticence, paranoia, suspicion and reserve until she was prepared to offer us assistance. Another half-hour after that, or thereabouts, to bumble my way back to the room which housed the draykoni, Ylona striding along in my wake. She had camouflaged her face, I think, for nobody paid her any attention.

She was intrigued by the matter of the captives, and I think it was this that encouraged her to help us, more than any sense of responsibility. Either way, she was efficient. She took one long look at each of the two bound draykoni, and snapped into action at once.

'It's a circuit,' she told us, darting about the room. Those energy collectors were stationed all around; she went from one to the next to the next, tinkering with them, adjusting things, frowning in concentration and rambling as she worked. 'They both drain and power each other — mutually dependent — *quite* clever really, and hard to disrupt, for they adjust for interference and cover for each other… ah, there we go.' A harsh pulse of energy pounded through the room, the walls shook, half the energy collectors went dull and silent all at once, and one of the draykoni — a copper-coloured male — slumped to the floor.

'And there!' she said next, and it happened again. When she was finished, all the devices were dead-looking and quiet, and both the draykoni were free.

'Good,' I muttered, pleased but stymied. Their bindings might be dissolved, but how were we going to get them out of there? They were both unconscious and both enormous. Dead weight. They patently couldn't walk far.

Happily, Gio chose that moment to appear.

'How did you find us?' I asked, after I'd had a moment to finish feeling delighted to see him and remember the practicalities of the situation.

'Hyarn.'

'Wha... Dwinal's Hyarn?'

'He isn't Dwinal's anything, apparently.'

Well, that explained the convenience of Unaris's appearance. 'We need to get these back to the Seven,' I said tersely to Gio. 'I'm so glad you're here.'

Gio looked at the copper creature, a gigantic beast, and then at the slightly (but only slightly) smaller sea-green female. 'Impossible. I can't carry those so far.'

'Nindrinat—'

'I had Eva's help and it still almost broke us.' He looked around. 'Ylona?' he called.

Ylona immediately developed the chagrined look of a woman realising she ought to have beat a hasty retreat at least two minutes ago. 'Under no circumstances!' she proclaimed. 'Those creatures are enormous!'

'Then we need more help.' Gio was unflappable, inflexible and rather imposing, and I felt inordinately proud of him.

Ylona sighed deeply, muttered something unflattering about Gio's parentage (not altogether unfair, considering his ancestry), and capitulated. 'Moment,' she said, and disappeared.

She returned soon afterwards with two other Lokants, neither of whom I recognised. They were a bundle of efficiency between them, for the four had the copper drayk out of there within five minutes. The green-scaled female soon followed, and Ylona and team reappeared, panting for breath and weary but sound enough.

But Gio was still absent. 'Where—' I began.

'Coming,' Ylona answered shortly. 'He ran into a friend.'

That mystified me, but not for long. Gio reappeared a couple of minutes later, with Nyden. Drayk-shaped Nyden, dragging along with him a few objects which looked worryingly like bleeding body-parts. 'Found Nyden,' said Gio unnecessarily.

'Where…?'

'HQ. We left the other two there for now. Made them as

comfortable as possible. Best we can do for the present.'

'Mm.' I could not take my eyes off Nyden, who had an arm hanging out of his mouth and a couple of chunks of leg tucked under one great foreleg. 'Those aren't…?'

'Rastivan, I imagine,' said Gio, sparing a brief, expressionless glance at Nyden's horrific trophies.

'Oh.' I swallowed. If I admit to experiencing a surge of nausea, shall you think less of me? I do not deal *especially* well with the bloodier aspects of our adventures. And while I am more than aware of the capability for violence that I possess in my more ferocious aspect, I have indulged in it only at dire need. Nyden's way of revelling in it positively turned my stomach.

'Did he… did he *quite* deserve that?' I enquired of Nyden.

Ny cast me a withering look, his jaws tightening on the severed arm. *Yes,* he said in my mind.

Right, then.

'Eva wants a report,' Gio said, happily diverting my attention from the macabre spectacle Nyden made.

'Where is she?'

'Plaguing Hyarn. She's hoping he can find out where the island's got to.'

My befuddlement must have shown on my face, for Gio blinked, thought, and said: 'Oh, yes. I suppose you haven't heard about that yet.'

'The island?' I repeated. 'You don't mean Orlind…?'

'Vanished,' he confirmed. 'Whisked away into the night. Has to be Grandmother, of course. Eva thinks she is trying to build a new Library on it.'

It took me a couple of minutes to wring a more coherent version of events out of Gio. I was joined by Tren, who was as appalled by the news as I, but who took it rather better in stride. 'Tricky folk,' he murmured when Gio had finished. 'I think we ought to have seen that one coming, though.'

He was right: we should have anticipated something of that kind. Of *course* Dwinal wanted to build a new Library. Of *course* that's what she had meant all along, with her talk of a "new establishment." And if she was going to start a new Library, why wouldn't she aim for the very top?

Pinching the actual, physical island upon which the *old* best-ever-Library had been built was unexpected, and I don't think any of us imagined that might be possible. But no matter. All we had to do was find it and go steal it back. Simple, right?

'I had better go with you,' I said to Gio.

'Me, too,' said Tren.

Nyden spat out the arm. 'That one is for here,' he muttered.

Poor Avane stared at him, the look of utter horror on her face probably reflective of mine. 'Nyden,' she whispered. 'What are you doing?'

'Scattering the traitor.'

'What?'

'Scattering the traitor's bones. Then he can never be revived.'

Avane approached, and laid a gentle hand on Nyden's flank. 'Ny. I think you need to put all of those… things… down.'

'I am putting them down. One piece at a time.'

Avane swallowed, and backed away again.

Nyden snarled, transferred one of the legs to his jaws, and chewed off a piece.

Right, then.

'Shall we go?' I said to Gio.

'Please,' said Tren fervently.

We went… but not alone. 'I need to see Eva,' Nyden announced. 'I have important information.'

Even cool, impassive Gio winced. 'Is it really that impor—'

'Yes.'

'Maybe you could leave the parts behind—'

'No.'

Gio got a grip, folded his arms, and said sternly: 'At least shift your shape. I am not at all interested in dragging you around unless you're more portable.'

Nyden's black eyes narrowed, but he heaved a sigh and Changed human. He was still rolling his eyes when his form solidified. 'Fine,' he said, and walked towards us.

To my dismay, he retained his grip on the bits of Rastivan's legs.

Gio rolled his eyes, too, but he made no further attempts to reason with Nyden. 'We're going,' he announced.

And away we went.

EVA

The Island

I had an hour or two of blissful peace, during which I consulted quite productively with Hyarn as to plausible locations for the stolen Island of Orlind.

We were on the verge of drawing one or two useful conclusions when all that lovely peace was shattered by the arrival of some of my dearest loves.

Tren I greeted with unalloyed delight. Everything is better when he is around, literally every single thing in life. He greeted me with a joy to equal my own, and that was lovely, and how wonderful and beautiful and there was Ori, too, with Gio, all of them positively bursting with news (good news, I hoped).

And there was… Nyden. Dishevelled, clothes torn, hair askew, and incomprehensibly clutching a pair of bleeding stumps under one arm. His pockets bulged with further, deeply unpromising burdens.

I surveyed all this with sky-high brows, and looked helplessly at Gio. 'Why?' was all I could find to say.

Gio glanced at Nyden, and gave a vaguely apologetic shrug. 'He insisted.'

'Eva!' said Nyden importantly. 'It's a trap!'

'Another one?' said I, as placidly as I could manage. 'Do elaborate.'

'Isn't everything a trap?' muttered Tren, and I could not

disagree with him.

'Rastivan. He found us deliberately. Dwinal told him to.'

This was not the good news I'd been hoping for. 'Tell me everything,' I ordered.

He did, and the emerging picture was every bit as unpromising as I was hoping it wouldn't be. 'Any idea why…?' I tried, without much hope. 'Why would she want us to know about the captives? Why hand over Rastivan? How did she manage to retract his ability to Change?'

'No idea,' said Nyden, and I sighed.

'Rastivan said nothing else useful, I take it?'

Nyden looked shifty. 'No.'

'Can we talk to him again?'

Nyden would not meet my gaze. 'Erm…'

I looked again at the sundry severed parts in his collection, and felt a headache coming on. 'I see.'

Making no reply, Nyden devoted himself to tucking a thigh bone out of sight beneath one of the tables.

Tren sighed. 'He is scattering the pieces,' he told me in a low voice. 'You know, so nobody can revive the man again someday.'

'Of all things, the most helpful,' I observed.

'Oh, quite.'

I raised my voice. 'Nyden. We are going to need those parts back.'

That won me a fine show of outrage. 'He is a *traitor*,' Nyden snarled.

'I realise.'

'But—'

'Tough. We need him.'

Ny became sulky. 'You don't need him. He told me everything he knows.'

'Even if that proves to be true, you have gone too far. *Too far, Nyden!* This is cruelty beyond justification.' I felt a stab of guilt that I had left Ny alone with Rastivan, knowing that he would inflict a harsh fate upon the betrayer. There was harsh, and then there was *harsh*.

'I don't know where they all are,' Nyden muttered.

'Better get to work on finding them, then.'

Hyarn gave a slight cough and backed away. Was he trying not to vomit? I couldn't blame him.

'What other news is there?' I said, looking to the others. 'Some good news, please. Please?'

'The best!' said Ori enthusiastically. 'We found the captives.'

'I know. Did you get them out?'

'Yes!'

I brightened up at once. 'All of them? Good. That's such a relief.' I could cross that off my mental list of *things very, badly, deeply urgently to be done.*

'They are both at headquarters,' Gio said. 'Untended for the present, but they're stable.'

'Both?' I echoed, suffering one of those unpleasant sinking feelings you get when the day unravels around you. 'What do you mean, both?'

'Both of them,' Ori said with a tiny frown. 'A male and a female, neither familiar, taken from—'

'Two?' I interrupted. 'Only two? What about the other fourteen?'

My two fine, young gentlemen blinked at me like I was crazy.

'Fourteen?' said Tren. 'There are fourteen more?'

'According to Rastivan.' I raised a brow at Gio. 'Did you not tell them?'

'I didn't think of it. I caught up with them late, we were busy getting the two out — I forgot they wouldn't know.'

I looked accusingly at Hyarn. 'Was it not your duty to accommodate Dwinal's "guests"? Where have you put the rest?'

He looked pale and worried. 'I… thought I was,' he said in a helpless fashion I did not like at all. 'I know nothing of any others.'

The headache grew a little worse. I took a deep breath. 'All right. Two down, fourteen to go. Any idea where the others might be?'

They hadn't, of course, and their source had vanished into the wind. Hyarn continued to deny all knowledge. But Dwinal had made certain we knew about all the others, for some reason of her own. I began to feel that the two Ori and Gio had just rescued had been planted in our way, like bait. A little victory, to buoy us up, keep us focused. Keep us running after the other fourteen.

But was Rastivan even to be trusted? Maybe he had fed us a lie, Dwinal's lie. *Were* there sixteen? Were there any more at all, even? Perhaps there had only ever been three.

No, I doubted that. Dwinal's plans were on such a grand scale, a mere *three* enslaved draykoni could not possibly be enough. Rastivan was probably telling the truth, more or less, about the others. But why had Dwinal fed us that information? What did she expect us to do about it? Something that played into her plans, obviously, but *what*?

We would spare no effort to find the rest and free them, of course. But how could that possibly benefit Dwinal? None of it made any sense and I was driving myself mad trying to figure it out.

I took a few deep breaths. 'Right,' I decided. 'It's no good trying to second-guess Dwinal. We just have to proceed as best we can. Right now, finding the rest of the captives is of paramount importance, whatever the outcome. And finding out what's happened to the missing island is no less vital. Hyarn?'

He nodded, his face still averted from Nyden. 'I've been thinking,' he said. 'I may know where the island is.'

"Where the island is" turned out to be… directly next door. I am not joking.

'Something odd happened earlier today,' Hyarn explained. He then went on to describe what it was, but since it came attendant with a deal of Lokanty jargon we had no hope of understanding, I was not left with much comprehension of what he was talking about.

The gist, though, proved to be as follows:

- You may think it shouldn't be that easy to just walk off with an entire island, but… well, no. You'd be right. It isn't a case of waving a magic wand and tada, a spit of land obligingly toddles off. The *Libraries* are equipped with the means to move around, so therefore: if you want to relocate a piece of land, use a Library.

- The "odd something" Hyarn noticed was the inevitable impact upon a Library like, for example, Sulayn Phay when it has been hitched up to a floating island and is subsequently being used to tow it away somewhere. Islands are heavy.

- This process is slow. Therefore, the island (and the Library) cannot yet have gone far. *Therefore!* Both must still be somewhere in the environs of the coast of Irbel.

This I relayed to Llandry with all possible speed. Good woman! She leapt to the task of discovering its whereabouts.

'We should be able to find it fairly quickly, I hope,' she confided, sounding jauntier than she had the last time we'd spoken. 'We have a lot of people here.'

'Do you?' I said, in some doubt, for though I knew she had collected the entire citizenry of both Nuwelin and Anshalin about her, I also knew that those two villages were not blessed with a bustling population.

'I've mustered Eterna's colony.'

'You've… is that safe?' Eterna is not the worst person I have ever known, but it's safe to say that she is not the easiest person to work with.

'Maybe not,' said Llandry, cheerfully enough. 'But desperate measures.'

'How did you convince her?' She being notoriously difficult to persuade into any course of action she hadn't chosen to embark upon voluntarily.

'You know those sixteen enslaved drayks? About half of them were hers.'

Oh. 'That would do it,' I said.

'Mm. When I told her that the person behind her missing people had just stolen Orlind, she became all kinds of enthusiastic about helping us out. She's rather taken over the operation by now. I hardly have to do anything.'

'Sounds great, until she starts trashing things.'

'When she does, we are ready to intervene.'

I noticed that Llan said *when,* not *if,* and did not feel encouraged by the term. But she was right: desperate measures. And goodness, we could certainly use the manpower.

'Let me know when you find something,' I said. 'Something large, watery and Orlind-shaped, in particular.'

'Will do.'

Good. Excellent. So.

'I've previously wondered,' I said to Hyarn, Tren and Gio, 'why Dwinal was ever bothered about becoming Lokantor here when she does not seem to care for the post. Perhaps this is why, hm?'

Tren looked sceptical. 'So she could use it to steal Orlind?'

'Why not? She's probably been planning this for ages.'

'True. Possible.'

'What I am wondering is,' I continued, with a narrowed-eye look at Hyarn, 'once we find the island, how do we get it back again?'

'Only the Lokantor can move the Library,' Hyarn said, confirming my worst fear in seven brief words.

'Right, then,' said Ori. 'So we locate the island, help Ylona to stage a coup, overthrow Dwinal as Lokantor and install Ylona in her place, have the new Lokantor put Orlind back and… we're done!'

'Find and rescue the other fourteen draykoni,' Tren reminded him.

'Oh yes, and that.'

'And do something about Dwinal,' I added. 'We can take the island and the Library off her, but will that mean she'll meekly go home and never bother us again? I doubt it.'

'That too, then,' said Ori.

'Easy work,' said Tren, cracking his knuckles. 'We'll be home by tea time… in about a year.'

'We will need more help,' I agreed.

'How nice that would be,' said Tren with a wry smile. 'If only there were someone we could ask.'

He and I exchanged identical looks of mingled resignation and chagrin.

'Limbane it is, then,' I said.

Rikbeek found Limbane delicious, it seems, and recognised the name. He stirred awake the moment I spoke those syllables aloud, and began to salivate.

You had better behave, I told him.

Hmph, said Rikbeek.

I reconsidered. *You had better mostly behave.*

I don't think Rikbeek knows how to smile, or he would have done so just then. Broadly.

My meeting with Limbane did not go well.

'*What?*' he snapped.

As I had only proceeded as far as revealing that Dwinal had taken the island, this was not promising.

I explained the rest.

'You,' he said in a fashion disagreeably thunderous, 'were supposed to prevent catastrophe!'

'Oh, was I! I thought I was merely meant to convey information.'

'Did I need to spell it out?' he bellowed. 'Obstruction is your natural talent! Getting in the way is what you do! Yet all this has gone on right over your blessed *heads*!'

Once, I might have been goaded by such unfair accusations, such unflattering reflections upon our characters. I would have become angry myself. Instead, I couldn't be bothered with Limbane's childish anger. In fact, I couldn't be bothered with Limbane.

'These problems must be resolved,' I said calmly. 'Will you help us, or not?'

'I don't see that I have any choice,' said he with (perhaps) pardonable bitterness. 'She cannot be permitted to build any such structure anywhere, but especially upon that island.'

And I realised he was angry because he was worried. Limbane! Afraid! Dwinal may have hatched an absurdly ambitious plan, but she was coming awfully close to pulling it off. And without the approval of the Lokant ruling council. If she succeeded, she would build a Library more than mighty enough to challenge the council for power. Governing bodies don't usually like being overthrown, as a rule, and Limbane would positively despise being rendered irrelevant.

Part of me was tempted to dismiss all of it as mere Lokant politicking and leave the whole mess in Limbane's hands. What did it need to matter to us, provided we got our island back? Let Limbane take care of the rest of Dwinal's plans.

But that would not do. What I'd said before was true: if she wanted the island of Orlind that badly, she would come back for it. And she *did* want it. Where else could she find such a perfect place to host her new "establishment"? A Library populated by Lokants and draykoni alike, mixing and mingling their unique powers, would need the right conditions for both species to thrive. It would need the Library structure itself, and the *amasku* which only Orlind could provide. Without Orlind, Dwinal would simply have to abandon her mission. And that seemed about as likely as the Darklands abandoning the NightCloak.

Could I rely on Limbane to deal with her? To make sure that she was never in a position to come after our worlds again?

Hah. What kind of a fool relies on *Limbane*?

'*Ow*,' said Limbane in sudden annoyance, slapping at his neck. I saw a tiny flash of red: he was, once again, bleeding.

Satisfied? I enquired of Rikbeek.

I received in response a glow of smug contentment, wordless but profound.

Limbane's gaze focused on me and his eyes narrowed. Suspicion.

I mean, whatever else Limbane may be — annoying, aggravating, obnoxious — he is not stupid.

'Carrying any passengers, Lady Glostrum?' he asked of me, in a tone of mild interest. 'Small, swift, *biting* passengers, by any chance?'

I decided it was time to go. 'I will see you at Sulayn Phay,' I told him firmly.

He replied only by way of a sour look and a dismissive wave.

'How did it go?' Tren said a little later.

'Limbane would be delighted to help us. He is on his way at this very moment, bringing all his best and brightest people along.'

'Really…?'

'No.'

'Did he refuse?'

'No. I think he will show up, but I do not know when, or how, or what he plans to do when he gets here. So, I think we are on our own for the present.'

Tren shrugged. 'Not an unfamiliar situation.'

'It's lucky that we are a brilliant bunch, equal to anything.'

'Isn't it, though?'

'So what are we going to do?'

Tren thought deeply for a moment, and then said: 'I have no idea.'

'Me neither.'

'Excellent.'

We were saved by Hyarn, who was rapidly winning his way into my good graces. We had convened at the schoolrooms, noticing in passing that Dan and Tynara were nowhere in evidence. Not a promising sign, that, either. Where were they? What were they doing? We enquired of the students and found that no one had seen or heard from them in a while.

No one had seen or heard from Dwinal in a while, either. Were any of them still in the Library? If not, where were they?

And why (my suspicious mind insisted on asking) had Hyarn

been left behind?

Regardless, Hyarn found us there — and when I say "us" I mean Tren and I, Gio, Ori, Nyden, Avane, Adonia, the students, everybody. He was a little out of breath, as though he had been running, which made no sense considering he merely had to translocate. Perhaps he was breathless with excitement, for he immediately said: 'I think I know what became of the other fourteen.'

We, of course, all leapt upon him at once, eager for more information.

'I have been talking to Dwinal's supporters — the few I could find. I picked up a rumour, a thought. There *were* more draykoni and they were probably housed in the same hall in which you found the other two. But they've been moved out of the Library. It happened not long ago.'

'Where could they possibly…?' I began, but the rest of my question went unspoken, for I knew the answer.

'The island,' said Hyarn. 'It is the only place they could possibly have gone. I believe, in short, that Dwinal and her supporters have simply moved out, and taken the remaining draykoni with them.'

Yes. It made sense. What else would they do, now that they had carried their point of securing the island of Orlind? That would explain the absence of Dan and Tynara, too.

I know I said that all of the students were there in the schoolroom with us but it occurred to me that I was wrong. There weren't enough of them. All right, an oversight on my part, but I had other things on my mind — my first thought wasn't to take a head count.

'Is it me or are we down a few students?' I said aloud.

'Eight,' said Faronni.

I noticed that she looked dismayed. 'What happened?' I asked her.

'Tynara held a series of tests. She said there would be a special reward for those who passed.'

'You did not?' I guessed.

She shook her head. 'All of us here failed.'

Fostiger was one of those absent. The names of the rest, I did not know. 'The ones who passed must have been the most talented, according to Dwinal's definition. Or at least, those best fitting her requirements. They've been taken to the island.'

Faronni nodded. 'I felt like such a failure, but now…'

I mustered for her a reassuring smile. 'I think you received the better outcome.'

All right, so Dwinal had taken the rest of her captives, the best of my students and all her favourite followers and decamped to the island. But now what? She couldn't seriously expect that she would be left in peace to build her new Library undisturbed, stationed as she was right next door to Sulayn Phay, and in the middle of the oceans of the Seven Realms. Did she plan to leave the island right there, not all that far off the coast of Irbel? She must know there would be opposition. Strenuous opposition.

'Is the island still there?' I asked of Hyarn.

'Nearby? Yes, it is still in tow, and we are still in your Cluster.'

I hoped, then, that Llandry would soon find the island. 'Some things aren't making sense,' I said, that headache still beating at my brow. 'She can't just sit there forever. But neither will Sulayn Phay, will it? Just how do your Libraries move from world to world — or Cluster to Cluster?'

'It is hard to explain—'

'I do not need the details. In general terms, please. You do not *sail* from place to place, that cannot possibly be the case.'

'No, no. It is a form of translocation, much the same thing we do individually, only on a grander scale.'

Which was much what I had been thinking, alas. 'So at some point, Sulayn Phay will translocate away from the Seven and off into some other Cluster of worlds?'

'Exactly. It is under the Lokantor's direction.'

'Mhm. And could a Library do that with an island in tow, would you say?'

Hyarn gave me a troubled look, and thought. 'No,' he decided. 'Too much extra weight. Consider how much harder it is for you to translocate when you have passengers to take along. For most, one or two or perhaps three extra people is the most we can manage. This Library is a strong, proud structure, but I do not believe it is robust enough to drag the entire island of Orlind around with it.'

'That is reassuring,' I murmured.

'Is it?' said Tren. 'What if there were two Libraries here? Three? How much extra weight could they carry between them?'

And we all stared at him in utter horror, because he was right. He was *right*. 'She has supporters elsewhere. Other Libraries, other Lokantors. What might she promise them, if they help her to build her new Master Library? All manner of powers and privileges, I am sure.'

'Right,' said Tren grimly. 'So the whole lot of them are sitting out there ready to go, the moment enough additional Libraries arrive here to help her take Orlind away with them.'

'But only Dwinal can order this one to move,' I pointed out. 'She is still Lokantor here. She will have to come back.'

Something in my pocket buzzed, and I jumped and grabbed for it. Llandry's voice box. 'Llan!' I practically yelled. 'Tell me you've found it.'

'We have. It's not far out. Due northeast from its old position. But Eva, it's not alone out there, there's a building stationed right by it — incredible place, vast, all built on its own, separate island. We think it must be—'

'A Library. It's Sulayn Phay, that is where we are. Where are you now?'

'On the coast, as close as we can get to the island without being seen, because it's not empty anymore. There are people there, and they're building, impossibly quickly. I have no idea how they're managing that.'

'New Library,' I sighed. 'Llan, listen.' I told her everything we had learned and all that we had concluded, finishing with: 'If any other Libraries show up you must te—'

I stopped speaking because Llandry had gasped, and I had patently lost her attention for a moment. 'There's a second,' she said. 'Just popped out of thin air, the way you do when you're translocating.'

I may have said a foul word, but it would be unladylike to reproduce it here. I felt briefly frozen with panic. What to do? We were rapidly being outmanoeuvred. If Dwinal managed to get away with the island, we could have no way of following, or of figuring out where she had taken it. Was two Libraries enough? Were they waiting for a third, or a fourth?

What should we do?

'Llan,' I said tersely. 'I think you need to get back to Orlind. Take everybody and get over there. We can't let her take the island out of our Cluster — certainly not without us.'

'Agreed,' said Llandry, but she was doubtful. 'But if it takes us with it, we'll have no way to get back.'

'You will, because we're going to join you. We are on your doorstep, after all. I'm bringing as many Lokants as I can get hold of. Go.'

Llandry made no further objections, and I stuffed the box back into my pocket. I relayed everything Llandry had said, but skipped over my half of the conversation — they had all heard.

'So,' I concluded. 'I need everyone who's willing to go. And Hyarn, we need you to guide us out of this place. If you have anything so convenient or commonplace as a front door, I'd love to know where it is.'

'There is a way out, of course,' he said. 'I will get you there.'

'Great. Volunteers, then?'

Not everyone was willing to go. Most of the students declined, not much to my surprise, but that was well enough. Many of them were incapable of translocating, and those who could do it at all were not yet able to manage the art very well.

Faronni was eager to go, though, which surprised me. I raised an eyebrow.

She hung her head and uttered the word "Fostiger" in an abashed tone.

Ahh. 'We will try to get him out,' I promised her. 'Assuming he wants to be retrieved.'

Tren and Gio and Nyden and Ori and Avane and everyone else were all in favour, naturally, but since only one of them could translocate, I needed to do better. 'Hyarn, who else can you rustle up? There must be more of you who'd rather not see Dwinal crowned queen of all the worlds.'

'I will do what I can,' he promised.

'I hope Limbane shows up soon,' I muttered, for now of all times would be convenient.

'Ylona,' Tren pointed out.

Oh, yes. Ylona! 'You're a genius,' I told him with a kiss.

'I know.'

See, not only would Ylona be able to deliver plenty more translocation-handy Lokants, standing by to pull everybody out of Orlind at need. She was also the person who could stop Dwinal from using Sulayn Phay to steal the island in the first place.

But the conversation did not go quite as I was hoping.

'No,' she said, once I had laid the problem before her.

'No?' I was too shocked to know what else to say. No? What did she mean, just *no?*

'So Dwinal is gone? Good riddance to her!'

'I don't think she will just cede the Library to you,' I pointed out, having recovered my wits. 'Already she plans to use it to carry off Orlind, dragging all of you along with her. And then what? Peace and harmony? Doubtful.'

Ylona's eyes narrowed. 'What do you care for Sulayn Phay? Not one whit, I'd wager.'

'Not even half a whit,' I acknowledged without a blink. 'But I do care for the fate of Orlind. That's our island. I want it back.'

'It wasn't always yours. Where do you think it came from in the first place? Galywis and his disciples dropped the island in your Cluster to begin with. Why shouldn't it be reclaimed now?'

'How do you know that?' I was fascinated by this confirmation of an earlier suspicion, temporarily distracted from my purpose.

'I had productive ancestors.'

Focus, Eva. 'Be that as it may, it cannot be argued that the island is more ours than anyone else's, by this time. It has been part of our Seven Realms for… how many centuries?'

'Can't it?' was all that Ylona said, with an ironic quirk of her lips.

I blinked. 'It is certainly more ours than Dwinal's.'

'That, at least, is perfectly true.'

This acknowledgement did not leave her much moved in our favour. 'Are you not concerned by the prospect of Dwinal's building such a Library?' I tried.

'Not as much as some. So the outcome might be disastrous — the same could be said for virtually every endeavour undertaken throughout history, however grand, however modest. The outcome might also be wonderful. I admit, I would rather see such a construct in other hands than Dwinal's, but just because she builds it does not mean she gets to keep it.'

'I just want our island back,' I said, unwilling to embark upon a long debate about possible consequences. 'And I need you to help us achieve that. Please.'

Ylona looked, at last, a little weakened, but she was not conquered. 'I cannot,' she said simply. 'Whether I will or no.

What you want of me, I imagine, is to block Dwinal from absconding with the island. Is that right?'

'Yes. If she is no longer Lokantor—'

Ylona held up a hand. 'Exactly. Do you think it is so easy, to take over that post? If it was, the role would change hands rather more often, and much more violently. It is possible for a new Lokantor to be appointed in the absence of an old one — Dwinal is not the first person to walk out on the job — but it is a lengthy process. The Lokantor must be absent for an agreed length of time, a challenger must accumulate enough support to justify their claim… I cannot simply usurp Dwinal's post at will. I definitely cannot do so in time to get in the way of her plans out *there.*'

Well, damn.

That neatly scuppered all my hopes. How else could we hope to block Dwinal?

LLANDRY

The Stolen Island

I may be used to writing in my own journal by now, but there is something odd about writing in someone else's. Eva has put her precious book into my hands and asked me to recount what happened when Pense and I and virtually every living draykoni high-tailed it over to the stolen island of Orlind. She was stuck at Sulayn Phay at the time, futilely trying to wear down Ylona, and of course it must fall to someone else to tell this part of the tale. But does she not realise how poor an affair my writing will seem after her elegant, witty prose? I doubt that it entered her head, generous as she is.

No matter. Perhaps nobody cares. All that is important is to make a record of events.

We may have felt some doubts about Eva's order but it came as a relief, having something to do right away. We had been dithering and doubting and arguing amongst ourselves for some time. Everyone agreed that *something must be done,* and that we must not let the island be carried any farther away from us. But the fact that we had entirely lost control of the place escaped nobody. What would come of an invasion, if we were to mount one? Even Eterna hesitated. I think she is more afraid of the likes of Dwinal than she would like to admit.

Eva's revelation that the island stood in immediate danger of being whisked off to the other side of somewhere did not reassure me, but it certainly heightened the urgency of the matter. A decision had to be made; Eva made it; we acted upon it. The prospect of imminent Lokant aid did not hurt.

Away we went. Can I describe how it felt, to fly like that? The air around me was so full of draykoni I could hardly see the sky. We have never come together like that before, never acted in such concert. I suppose it couldn't last.

We left the coast of Irbel behind and flew like the wind, covering the mile or two or three (I do not excel at measuring distances) as fast as we could. Sulayn Phay grew larger in my vision, and what a vision it was. I had never before seen the outside of a Lokant Library. The nature of translocation means that, upon visiting, one is always smartly transported into the middle of the Library, and straight out again the same way. But oh my, they are incredible to behold.

Sulayn Phay was a monolithic structure crouched atop a rocky spit of land just large enough to contain it. How can I describe the Library? My pen feels unworthy to the task. Its sheer size was impressive enough. Accustomed as I am to the glissenwol trees of home and the simple houses and bridges we build up and down their soaring trunks, I struggled to take in the vastness of Phay. It looked like a town all by itself. For all that its interior can sometimes seem stark, even clinical, its exterior was all beauty: spires and turrets and other features I have no words for, all built from smooth white stone (or something like it). The only thing it lacked for was windows, which struck me as odd.

Next to it, our poor beleaguered island looked sadly bare indeed. A rough little piece of land, comparable in size to that which hosted Sulayn Phay (if not a little larger), but otherwise unimpressive. But it was swarming with people, and somehow, building was proceeding apace. Foundations were going up, walls were partially built. What arts were these, that could draw the beginnings of so proud a building out of nothing but the bare earth of Orlind? For so it appeared, as we flew en masse towards Orlind.

The second Library was smaller than Sulayn Phay, which is not saying much. It was still vast and magnificent, composed of near infinite towers reaching like scattered fingers into the sky. Were the two of them powerful enough together to carry away Orlind? They could be. They looked it.

We flew faster.

What do we do, when we reach Orlind? That was Meriall's voice in my mind, and unfortunately she echoed the same question I was turning over myself.

Pense? I asked privately, a little desperate. Eva had issued her orders with her usual crisp, brisk confidence, the kind that sends lesser beings scurrying to obey without question. But now I wished I *had* questioned, because here we were hurtling towards the island with no notion whatsoever of what to do when we got there. No way to predict how our arrival might be greeted, either. How far behind us would Eva's Lokant reinforcements be?

I do not like the look of it, Pense said, as grim as I had ever heard him.

Well, no. That went without saying.

We braced ourselves as we neared the familiar, ragged coast of our island, awaiting… something. Some manner of response, possibly hostile; and who would blame them, if it was? What would *you* do, if you looked up to see a horde of angry-looking draykoni bearing down upon you? We were fully prepared to encounter resistance of the most forceful variety.

But none came. We were spotted; people looked up, shouted things to each other, pointed at us. But they went on working. Nobody seemed concerned by our rapid approach, not even a little.

I do not like the look of it either, I said to Pense, and to Meri I said: *I don't know, Meri. See what happens.*

It may sound odd, that I would have been less troubled by a violent objection to our appearance than I was by its absence. But it made my skin creep, for it proved that they did not in the least bit fear us. Not even in all our numbers, and all our indignation at their having *stolen our home.*

There are draykoni down there! It was Larion who announced the discovery, and he was far enough off that I couldn't see him. Somewhere to my right. I veered that way, Pense at my side.

Soon enough, I saw what he meant. Gathered in a knot on the eastern edge of poor Orlind huddled a number of drayks, perhaps ten (I thought), or twelve. I now know, of course, that there were fourteen — the fourteen missing draykoni Rastivan had spoken of, and which had vanished from Sulayn Phay right under Eva's nose.

They were clearly in distress. Not because they were fighting or screaming or anything like that, but because they were too quiet, too still. We dove as one, every one of us who had seen them, and as we came in to land around them we felt it: a sickening *pull* about the energy of the place, that beloved, beleaguered *amasku* we had poured so much time and effort into mending. It was not corrupted again, not quite, but its patterns were not as they should have been. Somehow, it had been co-opted into serving as a binding force; not a life-force anymore, but a prison.

That put paid to the theory that Lokants didn't understand the *amasku* all that well. They may not be able to experience it the same way we do, and their comprehension may not run as deep, but that day proved that they can manipulate it in ways we have never even thought of.

What's more, the heart's energy of each draykon there was depleted. Like the waning light of a dying sun, it pulsed feebly through them, in danger of going out at any moment. They had been sucked virtually dry.

I paused only to note that there were no Lokants nearby — odd, I know, but I did not consider the peculiarity of it just then — and Changed human in an instant. I dragged out my voice box and, hands trembling so much I almost dropped it, I hastened to get hold of Eva.

To my relief, she answered almost at once.

'Llan?'

'They're here. Eva, the missing fourteen are here, and it's bad. They'll die soon if we don't release them but I don't know *how* because it's like… it's like the entire island's been turned into an energy collector. I don't…'

And I almost dropped the box again, because I suddenly realised why nobody was concerned by our appearance in numbers that should have been daunting. Why the incumbent Lokants' reaction to our bearing down upon them, en masse, was merely to note the fact and carry on building.

'Llan?!' Eva was shouting. 'What's the matter?'

'They're bait,' I whispered. 'Rastivan was planted in your way because this whole thing was *bait.* Eva, we were meant to leave the island, so they could move in on it — but then we were meant to come flooding *back*. Orlind is functioning as an energy collector and here *we* obligingly come, a hundred drayks all ready to be drained. They're using these fourteen to power the building and now we've given them a hundred more…'

There was an awful silence for several seconds, and then Eva began to curse. 'Get out of there,' she said, frantic. 'I should have realised — it's my fault — *go*, Llandry.'

'But the island—'

'Forget the island! GO!'

It was too late, of course. Once we had so obligingly flown into their trap, were they likely to let us turn around and fly away again?

I did not even have time to warn the others, could not even close off the voice-box before the trap sprung around us. *Amasku* encircled me like a vice, no longer the friendly, rejuvenating life's energy it ought to be but a net to bind me tight, winding me up in its coils with suffocating force. I could not move, could barely breathe, and I felt a spreading weakness in my limbs that slowed my heartbeat to almost nothing.

I did not notice myself sink to the floor, did not see my friends and family felled like a forest of saplings around me. I could see nothing, sense nothing; there was only the *amasku* and a creeping lassitude that soon carried my consciousness away.

EVASTANY

On the Small Matter of a Total Disaster

Do not try too hard to imagine my dismay, my fear and my self-reproach after that desperate call of Llandry's. Believe me, you cannot curse me more brutally than I cursed myself. How could I fail to see that coming? I, who knew full well that there is a clear, cold reason behind everything a Lokant does? Who knew that Dwinal must have some scheme in mind, who even knew that Rastivan had been sent to us on purpose!

Abruptly, everything was horribly clear. Llan was right. Dwinal had thrown a mystery paired with an emergency in our path, and everyone had gone running to deal with it — leaving Orlind conveniently empty, unguarded. She and all her people had quietly moved in and taken it over, while *we* and the draykoni were running merrily around in their wake, blind and foolish, too late and too stupid to do anything meaningful to oppose them.

Then she had waved the prospect of the missing fourteen under our noses and we had bitten — again. She had made a few flashy, carefully calculated gestures: moving the island a ways out, so we could see what was happening, so we could take fright at the prospect of its imminent disappearance out of our Cluster altogether. Making sure that a second Library made itself nice and visible in plenty of time to attract our attention, so that we could helpfully panic about it.

Then put the missing fourteen somewhere suitably obvious, so that the enraged draykoni would see them the moment they went flying back in to reclaim their home.

Dwinal is nothing if not efficient. If all she'd wanted was to steal Orlind, the island would be long gone by now. She would have lured out the draykoni, moved her helper Libraries in and whisked the island away, and that would have been that. We would have been left standing, helpless to intervene, powerless to follow.

Everything she had done had been designed to manipulate the displaced draykoni of Orlind, probably with the full realisation that they, once properly motivated, would mount an attempt to win back the island — and bring plenty more draykoni along.

Ylona and Tren stood by in wide-eyed silence as I cursed and cursed, the voice-box trembling in my shaking hands. Tren wisely retrieved it from me after a little while and tucked it into his own pocket, then took both of my hands in a stabilising grip. 'Eva. Calm, love, and tell us what's happened.'

I told them. They were not much better pleased than I was, though at least they refrained from employing the kind of foul language to which I had resorted.

'Hyarn,' I spat, moved to consider another possibility. 'Without his interference, we would have behaved differently, wouldn't we? He's a traitor too, a lying, manipulating—'

'He is my brother,' said Ylona coldly. 'And he is no traitor. At least, not to you. He was planted with Dwinal all along, charged with espionage. Sabotage, if he could manage it. He grew tired of the assignment at last, but he performed his role well.'

Another twist in this vilely complicated tale, another truth I had failed to grasp until I was bludgeoned over the head with it. I could almost have wept. 'Is that why he killed Galywis? To win trust? Was it a test she set him?'

'In part. It was not a duty he relished, but needs must.'

Oh, tangled webs. How did I become so wound up in them? How could I still be so blind that I couldn't see more than a foot in front of my own face, no matter how hard I tried?

Well, a more unproductive line of thought would be difficult to imagine. I put my self-reproach aside for a while — there would be more than enough time to wallow in my own failures later — and turned to Tren.

'We have to fix this,' I said.

'Immediately,' he agreed.

I looked at Ylona. 'Do you think your brother could talk you into assisting us?'

She looked back at me, and then at Tren. A tremor of some unnameable emotion crossed her face, and then she dropped her face into her hands and made what sounded like a growling noise. Frustration, I think. 'No,' she said upon a long sigh. 'I suppose I cannot let Dwinal destroy the entire extant population of draykoni just for the sake of a new Library.'

The phrasing struck me as odd, and I had to wonder what, in Ylona's mind, *would* be worth decimating the draykoni for. That is an implication she probably did not mean to make.

Probably.

She produced the kind of superior voice-box Limbane is sometimes seen to wave around and spoke terse words into it. Hyarn appeared moments later, looking stricken.

'I had no—'

'No time,' said Ylona, ruthlessly cutting him off. 'Take some flyers, as many people as you can gather, and these two —' (this last said with the kind of look at Tren and me that said *please get these idiots out of my hair*) — 'and head out the north door. Dwinal's gambled a lot on the timing of this thing and she's about to lose. She'll need a third Library to move that island and it's not here. We've got time—'

'It's here,' interrupted Hyarn.

Ylona gave him a flat stare. 'Then what are you waiting for?'

Hyarn left, dragging me and Tren with him. What Ylona planned to do I was left to imagine.

The next few minutes passed by in a blur. We charged through Sulayn Phay in Hyarn's wake, periodically translocated hither and thither. All the while he had a voice-box in hand which he talked into as he walked, and it seemed like more Lokants joined us with every few paces that he took.

What Ylona referred to as "flyers" turned out to be some of those flying machines I once saw during our battle for Orlind, when Krays was still alive. Those were Irbellian inventions, and as marvellous as they were, the Lokant variety naturally left them in the dust. Sleek, smooth, fearsome-looking machines, these.

We were piled into one with Hyarn and a few others, then the machine hummed with building power and made ready to rise.

'Wait!' I yelled over the noise of the engines. 'Where's Nyden? We need Ny!'

'Why?' bawled Hyarn.

'He's the only Elder we have left! If there's any chance of breaking the lock on the island—'

'It would be the heights of foolishness to take another draykon to that place! We'll have to disrupt it from Dwinal's end.'

He was right, but somehow I fretted over it. I ought to be glad that Avane and Nyden had escaped the fate of the rest of our friends, safely at Sulayn Phay as they were.

...although that was rather a point. Where were they? I didn't recall seeing either of them in a while. Were they all right? Had they ended up at Orlind, after all?

I had no time to think about it, or to argue further. The flyer rose up into the air and sped towards the island at a pace that sent my hair streaming back in the wind, made my eyes sting. All around us more flyers were taking off, filling the chill air with a low, fierce thrumming of noise and machine-power. I saw the third Library that Hyarn had described: bigger than either of the others and awash with colour, what a glory. I could have stared at it forever, and spared a moment's bitter regret that I saw such wonders only under the kind of urgent conditions that gave me no time to appreciate them.

And I regretted — I regret — that such marvels are built and owned and led by people like Dwinal. How odd, that such beautiful, fantastic creations should be the product of such rotten souls.

We reached the island faster than I would have believed possible, and the flyers landed on the southern shore. Lokants streamed out and headed en masse towards the new Library, its as-yet modest walls gleaming white in the distance. Ylona's people, and Hyarn's, ready at last to oppose Dwinal directly; ready to make it war.

I turned my back on it all. Lokant clashes were emphatically not our business, and we could do nothing to help there. I lost sight of Hyarn almost at once.

'We need to find Llandry,' I said, and pointed. I'd kept my eyes open while we were flying towards the island, and I'd seen a glimmer of massed colour north-eastwards: a small sea of felled draykoni, or so I hoped.

'Go,' said Tren. 'I'm with you.'

We went.

YLONA

That Bitch They Call Dwinal

Let me begin by saying that this is ridiculous.

I do not keep diaries. I keep journals — the *scientific* kind, full of data and observation. This habit of recording one's escapades is ridiculous, for who could possibly care? And the language! The style! To call it merely *popular* would be an act of generosity.

But I owe a small debt to Lady Glostrum and Mr. Warvel, much as I hate to admit it. Dwinal had become a plague on our society, and the tentative efforts of the likes of Limbane and his ilk did little to combat her worst excesses. Nor could I do much better. Hamstrung by the Council as I was, I had to obey its strictures to a certain degree, or how could I claim to be any better than Dwinal? How could I propose myself as a worthier leader? Oh, the frustration of mounting such a feeble opposition! Mere political manoeuvring! How ineffectual against such a woman!

No such constraints bound the actions of Lady Glostrum, Mr. Warvel and their various friends. *I* could not simply have the woman taken out and shot, and neither could Limbane. But the people of the Seven Realms, as they call it, are not part of our world. They are not bound by our rules. And since they are able to take rather more direct action against such poisonous types as Dwinal — and indeed, *did* — I feel it incumbent upon me to play their games if I must, and contribute my mite to the melodramatic excesses of this idiotic account.

I do so secure in the knowledge that my own kind will never, ever read it.

I sent away my brother, and dismissed her ladyship and her fiancé along with him. What did I need the two of them for? They could not help me; they would only get in my way. Let them complicate Hyarn's day instead. Who knew? Once conveyed to Orlind, they might find a way to be useful after all.

My errand was different, and particular. See, Dwinal might have been making herself scarce but I knew she would have to show herself sooner or later. Only the Lokantor of Sulayn Phay could issue the order to translocate. Nobody else could ever have the authority. You may be wondering how this can be the case; I understand from Lady Glostrum that much has been said about Lokant affairs in this and other accounts, and you are likely to be aware just how much delight we take in interfering in each other's business. (Whether or not she had any right to detail such matters and make them publically accessible is a matter I shall investigate another time.)

If we can break into each other's quarters, no matter what measures are taken to keep us out; infiltrate each other's Libraries, whatever the fiendish complexity of the relevant security systems may be; how is it that I could not find a way to take over the leadership of Sulayn Phay, at least for a while?

Well, I am not going to describe the obstacles in detail, for it is none of your business. But I will tell you this much: the Lokantorship of a Great Library is bound into the blood. It is biologically determined. In order to take over Dwinal's duties, I would have to have *become* Dwinal — usurped her blood and flesh, made myself identical to her.

I may as well hint that even that is not, perhaps, entirely beyond me. But it would take an inordinate amount of time to pull it off, and time I did not have.

Instead, I lay in wait. There was no real need to overthrow her entirely, not right away. I merely needed to prevent her from issuing the order to translocate. As clever as she is, she is still a creature of flesh and blood herself. She is still fragile. She can be hurt.

And she can be tricked. Her ego is both her blessing and her downfall, for while it drives her on to greater and greater heights of achievement, it also blinds her.

I have spent a great deal of time studying the oddity that is Dwinal. I flatter myself that I understand her better than anyone.

At the heart of each Library, there is a hidden room wherein the controls reside. Once Dwinal's third Library was in place and ready to go, she would come back to Sulayn Phay. She would come back to that very room, and issue the command to depart.

So I broke in. That may sound impressive, but the security was not especially fiendish. Why should it be? Only one person can make any use of the room anyway.

I hastened to station myself there, for she would turn up at any moment. She must. By my brother's account, she had two Libraries out there besides my own, beloved Phay. Three was almost certainly enough. Her gamble had almost succeeded, but could still fail; she would not wish to delay.

Nor did she. I had barely settled myself in her beautiful, plush chair before a faint *whisp* of air near my ear announced the presence of a recently translocated person.

'Hello, Dwinal.' I said it with my most charming smile.

She looked dishevelled, which is not unusual for her. Some rely on a carefully cultivated appearance to impress; clothes chosen to impart the desired impressions, fastidious grooming to create a sense of efficiency. Dwinal relied on personality alone, and why not? She could get away with it. She wears black for the most part, but not because she wants to appear intimidating. It is because black is the most practical of colours, and if she always wears the same shade, she never has to waste any time thinking about her clothes. Her hair is her one vanity, for she wears it very long, albeit tied back in a hasty tail.

She is nothing if not focused.

So she appeared on that day, unchanged and unalterable, save that the shadows had deepened under her eyes. Always a mess of wrinkles, her face that day looked like a crumpled paper bag. Would it be ungenerous of me, rather younger as I am, to say that she looked every one of her advanced years?

It would be highly ungenerous, but I am unrepentant.

'Good morning,' said Dwinal, as though we had encountered one another in the corridor, or at a restaurant. That is another of her affectations: the appearance of always *knowing*, of being surprised by nothing. Unflappable calm. Unshakeable imperturbability. And it works, curse it, for study her though I might I have never learned to tell when she is genuinely forewarned and forearmed, or when she is only faking it.

Oh well, two can play at that game. I tried to look as though her total lack of surprise was of no surprise whatsoever to *me,* for her cool unconcern rattled me, and I would not have had her know it. 'I have come to get in your way,' I offered.

'Yes,' said Dwinal.

That was it, just "yes". I suppressed the frown of annoyance that threatened to burden my brow, and tried again. 'It is a poor scheme, you know. The costs are far too high. It will never answer.'

'Answer what?'

'The Council will never permit it. A new Master Library? The project must be theirs or no one's, preferably the latter. You have already made enemies among them.'

This was a salient argument. Believe me, the Council are full of ways to make one's life difficult, if they so choose. They can and will be ruthless about it, at need. But in answer Dwinal merely smiled, with a faint, mocking tilt to her lips that I found troubling.

I made a note to talk to Limbane, for unless I miss my guess, Dwinal was secure in the knowledge that somebody on the Council was safely in her pocket. Perhaps more than one somebody.

This boded worse and worse. 'It is too bad, using the draykoni as fodder,' I tried. 'They are creatures of infinite value, unique, powerful beyond reason. Does it not strike you as sadly limited, to use them as a mere source of power?'

'They are flawed. They will be improved.'

'How?'

Dwinal looked at me, impassive. I could not tell what she was thinking. 'Why do you ask, when you can only oppose me?'

I rolled my eyes. 'What else can I do, when at every turn you have opposed *me*? If I knew what you were about, perhaps I would feel differently.'

She was silent for a time, considering. Then she said: 'The Draykoni Project had great potential, but was poorly executed. Its earliest products are fatally flawed, and cannot be mended. They are best eliminated. But remarkably, those flaws breed out over time. Think of it! A product which self-corrects! A creation which can breed with other races, and not only will it maintain reasonably full use of its own powers, it will absorb others into its own system, adapt itself into something new. Something more, with all the strengths of both races and none of their weaknesses. Have you met my students?'

This question caught me off guard, appearing as a swift apropos-of-nothing change of subject at the end there. I nodded cautiously. 'Some of them.'

'Some of them are as nothing,' she said, contemptuous. 'But some of them… they could change everything. They *will* change everything. They will be greater by far than the sum of their parts. Greater than the draykoni, flawed and weakened and limited as they are. Greater than our kind. And the Library that can house and support and produce such a creation must be great, too — *truly* great. Truly a Master. The Council, blind and hidebound, will never see its potential.'

My mind raced with speculation. Eliminated? She did, then, mean to use up and discard those eldest of the draykoni race, the ones she considered irretrievably flawed. But the others were destined for a different purpose. What use would she make of them? She would use them as teachers, perhaps — she was already doing so. Tutors to coax the best from her precious students.

And what else? Her talk of *breeding with other races* bothered me, for I envisaged a most unpromising programme of cross-breeding draykoni with Lokants, like packs of animals. Those who already boasted a fine complement of mixed powers would be prized, of course, by such a project. People like Lady Glostrum, a partial Lokant who wielded our arts with confidence and skill, despite her poor training. Her draykoni blood might not be strong enough to permit her to shapeshift, but she possessed virtually every other advantage.

Dwinal would want plenty more like her.

She was watching me with that impassive face, waiting. Expecting. She was losing her grip on her composure, for I detected a glimmer of triumph in her air, of sanguine anticipation. Who could fail to be inspired by such a vision, after all? What Lokant could resist the prospect of so intriguing a puzzle, a project so replete with potential advantage?

And she was right, to a point. It was a seductive prospect. What might we accomplish, with the kind of Library she sought to build? How great *could* those students of hers become? The products of our best features and our most brilliant creations…

believe me, no Lokant could hear all of this and not feel tempted.

But she could not win me over.

'Your methods leave something to be desired.'

Dwinal's face darkened. 'Methods may be adjusted.'

'Upon my recommendation?'

'Within reason.'

She was eager to recruit me to her cause, and for the first time I wondered whether she really had expected to find me here. Whether her air of unsurprise was not a pretence after all, but the plain truth. Perhaps she had arranged things this way, manipulated me, given me credit enough to realise that I would figure her out, that I would put myself in her way.

After all, I was complicating her life rather a lot. I took great pride in doing so. *I* was the person who proposed to wrest from her a Lokantorship that she no doubt found convenient and useful to hold. I was the person who had stolen some few of her supporters, who had altered the minds of many long devoted to her cause. I had made of myself a sponsor to the likes of Gio, her wayward grandson, and his meddlesome new friends.

And just now, I was the person standing in between her and the fulfilment of a plan to which she had devoted years of her life.

I enjoyed the power of that moment. I felt her hope, try though she might to conceal it. I delighted in her confidence, her smug certainty that she had arranged everything just *so*, that of course I would see the sense of her arguments. I was a Lokant, a leader, one of our brightest lights and most accomplished scholars. How could I fail to be convinced?

'I will turn over the Lokantorship to you,' she said. 'Of Sulayn Phay.'

This was said with an air of growing triumph. It was the clincher, the leveller, the one thing that would tip me over the edge and sway me to her cause.

Another version of me would have taken her offer without thought. In another time, another place, I might have felt that I could better influence her actions by joining her than by opposing her. I might simply have listened to that part of me to which she primarily appealed: my zealous side, my obsessive scholar side. I might have taken the more interesting road, whatever the cost.

But I could not. Alas, that I could not! For while much was gained by opposition, at least as much was lost. She was not wrong to suggest that such a Library, and such Librarians, might prove to be the very greatest of our achievements.

I looked into her tired eyes and minutely shook my head. 'My father,' I said softly, 'would never approve.'

She became angry. 'Your *father*! What can he have to say to any of this? Where has he been all this time? Dead, that's where! He is *dead!*'

And I became angry, too. 'He died in the conflicts over the last "Master Library." He and many others, in case you have forgotten! Your people, and mine! What do you think you will set in motion, with these mad ideas of yours? Ambition without reason! Only disaster can follow!'

'There need not be disaster if only we would stop opposing one another! If we could but *agree*, and work together, we will achieve our highest potential without paying the price of war!'

'A fine proposition! What you mean is that if we could only agree with *you*, and do whatever *you* say, then we need never fight again! How simple! A beautiful resolution! If everyone had let Krays have the Master Library eons ago, there need not have been any war! You are quite right, it is all *our* fault.'

'He would have made a flawed Master Lokantor, it is true, but the cost of opposition—'

'He was a madman!' I shouted.

'And you are not?' Her head tilted; her lips twisted cruelly. 'What right have you, to take the moral high ground over me and mine? Do not think I am unaware of your history.'

She had me there, curse her. 'I do not claim the moral high ground,' I said, fighting to regain control of my temper. 'When something needs doing, I will get it done — even if it means breaking some rules. But up to a point, Dwinal. Up to a point! For you, there is no limit.'

'That is why I shall always be greater than you.'

There was no warning (except for the sheer melodrama of that statement, clearly designed to close the argument forthwith). Tired of waiting for me to come around to her way of thinking, she took the expedient of shoving me out of her way, physically *and* mentally.

And I was in trouble, for it was like being hit with a wall. She hauled me out of the chair and hurled me away, proving herself far stronger than I had ever imagined. At the same time, she hit me with a brutal compulsion, as staggering and as unavoidable as a punch to the face.

It could not hold me long, for I am no weakling. But for a few brief, vital seconds, I *had* to get out of her way. I could not help myself. Nothing in the world was so important to me in that moment as retreat. I was at the door before I knew where I was, bruised and aching and bewildered.

There I stopped, but too late, for Dwinal had taken the chair and was intent upon the controls which I had so zealously guarded only moments before.

What followed was… not pretty.

We fought. I am no weakling, as I said, and when prepared to encounter an attack I will not so easily succumb. But Dwinal is something else again. Perhaps it comes from her sheer, ruthless brutality, her willingness to do whatever is necessary to achieve her goal. She took everything I had and weathered it, barely slowing down.

It is an attitude I can match, if I have to. We fought with the savagery of wild beasts, and if it were not for the fact that neither of us was armed with anything sharp, I believe one of us would have died — perhaps both. As it was we tried our best to cripple one another, and almost succeeded.

In the end, though, for all the bruises I took and all the damage I delivered, I could do no more than distract her. She was weakening, but so was I; one more well-placed punch, one more psychic attack, and I would be unconscious.

I was therefore very glad indeed when my brother appeared.

Did I say that I had no need of him? I suppose I was being an overconfident fool. It would not be the first time.

'*Hyarn*!' I shrieked. In my urgency I forgot that he was not yet exposed, that he still purported to be among Dwinal's supporters. 'Help me!'

He hesitated. Unsure, I think, whether it was the right time to abandon the masquerade, whether more might yet be gained by a continued pretence. But his sister entreated him, a sister dishevelled and bruised and by no means certain of winning her battle.

So he helped me, and Dwinal screamed in fury, for she had not yet come to view him with suspicion. Clever brother, mine! To live so long by her side, subverting her efforts where he could, and yet go unsuspected!

Between us, we made short work of her. But even we two, powerful as we are, determined as we were, could not wholly subdue her. Hyarn swung, and his fist failed to land, for where Dwinal had stood the moment before there was only empty air. She had translocated.

'I suppose she would, at that,' panted Hyarn. Kind soul that he is, he came to tend to my hurts before he bothered about his own.

'At least we deflected her.' I was exhausted to the point that I could barely speak, for to wage a battle on two fronts like that — the physical and the mental — is utterly draining.

'For now. She will return.'

'With help.'

'Undoubtedly.' Hyarn sighed, looking terribly old. 'We had better stay.'

'And summon aid.'

'Lots of it.'

NYDEN

About Rastivan. Again.

I do not see why I am only asked to talk about Rastivan.

Rastivan! That wretch! That filthy, sneaking, betraying, snivelling coward! He is unworthy to call himself a draykon!

But that is all anybody wants to hear about. *Tell us what happened with Rastivan, Ny,* they say. *We need to hear all the details. Write down everything.*

Fine. But only because Avane asked it of me.

And only because she promised I could talk about her at the end.

Remember, Avane. You promised.

I had mostly finished scattering the traitor's parts when Eva got hold of me. *I need you to collect all that back up again, Ny! That wasn't fair of you, Ny! That was too cruel!*

Too cruel, huh. Why was it not "too cruel" of Rastivan to betray us? I felt a tiny bit like biting off her head, but of course I did not. That really would be too cruel.

Eva scares me.

There, I have been honest. They told me to be honest, didn't they? I don't like to admit it. She is a human, and insists on clinging on to that shape. As if it's all that great. But I am glad she doesn't adopt a draykon shape after all, because if she can terrify me as a mere spindly human, what would she be like as a drayk?!

It is something to do with the way she looks at you when she is displeased. A winter-cold quality to her voice when she says things like, *Nyden! I am displeased with you!* A look in her eye that says, *if I were not such a fine lady I would have you minced and fed to my pets.*

She would, too. For all her talk of *too cruel,* when she is truly angered with you she will feed you to Pensould. Just ask Krays.

Anyway, I am trying to explain why a mighty *dark-as-the-night-and-twice-as-cunning* fellow like me consented to obey her order. I could have refused, and if I had, I do not think anybody would have been able to reassemble all of the rancid Rastivan's parts. I had scattered them too far and wide, and hidden them too cleverly.

But I did not refuse, because I do not want to be minced and fed to Eva's pets. Or to Pensould. And because Avane agreed with Eva and how could I resist that?

She promised to help me, and so off we went together, with a trifling assistance here and there from Gio. It took us a while, and Avane only threw up the contents of her pretty stomach three times over, is that not wonderfully resilient? I was so proud of her I could almost have burst with it.

We were delayed for an hour or two by the persistent absence of Rastivan's left forefinger. I could have sworn I had left that one in a dining room at Sulayn Phay but it turned out I had dropped it on the street outside Eva's headquarters instead. Perhaps I was hoping she would find it, when next she stepped out for some air, and promptly lose her lunch.

Reviving a dead draykon is no easy task, I need not tell you. Raising the dead cannot possibly be *easy.* How wonderfully macabre it sounds! Avane and I worked together on the project, and we made a beautiful team. I have no doubt she felt it, too. Afterwards we were exhausted, for it is necessary to employ one's own energies in order to reinvigorate those of the deceased. But it was a successful venture. Rastivan's severed bits and pieces knitted themselves back together, his ravaged body healed over, and he began to breathe again.

We conducted this procedure in a tiny antechamber at Sulayn Phay. It was a featureless little space, somewhere out-of-the-way that we seized upon because it was the first convenient spot that we found. It had no real furniture, the walls were the colour of vomit and it stank of some repellent substance I could not identify, but it served our purposes.

Rastivan awoke. His nose wrinkled as he encountered that delightful aroma, and I congratulated us for inadvertently ensuring that his waking should be as unpleasant as possible.

He began to shiver, and it occurred to me that it was a bit cold in there.

Avane fussed over him at once, while I sat back on my haunches and fixed him with a murderous glower. This I could not help. I may have been instrumental in returning him to life, but that did not mean I had to pretend that I liked it. I wanted to kill him again, but Avane was right there and I had already made her throw up thrice. By that time I was beginning to wonder if she really, truly liked me after all, so I left Rastivan in one piece.

He should consider himself lucky.

'Keep him away from me!' said the traitor, staring at me with a white-faced horror that gratified me deeply.

'There, there,' said Avane. 'The nasty thing won't come anywhere near you.'

That did not gratify me at all.

'Nasty! Avane, he sold umpteen draykoni to Dwinal!'

'Yes, and that was very bad indeed,' Avane agreed. 'But he did so under foul coercion, and he is sorry for it now. Aren't you?' This last she said with a winning smile at Rastivan, and my heart contracted, for he would fall in love with her on the spot. He had to. And what if she decided she liked him better than me? What if ripping a man to shreds and scattering about his parts turned out to be worse, in her estimation, than merely handing sixteen of one's kind over to an abominable creature like Dwinal? More than sixteen! There is Nindrinat, too! Seventeen. What could be worse than that? But Avane might not agree.

I was so worried I forgot to talk. Anyone who knows me will realise that is a bad sign indeed, but Avane did not even notice.

'Those draykoni are in deep trouble,' she said to him. 'We have only been able to extract a few of them. The rest are trapped on Orlind, bound and in distress. We need you to help us.'

I scoffed. What could Rastivan do to help? He was the reason they were in trouble!

But I could see that he was swayed. Perhaps it was the fact that I had already torn him limb-from-limb once and I was sitting nearby, obviously dying to do it again. Or maybe it was Avane's sweet loveliness that turned his black heart. Either way, he fell to blubbering and begging forgiveness, an attitude he occasionally interspersed with justifications of the *but she threatened me!* variety. Pah.

'I will threaten you again, if it would help.' I said this with my teeth showing, and the effect upon Rastivan was profound, if I do say so myself.

Avane shot me a *shut up, Nyden* look.

I shut up.

'What did she do to the people you sent her?' Avane asked of Rastivan. She was kneeling by his side, the weakling being still stretched upon the floor where we had put him. I hated to see her like that, bending over him all tenderly, caring for him like he was worth something. 'How did she trap them?'

'I don't know,' he said, eyes wide as he stared at Avane. He was falling in love with her! I knew it!

The bastard. Next time I would eat him. Watch Eva try to bring him back from *that.*

'Are you sure? Is there nothing you can tell us?'

He licked his lips. They were probably dry and no wonder, I suppose he had not had anything to drink in a while. You know, being *dead.* 'She had help.'

Avane stiffened. 'What kind of help?'

'There were five of us. The others were all Elders, but not me. My job was to find sleeping draykoni and deliver them to her. Live ones, too, if I could. But the other four, they were there to subdue the ones I brought in. They worked together, made a — a kind of vortex of *amasku.* It made me dizzy just being near it. Nobody could fight it. It was twisted somehow, she'd twisted it.'

'Who are the other four? Where are they?' Avane looked electrified, and sickened. She looked once at me, and the look of anguish in her beautiful eyes cut me to the quick.

Yes, I have a heart. Really. I may be darker than the night, but I am soft as cloudy wood-moss in the middle. All right? Satisfied? Let's move on.

'I don't know! Really, I do not. They were not woken by me, and I did not see them often. When I did see them, they were always with Dwinal…'

Avane sat back on her heels. She shook her head, at a loss. 'I don't know if it's enough to help,' she said to me. 'But Eva needs to know about this, at once.'

I regretted that Gio had sauntered off somewhere, for we could have used him at that moment.

I knew one thing: I have not seen any other draykoni wandering around Sulayn Phay. Other than my own friends, of course. That may mean they are usually absent from the Library, so we are not likely to encounter them. Or it may mean that they are so well camouflaged that even I cannot spot them…

'We must find Eva.' Avane scrambled to her feet, and held out her hand to Rastivan.

The process of helping him up was not easy, and I revelled in his sheer unattractiveness as he staggered about, weak-legged and grey-faced. Hah. As if Avane could ever admire that!

Once he was on his feet and mostly stable, she looked expectantly at me.

'What?'

'Either you help Rastivan and I find Eva, or the other way around.'

Oh. The man could hardly walk, so "helping him" would doubtless consist of supporting him. Which would mean being near him. Touching him.

I was torn. I didn't want to touch him myself, ever again. Who knows, cowardice might be contagious! But I definitely didn't want Avane getting anywhere near him, either. What if he hurt her? What if she fell for him?

'*Ny!*'

'Right! Sorry! I'll find Eva.' I hated to say it but I could by no means trust myself not to bite Rastivan's head off if I were left in close proximity with him, so it would have to be the other option.

I turned my back before I could see Avane go to his side and put his arm over her shoulders.

[Edited to add: *Nyden was so caught up in the tale, he forgot to capitalise upon his promised opportunity to rhapsodise about Avane. Later, he was most upset to realise this. I have therefore consented to permit him to insert it prior to the book's publication, in hopes of shutting him up.* - Lady Glostrum].

Have you ever seen Avane? Probably not. Picture a glorious sunset. Picture the most beautiful dawn you have ever experienced. Imagine a serene cove, waters lapping gently at a white beach… imagine a sun-kissed forest, dew twinkling softly upon tender, unfurling leaves… none of this comes close to encapsulating Avane's pure perfection.

And that is only to touch upon the subject of her face. What can I say about her heart? Purer than pure! Is there no one she cannot love? No deed so foul that she cannot forgive? She puts all others to shame, casts all other women into the shade—

[*And that's enough.* - Lady Glostrum].

EVASTANY

The Tangled Web is… Still Tangled.

So there we were, camped out on the edge of the contested island of Orlind, surrounded by draykoni taking a nice, comfortable nap while *we* were tearing out our hair trying to find a way to rouse them.

What did we imagine we could do? Tren and I are both draykon enough to wield the arts we call "Sorcery" and "Summoning" with prodigious skill, but… that's about it. We know nothing of the deeper arts the draykoni employ. There was, on that day, one single advantage to this state of ignorant incapacity; that being that we were largely impervious to whatever twist in the *amasku* was keeping our draykoni companions bound in slumber.

But so what? That merely left us free to run in circles around them, flapping our arms and generally getting nowhere. Nor was it a balmy day on Orlind. Clouds had settled over the sea and drifted landwards, bringing an endless, drizzling rain with them. The air was dank and chill, my silken garments were increasingly soaked and I was *not* dressed for such nonsense.

I tell you, I have rarely felt so ineffectual in my life, or so surplus to requirements. It is not a pleasant feeling. I trust I will not have to repeat it in a hurry.

'What we need to do,' said Tren wisely after a while, 'is find out how this was done, and by who.'

'Or whom,' I put in.

Tren stared at me. 'Is this really the time?'

'For impeccable grammar? Always.'

He left that unanswered. After a short pause he continued: 'Whoever it was that said we have to unravel this from Dwinal's end was right.'

'That was Hyarn.'

'Then Hyarn was right. We can do nothing for them from here.'

'All inarguable, but what does that mean? Do you happen to know where Dwinal is, right now?' I waved an arm at the bleak expanse of bare island that stretched away before and around us. In the distance we could see the pale walls of the new Library bravely glinting through the rain, and of course there would be Lokants aplenty over there manning the whatever-it-was that accomplished the building. Would Dwinal be somewhere among them? Maybe, but probably not. She did not strike me as the type to get her hands dirty overseeing the peasants who carried out the menial labour. She would have other people to do that, while she… did something else.

'We can probably figure it out,' said Tren, with that appalling optimism of his.

'Really!' I snapped. 'Feel free to try. But we have not covered ourselves in glory trying to work out what these people are doing ahead of time, have we? In fact, we have got it wrong at almost every turn! The sad truth is that Dwinal is a lot smarter than we are. But if you want to take another shot at her, go right ahead.' I folded my arms and glared at poor Tren, while the cold water dripped out of my bedraggled hair and slid down my nose.

Anyone who is much acquainted with me will know one or two (or three) salient facts about my character, namely:

— I do not like being wet.

— I do not like being cold.

— I *do not* like being made a fool of.

Being obliged to suffer all three unfavourable states in one go did nothing desirable for my mood.

Tren, however, is used to me by now. His response to this display of irritability was to enfold me in a tight hug. Then he said: 'Take a breath. We can do this.'

I took a breath. I cannot say I found it as revitalising to my spirits as Tren appeared to expect, but some combination of those things was calming, and I managed not to claw his eyes out. 'All right. What is your best guess?'

'Let's think about what we know. First, these draykoni do not appear to be vital to Dwinal's plans immediately, so perhaps the urgency to release them is not as great as we've been assuming. Agreed?'

'I suppose.' I cast a dubious look at the nearest of the draykoni, which was poor Pensould. I hated to see him like that. I called it slumber but it was nothing like sleep, not really. Not restful, not rejuvenating. It was draining for him, and I have no doubt it was a deeply unpleasant state.

But Tren was right. Nindrinat had recovered, and quickly, though she had been kept in that state for some time. Pensould and the others would not deteriorate too far over the course of another hour or two.

'Next. Hyarn took a lot of Ylona's people out here in order to… what? I don't know, but if it were me I would want to achieve two things: interfere with the progress of building that Library, and make sure Dwinal doesn't manage to make off with the island.'

'Right. And those three Libraries are instrumental to the latter.' The three Libraries were visible from where we stood, just about. Sulayn Phay loomed large behind us; the other two were more distant, but still unimaginably huge. Just looking at them made me feel inconsequential, outfaced and unpleasantly awed, so I tried not to.

'Yes, so if I was Hyarn I would want to make sure at least one of those Libraries is unable to perform its intended purpose.'

'He might have gone to treat with one of the other two, to talk them down.'

'Or more simply?'

I narrowed my eyes at him. 'Don't test me!'

He smiled, all patience. 'Try this. If you were Ylona, what would you be doing right now?'

'I would be trying everything I could to take over the Lokantorship, instantly and without delay.'

'Which she says is not achievable. If you were Dwinal, what would you do next?'

'That depends on the status of her plans. If the other two

Libraries are ready to go—'

'—and they seem to be.'

'They do. Then I would hasten forth to bring Sulayn Phay in line, and off we would go.'

'So Dwinal is either: checking with the Lokantors of those other two Libraries to make sure they're in line with her requirements and ready to go, or she is back at Sulayn Phay, preparing to depart.'

'This does not help us much, Tren. If the latter, we are too late. In any case, how are we to intercept her at any of these points? What would we do if we did find her?'

'I—'

Sadly I will never know what brilliant plan Tren might have been about to advance, for he spotted something over my shoulder and stopped dead, his next words left forever unspoken. His eyes widened. 'Oh no, is that… it is! What in the world is Ny *doing*?'

I whirled, just in time to see the great, dark shape of Nyden, airborne and bearing down upon us at speed.

'Oh no, he mustn't come here, he'll be trapped like the others!' I waved my arms and jumped about and generally tried my best to signal *do not approach! Danger!* But to no avail. Nyden flew on, unperturbed, and landed in a spray of earth about ten feet away.

'Nyden, you prat, get out of here!' Tren ran at him, as though he intended to shove Nyden straight off the island again.

'I know.' Nyden got up, slowly. He was already affected by the draining whirl of *amasku,* for he staggered and almost fell over again. 'I have news.'

'It better be vital news!'

'It is!' And he told us, in as few words as he could manage, about Rastivan's latest revelations. I was so proud of him for obeying my orders I felt like kissing him. A meekly co-operative Ny! Wonders will never cease!

'Wherever those four drayks are, they are probably responsible for this mess.' Nyden weakly gestured a wing at the array of felled draykoni, his black hide glistening with rain. 'Kill them, and you'll free us.'

Us. I wanted to protest that it was too soon to be counting himself among them, but Nyden was fast succumbing. He slumped to the ground and stretched out, casually, as though preparing for a pleasant snooze. His eyes closed. 'I left Avane with Rastivan,' he said around a yawn. 'Make sure she's all right.'

I replied that of *course* we would check on Avane — once we had finished tracking down these mythical (and remarkably well-hidden) draykoni, doing something about the elusive Dwinal, and saving the island of Orlind, but Nyden was out cold before I had spoken more than about three words of this.

Tren and I stood for a moment, staring at Nyden's inert (but gently breathing) form with mixed feelings.

'Idiot,' I said after a while.

'Prat,' Tren agreed. 'But it *is* vital information.'

I cracked my knuckles. 'So. If you were an Elder draykon who's survived the twin threat of Galywis and Dwinal, and you were inexplicably happy to lend yourself to a scheme that involves draining the rest of your kind for every drop of *amasku* they can muster, and you're presumably expecting to get something nice out of Dwinal for it later… where would you be at this moment?'

'I am surprised they aren't here,' Tren said, looking around. 'Watching over the flock. Making sure nobody gets out. Bringing others in.'

'Indeed. Perhaps they cannot approach too closely, for fear of succumbing themselves.'

'So they're doing something… else.'

'Wherever Dwinal is… maybe we'll find them too.'

'Back to square one,' Tren sighed.

But we weren't, because I was having ideas. These draykoni had been involved all along, we just hadn't seen them. Or heard of them.

Well; *we* hadn't heard of them, but others had.

There are rumours, Ylona had said. *Whispers that there are draykoni hidden amongst us, shapeshifted to look like us.*

'They look like Lokants,' I said.

Tren blinked at me. 'What… oh. Of course they do.'

'Do you remember, from Llandry's journal? She said Eterna once appeared before them in human shape, and they never saw her coming. They never even sensed her. Llan only knew it was Eterna at all because she had previously encountered her human form.'

'So draykoni *can* camouflage themselves very well indeed, even from other draykoni.'

'If they are very old and very powerful, yes. Which means—'

'We've already met these people.'

I nodded, feeling grim as winter. 'Oh, yes. We've met them, all right.'

ORI

Treachery, Fakery and Other Adventures

Gio found me in the schoolroom.

I'd been in there talking to the students. Some of them had spent rather more time with Dan, Tynara and the like than the rest of us had; I suppose I was harbouring hopes they might have picked up something useful over the course of their lessons. I mean, besides what they were supposed to be learning.

I was destined for disappointment. Susa frowned and said: 'They didn't talk to us.' Faronni echoed that, and elaborated: 'Actually they barely spoke at all. Mostly they gave us books.'

And so I was reminded. A person might be an expert in a given art, and yet have no aptitude whatsoever for teaching it successfully. Books? *We* could have given them books, and left them to study the texts alone. We'd requested help because we wanted more than that for our students. Dan and Tynara's apparent lack of interest in teaching their own arts at a school inaugurated (in part) for their purposes was puzzling, but perhaps they were simply inept.

Either way, nobody knew what the two of them did when they weren't "teaching", and nobody had ever heard either of them refer to Dwinal. Or anything much else.

Anyway, Gio had wandered off for a while — actually we both had. I didn't know what Gio had been doing but there wasn't time to ask, as I was too busy greeting him like he was a shower of rain and I had spent the past twelve years in the desert.

He bore this for a short time, then withdrew from me and said: 'Llandry's been caught.'

'What? How? Where is she?'

'She is on Orlind, with the rest of the draykoni.'

That was news to me, too. By the time Gio finished telling me what had happened, I was in a fine state of mild panic and itching to dash out there *right away* and do something about it!

Yes, with hindsight I should have asked more questions. I ought to have done more than note in passing that Gio seemed oddly calm about it all, and write it off to a slight excess of his typical impassive composure. I should have asked how Llandry had been caught, and what had felled so many draykoni.

I also should have asked why we needed to take a flyer out there; why we couldn't just translocate, as we would normally do.

But I didn't. Llandry is like my sister. There's nothing I wouldn't do for her, or if there is, I can't call it to mind right now.

So I was an idiot, and I let Gio take me out there. I did not pause to think about what I was going to do once we reached the island. I was a hot-headed fool, and I deserved what I got.

What happened was predictable (or you will find it so, having read Llandry's account). Gio whisked me out there sharpish, me all brimming with confidence that he and I would make it right, somehow. After all, is there anything we cannot achieve, if we are together?

The moment I stepped out of the flyer, I was a goner. That vortex of *amasku* scooped me up like a leaf in the wind, my mind turned inside out like a glove, and I was face down in the earth in seconds.

We made a fine sight, I dare say. So many fierce, elegant draykoni gathered in one place, scaled hides glimmering in every imaginable colour. Has there ever been such a vision?

Shame that every last one of us was comatose.

EVASTANY

The Vortex

All things considered, I was a bit more suspicious than poor Ori had been when Gio showed up.

He came striding towards us over the bare earth of Orlind, all grim and purposeful and with his red coat billowing in the wind. He looked like a vision out of some hero tale. 'Where is Ori?' he said, the moment he was within earshot.

I waved an arm towards the Library I thought was Sulayn Phay. 'Somewhere in there.' It disturbed me that I could not answer the question more accurately. When was the last time I saw Ori?

'He is not. I have searched everywhere.' He stopped in front of us and stood there like a wall of rock, absolutely *not* moving until we answered his question to his satisfaction. He had a tight-lipped intensity about his chiselled face that revealed a degree of tension I have never seen in him before. Gio was desperately worried.

If it was Gio.

I opened my mouth, but could think of nothing to say except "oh dear me" or perhaps "are you really Gio?", so I shut it again.

Tren's thoughts were running along similar lines as mine, for he gave vague voice to my second question. 'Gio?'

'Yes?'

Tren stuck his hands in his pockets, adopted a pose I can only describe as Sceptical Swagger and surveyed Gio from his perfect white hair down to his shiny black boots. 'Really?'

'I don't follow.' Gio was not even looking at Tren. He was gazing behind us at the litter of felled drayks, his eyes restlessly scanning through them. He soon abandoned this approach and walked off towards them, his pace quickening to a jog. 'Help me search!'

'He is not here!' I called after him. We had searched among them enough, hadn't we? Neither of us had caught a glimpse of Ori's draykon form, and he is distinctive with his golden scales.

But I was to be proved wrong, for it did not take Gio long to discover our error. Ori was there all right — in human shape. He was tucked behind a great mountain of a beast whose red hide was so eye-catching, we had never noticed Ori's slight form lying nearby. Compared to the size and grandeur of the creatures around him, he looked frail and so, so young, crumpled and discarded like a sheet of paper.

Somehow, seeing him like that crystallised all the anger and frustration that had been building within me. Maybe it was the way he was lying there, curled up as though trying to protect himself from something.

'How long has he been here?' Gio said, in a half-broken voice, and I no longer wondered whether he was really Gio.

Neither Tren nor I knew the answer to that, and we did not try to advance one. 'We need to break this vortex,' said Tren grimly.

'Instantly. Time to think.'

I shared our shiny new theory about the draykoni Lokant-lookalikes with Gio, who greeted it with indifference.

'Yes,' he said.

'You already knew?'

He looked blankly at me. 'Did not you?'

Ouch.

'All right,' I said, folding my arms. 'Who are they?'

'I don't know.'

'Excellent.'

'They could be anybody.'

'I know.'

I clawed a bit at my hair, and sighed. 'How are they doing this?'

'This? Oh, they aren't. At least, they probably set it in motion but it's maintained by something else. Has to be, or they'd be trapped in it like the rest.'

Aha. Aha! 'Something that's both able to affect the *amasku* but is impervious to its effects!'

'The collectors!' said Tren. 'That's what they were for!'

Those energy collectors. We had encountered them before. They are curious devices, constructs fitted with draykon bone, designed to pull and absorb *amasku.* Krays distributed several around the island of Orlind some time past, and Galy redistributed them. Under Galy's direction, they were employed to keep what was, at the time, corrupted energy cycling around the island, keeping it in an eternal loop that prevented it from spreading beyond the borders. Llandry encountered quite some trouble recently when she discovered they were missing.

Well, they were missing for a while. Probably they were being altered somehow, their functions a little bit adjusted. And then put back, buried again, and that clever loop Galy had designed was now being used to keep an eternal vortex spinning around this place, coupled with a drain upon the energy of any draykon caught in it… cruel, cruel. Their own life's energies were feeding the very trap that had caught them.

'We probably don't need to find them all,' I said, already searching the horizon as though I expected to see one sitting in some conveniently obvious spot. 'The circuit is important. Dislodging one or two might be enough to loosen its hold.'

'Right.' Tren strode out and I followed suit. We had no idea where we were going or how we were going to find the collectors, but it felt good to be doing *something.* I was filled with a restless urgency, a need to act. How long had we spent trailing uselessly behind Dwinal and her repulsive followers! Always just too late to realise what they were doing, always too gullible to spot their ploys ahead of time. And here was the result: almost all of our friends and loved ones, trapped in sleep until we finally figured out how to release them.

Now we knew, and nothing was going to prevent us from getting them out. The fact that the authors of the hideous vortex could not safely come too close to it was to our advantage, for the site was as yet uncontested. We needed to fix the problem at once, and get to Dwinal.

Which reminded me. 'Gio, where's your grandmother?'

'No idea.'

'Please find her and ruin her day. Tren and I will deal with this.'

I wanted to be the one to wreck Dwinal's plans, but I had to admit that Gio had a far better chance of tracking her down than I had.

'No,' he said flatly. 'I am not leaving until Ori's free.'

'But Dwinal—'

'Can wait.'

I cast a speaking look at the three Libraries assembled around us. They had formed up into a three-point circle around Orlind, the far-most one out of sight save for the tops of its turrets. They looked ready to leave.

'We'd better hurry, then,' was all that Gio said.

Indeed.

'The collectors,' said Tren, declining to participate in my efforts to persuade Gio. 'They have draykon bone in them.'

'Presumably they still do, yes.'

'Do you remember when Llan told us about how she found Pensould? He was nothing but a pack of bones buried underground but she sensed him somehow. Sensed the *bones.* Surely we can do that.'

'Llan is full draykon,' I said, dubious. 'We are far from it. If they're buried deep, I doubt we can feel them.'

'They won't be buried deep. Who digs a twenty-foot hole when two feet will do? Try it. Can you sense the draykoni over there?' He nodded at the sleeping captives. We had wandered perhaps fifty feet away, and that was too far, for me. I tried, but though I could see them with my eyes, I could not find them with what Llan calls the *other* senses.

'Well, I can. If I can feel those, I can find a collector buried a couple of feet deep. We just have to get near enough to them.'

I started walking. 'Let's hope we don't have to circle the entire island.'

'Doubtful. All these drayks were caught as they flew in from the coast of Irbel, which means the vortex was positioned to capture them as they arrived. No need to cover the entire island. We just need to follow the coastline until we find one.'

The theory seemed sound, so off we went. I tried to ignore the way my sodden trousers clung to my legs, the water dripping into my eyes from my straggling hair and the unpleasant sensation of my heels sinking into the waterlogged earth, but I won't lie. It was a slog.

But a successful slog, for we found one about ten minutes later.

'Freshly turned earth,' said Tren in triumph, pointing at a patch of ground far enough ahead that I couldn't see what he was indicating. I saw an expanse of flat, rain-soaked ground so absolutely unbroken I had to wonder if hope was making Tren hallucinate.

But no. He really could sense those collectors, it seemed, for he broke into a run and headed unerringly for a spot almost at the water's edge. The tide was in, and sleet-grey seawater lapped only a few feet away from an oblong patch of ridged earth.

It looked disturbingly like a grave.

'How do we—' I began. I was going to ask with what we were going to dig, but I shut my mouth, because my dear Tren and poor desperate Gio attacked the earth with their hands. They clawed up mud and dirt with their fingers, heedless of the mess they made of themselves and their clothes and I stood, speechless in awe and disgust, for approximately three seconds.

Then I sighed, bid a wistful farewell to my fingernails, and joined them.

Happily, Tren was right about the depth. It was not long before he crowed in triumph, for there emerging from the ground was something metallic (I think?) and sort of oblong and tucked into a nook at one end was a chunk of pretty, silvery, indigo draykon bone.

I pitied the poor creature whose parts had been broken up and put to such abominable use.

Tren wasted no time. He grabbed the piece of bone in a white-knuckled grip and tore it out by sheer brute force alone.

I was impressed.

He made as if to throw it away, but thought better of it and put it into the pocket of his long black coat. I noticed in passing that he looked every bit as gorgeous with his dark hair plastered to his head and water dripping off the end of his nose as he did when perfectly groomed, and spared a moment's regret that I almost certainly did not.

'Right,' he muttered, and shut his eyes. What was he doing?

'The vortex is still up,' he continued a moment later, and flashed me a weary smile. 'On we go.'

He could sense the vortex, too? I felt deaf, blind and dumb in comparison, but deeply relieved to have him along. We'd never had cause to compare our respective aptitude with the draykon arts before; intriguing, to find Tren more adept than I. And galling, but only a bit. Honest.

We ventured forth, following the curve of the coastline on and on. But we had not gone far before Gio stopped, tension wrought in every line of his body, his head up and listening.

'Trouble,' he said tersely. He turned and searched the skies in between us and the Library of Sulayn Phay. After a few seconds, I heard it too: the whine of an engine.

A flyer appeared in the sky. It looked delightful from that distance, almost like a daefly: all delicate grace, pale hues and sleek wings. But I had no trouble believing that this airborne beauty heralded a problem for us.

A big, huge, vast problem, for we swiftly learned that these flyers not only flew; they could also shoot.

I discovered that the one urgent, tumultuous emotion I had not experienced during those few hours was knee-weakening, gut-clenching fear, and I instantly set about making up for the lack. By the bucket load. Tiny, speedy, life-ending missiles slammed into the earth around us, *thud thud thud,* spraying great spurts of mud into the air. We ducked (as if that would help) and ran (as if that would help either). What else could we do? Panic stole my breath and my wits in equal measure, and I felt acutely vulnerable, pinned as we were on open ground at the mercy of the flyer in the sky. Every second, I expected to feel a flash of pain and a warm flow of blood as one of those missiles tore through my body.

My heel sank deep into the wet earth and I stumbled. I might have been done for, but Tren barrelled into me, hauled me up and kept me moving. What would either of us have done without Gio? All we could do was keep running until we were, inevitably, mown down.

But Gio had come prepared, whether for an incoming flyer specifically or for threats in general I do not know. But he turned out to be considerably more *armed* than I had ever suspected, for when next I glanced in his direction — terrified that he might already have fallen — he was standing stock-still, arms raised, face intent as he pointed a weapon at the flyer which I must assume was some manner of gun. It was unfamiliar to me: an innocuous-looking object, rounded to fit comfortably in the hands (I suppose), made from something pure white and smooth. It tapered slightly at its business end. That was all, but though it was featureless it was certainly functional. It shot *something* at the flyer and whatever that something was, it hit a wing. The flyer went into a spiralling descent and plummeted into the water with a terrific splash.

'What is that?' I panted. Why did I even ask? What did it matter? I think I was becoming slightly hysterical.

'Something I shouldn't have,' Gio said. 'I stole it from Grandmother.'

Interesting.

'Come on,' said Gio. 'That was no coincidence. They'll have some kind of tracker on those collectors, and they'll know when they are disturbed. There'll be more flyers. We need to hurry.'

At that point, we hardly needed to be encouraged to pick up our pace. We went on at a run, and I no longer cared that I was chilled to the bone and looked like some drowned thing. All that mattered was finding the next collector and wrecking it, and the next one and the next, until the vortex spun itself out.

Rikbeek, though, had other ideas. At least as fond of being wet and cold as I was, he had been making his displeasure felt for some time. I had ignored it.

He resolved this communication issue by biting me.

'*Ouch*,' I shrieked, for the nasty little beast had made it a good, deep bite. The pain was intense, and the flow of blood no doubt swift. I tore him free of the breast-pocket in which he had been hiding, tearing the pocket from my favourite blue shirt in the process, and tossed him into the air.

Keep watch, I ordered him. *If our friends down there begin to stir, inform me at once.*

Normally I make at least some effort to coax Rikbeek into obedience, or he grows stubborn and intransigent. But we had no time for that, and I was angry with him. He'd left a weal on the left side of my torso that smarted and stung and might actually scar.

It rains, he said in reply. *Water from the sky, cold.*

Tough. I kept my will on him, forcing him back into the sky when he tried to return. He'd made his choice, and anyway I needed him up there. I watched the tiny, dark shape of his body and out-flung wings vanish into the curtain of drizzle and felt a vindictive satisfaction.

'*Here,*' said Tren and fell to his knees before me, so abruptly that I almost fell over him.

'Let me have that thing you shouldn't have,' I said curtly to Gio. 'Someone ought to watch for more flyers.'

He looked at me, all tilty-head puzzlement. 'Why you? Shouldn't I do that?'

'You dig better than I do.' Which was true. I lacked the muscular development that the gentlemen sported in their arm areas, which hampered my efforts to keep pace with them.

I didn't add that I badly wanted to try out the shooty-thing, because I thought that might give Gio an excellent reason to refuse.

To my mingled terror and delight, he accepted my logic and put the sleek, white shooter (I am calling it a shooter because I have no idea what its name is, and shooting is what it does) into my hands. There turned out to be a cool, round tab underneath that felt like metal.

'To fire, squeeze both sides at once and touch that tab,' he told me, and left it at that. He fell to with digging, and I turned to face the dark, looming outline of Sulayn Phay, all ready to fire at the first sign of incoming trouble.

I hoped.

Trouble was not long in coming. I do not know by what means they were monitoring those collectors but it was clearly efficient.

When we dug up the first one, they sent one flyer.

When we unearthed the second, they sent… a few more. I counted ten tiny, dark shapes in the sky before I stopped and focused on the problem of how to deal with them. At least ten flyers versus me with my one shooting device?

How do I get myself into these messes?

I don't know that we expected to be left to wreck the vortex entirely unopposed, but this level of opposition was far more than we were prepared for. The shooter, held before me at arm's length and aimed at the sky, began to shake, and I realised my hands were trembling. My whole body was a-quiver, in point of fact; my heart pounded fit to burst; I couldn't swallow, couldn't breathe.

If you have never witnessed your own abrupt, premature and violent death winging its way towards you through a rain-sodden sky, I do not recommend the experience.

I tried to fire, but it proved harder to accomplish than I was hoping. *Squeeze both sides at once and touch the tab.* That required a degree of control and composure that I had temporarily lost, and I regretted volunteering myself for a duty I could only prove inept at carrying out. That said, what matter if Gio was holding the shooter? Even he could not hope to prevail against so many foes with such minor equipment.

The flyers soared closer and I tried again to fire — and again. I fell to a fumbling, frantic assault upon the shooter and almost dropped it altogether, my hands wet with rain and slippery with sweat.

Then it jolted in my hands and I *did* drop it — but not before it had fired a beam of something indefinable in the general direction of the massed flyers.

It hit nothing.

'Missed,' said Gio laconically from behind me.

How did the man remain so *calm?*

'Are we making any progress back there?' I made sure my voice was as calm as Gio's as I bent, with a fine show of nonchalance, to retrieve the shooter.

'Almost there,' panted Tren.

Well, good. We might manage to release the draykoni, just in time to get the lot of us mown down by Dwinal's fine fellows.

I fired again. It only took me five attempts that time, and I hit a wing! Down went a flyer with a *boom!*

Of course, there were still at least nine more. And now they were close enough to fire, for the first missile hit the sand several feet in front of me and sprayed earth into my face.

'I can't find the *bone…*' gasped Tren, and I grimly resisted the temptation to run and help, or simply to run at all. I fired the poor, beleaguered shooter again and again and hit nothing, nothing…

Then I was down in the sand with my eyes to the sky, for one of the damned things had hit *me.* Dazed, I became aware of an intense pain in the right side of my torso. I was shuddering, with shock as well as fear, and my breath came in shallow, too-fast gasps.

'Eva!' Tren's voice, but he sounded so far off. I tried to muster a reply but my lips would not work.

The flyers soared overhead and… and turned. They turned,

and began barrelling away again. Where were they going? As I watched, two of them exploded in pretty puffs of flickering fire and fell out of the sky. Then a third followed.

'What…' That was all I could manage, one syllable, before I lost the battle for wakefulness and fell into a far more comfortable blankness.

TREN

On Catastrophe

When will you stop getting into these messes?

You asked the question, my love, and I can tell you the answer right away.

The answer is: never.

And that's okay. I love you anyway. Just try not to actually get yourself killed, all right? You were not trying very hard on that day. You thought yourself harm-proof, I am sure of it, as you stood there standing guard over your weary diggers while death descended from the skies.

I have never been more proud — or more annoyed.

I may have muttered something like *damned fool* as I hung over your poor bloodied body splayed lifeless in the wet sand. I had a fistful of draykon bone and the draykoni were stirring around me, but what did that matter, when you were dying?

The air was full of fire, too. I called your name, over and over, and I thought I saw your lips move, but if you answered me I could not hear it over the tearing noise of flying machines exploding into flinders overhead. You had not chosen a convenient spot in which to play dead, sweetheart, for debris rained down around us and I tried to shield you from it, but I had only my own body with which to protect you and what use was that? I would only get us both killed.

What you did not see, my love, was the second wave of flyers emerging from one of the other two Libraries stationed around the island. Neither Gio nor I saw them either, not until they were almost upon us. And we thought, in that moment, that we were done for. A single, intense look was all we had time to exchange, but his face said: *this is it, then.* And I knew that mine did, too. I swallowed, and forced my hands, shaking with exertion as well as fear, to wrest the elusive chunk of bone from the broken energy collector.

I knew as I did so that it was enough, that the gap we had opened up in that terrible circuit was enough to cause a faltering in the whirl of energy. It did not dissolve around us, or anything so dramatic; I sensed only a flicker in the pattern, like a missed heartbeat, and I hoped desperately that it would be enough.

Then I turned and lay down beside you, for if we were to be shot to pieces I would far rather be exploded into bits at your side. Is that not romantic? Having lived through that day I propose that we confine our romantic gestures to safer activities for the foreseeable future. Motion passed. I do not need to ask if you agree.

I wondered, as I lay there, why it was deemed necessary to bring out another wave of flyers, for were the ten (or nine, your having shot one down, my marvellous love) enough to deal with a mere three, virtually defenceless people? Perhaps they intended to slay all the draykoni after all, rather than risk their returning to vengeful wakefulness. That made a miserable kind of sense, so I shut my eyes and waited to die.

Dying has few advantages, but one of them ought to be its blessed, blissful peacefulness. Seconds passed, maybe minutes, and my world was no less rent with execrable, unbearably violent *noise.* I was confused by this, confused still more when my eyes opened upon command and focused upon a sky full of chaos.

The flyers, you see, were no longer shooting at us. They were targeting *each other.* There was full-blown air battle going on up there and it was brutal. Those lovely, delicate machines were cheerfully blowing holes in each other and ripping each other's wings off. As I watched, another toppled in a crumpled heap to the ground and lay there smoking, flames rippling over its sleek metal surfaces.

'Gio,' I managed to utter. I could not see him but I hoped he was close enough to hear me. 'What in the *world* is going on up there.'

Silence, for a time — actual silence, for the battle had been swift and brutal and quickly wore itself out. I watched with bemused interest as a trio of flyers beat a hasty retreat towards Sulayn Phay, one trailing smoke from its left wing.

Then Gio spoke. 'It's my guess that Grandmother was deceived. One of those Libraries most certainly was not here to help her.'

It filtered through to my dazed, shocked mind that I was not dead. I was not, but you, my love, might be. I rocketed into motion, another wave of terror setting my whole body to shaking, until I ascertained that you still breathed, still lived. You were stark white, however, and bleeding, and I had never seen you look so small and frail and fragile.

Gio was as unscathed as I, and I smothered a sudden, fierce wish that one of us had been hit rather than you. It was unworthy of me.

'We need to get help,' I said, and my voice shook almost as much as my hands.

'I am help,' Gio said, still so cool, so untouched. He was help, of course he was; though you have never mastered the Lokant art of healing, my love, Gio is something of a master at them all. And thank goodness that he is, for he tended to you with a brisk efficiency which soothed me in ways nothing else could have done. Your bleeding stopped, your colour improved, and your breathing deepened.

Gio sat back, and ran bloodied hands through his hair. His hands shook, the barest tremor, and he took the shuddering breath of a deeply rattled person. He may look inhumanly composed, my love, but he is human enough. I never thought to encounter the person who could outdo you for iron control.

'She needs more consistent care,' he said to me. 'But she is stable now. She won't die.'

I gripped your limp hand and kissed it and my eyes were so blurred I did not notice when Llandry came up behind us. When she spoke, I jumped about a mile.

'You've made a terrible mess of my island,' she said. She sounded weak but hale, and I swept her up in an impulsive hug because I was so full of gladness I had to take it out on somebody.

'*Ouch*,' she breathed after a moment and I released my bone-crushing grip. There was Pense behind her, still in his draykon form, groggy but sound. In the near distance I saw all the draykoni of Iskyr and Ayrien rousing themselves, dazed and befuddled for the moment but anger must soon follow.

Gio looked longingly in their direction, and then back at you, my love. He was clearly torn. 'I need to get her to an infirmary.'

Llandry read that look, and interpreted it in an instant. 'Ori's there somewhere? We will find him.'

Cool, undemonstrative Gio actually grabbed Llandry's hand and kissed it. I did not see how she received this uncharacteristic salute, for Gio grabbed you, love, and me, and whisked us away from the wreckage and the smoke and the pouring rain, and that was that.

LIMBANE

About That Third Library

Yes, yes, her ladyship has even talked me into contributing to her memoirs. I will not go so far as my colleague Ylona, and term the project *absurd,* for historic value has been wrung from far cruder documents. Nonetheless I am a busy man and I do not have a great deal of time to devote to such a project, so I will keep my remarks brief.

That third Library? That was mine, Estinor. I was initially surprised that her ladyship did not realise this fact at once, but she could not be expected to recognise the structure at sight. Nor could she be expected to follow my line of reasoning without elucidation, so I must excuse her lapse of understanding.

[Too kind, Limbane. Aware as I am that I lower the tone of my report in so saying, and damage its academic credibility still further: I hate you too. — Eva]

Upon receiving Lady Glostrum's information, it was forcibly borne in upon me that matters had proceeded to a state of grave urgency. Accordant with my duties as a member of the Lokantor Council, I took action at once, and depressed Dwinal's inappropriate pretensions in full compliance with the Council's established protocols for the interception, detainment and incarceration of aberrant Lokantors.

No, Lady Glostrum, I will not elaborate. I refuse to trivialise this account with an absurd dramatisation of the facts.

[Upon reading this I reminded Limbane that I had *almost died* in the course of cleaning up the mess he had summarily failed to deal with. I also showed him my wounds. It was a brutal tactic and I am not proud of it, but it succeeded and that's all that matters.— Eva]

Fine.

Here is what happened.

We, the Council, had been watching Dwinal for some time, and we were desirous of performing some intervention which would clear her out of everybody's way. But though her practices were often questionable, she was far more devious than I would like. On the face of it she was always beyond reproach, and therefore it was never possible for us to pursue her. Even had it not been so, Council protocol bound my hands at every turn. Ours is an advanced society, enlightened; we do not believe in capital punishments. A criminal must be given the opportunity to repent and reform. Such elasticity of moral fibre ought to be possible, ought it not? For such well-honed intellects as we possess must be capable of understanding their errors, and subsequently of reforming their judgements and choices for the future.

It is of no use to argue that the entirety of our long history proves this optimistic attitude misguided. Oh, I am fully in support of this approach in most cases; I am no savage. But when one is faced with the guile, the cunning, and the unapologetic amorality of Krays and Dwinal, of what use is it to suggest that, with the right guidance, they will meekly abandon their inconveniently selfish ways? That they will someday be instilled with a new appreciation for our system of rule and law, and come to act responsibly? The whole notion is preposterous.

Something agreeably permanent has already been done about Krays, and what a recommendation for the advantages of savagery that was. I confess, I had been living in hope that her ladyship and friends might find it possible to dispose of Dwinal in much the same fashion, but I came to realise that they might require a little assistance in order to carry it off. Dwinal is much slipperier than her former husband.

When her ladyship brought news to me of Dwinal's plans, I saw my opportunity to dispose of Dwinal once and for all.

I hastened to the designated spot off the Irbellian coast with all due speed. We were slower to arrive than I might have wished, for I have never had occasion to convey my Library to that particular area before, and we lacked the infrastructure to transport ourselves there more expediently. When my beloved Estinor came to dock off the shores of the stolen island of Orlind, I observed that Sulayn Phay remained in residence, and that a second Library was anchored nearby.

I had expected to encounter some manner of opposition from Dwinal's forces upon our arrival, and was surprised to find myself mistaken. Having read the pertinent excerpts from Lady Glostrum's account, I have since concluded that Dwinal was, indeed, anticipating the arrival of some one or two more such structures, and mistook my Estinor for one of those. Her ladyship is not alone in struggling to tell our Libraries apart, when there is nothing by which to judge them save a glimpse of some part of their exteriors. The same problem frequently afflicts my own people, and for the same reasons. How useful a peculiarity, on this occasion.

Dwinal was pressed for time. She was aware of the efforts of her ladyship's friends, and the likes of Ylona Duna, to disrupt her plans, and was naturally anxious to withdraw from the Cluster as soon as possible — provided she could do so with Orlind in tow. Upon seeing that third Library emerge, then, she hastened to Sulayn Phay, with a view to issuing the order to depart. There she encountered the siblings, and was repelled.

This meeting I missed, chancing to arrive shortly after Dwinal had fled Sulayn Phay in anger. It was not difficult to guess where Dwinal might then go: to the Lokantors of the other two Libraries, her supposed allies. She would first seek to determine whether the island might be moved with two alone, thus obviating the need for Sulayn Phay altogether. If that failed, she would recruit some other aid — perhaps choosing among those four camouflaged draykoni whose loyalty she had won, for what better way to overcome a mere Lokantor? — and return to conquer Sulayn Phay.

We found her within the second Library, in the Lokantor's private quarters. The Lokantor — a youngish, energetic man known as Vabind, all stooped shoulders and mismatched clothing — was also present, which simplified our errand nicely. The two were engaged in heated argument when I arrived.

Dwinal looked at me with the eyes of hate, uttered the syllable "*You!*" in sepulchral tones, and immediately leapt at me.

I own myself surprised. Dwinal has always been more in favour of the subtly manipulative approach to winning her battles, and prefers to prevail by wits than by brawn. I attribute her unusually aggressive attitude to the effects of pressure, and perhaps of surprise, for she could never have expected to be brought face-to-face with *me*.

I had arrived equipped to subdue her with all possible speed, and with the Council's full permission to use all necessary force. I had with me a device which delivers a swift, ferocious charge of energy into the body of an assailant, sufficient to render the unfortunate soul unconscious in moments. And within moments, Dwinal lay senseless at my feet.

Vabind judged it best to co-operate, after that.

The young Lokantor, Vabind, I turned over to the Council. I had every intention of doing the same with Dwinal, of course, in accordance with policy. Unfortunately, she proved remarkably resilient and recovered from the effects of the shock I had given her with unusual speed. She escaped captivity at an unfortunate moment, and suffered still more unfortunate consequences. A more detailed account of the occurrence may be found in my report, filed within the Council's archives.

[Better, but vague. Moreover, I suspect some part of the above to be a pack of well-phrased lies. Such deceit, Limbane, is beneath even you. - Eva]

You are difficult to please, your ladyship, and disconcertingly astute besides.

I have not been fully truthful, perhaps, but I hesitate to proceed any further with my narrative. It requires an acknowledgement of certain actions upon my part which I was not fully authorised to perform. Actions which fly fully in the face of Council protocol, in point of fact, and I should not like such an account to fall into the hands of my enemies.

I am assured that this book will not receive distribution outside of the Seven Realms, however, which must be reassurance enough.

Having subdued Dwinal, what then was I to do with her? I do not think she much feared Council interference, for she knew what the procedure would be. She would be brought before a panel of judges, some of whom she had (I have no doubt) already corrupted in her favour. She would appeal to the rest by outlining the ground-breaking nature of her academic goals, and the scientific possibilities that would open up to us were she to succeed. She would downplay the brutality of her methods, and point out — rightly enough — that there was little proof of her worst excesses. Few would be courageous enough to testify against her, for fear of the punishments she would deal out upon her inevitable release from incarceration.

Could there be any doubt of the outcome? Not in Dwinal's mind, nor, alas, in mine. I had little faith in my fellows to convict her at all, let alone to take the appropriate steps to ensure she would remain incapacitated for the remainder of her lifetime. I came down upon the side of Hyarn, in this instance: if Dwinal were permitted to continue with her projects, a new era of war would indubitably follow.

I also knew that Dwinal would never relinquish her goals, not so long as she lived.

I could not, then, turn her over to the Council for judgement, as I did with Vabind. For Dwinal, I felt obliged to make special provision.

I took her out of Vabind's Library (I forget its official name and cannot be bothered to look it up. It cannot be considered relevant, for the purposes of this account). Upon arrival, I had observed a rather large number of draykoni occupying one portion of the island, and it occurred to me that many among them had more than sufficient reason to feel displeased with Dwinal. This circumstance having operated to my advantage before, I presumed to make use of it again.

When Dwinal awoke, she found herself neatly deposited upon the edges of this fine community of draykoni. I do not imagine she was given much time to regret her misfortune. Precisely which draykon belly (or bellies) are now hosting the remains of Dwinal I do not need to know. I only hope, with the utmost cordiality, that the fine ladies and gentlemen in question found their unorthodox repast satisfactory.

There, Lady Glostrum. Will that do?

[I consider it a poor effort, but for a man unused to writing with lively energy — so accustomed as he is to the dry, dusty tone of academic report — it is not absolutely terrible. I award you a bonus point for using the word *sepulchral*. — Eva]

None of it will do, I fear, for her ladyship was rather angered with me. That, however, I will leave to her own pen to relate, for I have done. No doubt her effusions will far outdo mine for colour and wit, though I do not dare hope that she will refrain from roundly abusing my character, and condemning me at last to the fires of eternity.

If it helps at all, your ladyship, I do make some small apology for my (as I believe you termed it) *dastardly, irritating bloody secrecy.*

EVA

Ouch, and Confound it All.

I was, indeed, rather angered with him. In fact, when I contrived to get him before me I greeted him by way of a roar. '*Limbane! How could you!*'

I wanted to make a roar of it, that is, but since I was still flat on my back in a white-blanketed infirmary bed and suffering the agonising discomfort of a deeply-torn wound in my side, it emerged more as a hoarse whisper. Nonetheless, I believe he received the desired impression: I was most seriously displeased.

'How could I what?' he said, characteristically uncomprehending. Perhaps he thought I would be pleased, dear soul.

(Which is not to say that it was not kind of him to visit me. I had not expected it. I give him due credit for not being entirely heartless).

'Secrets!' I bellowed (softly). 'You could not have told me you had made arrangements to intervene? That the third Library would be yours? We thought we were done for! All was lost! And besides that you almost arrived too bloody late!'

He held up his hands and made pacifying gestures, an attitude which has always infuriated me. I believe he was a trifle concerned, for I was working myself into a fine fit of fury and it cannot be deemed a helpful state of being for an invalid.

'Forgive me,' he said, and those two words took me so much

aback that I was rendered speechless. 'I ought to have notified you.'

'Why did you not? You had a voice-box connection straight to me! You could have informed me of your plans in a mere two minutes!'

His brow wrinkled. 'A voice-bo— oh, I see what you mean. Yes, I confess I forgot about it. I am not used to working with others much, you see, let alone those who are not — I mean, who exist outside of my own society. It did not occur to me to recall that you would still be at Phay, caught up in the midst of it all.'

And I sighed, for there was no use trying to explain. He had not said it in so many words, but it was evident that he had not imagined that we might be able to help him. Or he had forgotten us altogether, which is just as likely. So he had done it his own way, and I wanted to punch him, for had we known that such considerable help was on its way, we could have shredded the vortex and released our friends slightly later, in peace, and without being shot at.

And I wouldn't have a gaping hole in my side.

That made it hard to forgive him, even if he was being unusually apologetic. I still haven't, quite, but then the wound has not yet fully healed. Perhaps I will relent, when it does. It will probably depend on the size of the scar, and its relative lack of aesthetic appeal.

The important point, of course, is that the day was won. The draykoni were severely compromised in ways we could not have foreseen, but they are freed and restored to their customary state of health. Eterna was in favour of burning one of the Libraries by way of recompense, and I did not necessarily think it a poor idea, myself. But no agreement could be reached as to which Library to choose as the target of their justifiable wrath, and since they were eventually outfaced by the sheer size of all three, the project was regretfully abandoned.

The island of Orlind was restored to its customary position, and anchored there once more. Limbane saw to that, for which we are all grateful, even if he is irritating beyond words. Llandry and her fellows are restored to possession of it, and His Aggravating Lokantorship even saw to the cleaning-up of all the wrecked flyers which were left littering the sands, and the removal of the fledgling Library Dwinal had been building upon it. Was that not helpful of him? I begin to think him altogether reformed, or I would if he was not so adept a secret-keeper. I suspect him of duplicity. I cannot help it.

Identifying and ensnaring the four draykoni traitors was a more difficult task. Rastivan and Avane were of great use there; Avane was Avane, and even a damaged, paranoid soul like Rastivan could not resist her sweetness or her relentless insistence upon caring for *everything,* even a traitor like himself. He told her everything he knew, everything he suspected, and everything he had heard. While Tren, Gio and I we were out digging up collectors and getting shot, Avane and Rastivan were quietly working out the identities of the four, and tracking them down.

Dan and Tynara were two of them, which by this time may come as no surprise. The two Maevals were the others: Unaris and Lania, both dedicated to showing up at just the right moment, with just the right information. Our two detectives took their information to Llandry, who deliberated a great while as to how to respond. At length she judged it a matter for the attention of all draykoni, and duly shared the news. With Limbane's help (again), the four of them were retrieved and handed over to the draykoni, who did… something to them. I don't know how they chose to deliver justice, or what their idea of justice for that betrayal might be. I did not ask, and I do not plan to. Bearing in mind Nyden's idea of a fitting fate for Rastivan, I imagine I will not like the answer if I do.

Why did they assist Dwinal? I think that Rastivan's tales are the key. Out of fear — and hope, for they were Elders, and she made them know their danger. If you were told that your mind balanced always on the brink of disaster, and that you might slip into insanity at any moment, would you not be afraid? And if that person promised that you could be cured, and *would* be, in exchange for your aid — would you not agree? Many would not, perhaps, but some would. Some did. I leave it to the reader to decide how far they deserve to be condemned.

For my part, I cannot muster much sympathy for them. I only need to remember the sight of stolen Orlind, littered with the felled bodies of so many of my friends, so many great and fierce and proud draykoni, to lose what little sympathy I am able to feel.

And so all was resolved and made right, more or less, but

there is the small matter of the manner of the resolution. I could not forgive Limbane for his secrecy, nor could I forgive him for swooping in at the last moment and fixing everything with no reference whatsoever to the rest of us. He practically waved a magic wand! Wretched stealer of credit! Waster of our efforts! I told him all of this, and he stared at me with that amused glint in his eyes which I desperately hate, for he was laughing at me.

'I could not have done it without your timely information,' he assured me. 'It was your intervention that made the difference, and just in time.'

This was generous. I acknowledge that freely. And coming from Limbane, of all people? All the juicier.

But still. One has principles.

'Very well, Lady Glostrum,' he said gravely. 'If it will make you happy, I will put it about that you and your friends were instrumental in overpowering Dwinal. Neither she nor Vabind will be in much of a position to contradict us.'

This was more than I had hoped! There remains this book to record the true course of events, which is a trifle inconvenient; in this I have been too clever for my own good. But as far as Lokantkind is concerned, Tren and Ori and Gio and Nyden and Avane and all the rest of us — and *me,* absolutely including me — are the heroes who rid their world of a persistent threat. It may not be strictly the truth, but it is quite what we deserve, so I am entirely at peace with the deception.

Except, perhaps, on Ylona's account. She congratulated me upon my heroics and their spectacular success, and I felt a twinge inside — of guilt, in a mild way, and alarm, in case she should come to learn the truth.

But the truth is written only in this book, and I am secure in the knowledge that she will never, ever read it.

ADDENDUM

Three moons later, this manuscript is on its way to the printers. It is not intended for mass distribution, but I do intend to finance the production of some few copies, for addition to those Libraries — no! I mean *libraries*, the ordinary kind — that might benefit from its contents, in years to come.

My wound has healed and I am once again hale. But I have a scar the shape of a crescent moon marring the flesh above my right hip, which sounds a bit lovely but I assure you it is not. It is unsightly in the extreme, and I have therefore made my peace with never forgiving Limbane so long as I live.

We returned to a water-ruined headquarters and a mess of wedding plans left partially completed. The former was resolved by the simple expedient of paying lots of other people to make the problem go away. The latter we resolved by dismissing my planner and eloping. After so much chaos and complication, I could not face another conversation about the exact hue of the ribbons tying up my bridal bouquet.

Gio and Ori took inspiration from our approach, and did themselves some eloping, too. Is that not wonderful news? They are both installed at our (thankfully refounded) school as tutors, for the foreseeable future. Since we succeeded in retrieving our thieved students from the island (Fostiger among them, much to Faronni's relief and delight), our school retained its full complement of eager pupils (mostly eager, anyway). We secured more tutors, both draykoni and Lokant, and the place is thriving.

Nyden, however, we did not re-employ — though we thanked him most sincerely for his efforts, of course. Not everyone is cut out to be a teacher. Nyden is restored to Orlind, which may or may not have made Llandry very happy. But since Avane went with him, I hope she is not too heartily displeased with me.

I have taken steps to expand our school into a larger organisation. At the moment we are calling it the Bureau for Lokant Heritage Investigation, Training and Employment, which is a little unwieldy, but I trust we shall come up with a sleeker moniker in time. It is my hope that the Bureau will revolutionise the lives of partial Lokants across the Seven (and we are, at last, beginning to recruit from among the Daylands and Nimdre, as well. Our reach grows apace). We aim to turn out graduates skilled in all the arts available to them, and thereafter to ensure they are employed at the highest possible level, to use their unique mix of abilities for the good of our Seven Realms. A lofty goal, is it not? I am breathless with anticipation to see what comes of it.

My pen is about to be wrested from me, for Tren has come up behind me and seems intent upon securing it in spite of my *fervent* objectio

[You have written enough, love. The book is finished. It must go to print, and you must come to bed.]

Hmph. So he wrote in his gorgeous scrawl, and he is not wrong. In fact he is right, only I find it hard to relinquish this journal. I have grown used to recording my adventures, my thoughts. I enjoy the idea that the truths of our contributions, our struggles, our failures and our triumphs will be recorded for all of posterity, and read, perhaps, by our descendants, for many years to come.

It is hard to let it go, but so I must.

There are, after all, other journals. Empty ones, fresh of page and scent, just waiting to be filled with adventures.

Perhaps this will not be my last. But if it is: goodnight, sweet book, and dear reader, farewell.

More Stories by Charlotte E. English:

The Draykon Series:

Draykon
Lokant
Orlind
Llandry
Evastany

Seven Dreams

The Malykant Mysteries:

Death's Detective
Death's Avenger
Death's Executioner

www.charlotteenglish.com

Milton Keynes UK
Ingram Content Group UK Ltd.
UKHW010216030124
435363UK00005B/521

9 789492 824219